Before You Say I Love You

ALSO BY SARAH GATE

UNFORGETTABLE LOVE STORIES
Book 1: Before You Say Goodbye
Book 2: Before You Say I Love You

before you say I love you

sarah gate

Choc Lit
A JOFFE BOOKS COMPANY

Choc Lit, London
A Joffe Books company
www.choc-lit.com

First published in Great Britain in 2025

Cover art by Jarmila Takač

ISBN: 978-1781898482

To Lucky, who is my very own Stevie Licks,
and for Harper and Coco

CHAPTER ONE

Maddie didn't like winter, but she had to admit it looked glorious draped across the Hertfordshire countryside. The ground was crispy and glistening, the sky so icy blue it was almost too bright for her eyes. Maddie twisted her fist to hug her tweed jacket tighter. It had belonged to her brother, Bowie, so the jacket was huge on her and gaped. It was serving no practical purpose for keeping her warm and letting in far too much cold air, but wearing it comforted her in a way that was almost magical.

The bottom hem of the jacket hit her wellington boots as Maddie trudged across the garden. She'd begged Bowie's twin brother, Marley, to let her keep it when they'd sorted through Bowie's things. For a man irreparably devastated by his brother's death, he'd been surprisingly strict when they'd undertaken the task, adamant Bowie would not want them keeping things out of sentimentality when other people could make use of them. Maddie smiled in spite of herself. She and her brothers had always been close, agreeing on so many things, but the transmission of universal energy from people into things was not one of them.

Over the years they'd spent many afternoons sitting snugly beside the fire in their parents' living room, debating

1

the existence of fate and destiny. Her brothers had lovingly mocked her unwavering belief in star signs and the law of attraction — things they simply were never going to be able to agree on. Bowie had been a practical and logical person his entire life, with the exception of some little things he'd said towards the end of his days that had given him peace. Marley was right — their brother would not want her to hold on to something someone else could make use of if she wasn't going to use it herself. She'd therefore sworn to use the jacket, despite its swamping nature, and now reached for it whenever the weather turned cold. She also wore it whenever she missed Bowie, which was often.

Maddie stopped as she reached the gate of her parents' estate, nine acres of mostly rewilded landscape and forest, a gravel driveway, a wrap-around garden and, in its centre, a large country house built from grey stone, covered in ivy and Japanese wisteria. The lane that ran the length of the property was eerily quiet, as always. She closed her eyes, her arms resting on top of the wooden gate, and drew in a deep breath. Her mouth dried as the cold early December air hit the back of her throat. They were two days into 'Christmas month', as her nephew Benjamin called it, and winter was in full swing. Still, that was the least of her worries. There was so much lingering in the peripherals of her mind.

First, there was the prospect of another Christmas without Bowie. Maddie loved this time of year, but digging the tree out of the loft and hanging several dozen metres of Christmas lights hadn't felt the same since Bowie had died, six years ago.

Next, there was everything she had to do to renovate her parents' property before spring. She'd known long ago what she wanted to do with the money her brother had left her, and had finally taken the plunge and asked her family for their blessing last winter. Maddie, a former carer, wanted to open a 'recovery retreat'. It would be a bed and breakfast of sorts, but specifically for those who had been battling cancer. She'd loved being a carer. She'd enjoyed working with elderly people in care homes and as a private care assistant for people with disabilities, but her favourite job had been working with cancer patients in palliative care — helping improve the quality of life and manage the symptoms of people who had been told they would not win their battle, providing emotional and spiritual support to them and their family members. She'd been barely twenty-five when she'd had that particular job, but cancer had already been such a major part of Maddie's life, since Bowie had been diagnosed with non-Hodgkin's lymphoma when she was just a teenager. The job made Maddie feel useful and important, like she was making a real difference. Her passion had led her to achieve a degree in Cancer Care and her skills had come in extremely useful years later, when she'd stepped in to support her brother and their family through his terminal diagnosis and final days. Now, at age thirty-three, Maddie felt ready to return to what she loved to do most.

Bowie had confirmed what she had already known deep down, that she was very good at her job. He'd been grateful for the sensitive way she'd helped him keep his dignity. He'd taken a flippant comment she'd made about leaving the social care sector, because the pay was so bad, extremely seriously and left her a reasonable sum of money in his will, imploring her to do whatever she wanted to with it. Though she wasn't sure she was mentally strong enough yet to work with people who would definitely not survive, she knew there was important work she could be doing to help people who had been fighting cancer and its terrible symptoms. She could offer them peace and comfort, a safe and comfortable place to stay for a few weeks at a time, where they could be with other people who understood what this fight felt like. Though the retreat was specifically for people who needed time to process their journey and recover mentally, she would be there to help them minimally as a professional, if they needed it, but Maddie would mainly focus on running a service that provided holistic well-being in the form of plant-based nutrition, yoga and meditation. Her family home — with its high ceilings, big windows, pretty gardens and rural location — was the perfect setting.

Luckily, her parents had agreed. They'd been considering travelling for some time and — since her siblings had all left home — this felt like a good way to make sure Maddie was not left on her own. It would give her something meaningful to focus on. They'd drawn up an agreement that meant Maddie's new business was technically leasing the property from them. They hadn't wanted to charge her anything at all for the privilege, but Maddie had insisted. She was planning on transforming the property and she needed the agency to do so. She wasn't sure she'd have that unless she was officially paying to use the house and grounds. She'd ignored their protestations and had the paperwork drawn up. She'd triple-checked they were OK with the fact they would no longer have use of the property when there were guests there, which — since she was planning on operating in fortnightly cycles — was essentially half of the year. She'd had a professional mock up visuals of her planned renovations and insisted her family sign them off. All of that had taken a full year. Now, alongside helping her parents plan their impending expedition, she was knee-deep in renovations and working towards an opening date in March.

Maddie felt her heart-rate quicken and tried to force herself to stop panicking about the future and be present.

"Things always work out for me," she whispered, trying hard to quiet her mind. "The universe is my friend."

Maddie focused on her inhalations and the chirping of birds, hardy enough to endure the English winter.

"I'm just like a bird. I could fly away, but I'm strong enough to stay."

Suddenly, she was on the floor, her limbs tangled up with something that appeared to be squishy and pink. It was squealing — a high-pitched and frantic sound that seemed to bounce off her eardrums so that she couldn't help but wince. Before she had time to realise it was a piglet and close her arms around it, it wriggled free and took off back the way she'd just come — across the garden, sprinting towards her family home. Maddie watched it running at an impressive speed. She'd had no idea pigs could move so fast. She was startled, but the ground was freezing, so she forced herself to stand, brushing herself down. She was so distracted she didn't hear approaching footsteps.

"Have you seen a pig?"

Maddie jumped so violently at the sound of a strange voice she was sure she shot straight out of her wellies and into the air. She clutched her chest and glared. A man stood in the middle of the lane.

"Jesus Christ," she snapped, narrowing her eyes at the obviously irritated peace intruder. "Are you trying to give me a heart attack?"

He shrugged. "Sorry." He didn't look sorry. He looked impatient. He raised his eyebrows questioningly, as though waiting for something, but Maddie was still trying to calm the furious beating of her heart and couldn't remember what he'd said.

"Did you say something?" she asked.

"Yeah. I said, 'Have you seen a pig?'," he helpfully repeated.

"I have, as a matter of fact. It just knocked me over."

"Oh good, you found him? The speed he took off at, I was sure he was gone for good."

"He can certainly move, that's for sure," Maddie concurred, turning from the gate. She was ten steps into her walk back to the house when she realised the man wasn't following. "Well, come on then!" she called back to him. He nodded, bounded to the gate and cleared it with one high, sideways jump before falling into step beside her.

"Is your name Maddie?" he asked. She was too tired to answer verbally, so nodded. "We went to the same school. I'm a few years older than you, though. James Byron?"

Maddie had never heard that name before in her entire life, but she nodded.

"You don't know who I am, do you?" he challenged her with a grin.

"No," she admitted, a little grumpily.

"I don't blame you. I was an invisible teen."

Maddie almost confided in him that she knew how that felt — almost asked him if he still felt invisible now. But as she turned to do so, she got a proper look at him, and his appearance answered her question. He was tall — not quite six feet, but close — with a mop of curly black hair and eyes the colour of milky coffee. His lips were thin and framed by silver-speckled stubble. He had the bearing of a much younger man, but the crow's feet beside his eyes belied his youthful aura, as did the black skinny jeans and Chelsea boots — millennial indie-boy staples Marley also refused to give up. He was objectively beautiful. There was no way he felt invisible now. *Lucky bastard.* The next best thing to being what society deemed beautiful your entire life — like Maddie's sister Bluebell — was almost certainly being considered unattractive when you were young and then growing into a swan. Maddie, on the other hand, had always felt plain. Ordinary. Five foot six with thick, brown, shoulder-length hair — which she frequently wanted to chop off. She was entirely unremarkable. She ate like an average-sized woman and therefore she was one. She had once considered herself reasonably fashionable, but now she dressed like almost every other woman in her village, in jeans, T-shirts and — if she absolutely had to go out — boots. Wellingtons if she was trudging the countryside, ankle boots if she was venturing to the high street. Sometimes she would shove a patterned headscarf on her head, but only if she was feeling fancy. She had nice skin, which was lucky, because she rarely had the desire to put on much make-up. Perhaps, on reflection, that was why her skin looked so fresh. When people complimented her they typically told her she had a nice smile. Sometimes they commented on her skin tone — a shade her favourite foundation manufacturer called *caramel beige*. Maddie thought that was an apt description, because beige was both how she felt and how she had been treated her entire life. Her sister insisted that such treatment wasn't because Maddie wasn't spectacular — but because she was so good at making herself invisible.

"I knew your brothers," James continued. "Bowie and Marley. We used to go to all the same gigs before they went off to uni. They're cool."

Maddie agreed with a nod and didn't elaborate. She was still surprised how often she implied Bowie was still alive to avoid announcing his death to another unsuspecting fan of her brother's. She admonished herself every time, but couldn't help it. She couldn't bring herself to say the words unless she absolutely had to.

"They were a few years older than me and the only cool kids at school who didn't either bully me or ignore me altogether," James continued.

Maddie nodded, but said nothing.

"Jeez, how long is this driveway?" he added.

"The house is just beyond these trees," Maddie said.

"Is it a mansion?" His flippancy irritated her. She already knew how lucky she was.

"Dad owned a successful content-writing company and sold it for a good amount a few years ago," she explained.

"Nice." James nodded, falling silent. She wasn't sure if he'd run out of things to say or if he sensed she was annoyed. Either way, she didn't really care. She braced herself for an inane comment as the house came into view, but she still wasn't prepared for his brazenness. "'A good amount' is an understatement, isn't it?"

"He's a hard-working man and was very successful," Maddie said, feeling defensive. Ben Whittle was the best man most people had ever met. He'd sacrificed a lot to give his wife and children an exceptional life, including precious time making memories with them. Ben was incredibly family-orientated — he'd spend every moment with his wife, children and grandchild given the opportunity. It had once pained him to devote so many hours to work, but he'd done it because he'd had an opportunity to make them all extremely comfortable and he'd wanted that for them all, more than anything.

"I'm sure." James nodded.

Maddie felt anger swell within her. She'd met many people like James through the years — people who thought her father stumbled into fortune and that she was an entitled princess — and though she typically brushed off their commentary, for some reason, something about James saying it riled. How dare he comment on them when he had no idea of the hell they'd been through these past few years? She thought about telling him to fuck off, but the piglet needed to be caught and then removed from the grounds. Along with its owner. Maddie surveyed the area. She was about to suggest they head towards the wooded area when the front door opened to reveal her mother.

"There's a pig in the house!" she shouted. Maddie and James glanced at each other, then set off towards her. Emma didn't appear perturbed. If anything she looked like she found the whole thing funny. "It's dragged mud everywhere. Dad opened the door to feed the robin and it ran right in as if it lived here. He coaxed it into the orangery with a croissant. It's eating the strawberry vines."

Maddie groaned. The orangery was brand new, having been built just a few months ago. Her mother had always wanted one and Maddie felt like it would be a good addition to her planned renovations, so they'd split the cost at Maddie's insistence.

"I'll get him, don't worry," James said.

"Oh, is he yours?" Emma asked, leading them inside the house. She stopped in the foyer, looking disappointed. "I was hoping we could keep him. We've named him Pigglesworth Snortimer."

In spite of her annoyance, Maddie smiled at that. Emma's cheeks were rosy with excitement. A pig was the last thing they needed, but she was powerless when it came to her mother, especially since they'd lost Bowie. It had taken Emma such a long time to find joy in anything other than her new grandson, Benjamin, so when she was enlivened by something, it was difficult to say no. She wondered if James would let them keep the pig if they asked.

James shook his head. "He's not mine. He escaped from the farm where I work. I got sent to come and look for him."

Emma blinked dramatically. Clearly confused, James turned to Maddie, and before she could stop herself, she drew back with a flinch. She was fairly certain she hadn't been this surprised in a while. She wasn't sure what she expected a farm worker to look like, but James was *not* it.

"What?" he asked, searching himself, his eyes widening. "Is there a spider on my face?"

"We're vegan," Maddie said, as if that settled everything.

"Oh." James stopped fidgeting and eyed her a little sheepishly. "Sorry?" he tried.

"Was that a question?" Maddie asked.

"I'm not sure what you want me to say."

"Well, you can't take the piglet," Maddie said. Emma nodded her agreement.

It was James' turn to blink pointedly. "Excuse me?"

"I can't let you take the pig back to the farm," Maddie said.

"OK . . ." James held his head high so that his sceptical gaze rolled off his long nose like a ski slope. "I mean, you can't really stop me."

"Wanna bet?" Maddie braced herself.

James faltered. "It doesn't belong to you."

"Prove it." Maddie crossed her arms across her chest.

"I'll call the police." James mirrored her.

She shrugged. "And say what?"

"That there's a piglet here and it's not yours, it's mine!"

"You just said it wasn't yours." Maddie smirked.

"I don't have time for this." James unfolded his arms and took out his phone. "Take me to the pig, or I'll call them right now."

"You'd better get off my property while you call or I'll report you for trespassing," Maddie shot back.

"It's not *your* property, it's your dad's," James said, rather pointedly. His comment made Maddie's cheeks flush. His contempt for her privilege was clear as he eyed her, a satisfied smirk threatening to burst free.

She shrugged. "Then I'll get my dad to remove you." The threat sounded pathetic when she said it aloud. Her dad had never 'removed' anyone in his entire life. He was physically unimposing, logical and diplomatic. But James didn't know that. She thought her mother might laugh and ruin things, but she didn't.

"You brought me up here — and into your house!" James said.

"Prove that, too, while you're at it."

James opened his mouth to speak, but Emma, who had been watching them argue — like she was watching a tennis match — held her hands up to silence them both.

"Stop, please, we don't argue in this house." She sighed as though exhausted. Maddie's heart lurched threateningly and it took every ounce of strength she had not to hurl herself into her mother's arms. She often felt like this. It was something that had started in the wake of Bowie's death, an urge that had grown progressively more present in her day-to-day life. She'd given it some thought, and deduced it was because she knew how bad *she* was feeling about losing her brother, so she dreaded to think how devastated their mother must be. Everyone who knew Emma knew how hopelessly devoted she was to her children. Losing Bowie to non-Hodgkin's lymphoma had almost destroyed her. If it hadn't been for Marley and how desperately he'd needed her in those dreadful early days after his twin had died, Maddie wasn't sure Emma would be here at all. Maddie opened her mouth to apologise, but the front door behind her opened before she could.

"Marley!" Emma's face softened, the way it always did when she laid eyes on one of her children. Marley's cheeks were flushed pink from what Maddie assumed had been a brisk walk from the cottage where he lived with Autumn in the nearest village. He paused briefly to take in the scene, then beamed at his mother and strode into her arms, letting the old oak door slam shut behind him. He was alone. Maddie was disappointed. Nothing cheered her up like her nephew, Benjamin, or a visit from her friend, Marley's partner, Autumn. Still, Marley alone was a significant enough presence to lift her spirits a little. For a while, they'd all thought they might lose Marley after the death of Bowie, the twins having always insisted they could not live without each other. Maddie had also worried Emma might die of a broken heart. But Marley had survived. They had all somehow survived.

When Marley had finished hugging their mother, Maddie opened her arms to receive her brother. She held him close, like she always did, trying in vain not to notice the similarities — how much he felt like Bowie, smelled like him and even chuckled her name in greeting the same way.

"Dad called — something about a pig?" He caught the eye of the stranger standing in their foyer. He moved to introduce himself, pointing with obvious recognition. "Shit — James Byron?"

"Good to see you, Marley." James held out his hand.

"Fucking hell." Marley's profanity incited an exasperated tut from his mother. "I haven't seen you in years. How are you?"

"I'm good, thanks. You?"

"Not too bad." Marley nodded, his eyes crinkling at the corners. Maddie realised this might be the first time since Bowie's terminal prognosis that she'd heard Marley say those words in a way that didn't sound laboured, laden with sadness or disingenuous. She wasn't sure if that was because he really liked James or because he finally really was 'not too bad'. She hoped with all her heart it was the latter, and she wouldn't be surprised if it was. Marley had a wonderful life.

"Is this—?" Marley's eyes slid pointedly between James and his sister.

"No!" Maddie and James exclaimed together. James cleared his throat and shuffled uncomfortably.

Despite the fact she was hardly ever embarrassed by her family's nosiness, or coy about her love life, Maddie found herself blushing. Marley fought off a grin, his big blue eyes wide with mischief. Maddie shook her head a little bit. The message was clear. *Don't.*

"James works on a farm," Maddie said, eager to end Marley's teasing. Her statement was immediately effective. Marley's face dropped. Maddie continued, "A piglet escaped this morning. He was sent to come and find it. He wants to take it back there. To be fattened up. For *food.*"

Marley muttered something, and Maddie threw James an arrogant smile, tossing in a haughty eyebrow raise for good measure. He narrowed his eyes at her, his irritation palpable. Maddie felt smug. She did not like this man and he did not like her. This was a competition and she was determined to win. Was she acting like the spoiled little rich girl she was sure he thought she was? She didn't really care. Truthfully, all that really mattered now was saving the piglet. Winning against *him* would be a bonus. And she had drawn her best weapon — her family.

Her mother in particular was a lover of all creatures and would do absolutely anything necessary to preserve life. Checking the driveway for slugs before she drove down it was a regular part of Emma's routine. Through the years, Emma had nurtured many injured animals back to health. Maddie had once returned home in desperate need of a toilet only to find a one-legged duck swimming around in the bathtub. Emma's love for animals had rubbed off on Maddie and Marley — and their siblings, Bluebell and Pip — and Maddie knew it was something Marley was actively working to pass on to Benjamin. There was absolutely no way they would let James take this piglet back to the farm.

"Er—" James started, his eyes bouncing between Emma's worried stance and Marley's disapproving features. James liked Marley, Maddie could tell, and was torn as to what to do.

"Where is the pig?" Marley asked, looking around as though he expected to see it in the hallway.

"It's in the orangery with Dad," Emma said. "He's googling things pigs can eat and feeding it everything we have in a desperate attempt to stop it wrecking the place."

Marley rolled his lips in on themselves in a poor attempt to hide how funny he found the situation, and that prompted Maddie to do the same. She knew her calm, animal-loving father would be acting in devoted service to his neat and tidy wife, doing everything he could to protect her brand-new orangery from the pig, while also making sure it was safe from harm, stress-free and comfortable. It conjured up some pretty amusing images in Maddie's mind. Marley shook his head from side to side, as exasperated as he was amused.

"James, why don't we have a cuppa and talk this through?" He motioned towards the kitchen.

"I have to take the pig back," James said, though he stepped in the direction Marley pointed. Marley nodded flippantly, but threw his sister a reassuring grin. Maddie felt herself relax further. Marley was intelligent, imposing and charming — a deadly combination. He could convince almost anyone to do absolutely anything.

James wasn't taking that pig anywhere.

* * *

"It's my first day," James said, graciously accepting the freshly brewed coffee Marley was handing him. "It was literally the first thing that happened this morning. The pig escaped, and I was sent to find it. They'll be wondering where I am."

Maddie opened her mouth to say something cutting, but Marley shot her a warning glance.

"I don't really want to work there because I'm worried I'll get attached to the animals," he continued. "I eat meat, but I've never been part of the food system before. I don't know, I guess I've never really thought about it. I googled it and apparently sometimes farm workers have to put sick animals out of their misery. I'm worried about that, too. I don't want to watch animals die . . ."

James carried on talking, but Maddie was no longer listening. *She* had seen someone die. Bowie. Six years ago, she'd gone to bed with everyone else, given them a chance to fall asleep, then crept downstairs to meet Marley and Autumn. It had been a rough few days. Bowie had been in considerable pain, relentlessly begging his family to kill him. If it were up to Maddie she'd have given in to him earlier. Bowie knew it, too. They both agreed that euthanasia should be a human right and a choice for the terminally ill. He'd begged her extra hard to help him end his life, but she had insisted she wouldn't do it unless everyone in the family agreed. She hadn't realised until that evening it was actually only Marley's approval she needed. Marley loved Bowie more than anyone else in the world, and he'd have done anything for one more minute with him. If he thought Bowie was too sick to go on, then he was. Together they'd said their goodbyes and given Bowie the tools he needed to fall asleep and die. She hardly remembered anything after that, just blocks of commotion. Her mother's soul-shaking wail, her father crying, Autumn on the floor in the corner of the room hugging her knees to her chest. She remembered unhooking Emma's arms from around Bowie's neck and prising Marley's hand from around Bowie's wrist, hearing him sobbing 'I'm sorry, I'm sorry, I'm sorry'. The official story was that Bowie had been left alone for a short period of time and had committed suicide. Maddie had a feeling the others suspected there was more to it, but they'd never asked and, even if they did, she would never, ever tell them what they'd done.

Six years had passed since that night. Yet that morning, sipping coffee in the kitchen while James Byron word-vomited his justifications for eating meat, Marley's mask slipped. He was an actor, but there it was. Just a flicker of pain, a visual confirmation that Marley was reliving that extremely painful night, too. Marley straightened his expression in less than a second, but it was too late. Maddie's stomach lurched. Her brain flooded with memories. Bowie's pain. His eyes. His gratitude. She had loved him so much. She still did. She wanted to burst into tears, or go to bed and never get up again, or both.

Luckily, James' whining brought her back to the present. He was slouched dramatically over the kitchen island, his face set in a deep frown, while Emma tapped him gently on the back, as though he was a baby she was burping.

"I don't know how I'm going to work there now, actually, on reflection."

"Then get another job!" Maddie snapped at him. She couldn't help herself. All three of them planted their eyes on her, their faces contorted in surprise and confusion.

"He's explained all that, darling girl," Emma said. "Goodness me, where have you been these past ten minutes?"

Marley was watching her closely. Maddie suspected her brother knew exactly where she'd been, because he'd been there too, back in that bedroom, cradling a dying Bowie in their arms.

James rolled his eyes at Maddie. "For those of us who weren't listening, I'll repeat myself, shall I? I've tried finding another job, I really have, but there aren't any locally. I've just been travelling and I'm living in the house my gran left me half of. I can't sell it and fuck off abroad again because my mum owns and lives in the other half. So I need to save up some money before I can go travelling again. I'm back too late for seasonal work, I've tried every employer in a ten-mile radius. There's nothing except for the farm. It's my only option."

Emma winced at his bad language, but did not stop soothing him with motherly taps to the back.

"You are in a pickle," she said. James nodded, theatrically knitting his eyebrows as though in physical pain. Maddie resisted the urge to roll her eyes.

"Why don't you work here?" Marley said, refilling James' mug from the cafetière. Maddie reeled, planting her outraged gaze firmly on her brother. He ignored her.

"Absolutely fucking not," she said.

Emma shook her head, as though beaten.

Marley continued to ignore her. "Are you any good with a drill, James?"

"*Marley*," Maddie hissed.

"Er . . ." James hesitated. His eyes darted to Emma, who was slowly positioning herself between her children. She didn't offer him any reassurance, she merely sighed, and Maddie knew that was because there was nothing she hated more than a spat between her kids. James continued cautiously. "I'm not too bad with a drill, Marley, but why do you need someone to work somewhere like this?"

"Maddie is opening a recovery retreat for people who've had cancer in the spring," Marley said. "Mum and Dad are heading off travelling for a bit with our sister, Bluebell, who's currently in Asia somewhere, rescuing street dogs. The rest of us don't live here anymore. We have a lot of space that no one's using, so we thought it might be good to do something cool with it."

"It's been slow progress, to be honest with you, James," Emma said. "Marley is very busy with work and, if we're all being truthful, he's not very good with a drill. Ben's getting too old to be climbing ladders, I am hopeless at DIY. Poor Maddie is learning as she goes along and doing a lot of it by herself. We've been needing a helping hand for a while."

"I'm all right with a drill, aren't I?" Marley asked disbelievingly. Maddie and Emma both shook their heads. "Right. Well, that's news to me. Anyway, James, we'll pay you a good wage."

"And you'll get a room here to use as you want and your food cooked and paid for," Emma added.

"Is nobody listening to me?" Maddie butted in.

"I am, actually," James said, surprising her. "Look, guys, that's a lovely offer, but the lady of the house clearly does not want me here. This is her project. It would feel wrong to impose myself without her blessing."

Everyone turned to Maddie. She knew she'd regret meeting her mother's or brother's gaze because she'd just sink into their sky-blue eyes and give them whatever they wanted, so she planted her eyes on James'. They'd seemed lighter as they'd walked through the garden in the dazzling winter sun. In the shade of the kitchen they were chestnut brown. He fluttered his thick dark eyelashes at her and she wondered if he'd done it on purpose. He was handsome, there was no denying it, but there was something about him that she didn't like. A self-assuredness, a cockiness, an ugly confidence that made him unappealing. She was sure he felt he was better than her, and that he always thought he was right. His comments about her family home and personal situation had been flippant, rude and reductive. She did not want him here.

"Good, that's settled, then," she said.

Emma and Marley sighed and shook their heads, and Maddie almost changed her mind. She hated disappointing her family, but not enough to have James Byron under the same roof. "So what are we going to do about this piglet?" she asked.

"Oh, gosh, yes, the pig." Emma frowned.

"We can't let you take it," Marley said, slapping James heartily on the back. James opened his mouth to say something but quickly shut it as Marley shook his head forcefully. "How about you go back to the farm and tell them you can't find it?"

"I'm a terrible liar," James said.

"Tell them someone stole him," Emma suggested.

Marley nodded. "Yes, then you wouldn't be lying."

"What if they call the police?" James asked.

"They won't," Emma, Marley and Maddie said together.

"Darling, they don't care that much," Emma clarified.

"They're not going to halt operations to look for a pig," Marley concurred.

James looked unsure. "What will you guys do with it?"

"He can be our first resident," Emma said.

"Where will you put it?" James' features were heavy with bewilderment.

Emma moved to clear up the coffee cups. "He can stay in the orangery until we build him an enclosure." Maddie and Marley nodded along dutifully with their mother's plan.

James stared at each of them in turn, blinking theatrically. "But you said it was destroying the orangery."

"Well, he is, but that doesn't mean we want him to die," Emma said, putting the mugs in the sink and then wringing her hands at the very thought of it. Maddie was once again overcome by an urge to hug her mother. Emma was distressed by the impending death of any living creature and always had been. She was truly a pure soul.

"You're going to let the pig destroy the orangery instead of giving it back to me?" James spelled out the situation. They all nodded in unison. "You're not normal people, are you?" he said.

Maddie had had enough. She turned and stalked out of the kitchen, aware that her reaction would alarm her mother, but past the point of caring. Maddie was proud that her family was different and had no interest in being around anyone who thought it was a bad thing. She was tired and grouchy. She had enough to do without pig-proofing the orangery, a task that had been added to her ever-expanding list. She didn't have time to argue with a thirty-odd-year-old fuckboy brimming with audacity.

She took herself out into the garden and headed for the double swing, her favourite place to sit and contemplate. She'd allow herself five minutes alone and then she really must get on. She had sanding and painting to do, mood boards to create, furniture to order, guests to attract. James Byron and the pig had really set her back. She could do with the entire evening to catch up, but had promised Benjamin that she'd watch him in the pantomime he'd been cast in. She'd been looking forward to it for weeks. Sure, she was stressed now, but she'd have a good time when she got there.

She tried to quiet her mind, but it was almost impossible these days. She had thought giving herself a major project to work on would distract her from her ongoing and relentless grieving, but all it had done was add to her woes. She couldn't tell anyone, of course. Everyone she knew and loved had enough to deal with already. Plus, she had done a good job of convincing everyone she was all right, so she couldn't go back on that now.

From her spot on the swing, braced against the cold with Bowie's coat clasped tight around her, she saw the front door open, and James Byron step onto the wrap-around porch. He bid her mother and her brother goodbye, then headed for the driveway. It was snowing. Maddie watched him tilt his head back and stare at the sky. She could see him in her imagination, his fat black lashes covered with snowflakes. She was seized by a baffling and almost uncontrollable urge to call him over.

She ignored it.

CHAPTER TWO

Later that evening, Maddie launched herself out of her seat in raucous applause. On the stage, five-year-old Benjamin took his third bow, his cheeks tinged pink and his little fists tightly balled in what Maddie knew was an expression of excitement. There must have been nearly five- hundred people in the audience, but his eyes were glued to his mum and dad, Autumn and Marley. Maddie whistled and Autumn laughed, nudging her affectionately. They kept clapping and Benjamin kept bowing until the director of the pantomime came onstage and took his hand to escort him off.

"Look at him, lapping it up." Autumn's eyes were wet with proud tears. This was Benjamin's last show. Because of his age, another child would take over the role tomorrow, much to Benjamin's dismay. He would live on the stage if he could.

Ben was still clapping. "Our little extrovert." He beamed.

"He takes after his dad, I fear," Maddie joked. Autumn laughed.

"*Hey!*" Marley's eyebrows knitted in mock offence. They laughed harder, but Maddie saw Autumn reach for Marley's hand and squeeze it reassuringly. Marley locked his eyes on hers and Maddie bore witness to the kind of adoration she'd read about or seen in movies, but never experienced herself. Autumn and Marley had not been graced with an easy start. They hadn't exactly met in a conventional fashion — but goodness, how they loved each other now. Maddie knew them both so well — she and Marley had always been close and Autumn was a dear friend — but she still hadn't expected them to fall as madly in love as they had. Until he'd met Autumn, Marley hadn't been interested in monogamous relationships. His love for Autumn grew from nothing into everything across one summer, as they'd tried to navigate Bowie's terminal illness. Maddie still found it difficult to accept. In her mind now, there were two Autumns: Bowie's Autumn and Marley's Autumn. It was the only way she could forgive her brother and her friend for moving on together, despite the fact she knew Bowie approved because he'd told her — and everyone else — that he believed it was his purpose to bring Autumn into their family, to give Marley something to live for. Autumn had clearly done that and more. She and Benjamin were absolutely everything to Marley and he in turn was the centre of Autumn's and Benjamin's universe.

Benjamin, who Maddie often joked was part boy, part whirlwind, came tearing into the auditorium and threw himself into his mother's arms. She hoisted him up onto her hip. He graciously accepted congratulations from Nanny Emma and Grandpa Ben, before turning his attention back to Autumn.

"Are you proud of me, Mamma?" he asked, all giddy.

"I have never been prouder of anyone in the world ever!" Autumn said. Maddie knew she meant it, but she also knew Autumn was nervous about Benjamin's burgeoning love for the stage. He loved drama classes and rehearsals and had started suggesting she leave him there and go home like the other mums did, but Autumn did not like leaving him in the care of anyone except close family members. It was something she was fairly sure she and Benjamin would come to argue about, as he'd no doubt start seeking independence before Autumn was ready for it.

Benjamin turned his attention to Marley. "Did I make you laugh, Daddy?"

"All the way through," Marley said, having managed to laugh with the enthusiasm of someone who hadn't already seen the show dozens of times. Autumn and Marley had been at every single dress rehearsal and every evening since opening night.

"Aunty Maddie, did you laugh?" Benjamin pivoted his weight and Maddie opened her arms to take him from Autumn. He was getting a little too old to be carried, but nobody was going to tell him that. Benjamin had never once in his life been rejected when he'd requested affection. Maddie was sure a luckier boy did not exist.

"I laughed so hard Grandpa Ben had to tell me to be quiet because he couldn't hear," Maddie said, pushing his shoulder-length hair away from his face. People often mistook him for a little girl, but he liked having long hair, and as there was no practical reason to insist he got it cut, Autumn and Marley hadn't bothered. Maddie knew he wanted to look like his father, who was sporting a longer, shaggier mane of his own these days. Marley had openly confessed one night that it was an attempt to stop so closely resembling the twin brother he had lost. Marley and Bowie had not been identical, but they'd looked and acted so similarly that people confused them for one another all the time. In the wake of Bowie's death, just looking in the mirror had caused Marley great pain.

Benjamin wriggled for freedom. "I'm going to find my friends."

They watched him run off through the crowd.

"Your pain is finally over," Marley said to Autumn, slinging his hand around her shoulder.

"Ugh," she groaned dramatically. He laughed.

"Did you get bored of it?" Ben asked.

"Not watching Benjamin," Autumn said, shaking her head. "But I am sick of the sight of these other people."

Maddie chuckled. Autumn was an introvert. She liked being at home with her family and her books. Being around cast members and audiences every night was no doubt exhausting for her.

"It'll get even worse if he starts doing it properly, for a professional production," Marley said, rather pointedly. Maddie saw Autumn bristle. Emma and Ben glanced at each other, their eyebrows raised, then turned away. They hated it when Marley and Autumn bickered, and this was something the two were known to bicker about. Larry Ross, an old family friend, wanted Benjamin to audition for a part in an upcoming musical, and Marley was keen he should do it. Autumn was not so sure. She knew the Whittle's favourite family memories centred around performing when they were children, but the theatre was also where Bluebell had met her abuser when she'd been just a teenager. To Autumn, who had also suffered childhood abuse, it made sense that groomers would hang around places like theatres. Marley had tried to tell her things were different now, there were protocols in place, but when Autumn had asked him how they'd know for sure Benjamin was safe if they weren't with him personally, Marley hadn't been able to give her an answer.

"We can talk about this later," she said to him now.

"I thought we were going to be the type of parents who help him follow his dreams?" Marley shrugged.

"Marley," Autumn said, warningly. But Marley wasn't done.

"We all performed in shows every year from the age of four and we loved it, didn't we, Maddie?"

"Not professionally, though," Maddie pointed out. She was with Autumn on this one. Maddie thought Benjamin was too young. She was fiercely protective of him, and if it were up to her, he would never be out of the sight of a family member for the rest of his life.

"Does that matter?" Marley asked. "Benjamin isn't going to know the difference, he'll just be having fun. He wants to do it and he'll learn loads. We'll protect him from any pressure and anything that might cause him harm. It'll be better for him than sitting around at home in the evenings and at weekends. Maybe he'll even tire himself out."

Maddie knew that would be a compelling argument for Autumn because Benjamin was full of unquenchable curiosity at all times of the day and night. Then there was of course Benjamin's undeniable obsession with the theatre. He watched performances on YouTube in his spare time and told everybody he wanted to be an actor. He performed for his teddy bears in his room when he was supposed to be getting ready for bed. Autumn's parents had never shown any interest in her writing career, and Maddie suspected she would feel like she might be letting her son down if she didn't foster his ambition. There was also the little fact that she trusted Marley's parental instincts much more than her own, due to their very different family backgrounds. She was likely going to relent.

"We'll talk about this later," she repeated, searching the crowd with her eyes for her son. Marley rolled his eyes at Maddie. She should squeeze his arm playfully, but couldn't bring herself to do it. She wasn't sure what was wrong specifically, but she was angry at him.

"You OK, Mads?" he asked, his eyes softening with concern.

"I'm fine." Her voice didn't sound normal. Marley would now know for sure that something was wrong, so she offered to go and retrieve Benjamin and hastily pushed through the crowd in search of her nephew. She sighed as she did so, already anticipating a confrontation with her big brother. Marley was not the type of man who'd shy away from a frank conversation if he thought there was animosity brewing. In the early days of his relationship with Autumn, he'd argued with their younger brother on a number of occasions. He'd challenged Pip to confide in him the darkest criticisms of his mind so that he could either apologise or explain. He'd braced himself against the foulest of insults. Pip had accused Marley of not really loving Bowie. How could he declare he loved his brother when he'd slept with his girlfriend — and conceived Benjamin, it turned out. It didn't matter that Bowie had been engineering Autumn and Marley falling for one another in preparation for his death, Marley should have resisted. As far as Pip was concerned, Bowie was a better man than Marley, and Pip wished Marley had died instead. This feedback had temporarily torn their family apart. Autumn and Marley had taken Benjamin and moved out of the family home and into a cottage in the local village, where they had lived ever since. Emma was devastated. Maddie was angry Pip hadn't considered their mother in his rantings and had, in turn, fallen out with Bluebell when she defended their younger brother. Bluebell didn't wish Marley dead, but neither did she think she could ever forgive him. None of it had been helpful.

Maddie thought their focus should not be on the past, but on the future. Benjamin was all that mattered now. Loving him, protecting him, taking care of the people around him so that they could love and protect him. She realised, with a start, that was part of the problem. She was vehemently against Marley pushing Autumn into letting Benjamin perform aged five, and she wasn't sure she could trust herself in the heat of the moment not to call Marley an ignorant fool. Things had changed, sure, but not enough. Benjamin would never be safe if he was out of sight of the people who loved him.

* * *

Maddie found Benjamin playing with some of his friends and coaxed him away by promising she'd ask his parents if he could stay with her at 'the big house' tonight. She knew Autumn and Marley would likely say no, but it was the only way she could get him to comply. She swept him into her arms and they set about looking for their family, who were loitering by the front door.

"Ready, baby?" Autumn asked, pushing Benjamin's hair out of his eyes. Benjamin let his head drop heavily on Maddie's shoulder, nodding sleepily. He was clearly exhausted and all thoughts of the big house were apparently forgotten.

Maddie carried him to the car and fastened him into his car seat, tucking him under an old blanket of Bowie's he'd been sleeping with since he was a baby. He smiled gratefully at her in a way that was oddly mature. Benjamin did this sometimes and whenever he did, Bowie's face would swim across her mind unbidden. She'd always put it down to him looking like Marley and therefore also looking like Bowie, but it caught her off guard every single time he did it. She did not let her mind wander any further than that. She was a spiritual person, but even she drew the line at suggesting her dead brother had reincarnated as the love child of his girlfriend and twin brother.

"Love you, Aunty Maddie," he said, right on cue.

"I love you, too." Maddie kissed his head.

She bid Autumn and Marley goodbye before clambering ungracefully into the back of Ben's and Emma's 4x4, trying desperately to keep her mind off the enormity of the recovery retreat project, the pig, Bowie, and her own concerns about Benjamin embarking on a career in showbiz at five years old. She was unsuccessful. By the time they pulled up to the house, she already knew she had a sleepless night to look forward to.

They were halfway up the steps to the front porch when James Byron stepped out of the shadows, his eyes dark and sallow, his curly hair stuck up everywhere as if he'd been electrocuted. In the dim light, he looked like something out of a horror movie. Maddie felt undeniably self-satisfied. He wasn't so perfect after all. She bet he looked like crap first thing in the morning, just like everyone else.

"Hello there," he said. Maddie and Ben shouted the same expletive. Emma shrieked. James grimaced sheepishly. "I'm sorry. I've spent hours mulling over how to *not* cause you all to shit yourselves, and I'd decided on waiting on the steps, but then I sat on your lovely wicker porch couch and snuggled up under those blankets you keep in the basket by the front door. I was so comfortable I must have fallen asleep."

Emma was clutching her chest. "Jesus Christ, you nearly gave me a heart attack."

"So sorry." He shook his head, no doubt at himself.

"What are you doing here, lad?" Ben asked, pushing the front door open. James and her father had not yet met, but Maddie had spent so much of that afternoon ranting to Ben about his audacity that he likely felt like they already had.

"I came to speak to Maddie," he said.

Maddie frowned, her mind whirring. "Me?"

James nodded curtly. His hands were clasped behind his back like he was some sort of old English gentleman. He was after something, she could tell. Maddie sighed, folding her arms across her chest.

"Would you like a cup of tea, James?" Emma asked.

He looked as if he was about to nod, but Maddie spoke before he could move. "He won't be here long enough to finish it."

James widened his eyes at Emma. She shook her head knowingly, her mouth slightly upturned at the corners — and followed Ben inside. She held the door open for them to follow, but Maddie stood her ground until her mother gave in and shut the door, leaving them standing outside in the light cast from the porch. They stared at each other for a moment, perfectly still, with their shoulders pitched up high near their ears to protect them from the icy air. James blinked, then squinted, then narrowed his eyes.

"Are you pulling faces at me?" Maddie asked.

James shook his head. "No, I'm trying to keep my face alive."

"What do you want, James?"

"I need to reconsider the job thing," he said.

"Absolutely not."

"I promise you, I'll be no bother."

"No," Maddie said, curtly. James dropped his shoulders dramatically and stared, exasperated, at the sky. In spite of her annoyance, Maddie had to stop herself from laughing. She loved theatrical people and James was clearly one of them. Animated and dramatic in his movements and words, she was sure he'd be a blast to be around if circumstances were different, but she couldn't overlook the animosity between them, the way he had judged her home and her family, his self-confidence and how arrogant it made him. She also didn't like the fact he was a farm worker who had come to her house hunting a defenceless pig. Maddie, like her entire family, had been vegan since birth. Her moral stance on eating animals had only strengthened over time.

He interrupted her reverie. "Is this because of the pig?" he asked.

"No, it's your hair," Maddie snapped. "Of course it's because of the pig!" She thought about mentioning how he'd made her feel like she should be ashamed of her home — the only place Maddie felt like she could truly be herself and the only place in the world she wanted to be — but she couldn't be bothered to get into an argument about it. It was easier to put this all down to the piglet.

"I was just doing my job," he hissed the words at the sky, holding his hands up in what was either an expression of submission or a declaration of innocence. Maddie wasn't sure which.

"There is absolutely no excuse for working there," she said.

"How easy for you to say." He stared pointedly around the huge grounds. "How many millions has your dad got in the bank?"

Maddie clenched her teeth. She wanted to tell him she knew how lucky she was — in fact, she had spent a long time feeling guilty about it and that was part of the reason she was opening the recovery retreat — but she caught herself just in time. She reminded herself she did not need to explain herself to James, a man she did not like. "There must be other jobs."

"There aren't," he said. "Not close by, anyway."

"Then go further afield."

"I can't. I have a rescue dog who hates being without me for too long. I need to be able to pop in and see her every now and then or she'll lose her shit."

Despite herself, Maddie softened. She loved dogs. She'd wanted one for a long time, but the timing had never been right. She suspected James had sensed the shift in her mood, because he reached into his pocket and pulled out his phone to show her his lock screen — a picture of a scruffy looking, mismatched sort of dog.

"I found her on a beach in Morocco. Her name is Stevie Licks."

Maddie felt her mouth twitch before she could stop it. James continued to hold the phone up with all the pride of a father showing off his kid. Stevie Licks was white and sandy coloured, with sad brown eyes and gremlin-like ears.

"She's a lovely dog, but she's very attached. Mum can look after her, but she doesn't give her much attention, and besides, it's me she wants to be around. We're best friends. We travelled across Africa and Europe together in a van. She's not used to being away from me, poor thing. I'm trying to train her, but it'll take some time, so I need a job nearby."

Maddie shifted her weight onto the other foot and stealthily let her gaze wander from the phone to James' face. His eyes were wide with childlike hope. He was clearly desperate for her to say yes and not used to people saying no — that much was obvious. Maddie wasn't surprised. James was objectively good-looking and everything he did was laden with charm because of it. She suspected he'd learned to use his attractiveness to get what he wanted. She couldn't judge him for that. Bluebell had done the same. And Autumn. And Marley. She gave herself a moment to really question why she didn't want him around. There was the farmworker thing, sure. But there was also something else lurking in the pit of her stomach. Fear? Was she afraid of James? She realised she was. It wasn't that she was afraid of him hurting her physically or mentally, more that she was scared of everything that came with spending time with someone new. Maddie was a solitary creature. She had no friends except for Autumn, no significant relationship with anyone who was not a member of her family.

29

Aside from her working relationships with her colleagues and the people she cared for, she never met anyone new. She'd always been this way, but had retreated further into herself when Bowie died. She cared only for her family — there was no room for anything or anyone else. She already knew that the Whittles would adore James. If she let him work here and they grew to love him, he'd be an honorary Whittle for ever, someone new to love and care about. She wasn't sure she could handle that — she was worried enough about the brood she had already. It would be better for her if he just went away.

James wiggled his phone to recapture her attention. Stevie Licks stared back at her with eyes full of hope and desperation.

Maddie felt herself relent. "You can have a trial period." She expected James to jump in the air, but he fell to his knees melodramatically, instead. He held his hands together in a prayer-like gesture and gazed up at her.

"Thank you so much." Somehow she could tell that his relief and gratitude were sincere. She sighed.

"Get up off the floor, James. I need to tell you the rules."

"There are rules?" He stood, brushing down his trousers.

Maddie nodded. "Rule number one. You will not consume or wear anything non-vegan in this house."

James nodded earnestly.

"Rule number two. I am the boss. If I tell you something is wrong or it needs doing another way, you will hold your tongue."

He nodded again.

"Instances of mansplaining are punishable by death. Got it?" Another nod from James.

"Rule number three. Since she needs to get used to new people, your dog absolutely must attend work with you every single day."

Maddie could tell he was surprised by this one. It was an act of kindness he hadn't been expecting. Maddie wanted to tell him not to get used to it — she had the animal's best interests at heart, not his — but she didn't have the energy, so instead turned on her heel and headed for the house.

"When do I start?" he called after her.

"Tomorrow at 9 a.m."

"How long is my trial period?"

"It's a rolling trial period. If you get on my nerves at any point, I'll sack you."

As Maddie reached the front door, she heard her mother and father scattering in different directions, giggling as they went. She braced herself to admonish them for being so immature, but before she could step inside, James called out to her again.

"Maddie?" There was a gentleness in his voice she hadn't heard yet. A sincerity. She realised everything he'd said up to now had probably been guarded. She desperately wanted to go inside. She was cold and tired and hungry — but she couldn't help herself. She had to see what he had to say. Maddie turned, her hand on the handle. His palm was spread across his heart. "Honestly, I can't tell you how much Stevie means to me. She's all I have . . ."

He looked like he was about to get emotional but paused his thanks to prevent it. His discomfort with his own emotions frustrated Maddie. Her family didn't hide how they felt. Her dad and Marley cried all the time. Still, she understood. She was from a different world. An extraordinary one. Emma and Ben had raised their children to feel everything completely and express everything shamelessly. Men like James Byron thought any hint of emotion from a man that was not anger or indifference was unacceptable.

She shocked herself by smiling gently at him. "See you tomorrow, James."

CHAPTER THREE

Maddie was wrong. She slept like a baby. When she woke the following morning she felt refreshed and ready to start the day. It was only 8 a.m., but James was already in the kitchen sipping coffee with her parents. She wished she'd known — she wouldn't have come downstairs in her pyjamas. As she made her way to them, Maddie noticed several boxes over-stuffed with Christmas decorations sitting in one corner of the room. She winced guiltily. She knew her parents were eager to get them out and put them up, but they didn't want to get in her way. She did the calculation in her head. Christmas was three weeks from tomorrow. They were usually much better prepared than this. She made a mental note to get things in order as quickly as she could so that she could give them permission to get started with the decorating. But first, caffeine.

"Good morning, my darling," Emma said, pouring her a mug of coffee from the cafetière.

Maddie kissed her on the cheek. "Morning, Mamma."

Ben put his coffee on the table before him and held open his arms to receive her. Maddie bent down to hug him. "Good morning, love," he said.

"Morning, Pops."

"Morning, boss," James quipped, tipping his flat cap. Maddie picked up her coffee cup and wrapped her hands around it, rolling her eyes. She hated conversation first thing in the morning. Her father, who was excusing himself to visit the bathroom, nudged her pointedly as he passed.

"I think the first order of business should be to build a pen for the pig," Emma said to James. "We moved all of the furniture out and he's fine in the orangery for now, but he really is destroying the place. We need a dry-stone wall and a shelter. We have a load of rocks left over from when we replaced the wall at the bottom of the garden."

Maddie concurred with a grunt.

"I built a dry-stone wall once in Spain," James said.

"Oh, how handy!" Emma was thrilled.

"How big do you want it? I reckon I can knock up six metres a day."

Emma paused thoughtfully and then said, "I think perhaps twelve feet by twelve feet? Maddie, what do you think?"

Maddie grunted again.

"Marley will give you a hand when he can," Emma reassured him. "Pip is home for Christmas in a few weeks, too."

"What about Bowie, where is he these days?" James asked. Emma and Maddie snapped to attention. James glanced awkwardly between them, his eyes wide with uncertainty. When Emma and Maddie didn't answer, he opened his mouth to continue, but Maddie shook her head, so he closed it. He shuffled uncomfortably, shooting her an accusatory glance when Emma wasn't looking. She knew what he was accusing her of. Omitting something terrible from their conversation about Bowie the day before.

"Erm—" Emma had always struggled to talk about what happened to Bowie. He'd taken half of her heart with him when he died. She had taken for granted that she would never have to live without any of her children right up until the last eighteen months or so of Bowie's life. Even then, she hadn't believed it, not really. She was sure something would happen, a miracle cure of some sort. A reality without one of her children was not a future she could ever imagine, and the prospect of it had driven her closer to Bowie in the last few months of his life. When he'd died, Maddie had been certain Emma would not survive it.

Before anyone could answer, Ben sauntered happily back into the kitchen, whistling a tune and swinging his arms as he crossed the stone floor. Maddie's father, who had an uncanny ability to detect his family's feelings, picked up on the atmosphere immediately and froze before them.

"My goodness, what's happened?" he asked. James put his head down. Maddie and her mother stared at each other, and Maddie found herself wondering if this ever got any easier, if they would ever not be rendered speechless by grief.

Tortured by silence, Maddie took it upon herself to answer. "James asked about Bowie, Dad. Unfortunately, James, we lost Bowie six years ago."

James met her gaze and she saw flashes of accusation, humiliation and hurt. She felt in equal parts defensive and ashamed, but couldn't bring herself to confess to her parents that she'd had the opportunity to tell James about Bowie but hadn't. She didn't want anyone to know how much she struggled with saying the words aloud. Her mother would force her back into therapy, and she didn't have time for that.

James gave up waiting for her to say something and apologised. "I'm sorry, Mr and Mrs Whittle. I didn't know."

"Oh, don't be silly, how could you?" Ben said reassuringly. James' eyes flickered to Maddie. She met his gaze for a second, then planted her eyes on the floor. Ben continued, "He was a glorious man and we're honoured you remember him after all these years."

James threw Ben a small smile and nodded. The colour that had paled from his cheeks returned a little bit, although he graced Emma — who looked like she might burst into tears — with a concerned glance. They stood there for a moment, an awkward party of four, Ben's eyes on Emma, Emma's on the floor, James watching Maddie, Maddie watching James.

James coughed, breaking their trance. "I should probably get on. Can someone show me where the rocks are and where you'd like the pigpen building? If you have a wheelbarrow or a trailer or something, that would be great."

"I'll show you," Maddie said. She didn't really want to be alone with James — she knew she'd have to explain, and that was the last thing she wanted to do — but he'd seemed so shocked and hurt by her omission. She hadn't meant for this to happen and felt it was important she tell him that. James nodded, but seemed reluctant. Luckily, Ben and Emma were still too distracted to notice. Maddie pulled on her boots and Bowie's big jacket over her pyjamas, then motioned for James to follow her.

The moment they opened the side door, Maddie was distracted. A barrelling ball of fur bounded out of the treeline and careered towards them, her mouth wide open and eyes shining happily. This must be Stevie Licks. The dog launched herself at James, who caught her in his arms. She was big — he stumbled with the weight of her — but Maddie could tell by the grace of the action that they did this whenever they saw each other. He kissed her head and lowered her to the ground, where she snaked between his legs in a figure of eight. Maddie was sure she'd never seen any dog happier to see their human.

"This is Stevie," James said.

Maddie bent low and held her hand out for Stevie to sniff. "Hi, Stevie."

"Don't talk to her, Stevie, she's mean," James said. Maddie stood up straight, her mouth agape. James glared. "Don't bat your eyelashes at me," he said. "What happened back there was awful and all your fault."

Maddie softened. "It's complicated."

"What's complicated about it? I mentioned Bowie in the present tense yesterday — that was your cue to say 'actually, Bowie is no longer with us'. I'd say 'I'm so sorry', you'd say 'don't worry about it', end of conversation."

Maddie sighed. James made it sound so simple, but it never felt that way. She'd learned that talking about Bowie's death sometimes kicked up dangerously sad emotions, the kind that would incapacitate her from feeling anything else for weeks. It was easier to pretend nothing had happened — that her gloriously charming, funny, kind, sensitive, curious brother had not died — especially if the conversation was small talk.

"I didn't know you'd be working here," she said, defensively. "I thought we were just having a little chat and that would be the end of it."

"That doesn't mean it's not weird," he pointed out.

Maddie scowled. "Clearly you've never lost anyone in a tragic way."

James' gaze hardened in a telling manner. She got the distinct impression he was holding himself back, avoiding saying something that would silence her on this matter for good. He could have spat it at her, but he didn't. Instead, he fixed his eyes on Stevie — sniffing Emma's flower bed — and kicked the ground with his wellie. "Show me where these rocks are," he said.

Maddie took him to the rock pile, gave him a wheelbarrow, chose a spot for the pigpen, then left him to it. She told him there'd be lunch in the kitchen at one o'clock — her father made sandwiches every day and would almost certainly make extra for him — but James told her curtly he'd take Stevie for a walk at lunchtime instead. Maddie bid him an awkward goodbye, and left him to his work.

She had so much to do today and hardly any time. She pushed James and his mood out of her mind and headed for her bedroom. She quickly changed into an old pair of overalls, refastened her hair into a messy bun and put sunscreen on her face — a habit Emma had instilled in her children in youth that they'd all carried on into adulthood. When she was done, she stared longingly at her bed. The endorphins that had been present when she'd woken were long gone.

* * *

Maddie spent the rest of the day painting. In preparation for the big switch from family home to recovery retreat, they'd hired a contractor to erect dividing walls in several bedrooms, turning Ben's and Emma's room into three smaller rooms and Bluebell's into two. Maddie had spent the last few days painting every single dividing wall in the same vanilla-pudding shade they'd used on most rooms in the house at her mother's insistence. The paint was plain and nondescript. Boring but practical. This way, Emma had reasoned, they could swap out the furnishings whenever she felt like a change, without having to re-paper walls or paint over stubborn shades. Maddie had to admit her mother's cautious colour choice was going to make redecorating the house easier than if it had been tailored to a very specific Whittle taste. Still, the freshly painted plasterboard made the other walls look grubby, so absolutely everywhere needed at least the lick of a brush. Maddie was managing a room a day. With the rest of the work she had to complete, she reasoned it would take her at least a month to finish. Overwhelmed, she wandered aimlessly from room to room, mentally jotting down everything she still had left to do. She wondered, as she did so, if she had made a hasty decision when she'd decided to open the retreat.

Maddie knew this was a silly way to think. Her heart belonged to social care. It always had. Maddie, who was typically shy and avoided social situations, switched instantly in 'professional mode' the moment there was someone she needed to look after. She had good instincts and strong values, a soft heart and a brain brimming with knowledge. She loved caring for people and she thoroughly enjoyed being at home. She was combining her two favourite things and she absolutely knew it was the right thing to do. A huge part of her worry and frustration was fostered by her eagerness to finish the 'getting ready' part and plunge knee-deep into the actual caring. She was thoroughly overwhelmed. Most days, she couldn't see the wood for the trees. Today was one of them.

She visited Bowie's old bedroom last, pausing trepidatiously at the door. She hated this room, not because she didn't want to be there, but because it was the only place she did want to be. Some days, when her mood was particularly low, she was genuinely afraid she'd barricade the door and trap herself in there. She sighed, forcing herself to enter. The winter sun had bid farewell and the sky was moonless and cloud-covered. The bedroom was empty and pitch-black. Its emptiness didn't startle her the way it usually did. For a few blissful seconds, she could pretend her brother was there, just a few feet away, sleeping in his bed. She inhaled deeply. She knew it was impossible, but she was sure she could smell Bowie's cologne — sweet and spicy — every time she ventured here. She was afraid to paint, she realised, in case she covered up the scent. She forced herself to hit the light switch, bathing the nothingness in a soft orange glow. This room was the biggest in the house, stretching right across the back of the property. It had been Bowie's and Marley's room, then Bowie's and Autumn's, then Autumn's, Marley's and Benjamin's. Maddie scoffed inwardly. If these walls could talk.

Maddie loved Autumn and Marley with all her might, but every now and then she would become suddenly outraged by what they'd done to Bowie. And this was despite the fact Maddie knew Autumn and Marley being together was, in the absence of Bowie, for the best. Autumn's and Marley's betrayal was a serendipitous event that cemented them together and had kept them together ever since. But Maddie, the family's biggest believer in fate and destiny, sometimes struggled to find beauty in their story.

* * *

"I haven't been in here in years."

Maddie turned to find Autumn standing behind her in the open doorway. Every negative feeling she had dissolved in an instant. She opened her arms and Autumn marched straight into them. They tried to lift each other at the same time, bursting into giggles when their synchronisation got them nowhere.

"I didn't hear you come in," Maddie said. She pulled away, rubbing her friend's arms affectionately before she dropped her completely.

Autumn pointedly rolled her eyes. "We came through the orangery."

"Benjamin?" Maddie grinned.

"Benjamin." Autumn nodded. "That piglet is all he's gone on about since Marley mentioned him yesterday."

Maddie laughed. "He's a Whittle through and through."

Autumn nodded her head, sighing happily. Maddie felt a twinge of guilt for her asinine thoughts. Autumn was one of the best things that had ever happened to the Whittles. She had given Bowie so much joy, given Marley a reason to live, given them all Benjamin. Though she'd been Bluebell's best friend, really, Maddie and Autumn had bonded over the shared experience of helping Bowie end his pain and built a firm friendship of their own. In fact, as Autumn was introverted Maddie's *only* friend, she was her best friend by default.

Consumed with a sudden sense of gratitude, Maddie fought the urge to pull her friend into another hug. Right on cue, Autumn stepped away from her. She turned in a circle, staring wistfully at her former bedroom. "What's the plan for in here?" she asked.

"I don't know yet," Maddie said. Autumn smiled sympathetically. She was staring at the spot where Bowie's bed had once been, her eyes glistening with tears. Maddie and Autumn hardly ever talked about Bowie in the context of him dying. Their conversations were always about the things he'd said or done that had made them laugh, or how fully he'd lived life before he'd been given his terminal diagnosis, right before meeting Autumn. For some reason, it felt appropriate tonight. "I miss him so much," Maddie said, knowing she echoed Autumn's thoughts.

"Me too," Autumn whispered, touching her lips with her fingertips. Maddie tried not to think about how confused Autumn must feel about the way she'd adored Bowie and the way she loved his twin brother. She bet she also pretended there were two versions of herself. Bowie's girlfriend, Marley's girlfriend. They were the same wonderful, glorious person, but they were also two very distinct people. "Has it really been six years?" Autumn asked, shaking her head in disbelief.

Maddie nodded sadly.

"We were only together for six months. Can you believe that? He's been gone twelve times longer than I even knew him." Autumn's tears spilled over. Maddie didn't know how to respond. She wondered how she would feel in thirty years, when she'd lived more life without Bowie than she had with him. Still heartbroken, most likely. Broken in the way Autumn was. Like a mug with no handle, still functional in the way everyone needs you to be, but with a vital bit of you, the part that makes things easier, missing. Maddie stepped towards Autumn, holding her hand out for her friend to take. It was the permission Autumn needed to dissolve. She had not been raised in a home bursting with affection, the way the Whittles had, so she resisted at first when Maddie pulled her into a hug, shaking her head and covering her face with the sleeve of her jacket. "I love Marley so much, please don't think I don't," she mumbled into Maddie's shoulder.

"Autumn, you never shut up about him. Nobody who has known you for more than two minutes could ever accuse you of not loving Marley," Maddie joked. Autumn tittered a little bit, to Maddie's relief. She couldn't stand seeing anyone cry, never mind someone she loved. They stood in silence for a minute, embracing. Maddie was waiting. Her friend never wallowed for long. She hated showing anyone her true emotions, so Maddie knew Autumn would simply have to ruin this moment somehow. It was only a matter of time.

"Who's the sexy wheelbarrow-toting bastard in the garden?" she murmured eventually.

* * *

40

They were sitting in the kitchen with mugs of cocoa when the 'sexy bastard' in question popped his head around the door and declared he was leaving. Maddie nodded a farewell, but he'd already gone.

"What the fuck was that?" Autumn asked, stuffing a marshmallow in her mouth.

Maddie tried to act innocent. "What was what?"

"Why was he so frosty with you?" Autumn frowned. Maddie opened her mouth to speak, but Autumn cut her off. "Don't lie to me, Maddie. I'll know."

Desperate to buy herself a few seconds to consider how to phrase her confession, Maddie sighed and tried to sip her cocoa at the same time, accidentally blowing a mini chocolate tidal wave over the rim of her cup instead. "Smooth." Autumn giggled.

"I did something pretty shit," Maddie admitted, wiping at her jeans with her sweater sleeve.

Her friend was visibly confused. "He's only worked here a day, hasn't he?"

Maddie nodded.

Autumn laughed. "How've you managed to piss him off already?"

"I pretended Bowie was still alive when he asked about him yesterday. He asked Mum this morning where Bowie was and what he was up to these days. Mum got upset, so I had to confess. Now he's raging at me." Autumn blinked pointedly, her mouth agape. Maddie guiltily folded her lips in on themselves and nodded. "It's bad, isn't it?" she asked.

"I mean . . ." Autumn started, drawing in a giant breath as though she was going to launch into a sermon before blowing it out exasperatedly. She shook her head at her friend and softened her stance, reaching to pat Maddie's hand. "I'm not going to force you to talk about why you're still doing that after all these years, but I wouldn't be a good friend if I didn't tell you it really isn't normal."

Maddie nodded sadly, staring into her cocoa. She felt small enough to jump into the mug and drown.

"Your mother is a saint," Autumn added. "I don't think anyone, even someone who has only just met her, would ever be OK with upsetting her. No wonder he's pissed."

Maddie groaned and put her head in her hands. "I'm going to have to apologise, aren't I?"

"Yes," Autumn said.

"Fuck's sake."

"Why is that such a problem?" Autumn asked. "You did something wrong."

Maddie knew why Autumn was so surprised. Maddie was very self-aware and not a defensive person at all. If she owed someone an apology, she would say sorry, even if she didn't like them. Her reluctance was a hard confirmation of something she already knew — that she really wasn't herself at the moment.

"What's up, Maddie?" Autumn asked, her voice gentle. "Are you OK? Marley noticed you were quiet last night. He'd kill me for telling you, but he was fretting about it all evening. I was distracted and thought he was worrying needlessly, you know how he gets, but I can see what he means. Is something on your mind?"

Maddie didn't know how to explain what she was feeling and that frustrated her. She couldn't describe it. She was overwhelmed, but simultaneously consumed by a need to be productive. She was socially burned out, but she couldn't stand the thought of going anywhere on her own. She was lonely, but she had no motivation to date or meet new friends. These were feelings she'd been experiencing in some capacity ever since they'd lost Bowie, but they'd grown more prominent over the past few weeks, nudging aside the numbness she typically felt and casting her mind into chaos. Maddie found it unbearable, but she didn't know how to begin fixing it. She knew everyone thought she was getting better because *they* were. Their laughs were no longer forced and fake, their smiles were genuine and their playfulness full of soul, but despite the fact she was incredibly happy that everyone was slowly moving on, Maddie was feeling worse and worse. She didn't want to tell them because she knew it would hurt them — they loved her and desperately wanted her to be happy — so she'd tried to trap the feelings deep within. Now, she knew it was no good. Her upset had crept from wherever she had shoved it and crawled across her features in front of her brother, manifesting as frustration about the decisions he was making as a parent. Marley and Autumn were onto her. They knew her too well and were too observant, especially when it came to the mental health of the people they loved. Autumn often blamed it on being a parent — breaking generational trauma meant she needed to be attuned to Benjamin's every mood, so she could respond with gentleness and understanding — but her friend had been extremely caring and perceptive since the very early days of their friendship. Maddie wanted to lie, but there would be no point. Autumn would know. Maddie felt her eyes fill with tears. She knew she was wrong to try and deal with this herself but she resolved to stay quiet, even though she knew she was beyond regaining control of her emotions right now. She was definitely going to cry, so Autumn was going to know something was wrong. Still, it was better than confessing how bad things actually were. Better than being a bother.

"Oh, Maddie, come here." Autumn opened her arms and let Maddie fall into them. She felt instantly better. "You don't have to tell me anything, so long as you're safe and you know I'm always here for you, no matter what. That's all I care about."

Maddie nodded, grateful. She closed her eyes and silently asked for an answer, something to drag her out of the rut she was stuck in, the emotional ditch that had her focusing on all the things she didn't have instead of what she did. She sighed. She'd be fine, she was sure.

CHAPTER FOUR

It took James ten days to complete the pigpen and he proved himself very handy as he did so. By the time they were approaching the middle of December, he'd dug out and laid a proper foundation and built a small, sturdy hut for Pigglesworth to take shelter in. It was strategically close enough to the house that the installation of a weatherproof socket on the porch and the running of wires underground to install a heat lamp were relatively easy for an electrician to do. James organised all of that without the need for her intervention and Maddie was incredibly grateful. He really took ownership of the entire project, making toys and scratching posts so that Pigglesworth could entertain himself. He even made a sign, which he pitched on the enclosure gate. Pigglesworth Snortimer became the pig's official moniker, much to Benjamin's amusement.

Maddie, on the other hand, felt like she was wading through treacle. She was so unfathomably busy she'd managed to put up exactly three Christmas decorations — two Santa-shaped, stained-glass-window ornaments they hung every year from the kitchen windows and a T-Rex wearing a Christmas hat she'd bought Benjamin a few years ago because it made him laugh. It was dangling from the pantry door handle, doing just enough to convince her she was at least moving in the right direction, even if it was slow progress.

But at least James was drilling through his tasks. Maddie was aghast to admit he was doing a great job. He had taken a lot of the pressure off her shoulders because she knew he was capable and a hard worker. He respected her authority and did what she asked without complaining. He was a model employee. Still, their relationship had not gotten any better on a personal level. After her conversation with Autumn, Maddie had apologised profusely to James, even though it was not an easy thing to do. He had just brushed off her efforts and told her it was 'fine', then continued acting cold towards her. This enraged Maddie. She felt like she had swallowed her pride and tried to make things right. She had done it expecting him to scratch out the past and start their relationship again, and she knew that was wrong. His rejection embarrassed her. Sure, this was all her fault — perhaps she owed him more than one apology — but she thought it was rude of him to continue making a point of keeping her at arm's length. She'd tried in earnest to make small talk with him for a couple of days before deciding he was petulant and emotionally immature. She disliked him even more now than she had before.

But he did have a new fan in Benjamin, who had taken to following James around the grounds whenever he was visiting, asking him incessantly what he was doing and why he was doing it. James was quite obviously not used to being around children — the words he used were too long and spoken too fast for Benjamin's little-boy brain — but when Autumn and Marley insisted their son leave him alone, James was adamant he liked spending time with him and it was no distraction at all.

"He's a top bloke, that James," Autumn said one evening. She was dropping Benjamin off. He was spending the night. Autumn and Marley were making the most of Marley's most recent period of leave and a gap in Autumn's writing projects and heading out on a date. It was not something they could do often. Marley's role in a musical in London's West End meant he left the house early in the morning and was rarely home before midnight. What spare time they had together they preferred to spend with their son, but tonight Marley had insisted they leave him with his family and go out on their own. "Have you two made up yet?" Autumn added, stepping out of her wellies and into a pair of very high heels.

"We're all right," Maddie lied, avoiding Autumn's gaze by focusing intently on the vegetables she was chopping for dinner atop the marble kitchen island. For a week and a half now, ever since Maddie had cried in front of her, Autumn had been checking in more frequently. She called Maddie most evenings 'just for a chat' and had been sending her supportive quotes. Whenever they were alone, she would unsubtly check Maddie was feeling OK by asking her outright. While Maddie was happy to divulge on a surface level how overwhelmed she was and how those feelings had somehow tied themselves to not having Bowie here to guide her, she definitely did not want to talk about her situation with James, who, in truth, hardly ever spoke to her. He was by no means impolite — he made her a brew when he was helping himself to one and bid her good morning and good night — but he'd shown no interest in engaging with her beyond that. She knew it wasn't because he was quiet — he loved laughing and joking with her parents and brother. He just didn't want anything to do with her. He did, however, let her spend as much time as she wanted with Stevie Licks. James and his dog had been attached at the hip for the first few days, but Stevie was getting more comfortable with her surroundings and with Maddie and her family. She now spent most of her time roaming the grounds, begging for affection, which the Whittles were happy to give her. Her owner, on the other hand, remained aloof, at least when it came to Maddie.

Maddie was a people-pleaser, but this situation with James seemed to be consuming her more than it normally would. Also, he irritated her. How dare he pretend to be a nice guy to everyone else and treat her so terribly? She had zero interest in any sort of friendship with someone who would exclude a person because of a simple mistake. She was sure her flippancy continued to feed his opinion of her — that she was spoiled and entitled — but she didn't care. Most of the time, anyway. Sometimes she did, but whenever doubts crept in she reminded herself that James was exactly like so many men she'd known when she was young — arrogant, self-important and emotionally immature. She was sure he would bring nothing except drama to her life. She, on the other hand, was fantastic emotional support for people she loved — she was told so all the time. So who was losing out here, really? *James.*

Autumn disrupted her rumination. "James said he'd show Benjamin how to feed Pigglesworth and then bring him up to the house," Autumn said. "But as I walked away, I heard Benjamin asking James if he was sleeping at 'the big house', too. So prepare yourself."

Maddie lit the stove and groaned. James staying would not be a physical imposition. Maddie had cleared out Pip's old bedroom several months before and set it aside for any staff she might hire. This made practical sense, since that bedroom was opposite hers and at the end of a long corridor that she could cordon off to prevent guests from accessing it. Because they'd split Bluebell's old room and her parents' current bedroom into five smaller rooms, they'd gained three extra bedrooms, which meant there'd be bedrooms for her parents and siblings to sleep in whenever they returned to the family home. With Pip settled in London, Bluebell content travelling the world and her parents set on joining her abroad, it was looking increasingly unlikely that the Whittles would all be home at the same time on a regular basis. But, if they were, they'd agreed to time it with Maddie's fortnightly cycle for the retreat, so that they were only home during closed periods and would occupy the guest bedrooms. Pip's old room would remain a staff bedroom. For now, her mother had given James permission to use it whenever he wanted to in order to change, nap or stay the night if he had a late finish.

"He has Pip's old room, but he never actually stays," Maddie said. Autumn shrugged and opened her mouth to speak, but was interrupted by a piercing ringtone. It was the television on the wall in the kitchen, which had paused her most-watched YouTube video — *Relaxing Zen Music 24/7* — to alert them to an incoming video call. It was Bluebell, live from Thailand. She called Maddie most evenings at the same time, so they could chat while Maddie made dinner, then she'd call again in the morning so Maddie could eat breakfast while Bluebell had brunch. It was very early in the morning in Thailand, which meant Bluebell had most likely been out somewhere, living her best life. Maddie was envious. She adored her sister and did not begrudge her anything, she just really wished she personally had the same drive to enjoy life. Bluebell was not worried at all that people would think she was spoiled and entitled. She didn't care what anyone thought of anything she did. She was really taking advantage of their parents' insistence that their children live at their expense until they found something they wanted to do. Bluebell had been doing it for years.

"Hey!" She beamed, happy to see them both. They heartily returned her greeting, blowing kisses at the screen. Bluebell sat on the floor in semi- darkness. She was wearing pyjamas, her face and hair still made up. "You look fit as fuck, Autumn," she said. "Where are you going?"

"Marley's taking me out on a date."

"We have Benjamin for the night," Maddie added, her tone laden with suggestion at his parents' date.

"Gross," Bluebell quipped. Autumn gave her the middle finger.

"Did you book your flight?" Maddie asked.

Bluebell nodded. "I'll be on the plane home in ten days."

"The day before Christmas Eve! Excellent timing! I can't wait to have you back," Autumn said, grinning. "How long are you staying?"

"Until the spring at least," Bluebell said. "So long as I don't get bored."

"When have you ever not been bored in your life?" Maddie teased.

"True," Bluebell said. "But I haven't seen you all in an age. It'll be Christmas, Pip will be home, you're there, Mads, there's work to be done. I'll keep myself busy."

"I'm here, too," Autumn pointed out. "Just down the road. I'll keep you entertained."

"I figured, since you and Marley are making another baby tonight, you'd be too tired to hang out," Bluebell said, smiling provocatively.

"You know full well we're not having any more kids." Autumn rolled her eyes.

"Another nephew or a brand-new niece would be the absolute best way to get me to stay home," Bluebell said.

Autumn looked like she might be thinking that through, then folded her arms and pursed her lips. "No." Bluebell and Maddie laughed.

Never one to miss a cue, the door opened and Benjamin came running into the kitchen in his duffle coat and wellies. His face was flushed red from the cold and his breath was visible, quick and raspy, so they knew he'd sprinted to the house from the garden.

"Mamma, I fed the pig!" he shouted, throwing himself into Autumn's arms.

"Hurray!" Autumn said, holding her hand up for him to high five.

"I fed the pig, Aunty Bluebell!" he shouted at the TV.

Bluebell acted shocked. It made Maddie smile. Bluebell, who loved pigs, was excited to meet Pigglesworth, who Maddie had told her all about.

"Great work, buddy," Bluebell said.

"Aunty Maddie, I fed the pig!" he said.

"Wow!" Maddie dutifully reacted as though she'd just heard the news. Benjamin wriggled from Autumn's grasp, kicking off his wellies and running towards the living room, screaming his news to Marley, Emma and Ben from the hallway as he went. The three women exchanged knowing glances.

"I have enough going on with one," Autumn said, pointedly. Maddie and Bluebell laughed again.

Bluebell beamed. "I cannot wait to squidge him."

"Ten days," Maddie reminded her, but Bluebell was no longer looking at her. She was staring at the doorway behind them, where James was instructing Stevie Licks to come in and lie down. Once she had complied, he turned his attention to them, waving a little awkwardly at the television screen.

"I promised Benjamin I'd stay for dinner," he explained. "It was the only way I could get him to stop demanding I sleep over. I hope that's OK."

"Fine," Maddie said. They tumbled into silence. Bluebell and Autumn stared at each other through the screen, looking uncomfortable. James remained standing, straight and still, in the corner of the kitchen. Maddie pretended she was busy.

"I'm Bluebell," Bluebell said eventually.

James nodded. "I remember you from school."

"I remember you too," Bluebell said. "Didn't we kiss once on a school trip?"

"No," James said, blushing.

"Are you sure?" Bluebell frowned.

"I'd definitely remember that."

Bluebell squinted at the screen, as though trying to get a better look at him. "I'm sure we did," she insisted.

"I didn't kiss a woman until I was, like, nineteen," James said. "Whoever you're thinking of, it's definitely not me."

"Oh." Bluebell shrugged. "You must look like someone else. Well, nice to meet you again, James."

James was now blushing profusely. "Nice to meet you, too." He took off his wellies and then continued to loiter in the doorway. Maddie turned back to Bluebell.

"Are you going to sleep, sis, or are you hanging out here while I cook dinner?"

"I'll hang out with you," Bluebell said. She was brushing her long blonde hair with an extravagant, beaded hairbrush.

She was still watching James. Maddie knew why Bluebell had chosen to stay. Her sister would be curious about the obvious tension and wondering why Maddie wasn't being her typical warm and friendly self. She wanted to know what was going on. "Sit down, James," she said, eventually. "Can we get you a coffee?"

"Oh, yes, lovely, thanks."

Maddie rolled her eyes. Although driven by Bluebell, his request for a drink felt rude and inconsiderate. She was busy making dinner and he could see that. She felt subjugated. Maddie wanted to suggest he help himself, but Bluebell — who had a view of everything from where the television was suspended from the wall in one corner of the room — would likely say something about how rude she was being, so she stayed silent and put the kettle on. James took a seat at the kitchen table opposite Autumn, where he set about watching Maddie make him a coffee, while she simultaneously chopped vegetables for the curry she was making. Once he was served, the three women carried on speaking as though they were all in the same room. They discussed family and the things they'd do together when Bluebell got home. Bluebell insisted she didn't want to do anything, just sit in and spend time with them all. Maddie and Autumn laughed at that, exchanging knowing glances. Bluebell loved a party. There was no way she'd stay home. When Ben, Emma and Marley entered the kitchen and joined James and Autumn at the kitchen table, the chat continued without interruption, as though Bluebell was right there with them all. They talked about the news, pop culture and conspiracy theories. Bluebell told them all about the dogs she was taking care of, expressing her sadness at having to say goodbye. Every now and then, someone would leave to check on Benjamin, who was in the living room watching videos. Maddie, who was hyper aware of James' presence, because it was rare for strangers to witness these conversations, saw him watching the interaction with great interest.

Half an hour later, Marley re-entered the kitchen having checked on Benjamin, and clapped his hands together resolutely. "Right, love of my life, let's go. We're losing valuable childfree time."

"We're childfree right now," Autumn pointed out.

"Was he all right?" Maddie asked Marley.

"Watching pig videos." Marley rolled his eyes. "I wish he was this chill at home. He's constantly full of beans."

"I wonder who he gets that from," Emma teased.

Marley put on his coat. "I don't have time for this flagellation, Mum. I need to romance my girl."

"Woman," Autumn, Maddie and Bluebell corrected him.

"Woman," Marley repeated. He grabbed Autumn's hand and pulled her enthusiastically towards the door.

"See you tomorrow, loves," Ben bid them farewell.

"Be careful on the roads, they're icy!" Emma called after them. The door closed and the kitchen was silent for a moment while their absence was absorbed. Aware that Emma would be fretting, Maddie gave her mother's shoulders a squeeze.

"I don't think I've ever come across a family so close," James observed. They were the first words he'd spoken since his exchange with Bluebell.

Emma smiled. "That makes me feel very proud," she said.

"You should be." James nodded.

"Dinner is almost ready," Maddie said. Hearing him say nice things about her family made her uncomfortable when he was so rude to her.

"What are we having?" he asked.

"Vegan masala," Maddie said.

"Much better than the beans on toast I normally have." Maddie thought he was talking to the room, but when she glanced at him, he was looking right at her. "Thank you," he said.

Maddie nodded. She didn't know what to do. She was surprised by this elaboration, given he'd hardly spoken a word to her in almost two weeks. Before she could stop herself, she offered him a polite smile. He nodded in a curt but not unfriendly way.

"I'm going to go," Bluebell said. "I can't keep my eyes open. Love you all."

They chorused a goodbye and the screen went black. Emma looked bereft once more. Maddie smiled sympathetically at her mother, handing her an oven mitt and nodding towards the oven, beeping in alarm. The naan breads were ready.

After Ben and James had set the table, they coaxed a very tired-looking Benjamin into his booster seat and Maddie placed an unspiced version of the curry before him with some rice and naan. He tucked right in.

"Are you sleeping at the big house, James?" he asked.

"Not tonight, buddy," James said.

"Will you put me to bed?"

James' eyes darted to Emma for help.

"I'll put you to bed, darling," she said.

"I want James to read me a story."

"This is lovely, thank you for cooking it." James gestured to the curry. Maddie got the distinct impression he was trying to change the subject.

"You're welcome." Maddie passed him the rice.

"Will you read me a story, James?" Benjamin persisted.

"Benjamin," Emma warned.

"I can stay and read him a story if you guys are OK with that?" James said. "But I have to go after that, Benjamin, because I have to take Stevie home."

"Stevie can sleep with me," Benjamin said.

"Benjamin," Emma warned him again, shaking her head, albeit with a small smile on her face. "Eat your dinner before it gets cold. Be quick, now. It's almost bedtime." She turned back to James. "That's very kind of you."

They ate in silence for a while, the only sound their chorus of clinking cutlery. Maddie felt a sinking feeling in the pit of her stomach — a sadness that hadn't seemed quite this strong since the summer they'd been nursing Bowie — and tried to get it under control. She reminded herself that all was

OK — Bowie was at peace, her family were all safe and happy, Bluebell and Pip would be home soon, and work on the retreat was progressing on schedule. There was no reason at all for her to feel this way. It didn't make things any better.

"Are you OK, love?" Ben asked. "You're quiet tonight."

"I'm fine." Maddie pushed her plate away.

"Are you finished, Benjamin?" Emma asked. Benjamin, who had ripped a piece of naan bread into the shape of a pig and was noisily pretending it was eating his curry, nodded. "Let's get you in the bath, then," she said.

"Storytime is at seven thirty, James," Ben said. "Right after bath time, so we'll have a glass of wine in the living room, if you fancy it?"

Maddie hoped he'd say no. She enjoyed a glass of wine with her parents most evenings. They'd be leaving soon. She didn't have many nights like this left to enjoy. He'd be intruding.

"Sounds good," James said.

"Red or white?" Ben asked.

"Red?" James said, in a manner that implied he wasn't sure which was correct.

"Excellent choice." Ben pulled a bottle of red from the wine rack. Maddie thought about making her excuses and heading upstairs, but straying from their routine would alarm her father and prompt a future conversation Maddie didn't have the energy for. It would be much less effort to endure things for the evening, so she watched her dad pour four glasses of wine and then followed him to the living room, delivering Emma's to the bathroom on the way. Ben and Maddie took their usual seats, Maddie on the floor in front of the fire and Ben in the armchair by the window. James perched on the edge of the sofa, commanding Stevie Licks to lie down at his feet.

"How's your mum, James?" Ben asked.

"She's all right, thanks," he said. This was the standard answer he always gave every time anyone asked. Maddie got the impression he wasn't close to her, despite the fact they lived together. He changed the subject. "How's Pip doing?"

"He's well, I think. He's so busy. He calls me, blurts stuff out for ten minutes and then tells me he has to go and hangs up the phone." Ben chuckled, shaking his head. Maddie smiled fondly. Her little brother was a socialist political campaigner and human rights activist. He had a huge group of friends and a very active social life. He was living in shared accommodation in London and enjoying himself immensely. Maddie missed him so much her heart ached, but she had no desire to deprive him of his chaotic youth by telling him so. Pip was wild, but he was also family-orientated. If he had any inkling how deeply his family missed him, he'd be home in an instant.

"He sounds really cool," James said.

"He is, I think," Ben said. "Though I've long since accepted I'm no longer the arbiter on what is cool."

"He is cool," Maddie concurred, setting aside her dislike for James for a second to brag about her little brother. "Though he would tell me I'm not allowed to say that, either."

"The first rule of being cool is that it's not cool to be labelled cool," James said. Ben laughed. "I know that because I'm cool," he added.

"I thought it was fine if other people called you cool, just not if you called yourself cool," Ben said, thoughtfully.

"Dunno." James shrugged. "I'm too cool to think too deeply about it."

They tittered then fell into a comfortable silence. Maddie watched the clock. She couldn't wait for James to leave so she could have her parents and her home back to herself. She could just about handle having someone who didn't like her around from nine to five, but not in the evenings. This time was sacred to her. It was when she unwound. She stared out of the window, fretting. Outside, the snow was falling fast.

"I hope Pigglesworth is all right out there in this weather," Maddie said. She was talking to her father, but somehow James concluded her concerns were directed at him.

"He'll be warmer than we are," James reassured her. "But I'll look in on him before I go."

"If your farmer mates could see you now," Ben said. "Worried about the safety and comfort of a pig."

"I wasn't there long enough to make any friends," James said. He looked right at Maddie as he said it, as though it was important she knew that he meant it. "Thanks to you." He raised his wine glass to her. Maddie blushed and shrugged. "I'm really enjoying working here. Not only do I get to be with Stevie all day, but I've found it really rewarding helping Pigglesworth."

Maddie knew they were waiting for her to say something, but she had nothing to contribute. It had been Marley and her parents, really, who had floated the initial idea. She'd done nothing except relent because she'd been too tired for theatrics and thought his dog was cute.

"We're enjoying having you here, James," Ben said. "When are you planning on running away again?"

"I reckon by the time you open in spring I'll have enough saved up to tide me over on the next wave of my travels."

"Perfect!" Ben said, standing up as his mobile phone began ringing. He checked who was calling and Maddie saw his face drop. She panicked.

Something was wrong.

CHAPTER FIVE

Maddie leaped up from the floor and moved closer so she could hear the conversation better as her father put them on speakerphone. Behind her, James and Stevie were on their feet, watching Ben pace around the living room.

"Dad, don't panic," Marley said right away. "We're fine, we're not hurt."

"What's happened? Where are you?"

"Calm down, Dad, we're—" Marley tried.

Ben was not listening, nor was he calm. "I'm coming right now. Where are you?"

Marley sighed. "Pass the phone to Maddie, Dad," he said.

Ben did as he was told.

"Where are you?" she said straight away.

"Blossom Lane. We're fine, we just broke down. We're fine, Maddie, I promise. We're off the road and in the car — safe, just freezing. I don't want Mum and Dad racing down here and hurting themselves. The roads are treacherous."

James seemed to take that as his cue to jump into action. He marched over to Ben and put his arm around him, guiding him back to his armchair.

"I've only called to tell you because it's a four-hour wait for the RAC and we can't get a taxi," he continued.

"I've had two glasses of wine," she said. "One when I was cooking and another just now, so one of them is going to have to come with me."

"Can James drive?"

Maddie's eyes darted to James. He was nodding at her. Maddie had to work hard not to roll her eyes. Not at James — he was being helpful and she was extremely grateful, because she did not want her parents out on the roads in this weather — but at the universe in general. It seemed she was fated to spend time with this man. She wasn't sure why. Perhaps her will was being tested.

"Can you leave them at home and you two come instead?" Marley said.

"Fine, we're on our way."

* * *

They took her parents' 4x4 for ease. Despite that, the journey — ordinarily fifteen minutes — took them half an hour. Maddie and James spoke of nothing but the snow. When they weren't talking about the weather, they sat in awkward silence. It was torturous, but necessary. Maddie was grateful for his help, but she didn't want him to think all was forgotten. Her dislike of him was deep, and he'd need to do more than this to earn her forgiveness.

By the time they arrived, a fellow motorist had taken pity on the stranded couple. Autumn and Marley were sitting in the back seat of a silver Jaguar. Maddie was relieved. She'd been fretting they'd be freezing the whole way there.

James pulled up behind them and Marley and Maddie got out. As they did, Marley rushed towards Maddie.

"I need you to insist we still go out," he said quietly.

Maddie was confused. "What?"

"Autumn wants to wait for the RAC and then go home, but I need you to insist we go out and to drop us at the restaurant," he said.

"OK." Maddie was bewildered. The snow was coming down thick and fast and the RAC were on their way. It would make more sense for Autumn and Marley to postpone their evening and Maddie had presumed that's what they would do. There must be a good reason Marley was adamant they still go out, but for the life of her Maddie couldn't work out what it was.

James seemed to get it. "I'll insist," he said, nodding at Marley. Marley patted him gratefully on the shoulder.

Autumn climbed out of the back of the Jaguar, calling "thank you, thank you so much" over and over again to the lady in the driver's seat. She teetered precariously over to them in her heels, reaching out to take Marley's hand when he offered it to her. When she reached them she sighed. "Can we go home now?"

"No, don't be silly — we can drop you off!" James said.

Autumn shook her head. "No, it's fine, James. We're late for our reservation. I vote we cancel the RAC until the morning and call it a night. I'm cold and pissed off. I'm not even hungry anymore."

"It's not that late," James said, ushering them all towards the car. "We're so close to the restaurant now, it'll take us ten minutes, tops."

Autumn caught Maddie's eye and visibly gritted her teeth. Her friend wanted her to intervene and agree with her, but Maddie's hands were tied by Marley's plea, so she smiled sheepishly and climbed into the front seat of the car. Autumn and Marley got in the back.

"Ready?" James asked, starting the engine. Maddie saw Marley nod enthusiastically, reaching for his girlfriend's hand. Autumn rolled her eyes and stared out of the window. Maddie felt so sorry for her. She probably wanted to climb into bed and forget tonight had ever happened. Autumn, like Maddie, had no real tolerance for things that did not go according to plan. She would want to run back to the safety of her home and the predictability of everyday life. Once a busy socialite, the past few years had carved her into a woman who happily no longer prioritised adventure. The slow stability, comfort and mundaneness of an ordinary day was what was wanted.

Every morning, Autumn rose early to eat breakfast with Marley and Benjamin, kissed Marley goodbye before he went to work, took Benjamin to school, then sat at a vintage oak writing bureau and wrote books all day. She'd put dinner in the slow cooker at lunchtime and work until it was time to pick Benjamin up, at 3.15 p.m. Sometimes they went to the park, most of the time they went straight home and ate dinner together in front of the television. She'd put him to bed at 8 p.m. and work until Marley came home, usually some time between midnight and 1 a.m. Autumn didn't view writing as work. It was her absolute favourite thing to do. Her first published book — *Beans: An Extraordinary Pig Tale* — had been a realistic portrayal of what life was like for factory-farmed pigs. Then she'd written a book called *Henpecked*, about egg-laying hens. Both books had won awards. From there she'd moved into the contemporary romance genre, where she had excelled in writing love stories that subtly forced readers to consider important moral questions, not least euthanasia, a subject that felt personal to her, given what Bowie had gone through.

She was known as a master of character dialogue and an expert builder of sexual tension. She had been hailed particularly for the way she wrote the preceding moments before a big event, something Autumn liked to call 'the time before'. 'The time before' was essentially the moment before everything changed — the hour before a bomb went off, the minute before a man won the lottery, the seconds before two new lovers kissed — a pivotal moment in history, on a small or a large scale. Autumn loved these moments and spent a lot of time crafting them, forcing her readers to care deeply about her characters, before dragging them out of 'the time before' and into a completely different set of circumstances. She loved it. Work was not a drag for her, it was a hobby she happened to be good enough at to get paid for.

Every now and then she'd be asked to attend a book signing or give a talk on writing, veganism or feminism — the key themes in most of her books — which would take her away from home for a couple of nights at a time. When that happened, Maddie, Emma and Ben would step in to help Marley with Benjamin, but most days passed in the exact same way, and Autumn was glad about that. She felt safe and secure, she and Marley had built a home where nobody slammed doors or shouted. She was happy. She was pleased to indulge Marley in his desire for something different every now and then, but only if it came without drama. Marley knew this. He understood it and respected it. He would know in no uncertain terms that Autumn was frustrated and homesick. Maddie found herself wondering once again why her brother was so insistent that they go out.

* * *

James was right, the drive didn't take long. Once they reached the main road the snow had mostly cleared, blasted into oblivion by a steady stream of traffic. They took Autumn and Marley right to the door of their favourite restaurant, a pizzeria called Il Pomodoro, and bid them a hearty goodbye. Then, with James insisting he was happy to wait with Maddie for the RAC, they made their way back towards the stranded vehicle. It would save Autumn and Marley a job in the morning, he said.

"Should we go get a coffee or something before we head back to the car?" Maddie asked. She was usually in bed early and was exhausted at the very thought of what they were proposing to do.

"Good idea." James nodded. "There's a drive-through just up here."

They ordered soya caramel lattes with extra coffee and a jammy pastry each, then made their way at a snail's pace back to the car. James yawned the entire way there. Since her parents' initial fears for Autumn's and Marley's safety would have almost certainly subsided, Maddie offered to drop James at home and pick up her dad instead, but he shook his head, defiant. He was fine, he insisted. He just needed some caffeine.

They parked a short distance away from the car in a lay-by, where they could see the vehicle and would spot the approaching RAC. They left the engine running so they could have the heating on, pushed their chairs as far back as they could go, then Maddie put her feet up on the dash and settled back to eat her pastry. James was already part-way through his. He put the radio on, navigating to a station that played 00s hits. Maddie caught his eye and smiled, grateful that he hadn't chosen a channel full of songs she wouldn't recognise. Clearly surprised by the gesture, he smiled back.

"What a night." He dug further into his pastry. Maddie concurred with a nod. "I wonder if Marley has proposed yet."

Maddie reeled, blinking furiously, her mouth hanging agape for a few seconds, before it curved quickly into the biggest grin she'd displayed on her face in a long while. She shook her head, surprised at herself. She couldn't believe she hadn't realised. Of course that's what Marley was doing. "Oh, shit!" she said.

"You didn't catch on? Come on, Maddie. It was so obvious!"

"I was distracted, I think," she said. "And if you only knew how anti-monogamy Autumn and Marley used to be, you'd be surprised, too. The fact they ended up here — and with each other — is quite frankly astounding."

"They really love each other, huh?"

Maddie nodded, marvelling for a moment at how cordial they were being and how naturally their conversation flowed, given they did not like each other. She was finding James really easy to talk to. His effort was almost certainly not for her benefit — he liked Marley and Autumn and really wanted to help them out — but still, she appreciated it. Tonight would have been miserable, boring and long if he'd been his typical moody self.

"I wonder what it feels like to be loved like that," he said.

"I have no idea," Maddie admitted.

"Have you ever been in love?" he asked. Maddie shook her head. "Me neither," he said.

"When was your last relationship?"

"A long time ago," he said, sighing. "Back when I was in my early twenties. I've had some situationships since then. Bad sex, bad vibes, no risk of heartbreak because there's no real heart in it."

"Sounds like my entire dating history," Maddie said monotonously. It was James' turn to look at her. "I've never had a real boyfriend," she admitted.

"Never ever?"

"Never ever ever," she said.

"You're not missing much," he said. "Men are awful."

Maddie laughed at that, and she knew he was smiling beside her. She could feel the atmosphere thawing between them and found, to her surprise, she had no desire to stop it. It had been an age since she'd had an extended conversation with anyone who was not a family member. She continued. "Have you met my dad?" she asked in jest. "He's wonderful, and so are my brothers. Imagine growing up around all that gentlemanliness and then dating Average Joe. It was a real shock, I can tell you."

"Didn't Marley have a reputation once upon a time?" James said, thoughtfully.

"Oh, gosh, yes, he did," Maddie confessed. Marley was so devoted to Autumn now that Maddie often forgot about his days as a heartbreaker. They'd started when he'd realised girls liked him and he liked girls at around age thirteen and continued right up until the summer they'd lost Bowie. The summer he'd fallen in love with Autumn. "I can't tell you how many young women turned up at our house in tears over Marley when I was growing up."

"I'm not surprised," James said. "He always was a sexy bastard. They both were. I think it was the musician thing.

Every girl I knew was in love with either Marley or Bowie, depending on whether they preferred an introvert or an extrovert."

"Bowie was so well behaved compared to Marley," Maddie said, smiling fondly. "He wasn't too bothered about women, really, he only cared about music and Marley. Until he met Autumn, of course."

James snapped to attention and stared at her, and then she remembered, he didn't know.

* * *

Maddie told James the whole story. She tried really hard to capture how painful and complicated it all was, how fretful and frightening, how torturous and terrifying. Those had not been ordinary times or typical circumstances, and Bowie and Marley were not normal men. Their love for each other had transcended all reason. She knew she'd done a terrible job of explaining, because James still looked confused and a little disgusted when she'd finished.

"Autumn and Marley tell the story much better than I can," she finished.

"Right," he said. Maddie felt her dislike for James, which had been temporarily expelled, reappear in her periphery. She set it aside to defend Autumn and Marley. Doing so was much more important than her own capricious feelings. She could continue hating him later if she needed to. For now, she needed to protect those she loved from a judgement she knew followed them everywhere.

"I know it sounds weird. We all found it really hard to accept at first, but whenever I see them together I know there was no better possible outcome for Marley or Autumn, or for my family, who have Benjamin because of this entire mess. His presence in our lives as a result of their transgression and Marley's happiness made it really hard to stay mad. You said it yourself, they have the kind of love people spend their whole lives trying to find. We have no choice but to accept that Bowie wanted this for them, for all of us."

James nodded curtly.

"Don't fucking judge us, James!" Maddie snapped.

"I'm not!" James held his hands up in submission. Maddie glared at him. "I mean, it's an unusual story . . . but I promise I'm not judging you. I'm just a little in awe, I think. Of Bowie in particular, but of your whole family more generally. I definitely judged you guys in the beginning and I've been proven wrong. You're all so . . . *nice*. There's so much love and acceptance. I don't think I've ever seen anything like it before."

Maddie wasn't sure she believed him. She eyed him suspiciously. He kept his hands raised by his face, as though she were pointing a gun at his chest. Perhaps she was. They'd been so close to putting their initial arguments behind them, they'd bonded a little bit tonight, she felt. If she was being honest, she didn't want to go back to the stony silence they'd grown used to working in, but their budding friendship hinged on his understanding of their unique circumstance.

"I swear on Stevie," he said, a little frantic. "And she's the only thing I love in the entire world, so I would never say those words if I didn't mean them."

Maddie softened at his words. He seemed eager to prove it, but she had already known he would never lie if he was swearing on Stevie. She had to consider that perhaps she was being defensive here. She was hugely proud of her family — they were the only thing she had in the absence of any friends. She'd take on anyone who tried to ridicule them in a heartbeat and had likely jumped to the conclusion that was what James was doing, because so many people had done so before.

"I believe you," she said.

He let his hands drop. Maddie shuffled uncomfortably in her seat. She watched him from the corner of her eye. He sat dead still, staring out of the window in front of them, lost in thought. Maddie knew she had a choice. She could sit beside him in silence, or she could say something and set them on a different path. This was a 'time before' moment. Maddie pondered. It would be easier to work together if they got on.

"You don't love anyone except for Stevie?" she asked. James snapped to attention, turning to her, his eyes wide with surprise. He slowly shook his head. "That's sad," she said.

He nodded. "Yeah."

She didn't know what to say to that, so she smiled gently at him. He returned the gesture.

"Where did you go to uni?" she asked, breaking their lingering gaze to root through the dashboard for a packet of cola cubes she was sure she'd seen her dad stuff in here at some point. She found them and held out the bag, urging James to take one. He stared into her eyes, then down at the bag, then his eyes landed on her face once more. He seemed to recognise that she was holding up a white flag. When he didn't reply right away, Maddie thought about stuffing the bag into her pocket and reverting back to necessary communication only, but she forced herself to give him a minute. She recognised something in his stance, knew somehow that he, like her, didn't have many people he could talk to, that this didn't come naturally to him. In light of his admission that he didn't love anybody, she really didn't think avoiding talking to him was the right thing to do. For all she knew, she might be the closest person to him. Even if she wasn't, he had opened up to her. She wasn't going to mess around with someone's mental health. She was part of this now. To her relief, he stuck his hand in the bag, pulled out a sweet, and shoved it in his mouth.

"Leeds," he said. "You?"

* * *

They chatted for hours after that, pausing only to update her parents that they were safe. James did most of the talking. He talked her through the bars in Leeds, then segued into travelling. He'd worked all summer the year he'd graduated to buy himself a van he could camp in, and then left without a plan. He'd been on the road for years, stopping for weeks at a time to replenish his funds by working in beach bars or hotels. He hadn't needed much, just enough to buy food and alcohol. He'd loved it.

"That's the life for me," he'd said with a sigh. "Adventure, unpredictability and the open road. Though I'll have to buy a new van at some point. I had to sell the old one when I ran out of money."

Brexit had caused him some issues. He'd lost the right to travel indiscriminately and found he had to leave the Schengen area every 90 days, but he couldn't leave and immediately re-enter, the new rules meant he had to stay away for at least three months. That's how he'd ended up in Morocco, where he'd found Stevie. She'd been lying on the beach beside a dead sibling. He'd waited in his van and watched for hours to see if her mother would return, but she didn't, so he had picked her up and taken her with him. His intention had been to find her a home, but the two had bonded overnight.

"I fed her and settled her on a little dog bed I bought from a supermarket, but I woke up in the middle of the night and she'd climbed in my sleeping bag with me. She was snuggled right in, her head on the pillow, her little nose right next to mine. When I opened my eyes she was staring at me, as though I was the best thing she'd ever seen in her life. I asked her if she was all right and she licked the end of my nose. I knew there and then she was my dog."

The only thing Maddie felt that level of excitement and passion about was caring for people, so when James asked her what she loved to do, that's what she chose to talk about.

"This is my calling, I one-hundred-per-cent believe that," she said, grinning. "I've always known it, since my very first job. I love helping people in turmoil feel better. I like making sure they know they're cared about."

"You sound like exactly the type of person who should be opening a recovery retreat."

Maddie nodded. "When I recruit, I'm going to recruit based on values rather than experience. It's something the social care sector is trying to do more. If you hire someone who cares, nothing else matters, really. They'll learn because they'll want to do the best job they can. But if you hire someone with experience, who doesn't really care . . . well, we've all seen the news stories."

"Have you started recruiting?" James asked. Maddie shook her head. "I'll help with that too, if you like? I can help write the ads and stuff, if you need me to."

Maddie smiled, grateful. James smiled back.

The RAC arrived in the early hours of the morning. James told her to stay in the car in the warm and he'd get out and handle everything. As it was, there wasn't much to do. The RAC hoisted the car onto the back of their truck, then drove off into the night. They gave James a card to give to Marley and Autumn. James got back into the car and they set off home. Maddie texted Marley to tell him the car had been safely collected, but the text remained unread. She also called Ben and Emma, who were wide awake at home and sounded like they might be drunk. Maddie insisted they go to bed, but it was still snowing, and they said they wouldn't be able to sleep until Maddie and James were safely back at the house.

They parked up at 4.25 a.m. and were greeted at the door by Emma, Ben and Stevie. It had been a long night, and Maddie had truly never been happier to be home. Stevie was glad to see them both. Her parents said she'd been restless for an hour or so after James had left her with them, then she'd settled down, which was great progress. She wagged her tail so furiously her entire body rocked back and forth with the weight of it. Emma offered Maddie a glass of wine, but Maddie refused. She couldn't wait to climb into bed.

"I'm going to get off," James said, gesturing to the door.

"Stay!" the Whittles chorused together.

"You can't walk home at this time of night," Emma said, urging James towards the staircase.

"I'll get you some pyjamas," Ben offered.

"And of course you're not working tomorrow," Emma said. "So have a nice sleep in, and we'll see you whenever you feel well rested."

James looked hesitant. "Are you sure?" He looked right at Maddie as he said it.

"It's the least we can do after everything you've done for us tonight," Maddie said. "Thank you so much for all your help."

James smiled shyly, nodding his head in concession. "Shall I leave Stevie down here?" he asked.

"No, take her with you," Emma said. "I'm sure she makes an excellent little spoon."

"She does." James chuckled. "Though she's a little hairy."

James, Maddie and Stevie ascended the stairs together. Maddie was so tired she felt like her legs were dragging dead weights. She was even considering forfeiting brushing her teeth.

"Toothbrush," she said to James. He looked at her, confused. "You'll need a toothbrush?" she clarified.

"Oh, yes, if you have a spare one."

Maddie nodded and pushed open her bedroom door, which was right across the hall from Pip's old room, the one her family had agreed would always belong to resident staff members from now on. Currently James. She wasn't sure he'd been in there since the day Emma had shown him where it was and informed him it was his to use as he pleased, even if he wasn't actually living with them. That was a shame because it was a lovely room, big enough for a king-size bed, sofa, dressing table and en-suite bathroom. Her own room was an exact replica of Pip's but on the other side of the house. She stared forlornly at her bed as she picked her way through the mess, which was actually just piles of books. She dug out a new toothbrush from the bottom of her bathroom cabinet and took it back to a yawning James, standing in the doorway.

"It seems you have a book infestation," he said.

"It's a real problem." She sighed. "We're a family of readers and these are everyone's books, including Bowie's. We hauled them in here while we were decorating and I haven't been able to bring myself to get rid of them. So, here they sit, waiting for a new home."

"I knew you'd be a reader," he said.

"How?"

"You're 'book girl'," he said. "It's so obvious. Like, Bluebell is 'party girl' and Autumn is . . . also 'book girl', actually."

Maddie tried not to get irritated. "Woman. We're women. And I'm not sure I agree with the reduction of women based on their hobbies."

"I'm not saying that's *all* you are," he said, looking sheepish. "Just that it's part of who you are. And I don't only classify women, I classify men, too."

"What type of man are you?" Maddie asked.

"Guitar man," he said. Maddie smiled at that. "But actually, we can all be more than one classification, so I'm also 'travel man'. Marley is 'guitar man' and 'dad man'. Bowie was 'guitar man'. Pip, I'm guessing, is 'activist man'."

Maddie laughed because it was true.

"Your dad is 'dad man' and your mum is 'mum woman'," he continued. "That doesn't apply to all parents, of course, but it does yours. My mum is *not* 'mum woman'. Anyway, it's a tried and tested classification system. If I tried to set you up on a date and I said I was setting you up with 'gym man' or 'podcast man' you'd know the type of man I meant, wouldn't you?"

"Please never set me up with 'podcast man'." She chuckled.

"Gym man?"

Maddie shook her head.

"Guitar man?"

Maddie reeled theatrically because she thought James was joking, but he didn't carry on with the comedy. Instead he stepped back and blushed, fixing his eyes to the floor. He twiddled the toothbrush awkwardly and headed for his bedroom door.

"Anyway, I'm really tired, so I'll see you in the morning, yeah? Thanks for the toothbrush. Goodnight, 'book girl'. *Woman*! Goodnight, 'book woman'. Stevie, come."

And then he was gone.

CHAPTER SIX

Maddie thought she'd sleep in, but she didn't. By 9 a.m. she was in the kitchen and on the phone to her mother, who explained Marley had called them early that morning and asked them to bring Benjamin into the village for breakfast. The local café had a Saturday December breakfast deal — five snowflake-shaped pancakes and a hot drink for £7.50. Maddie wasn't sure why that information was relevant, but she nodded along anyway, gazing out of the window at the robin who frequented their garden. The snow had been washed away by rain and the roads were mercifully clear once more.

"He said they have news to share. I think he's proposed, Maddie!"

Maddie grinned, basking in the glee in her mother's voice. Emma, like the rest of the Whittles, had always presumed Autumn and Marley would never get married, because they had never shown any interest in it before. Her mother had a romantic heart, though, and would be thrilled by the prospect of a wedding, as would her father and her siblings. She really hoped that they were all right, that Marley had indeed proposed to Autumn, or else the disappointment would be monumental. Plus, a wedding would give them all something to look forward to. Despite the lack of confirmation, she already could not wait.

She was making a pot of tea when James appeared, fully dressed and ready for the day. Stevie Licks was hot on his heels. For a fleeting moment Maddie was worried they might descend back into not speaking, but he threw her an awkward little wave.

"Hi," she said.

His eyes flitted to the door. "Hello."

Maddie shook her head. "Please stay for breakfast. It's the least I can do."

He shoved his hands in his pockets and scrunched up his face. "I don't normally eat breakfast," he admitted.

"Tea, then," she said. "I know you drink a whole load of that."

He conceded with a floppy side-smile, let Stevie Licks out into the garden, then made his way to the table and pulled out the nearest chair, the one closest to the door. Maddie wondered if he'd done that on purpose, so that he could bolt from her company as soon as it didn't feel impolite to do so. She found herself hoping not.

"Any news from Marley?" he asked, accepting the mug she was handing him.

Maddie shook her head. "Not yet, but he did ask Mum and Dad to meet them in the village with Benjamin for breakfast."

James beamed. "Fucking incredible. How exciting."

Maddie nodded. She cut two bagels and popped them into the toaster, then took an avocado and a tomato from the fridge, chopping them up and setting them on the table. He'd said he didn't want any breakfast, but it felt rude to eat without offering him food at least once more. She didn't dare look at him, but she felt his eyes upon her the entire time, with the exception of one fleeting moment when he went to the door to let Stevie back in, then took her to the living room so that she couldn't sit and beg for food. She wanted to ask him why he was watching her, but it felt like a rude question. She forced herself not to meet his gaze, focusing instead on preparing a big bowl of chopped fruit while she waited for the bagels to toast. When she was done she set it all before him, handing him a side plate. He took it graciously.

"I mean, if you insist." He helped himself to half a bagel, smothered it with smashed avocado, then took a huge bite, closing his eyes and swallowing with a satisfied smile.

Maddie laughed. "Don't force yourself, will you?"

He opened his eyes, grinning. "Now that I think about it, not eating breakfast might be down to laziness, not lack of hunger."

"We have breakfast in the kitchen every morning and you never join us," Maddie pointed out.

His face fell, and he shrugged. "It never felt right."

Maddie didn't know what to say to that. They'd been on speaking terms for barely twelve hours, but not speaking already felt like a distant memory. Her opinion of James had changed somewhat through the course of the evening. The way he'd jumped to help her brother, how wholeheartedly he'd reassured her father, his eagerness to see their mission through to the very end and his banter with her in the early hours of the morning had all taken her by surprise.

"Well, from now on I hope you will," she said, pouring herself another cup of tea.

James nodded as she held the spout to his teacup. "Thank you."

They fell into a comfortable silence. James helped himself to a second bagel, loading this one with twice as much avocado and several chunks of tomato. When he was done with that, he plated himself some chopped fruit, sprinkling it with quartered walnuts Maddie retrieved from the cupboard. She watched him, working her way through a much smaller portion.

"That was all delicious," he said, rubbing his stomach when he was done. "It's the second cracking meal I've been served in a row, Maddie. You better be careful, or I'll be moving in."

Maddie barked a laugh and, for absolutely no reason at all, she felt herself start to blush. She pleaded with herself not to dissolve into an embarrassed mess, but she had been so isolated for so long she wasn't used to compliments from strange, attractive men, and her body was reacting accordingly. Maddie, who did not consider herself a fickle woman, was furious with herself. She stood rather suddenly, collecting the dishes from the table and waving James away when he tried to help.

"You've probably already gathered this, but preparing food and eating together is such an important part of our day in my family," Maddie said, hoping words would distract him from her reddening face and chest. "It always has been. No matter what we've had going on, even when we were nursing Bowie through his illness, we've all always eaten together. In fact, when we lost him, I think meals together were a big part of what kept us all sane."

He didn't say anything, so Maddie continued talking.

"I love to cook for my family. It really is my way of showing them just how much I love them, you know?"

James didn't answer. This time, his silence caused Maddie to look up from the pile of dirty dishes. He sat dead still, staring at the tabletop. She could tell from his form that he was tense and upset. His shoulders were slumped unhappily, his hands balled into fists.

"You OK?" Maddie asked, warily. She did not feel like she knew this man well enough to have this conversation with him, but he looked so sad.

He shook his head and rubbed his hand across his face. "I'm sorry."

Maddie abandoned the dishes and headed for the table, sitting down beside him. She poured them both another cup of tea. He took it graciously. She had the unsettling urge to reach out and take his hand, but she stopped herself. She knew enough to know this flippant approach to affection was not normal and not everyone was comfortable with it.

Although, on reflection, she realised she'd probably feel far more comfortable touching a stranger in sympathy than she would touching James. Too much had gone on between the two of them — their initial animosity towards each other, their thawing coolness across last night, then whatever *that* had been outside of her bedroom in the early hours of the morning. She'd stop short of calling it a flirtation, but it had been . . . something.

"What's going on?" she asked softly. She didn't know much about James, but she did know he had been away from home for quite a long time before his financial woes forced him to return to their village. She got the impression he didn't have many friends here, and because of how rarely he spoke about his mother and how dismissive he was when anyone asked how she was — plus the fact he'd declared he didn't love anyone the night before in the car — she'd deduced they were not close.

He sighed. "Did you know I lost a brother, too?" Maddie's eyes went wide. She shook her head. James met her gaze and nodded. "My older brother, Harry. We were in a car accident when I was fourteen. He didn't make it."

"That's so sad, I'm so sorry," Maddie said. She had once accused James of not knowing what it felt like to lose someone important in tragic circumstances and she felt terrible. He could have thrown that in her face back then, but he hadn't.

James swallowed hard. "We didn't pull together, like you guys. It tore my entire family apart. Dad blamed Mum because she was driving. He left us, left me there with her. She went into herself and I couldn't . . . I couldn't get her out of it. She feels she deserves to die and she's sitting there, in her bedroom basically all day and all night, waiting for it to happen. She has no desire to seek any joy from life and I can't pull her out of that. Dad met someone else and had a new set of kids, forgot all about us. Somewhere along the way, I learned people can love you and then stop loving you — because they're too busy grieving or they think they're protecting you or you remind them of your dead brother and they'd rather build a new family and erase the memory of you both — and that's the absolute worst thing that can happen to anyone as far as I'm concerned."

Maddie listened to him intently. He was picking at his fingernails and avoiding her gaze, and she knew somehow he'd never told this to anyone.

"I was eighteen when I realised there wasn't a single person in the world who cared about me," he said. "I lived with my mum and my nan until I went to university and I called them every day for the first few weeks and then I stopped just to see what they would do and we went a month without speaking."

Maddie felt like she'd heard this story before. She took advantage of the break in his monologue to consider this. Autumn. Autumn had a very similar story, though she'd known long before she'd gone to university that her mother, Katherine, didn't really care about her. Incidentally, they were reasonably close now she'd had Benjamin. Katherine came to visit with Autumn's sister, Lilly, as often as they possibly could. Autumn was of the opinion it was important that Benjamin knew his mother's roots, so she'd resolved to allow Katherine to foster a relationship with Benjamin, so long as she continued to make the effort to visit her grandson. Eventually, once enough time and effort had been invested, Maddie knew Autumn would agree to meet her mother halfway, in both the physical and metaphorical sense, but for now she needed reassurance that Katherine's attitude had changed, and Katherine, who adored being a grandmother, seemed only too eager to prove it.

"Mum, I kind of understood," James continued. "She'd been weird for a while. But Nan . . . I wasn't expecting it. I really thought she loved me. It's the saddest I've ever felt. I want nothing to do with that kind of depression ever again."

Maddie stroked her thumb across his forearm and realised she had, at some point, reached out and grabbed him.

He met her gaze, and she felt herself blush. Desperate to hide her complexion's confusing reaction, she dropped his arm and turned away, sipping her tea in such a manner that the mug hid her face.

"I'm sorry about the way I was when we first met," he said. "I was embarrassed and upset that I'd hurt your mum, but I know better than anyone how complicated these things are. I shouldn't have given you such a hard time about it, but I did and then I didn't know how to undo it. It all felt so complicated."

"What's complicated about it?" Maddie said. "I did something awful, you overreacted. That was your cue to say 'sorry, I took things too far'. I'd say 'don't worry about it', end of conversation."

She was glad when his face broke into a wry smile. "I don't normally let people use my own oversimplifications against me, Whittle, but I deserve it in this instance, so I'll let it slide."

Maddie laughed. "Don't worry about it," she said. His eyes met hers again and this time she held his gaze. She did it for no reason except to prove she could. She'd spent very little time with men outside of her family in the last decade or so, but she'd always considered herself the kind of woman who could look into the eyes of a handsome man without acting silly. Her earlier reaction when he'd stared at her had perturbed her.

She was banking on him turning away, but he didn't. Instead his eyes roamed over her face and down her neck to her collarbone, then back up. Maddie was surprised by the action, but also, disappointingly, thrilled. She felt something stir in the pit of her stomach, a flutter she wasn't sure she'd ever felt before. She'd read enough and heard enough to know it was desire. Before she had a chance to abolish the thought, she wondered what it would feel like to kiss him. His mouth twitched at the same time, and she wondered if he was reading her mind.

"Don't you dare kiss me without my permission," she heard herself say. Her voice sounded bolder than she felt.

"Do I have your permission?" he murmured.

"No," she said.

"Why not?"

"Because you're only doing it because you're bored."

He scoffed. "This is the least bored I've ever been in my entire life."

He leaned closer and Maddie had to stop herself from whimpering. He was so close she could feel his breath against her lips. She felt a jolt of anticipation radiate through her hips and pelvis, and was infuriated at her body for reacting this way. She and James had spent most of their time working together ignoring each other. They'd been on speaking terms for hardly any time at all. And yet her insides screamed at her. She wanted him in a way she'd never wanted a man before, there was no denying that. It was a primal, insatiable feeling she had never experienced before, a sudden desperation. She'd heard people talk about it — her sister specifically — but never felt it herself. She had an overwhelming urge to straddle him on the kitchen chair.

He whispered. "Let me kiss you."

Against her better judgement, she nodded.

Maddie hardly had time to take a breath before his hand was in her hair and his mouth crashed against hers. He kissed her greedily, as though he'd been deprived of her. There were no pleasantries, he shoved his tongue hard against hers and snaked his arm around her waist, dragging her off her chair and urging her to straddle his lap. The whimper she'd been suppressing escaped her, and James moaned in response. He used one hand to hold her to him and the other to pull her hair so hard that her mouth was ripped away from his, her head thrust back and her neck exposed to his lips and teeth. Maddie felt like she might die if he didn't take her soon.

She was dangerously close to begging when James let go of her hair and picked her up, slamming her against the kitchen wall. He kissed her hard on the mouth once more and held her there for a minute or two, grinding his erection provocatively against her. She could hardly move from the weight of him. She felt controlled and at his mercy, and was surprised to note this was turning her on even more. She wrestled him playfully for freedom, pressing her body even harder against his, but he trapped her tighter between himself and the wall, rocking rhythmically against her, somehow hitting exactly the right spot. He moved his lips and tongue to her neck.

Maddie felt a deep heat rising within her. She was suddenly overcome with shyness and wanted to stop, but she couldn't. It felt too glorious. James must have sensed her apprehension, because he stopped to look up at her, his eyes wide with desire.

"Are you OK?" he whispered. Maddie nodded. "Are you sure?" he checked again.

"Yes," Maddie said. "I swear, I am. It's just, this isn't like me. I don't do this kind of thing."

"I do, but it never felt like this before," he said, a little breathlessly. She didn't know what to say to that, so she just stared at him. "Do you want to slow down? Or stop, for now? It's fine, Maddie. I want you to be sure."

She was trying to decide what to do when she became aware of an approaching rabble. Her family was back far earlier than she had been expecting. Maddie's eyes went wide. He lowered her quickly to her feet and raced away, she presumed to the bathroom to sort out what was likely to be a very obvious erection. It had certainly felt that way. Maddie straightened her hair and tried to blow cold air on her face to soothe her burning cheeks, but she could see her reflection in the kitchen mirror, and she looked anything but composed. She sauntered over to the kettle and filled it. They'd want hot drinks and excitement, and she was as happy to provide it as she always was, if not a little disappointed to have been interrupted.

The back door opened and the kitchen was suddenly alive with animated chatter. Maddie quickly hugged her parents, then turned her attention to Marley and Autumn, asking them how their date had been and checking they'd had enough to eat at breakfast. She noticed the ring on Autumn's finger, but didn't say anything, convinced they would want to break the news to her. She decided to pretend she hadn't known. At some point, James re-entered the kitchen. Maddie caught sight of him and marvelled at how completely ordinary and unfazed he looked. Not at all like a man who'd been dry-humping her against the kitchen wall three minutes earlier.

Marley marched right over to him and held out his hand.

"Thank you so much for last night." He pulled James into a hug.

"You are very welcome." James hugged him back.

"Coffee, Mum?" Maddie asked.

"Yes please, darling. I let Stevie out through the double doors and Pigglesworth out of his pen. They've gone for a wander. I think they might be in love."

"You should write that in one of your books, Autumn," Marley said.

"I would but, just like most things that happen in this family, nobody would believe it."

They all laughed apart from Benjamin, who was glued to Autumn's leg, his arms wrapped around her thigh. He was staring at Marley, his pretty blue eyes following his father wherever he went. He was always a little bit like this when his parents left him for an evening. They were all hoping he'd grow out of it.

"Benjamin, did you have something to tell Aunty Maddie?" Marley asked. Benjamin nodded his head. She questioned Benjamin with her gaze. His eyes flitted to the diamond ring on Autumn's left hand.

"Mummy and Daddy are getting married," he said.

"Oh my God!" Maddie played along. "What incredible news. Congratulations!"

She abandoned her coffee-making to hug the happy couple, then her mum and dad, who were positively beside themselves. None of her siblings had ever gotten married.

This would give her parents something wonderful to focus on. Perhaps it might even fix her own broken spirit. Maddie tried to push the dark thoughts out of her mind. This was a happy day. Her anxiety could clear off for now.

"Tell me everything," Maddie said, gesturing for Marley, Autumn and Benjamin to join James and her parents at the kitchen table. She put a cafetière of coffee and a pot of tea on the table, a bottle of juice for Benjamin, a packet of biscuits, and gave everyone their favourite mug — except for James, who didn't as yet have one. As she worked, Marley told her the story.

"I couldn't bloody believe it when the car broke down. I'd hired out the whole restaurant, they'd filled the place with flowers, I'd booked a room at the hotel over the road and had an overnight bag in the boot, everything was set! I was really worried she was going to insist we call it a night — she was so desperate to go home and so mad at me for insisting we go out . . . until she walked into the restaurant, of course! She knew right away what was happening, so I got down on one knee there and then."

Marley reached for Autumn's hand and they stared at each other like they always did, as though there was nobody else in the room, in the world, even. It made Maddie feel a little teary. Until recently, Maddie had never anticipated her older brother getting married. When he had been young, Marley had avoided commitment like it was an affliction. Tormented by Bowie's illness and in constant search of distraction, he must have taken hundreds of women to bed over the years. He had never been interested in any of them, but there was something different about the way he felt about Autumn. She was pretty, of course, but Marley had never had an issue attracting good-looking women. She was also intelligent, funny and kind, but there had already been many clever, amusing and charitable women in Marley's bed. Autumn did have some rarer qualities, however. She was very emotionally intelligent, knowing exactly who she was and embracing the good and bad parts of herself at all times. She'd spent a lot of time getting to know herself and accepting her flaws

— especially in the wake of Bowie's death, when she had undergone extensive therapy. Autumn talked about the bad parts of herself and how they limited her fairly often. Most recently, she'd openly admitted she found it harder apologising to Marley than she did her friends after they'd had a fight, and it was because she unconsciously resented men as a collective. Her father had been indifferent to her since she had been a little girl and, when she'd been a teenager, her stepfather had tried to sexually assault her. She'd had to explain to Marley that she was struggling to say sorry for her part in their arguments because she struggled to be vulnerable enough to admit her mistakes in front of any man — even one she loved, and who she knew loved her back. Being vulnerable had once put her in danger, so Autumn didn't feel safe enough to let down her guard. Maddie knew working that out couldn't have been easy, and that Marley would appreciate the tremendous thought and effort Autumn had needed to expend to come to that conclusion and then apologise anyway. Her brother adored Autumn's self-awareness, it was a quality most people generally didn't care to possess.

But, as far as Maddie was concerned, none of that was enough to explain his love for her. It had to be fate. Autumn and Marley loved each other endlessly because they were supposed to spend their lives together. It was written somewhere, it had to be. Marley leaned forward and pecked Autumn on the lips. She put her hand to his cheek and stroked his face, then kissed the end of his nose.

"Aw!" Emma, Ben and Maddie chimed together. Autumn blushed, and Maddie laughed. Even after all these years, it didn't come easily to Autumn to be the centre of attention, especially if there was something soppy going on.

"Anyway, we'd really like to get married here, in the garden in the spring, before you open the recovery retreat," Marley said. Maddie blinked theatrically at him, her mouth hanging slightly open. "If you don't mind, that is. We'll help set stuff up. I promise we won't add to your workload."

"You're not joking?" Maddie asked. Marley shook his head, wincing guiltily. Maddie sat down at the kitchen table, feeling suddenly weak on her feet.

"We can find somewhere else, Marley, this is too much trouble," Autumn said.

"No, we can do it!" Emma insisted. "I think that sounds like such a lovely idea."

"It's not you who'll have to do most of the work, Emma, it's Maddie," Autumn said.

"And me," James chimed in. "I can do a lot of it. It'll take me no time at all."

"We can pay you extra," Marley said. "To work overtime if you need to, so we're not taking you away from Maddie's project."

"Sounds great," James said, catching Maddie's eye. "It'll be fine. I can handle it."

"I want to get married at home," Marley said. "This is where we fell in love. It's where all of my favourite memories are. It's where Bowie is . . ."

Marley's voice caught in his throat and he busied himself pouring his second cup of coffee. Maddie caught Autumn's teary eye and felt herself relent. She knew Autumn and Marley were blissfully happy, and that they believed Bowie was one-hundred-per-cent responsible for the state of their lives today. Without his intervention, there would be no Benjamin and there would be no them. She understood why they wanted to get married here, and she would move Heaven and Earth to make sure it definitely happened, despite her reservations.

"Give me a date and we'll do it." Maddie sighed. Marley stood up and reached his hand out for hers, pulling her into his arms.

"Thanks, sis," he said, rocking her gently.

"Don't thank me." She rolled her eyes at her brother. "You're doing ninety per cent of this on your own — I'm just giving you permission to do it. So, you'd better get James to teach you how to use a fucking drill properly."

Marley laughed.

CHAPTER SEVEN

They finished their coffees and then dispersed. Maddie went to her bedroom to shower and change out of her pyjamas, while Emma and Ben migrated to the living room with Benjamin, and Autumn and Marley stayed in the kitchen to call Bluebell and Pip and tell them the news. Before they went their separate ways, James bid them all goodbye and said he'd go home, if that was all right, and he'd see them all tomorrow. Emma told him to take tomorrow off, too, and they'd see him the day after. James' eyes flitted to Maddie and then back to Emma and he nodded, thanking her gratefully. With that he was gone. Maddie was surprised to find she felt relieved. Every time she'd looked towards him, since their fumble in the kitchen earlier, she'd found his eyes on her, and she was worried he was making it obvious to her family that something had happened between them. She really didn't want them to notice. They loved James, they'd get over-excited, get involved and make her feel weird.

Maddie hopped into the shower and stood perfectly still beneath the steaming hot water. She wasn't sure what to do next. She'd already decided she too would take the day off, but because she hadn't had a day off in months, she'd forgotten what it felt like to relax. She cast her mind back several months, to a time before renovations and grand plans. Back then she'd spent her free days reading in the garden. Sometimes she'd wandered idly down to the local café or pub for a change of scenery and a break from her parents. The ice had melted, but even still it was too cold outside to face the twenty-minute walk to the village. Plus, she was too tired.

She got dry in the shower cubicle to protect herself from the harshness of the cold marble bathroom floor and, without much thought, got back into her pyjamas and climbed into bed. She really wanted to sleep, but the messiness of her bedroom was distracting her by reminding her of everything she still needed to sort out, so she clambered out of bed and trudged across the corridor to the spare room. James' room, technically, though he'd only used it once. Maddie often slept in here when she needed a change of scenery. It had never felt wrong to her before because the room had been unused, but it felt a little inappropriate now. Still, she slipped beneath the duvet, adamant she'd rest there just for a moment or two. She turned onto her side and caught a whiff of a familiar scent. It took her a moment to realise the smell was James. Her insides lurched involuntarily at the memory of the weight of him pressing her against the kitchen wall. She groaned and rolled onto her back, trying and failing to move her nose away from the smell. Her fingertips and toes tingled with desire.

Maddie was suddenly wide awake. Her heart was beating hard with longing. Her bruised lips throbbed with want. She rolled her eyes at herself and gave her head a little shake. What on Earth was going on? She had so much to do, so many things she needed to focus on. She hadn't even liked James this time yesterday, and now she was lying in his bed, sniffing his pillow and pining for him. She felt ridiculous.

Carrying on with James was a really bad idea. She had no time to build a 'happily ever after' right now and neither did he. He'd be leaving the country in just a few months and she had a recovery retreat to build and open. This was the absolute worst time to start messing around with a man she barely knew. Which was exactly why she wanted to do it. She felt like she never got to have any fun anymore outside of her role as daughter, sister, aunty. She felt like she was forgetting who she was. This silliness could be something she did just for her. Something out of character, something the typically sensible and considered version of herself would never do. Plus, it had been a *really* long time since there had been a man in her life. She tried to work it out in her head. Five years? Her last sexual dalliance had been thoroughly unsatisfying, as had most of her conquests before that. There'd been a couple of men she'd liked in her teens, but they'd been as young and inexperienced as she had been. In her twenties, she'd dated a man called Nathan. They had never been official — he refused to put a label on things and she'd been too young and inexperienced to see that as the red flag it was. They'd had lots of sex but he'd had no idea how to give her an orgasm and she'd had no clue how to direct him. In fact, she'd spent a long time thinking she'd probably had one, until she'd spoken about it with Bluebell and her sister had informed her that she had not, in fact, reached climax.

Bluebell had bought her a vibrator the following Christmas, and Maddie had taught herself about pleasure. She'd tried to bring it into her relationship, but the toy made Nathan feel inadequate. She'd tried to give him pointers on the things she liked, but he had taken no notice. In the end, their passionless relationship fizzled out. Six months later, she'd gone to bed with a man who'd taken her on a date. It was the worst sex she'd ever had. No foreplay, two minutes or less of thrusting, then it was over. Her lover had shown no interest in satisfying her, so Maddie had gotten herself off beside him in the bed. Afterwards, he'd texted her to tell her that her actions had made him feel like his skills were insufficient. Maddie had tried to reason with him, but he'd told her he wasn't interested in seeing her again. Two months later, he'd drunk-dialled her and invited her to his house for a bootie call. She'd declined, so he'd called her ugly and said she was shit in the sack. She had slept with other men here and there, but none had bothered to make sure she was satisfied. Five years ago, deeply depressed after losing Bowie and sick of trying to find a man who cared a jot about any part of her, beyond what she could do for them personally, she'd resolved to stop bothering.

It wasn't because she believed the guy who said she was bad in bed, nor was it because she didn't want to have sex. She had needs and desires like everyone else. It was just that she'd been busy with her grieving family. Plus, most of the men she met could hardly hold a conversation with her that wasn't small talk, and she knew herself well enough to know that she probably needed more than that. She wished she could be more like Bluebell, who'd learned to separate sex from feelings and found it easy to fish out men who would consider her needs, but that wasn't who she was.

So relationships and all the fun that came with them were deprioritised and then fell off the agenda completely, and Maddie had been fine with that. Sex with a specific human had hardly crossed her mind in all that time. Until now.

Desperate for an explanation, she took some time to consider why this might be happening to her. She wondered if it was a weird reaction to Autumn's and Marley's engagement. Perhaps romance was catching. Or maybe it was the impending return of Bluebell. Maddie's sister would be home in nine days and she always accidentally made Maddie feel like she was thoroughly boring. Bluebell was the personification of 'main character energy'. She would crash home in a whirlwind and bring with her enough melodrama and theatrics for an eight-episode Netflix series. Or perhaps Maddie was — and this one scared her the most — lonely. Terribly lonely. Maybe she was reaching for the first young, good-looking, eligible man she'd laid eyes on for a while because her mum had her dad, Marley had Autumn, Pip and Bluebell were off doing God knows what with God knows who, and she was the only one on her own. She had to accept it was a real possibility, and probably the most likely scenario.

She spent the next half hour wondering what James was getting out of this, aside from the obvious physical release that came from having sex with a woman, of course. He was devilishly handsome and had admitted he enjoyed one-night stands on a relatively frequent basis, so why was he bothering himself seducing her? Maddie was no longer prone to ripping apart her appearance — she'd spent many hours doing that when she was younger and had grown out of it as she aged — but she still considered herself average at best. At the very least, she was sure he could pull far more attractive women than her. What was he thinking, this man who'd pressed his erection against her and moaned with such soul it had almost tipped her over the edge? Perhaps he wasn't thinking at all. Maybe he just wanted to fuck his boss, or fuck any woman, for that matter. He'd said he did this often, but 'it never felt like this before', Maddie reminded herself. It was feasible he too was caught up in the drama of Marley and Autumn. Maybe he saw her as a cold, strong, independent challenge, or — and this was her worst-case scenario when James' motivations were considered separate from her own — perhaps he thought he actually liked her. She did not have time for that, and neither did he.

In the end, Maddie concluded that the reasons behind what had almost happened didn't really matter. What had almost happened absolutely *could not* happen, so there was no point mulling it over. She was quite sure letting James fuck her would be wonderful for her self-esteem. She had been thrilled by his expressions of want — no man had ever made her feel so desirable — but it brought with it too many complications. Sure, it would probably be good for her physical well-being — if the prologue was a prelude to the main event, then she was sure the epilogue would see her exhausted, fulfilled and thoroughly satisfied — but there was too much risk involved. Broken hearts, bruised egos, the vapid predictability of their inevitable parting in a few months' time. She didn't have the patience for any of it. They had to work together, for crying out loud. She was his boss.

Once she had worked it all out in her head, Maddie drifted contentedly towards slumber. She lay on her side once more, her nose searching hopefully for the dulcet remnants of James' sweet and soothing scent.

She found it, and slept deeply.

* * *

Her family let her sleep, and so she stayed in bed all day. When she woke up it was dark and she felt refreshed, though she knew she'd struggle to go to bed at a proper time tonight. That didn't bother her too much. In fact, she quite liked having the house to herself at night-time. She could put the fire on, pour herself a glass of wine and read her book in the quiet. She checked the clock. It was 6 p.m. She pulled on her favourite pair of slouchy jeans and a jumper, and made her way downstairs in search of food.

"Hello, darling," Ben said as she entered the kitchen. He was sitting at the table eating a bowl of mashed potatoes and gravy. Everybody else was nowhere to be seen. "Mum has taken Autumn, Marley and Ben home. We tried to encourage them to stay, but they wanted their own beds. Shall we put the Christmas tree up tomorrow? And the decorations?"

Maddie nodded. She helped herself to a glass of soya milk and sat down beside her father. He chewed thoughtfully, and she knew he had something to say.

"Spit it out, Dad," she said. Her father turned to look at her, a slow grin spreading across his face. Whenever he gave her this look, Maddie could not believe Ben was not Bowie's and Marley's biological father. He had not entered their lives until they were seven years old and yet they'd adopted so many of his habits. They'd always thrown her the very same look whenever they were going to say something they knew she wouldn't like.

"Mum and I were going to tackle this conversation together," Ben said. "We're worried about you, love. Worried about leaving you here next spring, I mean. It'll be awfully lonely . . ."

"Dad," Maddie warned. "I've always been a loner, haven't I? I could have friends if I wanted them, it's just that I'm comfortable on my own."

"You've never really been on your own, though, love. Not really. We've always been here. I know Autumn and Marley will still be around, but those two are lost in their own little world half the time. I'm just . . . worried."

"I'll be fine," Maddie reiterated. She really meant it, too. She knew it would be weird being here in this big house with staff and guests, but she was sure she would get used to it. She'd be really busy making sure nobody had to go through the pain and indignity Bowie had suffered. By the time she added spending time with Marley, Autumn and Benjamin into her life, she'd have hardly any time left to be lonely, she was sure of it.

"You've always been very family-orientated, my love," Ben said. "My quiet and introverted little girl. I just wish you had a friend or two to confide in, you know? I'd feel better about leaving you if I thought there were people you could spend time with."

"Dad, *you* don't have any friends," Maddie pointed out. "Neither does Mum, really. Your whole life revolves around this family, it always has. And you're OK."

"We have each other," Ben said. "But even still, the older we get, the more we realise that's not OK. That's my point. Mum and I both wish we had more friends, that's part of the reason we've decided to go travelling. To meet new people, get out there a little bit more."

Maddie was surprised at this admission. She'd never heard her parents lament their friendless existence. She had always assumed they were content with the way things were. Her father's disclosure made her heart sink. Her poor dad. She wondered how long he'd been lonely and kept it from her.

"Now, don't get me wrong," he continued. "Your mum is my best friend in the entire world, and you kids are everything to me. But there's something friendship brings to your life that family doesn't, and it shouldn't be underestimated."

"Maybe I'll make friends when we recruit staff for the recovery retreat," Maddie said, forcing a hopeful tone. Her father looked doubtful, and she was desperate to appease him. "Or at the book club I just joined."

"You've joined a book club?" Ben asked. His face brightened a little bit, so Maddie felt obliged to expand on the lie. "Yeah. It's at the Duck Inn. In fact, I'm heading there right now."

Maddie marched over to the coat rack and picked up Bowie's jacket and her scarf. She'd been looking forward to a quiet night in, but that was off the cards now. Emma and Ben had quite obviously been discussing this in depth between the two of them, and probably with Marley and Autumn. When her mum got back, they would ambush her and force her to talk. Her social battery had not yet recharged, and she needed some time alone.

"Oh, excellent!" Ben said. "Do you want a lift down there so you can have a drink?"

"It's fine, I'm not drinking this time," Maddie said. "I want to keep my sober head on."

"Sensible girl," Ben said.

"I'm a woman," Maddie reminded him. He rolled his eyes and apologised, turning pointedly back to his mashed potato. "I'll be back later." Maddie bid him goodbye.

"Don't you need your book?" He stopped her just as she was about to leave. Maddie internally chastised herself. Her dad was no fool and it would certainly cross his mind now that she was lying. Maddie did her best impression of a woman who'd made an honest mistake and headed for the bookshelf in the kitchen. She pretended she was looking for something specific and then selected a random book. *Call Me by Your Name* by André Aciman. It wasn't the book she was in the middle of reading, but it would do. She waved it at her father and headed for the door. He nodded, watching her leave.

Her mum had taken the estate car, so Maddie clambered ungracefully into her parents' 4x4, silently thanking the universe for thawing out the village. The roads were both free of ice and cars, so she felt comfortable driving. She even dared steal a glance at the odd Christmas display as she passed by quaint gardens lit up with Santa-shaped ornaments and prancing mesh reindeer silhouettes. Despite the fact her hand had been forced by her desire to avoid a difficult conversation with her parents, she was quite looking forward to a night in the pub now that she was on her way. As she parked up and headed inside, she silently prayed that her favourite seat — the squishy armchair right by the fire — would be free. She knew, somehow, that it would be, and she was right. There was barely anyone in the pub, a couple of men on their own at the bar, and three women chatting by the window. Maddie ordered a small glass of red wine, curled her legs up under herself and settled in for a night of reading, pausing for a moment to admire the seasonal decorations — the most impressive of which was a real tree. It was host to an immense number of baubles and a monumental amount of tinsel. It appeared to be leaning to one side under the weight of the decorations. Maddie smiled, turning her attention to her book. She was only a few lines into her new novel when she was distracted by a nearby conversation. The women in the window were gossiping away animatedly, gasping and giggling their way through some sort of debrief.

"His older brother was killed in a car accident."

"I thought Harry was younger."

"No, he was older, I'm sure of it."

"Is that why he looks so brooding all the time?"

Maddie tried her hardest to ignore them, but she knew who they were talking about. This was an incredibly small village. It was highly unlikely there were two brooding men with a brother named Harry who had been killed in a car accident. She wished she'd brought her headphones with her, but the women were less than twelve feet away, and they were hardly being discreet. There was no way to ignore them, especially as they were talking about somebody she knew. She had no choice but to listen. The women continued.

"He is brooding, isn't he? Perhaps that *is* why."

"Carry on with the story, please. He took you out, you were supposed to see him last night, he had some excuse . . ."

"Yes, he said there'd been an accident, he needed to help out a friend. He said he'd see me tonight, instead. Then he texts me today calling the whole thing off."

"How irritating."

"It's his loss."

"I'm not sure it is, actually. He was the only eligible bachelor in the entire village. Plus, he was truly spectacular in the sack."

The women laughed, and Maddie was in equal parts envious and irritated. She was jealous that the women had people to mull over their confusion with and irritated that their discussion was encroaching on her reading time. Admittedly, it was also making her feel strange. Not possessive, as such, but . . . something. A little sick. Vaguely frustrated. Mildly confused. The women were talking again.

"Seriously, I've never met a man with such well-placed confidence. I was sure it was all talk, but he knows exactly what he's doing. He's a genuine sex God."

Maddie rolled her eyes and sank lower in her chair. She tried once again to focus on the first page of the novel, but even when the conversation moved from James and onto another man, she could not stop thinking about him. She was embarrassed to admit he hadn't been far from her mind since she'd woken up in his bed earlier this evening. She felt like a silly teenage girl. He'd thrilled her for a few minutes, that was it. She hadn't had to travel far to find another of his conquests. He was with women all the time. She had already decided this couldn't go any further. It infuriated her that, despite all that, she couldn't stop thinking about him.

She gave her head a little shake and forced herself to concentrate. She'd be annoyed at herself if she left here later having hardly read anything. Thankfully the book, one given to her by Pip, was so enthralling it stole her focus quite quickly once she'd set her mind to it. She was so consumed she didn't notice the pub empty of people. She shifted from side to side every fifteen minutes or so to prevent her hips and back from seizing up and drilled through the pages, marvelling at the author's poetic depiction of desire steeped in confusion. She couldn't wait to thank her brother for the recommendation.

She was so deeply distracted she didn't notice a man enter the pub, nodding yes when the barman asked him if he would like 'the usual'. She was blissfully unaware when he collected his drink and sat down in the window. She missed the moment when he looked over and realised who she was. She didn't know he was there until he'd sunk his pint and — having briefly mulled over what he should do — was standing up to leave. He kicked a chair over in his haste, and the clatter broke her focus. She looked up to find him standing there, staring at her.

"James," she said, closing her book.

"Maddie." He nodded, looking anywhere but at her. Stevie, who was sitting dutifully at his side, waited for Maddie to hold out her hand to her and then trotted over for a fuss. They were silent for a moment.

"How long have you been here?" she asked.

"Just a couple of minutes." Maddie's eyes flitted to the empty pint glass in his hand, and she knew he'd been hastily leaving. It did not make her feel good. He followed her gaze and winced. "I realised I forgot to . . ." He faltered when he saw the look on her face. She knew men better than this and would not fall for such bullshit.

"It's fine," she said, opening her book on a random page. She expected him to leave, but he didn't. Maddie moved her eyes from side to side as though she was reading the book. She figured he would get the hint eventually and go away so she could swallow her disappointment and convert it into rage, but he just stood there, watching her, for what felt like an age. In the end she raised her head to look at him.

"You OK?" she asked. He moved as if he was going to nod his head, but he didn't. Instead he continued to stare at her. "I thought you were heading off to sort out that thing you realised you forgot?" she said, a little bitterly.

"I was lying about that." He held up his hands in mock submission. "Hard to believe, I know. I was so convincing."

Maddie had to fight hard to keep her face straight. She locked her eyes on his, trying to force the memory of him moaning in her ear out of her mind. It was difficult. He looked dishevelled in faded blue jeans and a baggy green sweatshirt, but he was somehow still the most beautiful man she had ever seen. He was carrying a guitar on his back and it looked like he was fiddling with a plastic pick in his hand. His hair was curlier than usual and looked a little wet — she concluded he'd recently showered. She wondered if he'd thought about their tryst as she had. If he'd touched himself. She silently admonished herself, and must have shaken her head a little bit as she did, because his eyes were suddenly brimming with sorrow.

"Please don't look at me like that," he said, stepping towards her. "I'm not that fucking guy, I swear it. I'm actually pretty good at communicating the way I feel most of the time. When it comes to romantic partners, I mean. I don't know why I was planning on bolting. I can't explain it. Maybe it's because you're my boss, I don't know."

Maddie raised her eyebrows and blinked theatrically at him. "Then how *do* you feel, James?" she asked. He paused, looking thoughtful. Maddie tried not to be distracted by a set of manically flashing Christmas lights strung over a picture frame behind his head.

"Can I sit down?" He pointed at the chair opposite hers. "Sure." Maddie shrugged. He asked the barman to pull him another pint, ordered her another glass of wine, set down his guitar, then perched on the edge of the other fireside armchair, warming his hands in front of the fire as though he'd just stepped in from outside. Stevie lay down in front of the hearth. Maddie used the time to consider how she'd get home, given she'd be over the legal limit to drive if she finished the drink he'd just bought for her. She reasoned she'd call a taxi or ring her dad and ask him to collect her. She knew he wouldn't mind. James waited until their drinks arrived before he said anything.

"I don't know what the hell that was this morning or where it came from," he said. "I am so, so sorry."

"Why are you sorry?" Maddie asked, confused.

"The look on your face when I asked if you wanted to stop or slow things down . . . We'd been talking about me losing my brother and I know that's such a sad conversation for you, too. I don't know, I came away from it feeling like I might have overstepped the mark."

Maddie scoffed. "You did *not* take advantage of me." He narrowed his eyes at her, as though searching for further confirmation. She shook her head a little violently. He looked relieved.

"I don't know what to do now, it's all I've been thinking about all day," he admitted. Maddie felt a little sad at that. The dozen or so times she'd relived what they'd done that morning had been bursting with thrills in her memory. James, on the other hand, had considered it only from the perspective of having done something wrong. Maddie wanted to reassure him.

"It was a welcome distraction," she said, a little shyly.

"A completely unexpected one," James agreed. He blinked rapidly, hiding his face behind his pint, as if he was blushing. Maddie took a sip of her wine, realising he'd bought her a large one. Good job she'd already decided not to drive home. "Did you sleep today?" he asked her.

She nodded. "Did you?"

"Not a wink." He shook his head. "I couldn't stop thinking about it, worrying about it, wondering about it." He shuffled to the very edge of the chair and leaned forward, as though he was about to tell her a secret. Maddie leaned towards him. "Where did that come from?" he murmured.

"I don't know."

"I thought you hated me," he said.

"I thought *you* hated *me*."

He shook his head in disbelief and then sat back again, nursing his beer. She saw his shoulders rise and fall slowly and fathomed he was sighing away some tension. She did the same. For a horrible moment, when she'd caught him trying to leave, she'd thought he'd been trying to avoid her because he regretted their frolicking and wasn't adult enough to confront it. That level of immaturity from him would have devastated her. She was relieved.

Despite that, she was still adamant it could never happen again. As deliciously enjoyable as it had been, Maddie needed to devote every free moment she had to the house. She was confident she couldn't manage everything she needed to do and foster a situationship, so — as horny as she was and as wild as James' proximity was driving her — she needed to find a way to turn this into a friendship at the very most. He had not taken advantage of her, but he *was* right . . . there was a lot going on.

"Oh, God, what?" James interrupted her ruminating. Maddie realised she had been frowning and straightened her face. She shuffled uncomfortably and sipped her wine, watching him watching her over the top of her glass. She wasn't sure how he was going to react. He might be angry and upset. Perhaps he'd call her ugly, like her previous lover. He might feign relief in order to try to hurt her feelings and save face. Or perhaps he'd be visibly and *genuinely* relieved. That would be even worse. She didn't want him to regret what had happened between them. She wanted him to feel the way she did about it — that it was wonderful, but the sensible and adult thing to do would be to leave it at that. "You're killing me here," he prompted her.

"I don't think we should do it again," she said. His face fell, and Maddie had to stop herself from congratulating him on reacting in exactly the right way. He didn't look defensive or bruised, he just looked disappointed.

"Oh, really?" he said.

"I don't think it's a good idea," she said. He seemed to shrink a little bit, and she was worried he was jumping to conclusions about himself, so she rushed to make him feel better. "It's nothing you did or didn't do," she said. "It's just there's so much going on at the moment and I've been feeling . . . not great, but I need to devote myself completely to the recovery retreat and now the wedding. There's no room for anything else."

Maddie paused. She felt very suddenly completely and utterly overwhelmed. Autumn's and Marley's engagement and the silliness that had occurred this morning between her and James had been heavy distractions from everything else, but now the weight of her to-do list was looming in her periphery, just waiting to set itself back on her shoulders.

James nodded his understanding, eyeing her intently. "Are you OK?" Maddie shot for a confident affirmation, but her attempt at a nod landed somewhere between an uncertain shrug and shake of the head. "Convincing," he teased her.

In spite of everything, she laughed. "I'm sorry," she said.

"Do not apologise." He shook his head.

"It's not you, it's just not the right time for a situation-ship of any kind," Maddie reiterated.

"I totally get it." He nodded. "I know things have been weird between us, but how about a friendship, instead?"

Maddie beamed. She couldn't help it. A friend was exactly what she was looking for. She'd lied to her dad and told him she was coming here to meet friends, now it felt somehow like she'd manifested one. She was the type of person who looked for the meaning in everything and she felt like James' suggestion gave her the answer she needed as to why what had happened this morning had happened. They had dry-humped in the kitchen in order to fast track their friendship. In her wine-filled haze, this made perfect sense.

"Can we draw a line under everything and start again?" Maddie asked. She didn't have the energy to work through her initial annoyance at him for working on a farm, or his anger at her for misleading him about Bowie, or his refusal to treat her better after she had apologised, or the countless dirty looks they had thrown one another, the mutterings under breaths, the way they had ignored each other countless times . . .

"Absolutely," he said. Maddie smiled and James stood, gesturing towards the bar. "So, friend," he said. "Have another glass of wine and unload your worries. From now on, your burdens are my burdens, and mine are yours."

CHAPTER EIGHT

They talked until closing time, mainly about travelling. James told Maddie all about the countries he had visited, the people he'd met and the jobs he'd done.

"Honestly, it's the only time I feel like myself. It's so freeing, you know? Waking up each day with no real responsibility, nobody to answer to, never knowing who'll I'll meet next and where I'll end up."

"It sounds like a nightmare to me." Maddie laughed. He waited for her to elaborate. "I'm such a homey person. I always have been. Perhaps it's because I'm a little shy, I don't know. I was so young when Bowie was diagnosed, he was only twenty-one, Bluebell was nineteen, I was barely fourteen. Pip was so young he hardly remembers a time before Bowie had cancer. He was five, I think? Six, maybe? Gosh, he was as young as Benjamin. Bowie was so sick, we were always taking care of him, worrying about him, hoping he would recover soon. It took so much away from our family. Maybe that's part of the reason why I like being at home with the people I love close by. I'd wrap them all in cotton wool and keep them there if I could."

"I cannot imagine anything worse than being trapped here," he said. Maddie felt her face fall. "Not that I think you're trapped, or anything. Our circumstances are so very different. Home for you is a peaceful place, and I can see why. For me it's . . . something else, I don't know."

"My therapist would say you're running away," Maddie teased.

He grinned. "My therapist would say your therapist is right."

At one point, Maddie listed everything she had to do around the house before the recovery retreat opened and her new list of things she wanted to do before Autumn and Marley got married in the garden. James listened without interrupting, but she knew he was paying attention because she could see the tension building in his shoulders. He really was shouldering some of the burden. She felt better with every word she spoke. He quite clearly felt worse.

"Jeez," he said when she'd finished. "You weren't joking when you said you have a lot going on."

Maddie nodded despondently.

"Well, I can definitely help with some of this. Just tell me what you want me to do and I'll do it. I can definitely get more involved in the house renovations and wedding prep," he said.

Maddie smiled, grateful. But, despite his offer, she still felt she didn't have enough time. She felt guilty for taking the day off, even though it was Sunday and she'd worked every waking moment for the last few months. She knew she'd have to make the hours up at some point.

"I can work more weekends, too," James said.

Maddie wished she could turn down his offer, but she was not in a position to. "We'll pay you," she said.

"I know you will." He nodded. "We'll get it done. I promise."

Maddie believed him, and it made her feel so much better. It felt great to have someone she could offload to, someone she could burden without worrying about the impact it was having on them because she loved them so much and knew they loved her back.

"Time, kids," the barman called. "Any later and I'll lose my licence."

"Sorry, Oz," James said.

"Get home safe — it's really coming down out there," Oz warned.

Maddie and James each glanced at the window, and then at each other. Oz was not lying. The snow was falling hard and fast. Maddie knew already the roads would be a nightmare. Not that she'd drive anyway, given she'd been drinking, but it meant getting a taxi in their tiny village would be nigh on impossible. There was no way she'd risk their safety by asking her parents to pick her up, or Marley, who lived around the corner, to drive her home. She was stuck.

"I'll walk you back," James suggested. Maddie nodded, packing her book in her handbag and climbing into Bowie's old jacket. She was sure she got a whiff of him as she did so. She inhaled deeper, hoping to hold onto him a little bit longer, but the scent was either gone or had been in her imagination. She was tipsy, so the latter was more likely. James was watching her intently.

"Bowie," she said, as though that explained it. His eyes were still quizzical, so she elaborated. "This is his jacket and sometimes I feel like I can smell him when I put it on."

"Fair enough," he said, gesturing towards the door. Maddie followed Stevie out onto the street. The village was covered in a blanket of snow so deep it went right up to Maddie's shins. It looked like the front of a Christmas chocolate box. The streets were empty and quiet, the air thick with the scent of roaring fireplaces. It was so magical that Maddie couldn't be irritated, despite the fact her half-hour walk home would likely take double the time. It was freezing cold and the snow was still falling so fast she could hardly see in front of her face.

"Shit," James said. "I've never seen anything like this, have you?"

Maddie shook her head. The village Christmas tree was coated with such a thick layer of snow she could barely see the lights twinkling between the branches. "I need to get my wellies out of the car."

"Cool, then we better set off before it gets any worse." He was slurring his words a little bit, and Maddie realised he too was probably a little bit drunk.

They retrieved her wellies and Maddie put them on. She gave permission for James to leave his guitar in the car overnight to save him carrying it and then they set off in the direction of her house, kicking at the mound of snow before them with each step. Stevie loitered in the warmth of the pub doorway, watching them fight their way towards the main road. When she eventually joined them, she was smart enough to stay behind and let them do the work. It took them ten minutes to reach the road, a walk that would normally take no longer than three. They stopped, exhausted.

"We're going to die out here," James said, dramatically. He was panting and sweating from the effort, but his nose was red from the cold. His hair was soaked through and stuck to his head. Maddie realised she too must have looked disgusting, but was too drunk to care. James tried to take advantage of the height of the snow and sit back, but he fell further through it than he was expecting and landed with his legs sticking up in the air. Maddie laughed.

"I'm stuck," he said. "Stevie, help!"

Stevie obligingly started digging. Maddie reached out her hand and grabbed his wrist. She tried in vain to pull him out, but he really was stuck, so when he tried to assist her in assisting him, he pulled her on top of him instead. Maddie screamed.

"For fuck's sake," James said. The weight of her had pushed him further into the snow mound and he was now effectively completely horizontal. They were a tangled mess of arms and legs. She grappled for balance, searching for something to grab hold of to steady herself, that was not snow or a part of his body, but there was nothing. In doing so, she touched his chest and thigh. When her hand brushed his groin she stopped, blushing profusely.

"Wait," he said, catching his breath. "Can I grab your waist a second?"

"Yes." She nodded. He tried to bench-press her back onto her feet, but he overshot. Maddie fell backwards, landing with a thump.

"Shit, sorry!" he called out to her. She was laughing so hard she thought she might pee herself. There was a wall of snow between the two of them now, but she could hear him giggling. They lay like that for a minute or so, laughing like children.

"Do you think we're too drunk to know we're slowly freezing to death?" he called out.

"Potentially," Maddie shouted back.

"Then we should make a move," he said. From her snow ditch, she heard him digging his own way out. She could see bits of snow flying everywhere as he did so. Suddenly, his face was above hers. He stood cautiously and held his hands out, pulling her deftly to her feet and holding her close until he was sure she had her balance. Maddie felt herself blushing again. James either didn't notice or made a deliberate point of looking away. Either way, she was grateful he didn't see. "We're not going to get you home in this," he said.

Maddie agreed. "I'll call Autumn and ask if I can crash on their couch." She pulled out her phone and called her sister-in-law, but there was no answer. Maddie found Marley's number and dialled. This too rang out. She was starting to panic.

"They're probably exhausted after all the drama last night," James said.

"You're probably right."

"You can stay at mine?" James suggested. Maddie eyed him cautiously. He held his hands up in submission. "In a purely innocent and platonic, friend-like way. I have a spare bed."

Maddie hardly had a choice, but she still worried it would be a mistake to agree. They had only just declared their complicated relationship a friendship, *and* they were drunk. She enjoyed being close to James a little too much and her lips were still burning from the force of his kiss earlier in the day. Truthfully, she wasn't sure she could trust herself, but there was nothing else for it, so she nodded.

"It's this way." James pointed back along the route they'd just followed.

* * *

By the time they got to his house — a thatched, terraced cottage situated right by the village green — Maddie was sure she'd never been so cold in her life. With her permission, James put his arm around her to try to keep her warm, but her clothes were soaked through and the temperature was below freezing and dropping. By the time he let them into the house, her teeth were chattering so violently Maddie was worried she'd bite her own tongue off.

The living room was empty, but there was a 'recently vacated' feel to it. She presumed his mother had gone to bed shortly before. The lights were off, but there was a fire in the hearth. James, Maddie and Stevie all headed straight for it. They didn't say a word until they'd thawed out. Once Maddie had stopped shaking — and had texted her parents to let them know that she was with James and safe — she took the opportunity to look around the room. It was small, cosy and full of textures. There were two sofas, one brown leather and one cream fabric. There were ditsy flowers of various colours printed on the wallpaper and a sideboard stacked with old-fashioned china against one wall. The far corner was host to a Christmas tree, which was tastefully decorated with silver baubles. There was a knitted nativity scene on the mantelpiece and tinsel blue-tacked to the door frames.

"Well, that was fucking scary," James said, kneeling down to check on Stevie. Maddie concurred with a nod. It had been fun and games at first, but it had very quickly become unfunny. She really had started to worry that one or both of them would become hypothermic. "Do you want another drink?" he asked.

"Do you mind if I just go to bed?" she said.

He shook his head. "Not at all. Do you want a shower first?"

"Just a towel to dry my hair and some pyjamas if you have any?" she asked. James nodded and led the way upstairs to a small hallway. There were three doors, one to the left, one to the right and one straight ahead. James opened the door on the right and turned on the light to reveal a teeny-tiny box room, just big enough for a chest of drawers and a set of old bunk beds.

"It hasn't changed since I was a kid because I haven't been back long and, obviously, I'm not planning on staying," he explained.

Maddie nodded, surveying the rest of the bedroom. There was hardly enough floor space for the two of them, so she was relieved when James gestured for her to enter while he remained in the doorway.

"Mum has the master bedroom, across the hall. There's a bedroom downstairs at the back of the house Nan used to use, but we haven't cleared it out since . . . Well, you know," James said.

Maddie nodded, turning to him. He was leaning against the door frame. He looked embarrassed.

"I'm sorry it's so small," he said.

"It's lovely." She meant it, too. The walls were powder blue, the linen was cream and perfectly pressed and the curtains were a pretty lace she knew would keep out absolutely no light at all. They were impractical, but gorgeous. There was not a scrap of dust or a stray sock to be seen anywhere. It was almost as though nobody lived here.

"They're both clean. I usually sleep on the couch, so you can choose whichever bunk you want," he said, opening the top drawer of the chest and pulling out a towel. He handed it to her. "The bathroom is here, at the top of the stairs. I store things in here — boxers, T-shirts, joggers and stuff. Help yourself to anything you need." Maddie stopped surveying the room to look at him. He was turning to leave.

"James," she said. He stopped with one foot hovering over the edge of the stairs. "You could stay in here with me, if you like?" She saw him wet his lips and swallow, and could tell from his face he didn't trust himself either. But Maddie was feeling stronger now that she didn't feel so cold and vulnerable. She spoke her thoughts aloud, answering his questioning gaze. "It's not like we'll be in the same bed, is it?" she reasoned. "I'll be underneath you or on top of you or . . ." She stopped when his mouth twitched. "Forget it," she muttered, feigning irritation. James laughed.

"Oh, come on, I'd have to be a saint not to laugh at that!" he said.

"Choose which fucking bunk you want and shut up," she said, pushing past him and into the bathroom. As she closed the door, she heard him chuckling from the bedroom.

* * *

Maddie texted Marley and Autumn to tell them she'd called because she'd gotten stuck in the village but had found a friend to stay with, so that they wouldn't panic when they woke up to a missed call each. She used her finger to rub toothpaste over her gums and splashed her face with warm water. She was almost done towel-drying her hair when James knocked to tell her he'd left her some clothes to change into outside the bathroom door. On inspection, she thought about wearing the joggers and T-shirt for modesty reasons, but the cottage was warm and she was worried she'd just end up taking them off, so she braved boxers and the T-shirt. She was relieved when she re-entered the bedroom and found James in the top bunk, as she didn't fancy climbing up the wooden stairs while he watched her from the bed below. She was grateful when he closed his eyes as she entered the room.

"There's a dark monster under the bed," he said. "So you have to switch off the light and run."

"I'm not doing that," Maddie said, pressing the light switch.

"Spoilsport." He tutted. Maddie felt her way to bed and climbed in. They were single beds but double duvets, which made it exceedingly easy for Maddie to roll herself up in hers. She spent a couple of minutes turning from one side to the other, trying to get comfortable. "Do you have fleas?" he asked eventually.

"I'm getting comfy," she said, feigning annoyance. They tumbled into silence. Maddie wanted to move again, but she was afraid she was getting on his nerves. It wasn't that there was anything wrong with the bed, but it had been a really long time since she'd slept anywhere except in her own house. Actually, she wasn't sure she'd slept anywhere else since Bowie had died. James seemed to sense her anxiety.

"You OK?" he asked. She could tell from the tone of his voice that he, in fact, was not OK. He sounded timid and unsure, like a little lost boy trying to be brave.

"All good, are you?"

"It's weird for me, sleeping in here," he said. "After Harry died, I left the room exactly as it was. It was like that when I left for university, but when I got back, that first Christmas, they'd gotten rid of everything. Instead of being full of boy stuff and shared memories, it looked like this."

Maddie didn't know what to say.

"I normally sleep on the sofa bed downstairs with Stevie," he added.

"I'm sorry, James. You can go downstairs if you want to."

"No, this is good for me," he said. She wasn't so sure. He sounded upset. "Losing a brother sucks, ey?" he added.

"Does it ever get any easier?" Maddie asked. James didn't answer for such a long time that she began to convince herself he wasn't going to. His silence would be confirmation of what she already knew. This empty feeling, this deep despair, this desperation for one more moment with her brother — one last chance to tell him how much she loved him — would never go away. She felt her eyes fill with tears and buried her head in the pillow in case she needed to stifle a sob. She heard a shuffle from above and thought James might be getting out of bed. Her eyes flew open and she hurried to compose herself, but as her sight adjusted to the dark of the night, she discovered he'd merely rolled onto his front and slid his arm through the bars, so that his open palm was suspended in the air beside her head. He wiggled his fingers pointedly. Maddie thought about it for less than two seconds before she reached up and grabbed his hand.

"No, Maddie," he said, stroking her thumb with his. "I'm sorry to say it never gets easier."

* * *

Maddie woke a couple of times in the night but was soothed back to sleep almost immediately by the sound of James' gentle breathing. At some point she let go of his hand, but every time she opened her eyes it was still there, open and expectant.

As the sun rose, the light chased the shadows across the bedroom floor. Maddie lay still and silent and watched them for a little while. She needed to pee, but was afraid she might run into James' mum, or wake him up when he seemed to be sleeping so peacefully. When she saw his hand twitch, she took her opportunity to shuffle, and knew instantly her movement had woken him up. His breathing changed and it sounded like he had rolled over. He let out a little moan, and she heard him scratch his head. He yawned a couple of times and then she heard him sit up.

"You awake?" he asked.

"Yes," she said. He sat up and leaned over the railings to peer down at her. He was shirtless, bright-eyed and pink-cheeked. Despite their heavy night, he looked like he'd stepped off an album cover. Maddie groaned and covered her head with the duvet. He laughed.

"Not a morning person?" he asked.

"Not in the slightest," she said.

"Hungover?"

"A little bit," Maddie acknowledged her headache.

"Me too," he said. She heard him swing his legs towards the ladder and remained with her head under the duvet to protect his modesty as he descended, only peeking out from beneath the duvet when she'd given him enough time to collect himself. Her stomach flipped at the sight of him shirtless, lean and covered in tattoos. She was taken aback by how many there were. She'd known he had some because she'd noticed them on his arms when he'd rolled up his sleeves once, but she hadn't anticipated there'd be quite this many. She was also surprised by how toned he was, though she wasn't sure why, given he spent so much time at her house effortlessly lugging heavy things around.

"Nice tats," she said, hoisting herself up onto her elbows.

"Thanks. I'd lie and tell you they're all really meaningful, but friends don't lie to each other. Most of them are just pictures I like," he said. Her eyes landed on the writing tattooed across his heart — his brother's name, Harry. He sensed her gaze. "That's the most important one," he told her. Maddie nodded.

"I've thought about getting a tattoo to honour Bowie," she said. "But I've never settled on anything I like for long enough to actually do it."

"You should," he said. "It's just skin at the end of the day."

Maddie smiled at that. It was just like him to consider something so permanent so lightly. She had never considered herself an uptight person, but, next to James and his attitude to life, Maddie was wound up tight as a bobbin.

"Does it hurt?" she asked.

"Nah." He shook his head. He opened a drawer and took out a hoodie, pulling it over his head. Maddie tried not to admire his form, but found it exceedingly difficult. James was her indie-band, mascara-boy, teenage dream personified. He held a green-and-grey-striped jumper towards her. "Cup of tea?" he asked.

"Yes please," she said, pulling the duvet back and swinging her legs over the edge of the bed. She thought she saw his eyes linger on her form, but the moment was so fleeting she couldn't be certain. "Can I have some joggers as well?" she asked. She wasn't keen on potentially meeting his mother wearing boxer shorts.

"Sure," he said, tossing her a pair. Maddie pulled them on. He watched her as she did so, and she was sure she caught him this time. Yes, she was almost one-hundred-per-cent certain he was admiring her curves. She wasn't sure why that surprised her. He'd proven the day before he was attracted to her. Still, the level of his obvious admiration caught her off guard. He caught her eye, and blushed.

They descended the stairs and were met at the bottom by Stevie, who was thrilled to see them both. They basked in her kisses and then James led the way to a door at the back of the living room, which opened into a perfectly square kitchen. He let the dog outside, filled the kettle, put it on, then held up a loaf of bread and a box of cereal.

"Do you have soya milk for the cereal?" she asked.

"Shit. No. I didn't even think. Toast it is."

Maddie smiled knowingly. "Do you have vegan butter for the bread?" His face fell. He lowered the loaf despondently and shook his head. Maddie took the liberty of sitting herself at the kitchen table and watched him try to figure out what he was going to do next. He was staring about the room as though the absent items might magically appear if he willed hard enough. She found it too cute to put him quickly out of his misery, so she let him ruminate for a moment or two. Before she could put his mind at ease, he had a sudden idea. He took out his phone.

"Who are you calling?" Maddie asked.

"Marley."

"Oh, no, you don't have to do that!"

It was too late, he'd already hit the call button. Marley answered on the second ring. Maddie put her head in her hands. In her text message, sent in the early hours of the morning, she'd told Marley she'd stayed with a friend. She had not said that friend was James. Maddie knew her brother would delight in teasing her about this and, given the nature of her feelings for James, she would really rather he didn't.

"Morning, mate. I have your lovely sister in my house," James said. "But we have no vegan-friendly milk or butter. I need to take Stevie for a quick wander around the block and wondered if you could meet me at the door with a jot of each? I'll be about ten minutes."

Maddie parted her fingers to watch James listening to Marley's reply. She saw him wince, then blush, then he started shaking his head.

"It's not like that," he said. "We were in the pub and she got stranded here because of the snow." He caught her eye and threw her a sheepish expression. Maddie giggled and shook her head. She knew Marley would be battering James with silly questions, teasing him, probing him, trying to get him to admit that there was something going on between the two of them. She could see his gleeful face in her mind's eye as he paced joyfully around his living room. She knew he'd hang up the phone and run to tell Autumn, perhaps he'd jokingly tell Benjamin that Aunty Maddie had a boyfriend. "Yes, well, as I said, it isn't like that," James insisted. "Cool. See you in ten."

He hung up the phone and stared at the screen. Maddie playfully rested her chin on her hand. "How did that go?" she asked.

"Your brother is brutal," he said. Maddie nodded. "He went right in with the personal questions. Like, right in there."

"I'm afraid we're one of those families," Maddie said.

"He's your brother, so I didn't think . . ."

"He's, like, my very best friend," Maddie corrected him. "They all are. Marley, Bluebell, Pip, Autumn, Bowie when

113

he was alive . . . they're my siblings, yes, but they're also my ride or dies."

"That's really lovely and, if I had known, I never would have told him you slept over here," James said.

"Too late now," Maddie said.

"Should I leave the milk and butter? It feels like I might be inviting more teasing by turning up at his door in my scruffs."

"If you don't go round he'll turn up here."

"Right," James said, opening the back door and calling Stevie inside. He pulled on his boots and a coat, picked up the dog lead and bid Maddie goodbye. "I'll be off, then." He waved half-heartedly. "If I don't die of embarrassment, then I will see you in ten."

* * *

Maddie helped herself to a mug of black tea and set herself in front of the kitchen window. The garden was long, thin and overgrown. There was a mouldy summerhouse at the very end and what looked like a rusty swing halfway up. The sky was clear and icy blue, though it looked like even more snow had fallen overnight. The world was still and pretty. Maddie wasn't sure how she'd get home, exactly, but she couldn't wait to get back to the house. She had always loved the way the garden looked in the snow, and she knew the walk up the driveway would bring back precious memories of many hours spent building snowmen and making snow angels with Bowie, Marley, Bluebell and Pip when they were children. It didn't always feel good to dwell on such times, but she felt mentally strong today. Right on cue, a fluffy robin landed on the windowsill before her. Maddie smiled. Her mother thought robins were a sign from heaven. Maddie was inclined to agree. "Hey, Bowie," she whispered. It made itself fatter and watched her through the window. She puckered her lips and blew it a kiss, amusing herself by imagining how perturbed Bowie would be if he could see her now. He had not believed in any of this stuff, and they had debated it often.

"James thinks that robin is his dead brother."

Maddie jumped so violently she dropped her mug of tea into the sink. The robin was startled and fled. James' mother stood in the doorway. She was a slight woman, and apparently stealthy, as Maddie had not heard her come downstairs and enter the kitchen. She looked Maddie up and down. "Mrs Byron, it's nice to meet you," Maddie said.

"Byron isn't my surname," James' mother said. "That was his dad's name. I changed mine back to my maiden name when he ran off with another woman."

"Sorry," Maddie said, watching the woman dressed in a pair of fluffy pyjamas and a giant cardigan, drag her slippered feet across the kitchen to fill up the kettle. She was small, perhaps only just five feet tall, with ash-coloured hair and a face lined with exhaustion. She switched on the kettle and turned to face Maddie, looking her up and down again.

"You're the latest one, ey?" she said. Maddie blushed and shook her head, opening her mouth to deny being one of James' conquests. His mother snapped again before she could speak. "He's never brought one back here before, so he must like you."

Maddie blushed and stared into her mug. She thought about correcting his mother, but there didn't seem to be any point. She spoke about him with a level of disdain Maddie was not used to hearing from a mum. Relations between the pair were clearly not good.

"Are you the one he was with the other night?" she asked Maddie. Maddie shook her head. The woman scoffed at that. "I don't know how he does it. He has his father's charm, apparently."

For want of anything else to do, Maddie took a sip of the dregs of her tea. She hoped James had managed to escape the clutches of her brother and that he'd be back soon. She thought about making her excuses and heading back upstairs, but it felt rude. Maddie came across as confident, but she was quite shy and didn't like to do anything that might upset anyone or cause confrontation. She felt she had no choice but to suffer in silence, so she put her head down, stared at the floor, and waited for James.

"My name is Jennifer," the woman said.

"Maddie," Maddie said.

"He slept in his room with you," Jennifer noted, pouring two mugs of tea and stirring milk into both and sugar into one. "He hasn't done that since he left for university."

"Yeah, he mentioned that."

"Do you take sugar?" Jennifer asked.

"No, thank you," Maddie said. Jennifer stirred the second cup of tea and handed it to her. Maddie accepted it graciously, hoping Jennifer wouldn't notice when she didn't drink it. She had never consumed dairy in her entire life, except by accident, and wasn't about to start now. But she also didn't feel like James' mum would be impressed by her veganism.

"So, where did you two meet?" Jennifer said.

"He's working at my house," Maddie explained. "Greystone Estate? We're turning it into a cancer recovery retreat, and he's helping us do the refurb."

Jennifer's face changed. She seemed curious. Softer, somehow. "You're Ben and Emma Whittle's kid?" she said. Maddie nodded. "Your brothers were very kind to James when Harry died. They took him under their wing at school."

Maddie hadn't known this. She made a mental note to ask Marley about it later. In that moment, she felt prouder of her brothers than ever.

"Someone made a big donation towards his funeral. They sent it to the school, so I never knew who it was. I always thought that might have been your mum and dad?"

"I don't know anything about that," Maddie answered honestly. "And they'd never tell me, even if I asked. Bragging, even inadvertently, is not their vibe. That does sound like something they would do, though."

Jennifer seemed to admire Maddie curiously for a moment, before her gaze hardened and the atmosphere cooled once more. Maddie was taken aback by the sudden change in ambience.

She wanted to turn back to the window, but she was worried Jennifer would be eyeballing her from behind, so she kept facing her, her back against the kitchen counter, the mug of non-vegan tea in her hands, until James returned home five minutes later.

"Marley definitely thinks we've banged," James called from the living room. Maddie grimaced and stood up straight, holding Jennifer's eye for a few painful seconds before James appeared in the kitchen doorway. "Mum!" James said. "I didn't think you'd be up yet."

James unloaded his bounty onto the kitchen table — a carton of soya milk and a plastic container Maddie presumed contained butter. He gestured for his mother to put the kettle back on, eyeing the mug of tea Maddie had in her hands. Maddie communicated wordlessly with him through wide eyes and a little shake of her head. There was no need to make a scene.

"It's hard to sleep when you're making such a racket," Jennifer said. James rolled his eyes, busying himself popping a tea bag into a mug and two slices of toast into the toaster. Maddie didn't really have an appetite, nor did she want any more tea, but she was too afraid to tell James, given he had trekked through the elements and braced himself against a barrage of teasing from her brother to retrieve milk she could drink and butter she could eat. She watched Jennifer watching him, a look of contempt on her face. If she hadn't known it, she would never have guessed they were mother and son. They did not look alike and James' sunny disposition was nowhere to be found in his mother. Maddie tried not to judge Jennifer. She had lost a son in extremely tragic circumstances. Maddie knew better than anyone how death changed a person.

"Marley said he's heading to your parents' house in an hour and he'll take you home then," James said, subtly handing Maddie a new mug of tea and removing the one she could not drink. Maddie could tell from the look on Jennifer's face that she knew what had happened. She shot Maddie an accusatory glare. Maddie pretended she hadn't seen it.

"What are you up to today, Mum?" James tried.

"Nothing." Jennifer tossed the rest of her tea in the sink and headed for the door. "I'm going back to bed."

James nodded in a knowing manner, trying and failing to remove the sadness from his face. He waited until they'd heard her go upstairs and close her bedroom door before saying anything else. "She's a real mood hoover, isn't she?" he said.

The timing of the comment was impeccable. Maddie had never heard that phrase before, so it made her laugh. She didn't want his mother to hear and think they were laughing at her, so she tried in vain to straighten her face, but his obvious joy at making her giggle made that extremely difficult. Maddie wasn't only laughing at his comment, she was laughing at the ridiculousness of this entire situation. She marvelled at the randomness of life. Two days ago, she had hardly spoken a word to this man, now she was wearing his boxer shorts and drinking tea in his kitchen, forty-eight hours of solid drama behind them. They'd gone from indifference, to despising each other, to emotional support, to almost sex, to awkward reunion, to close friends in just a few weeks, and most of those transitions had taken place in the last few days. The whole thing felt like a story she would read and disbelieve, but also completely right. Now, exhausted and confused, Maddie was stuck in a spiral of amusement. Every time she caught his gaze she laughed harder and so did he, until she wasn't sure what they were laughing at anymore and she thought she might cry, instead. They had to put their heads in their hands and break eye contact in order to suffocate their snickers. It took Maddie longer than James, and his sudden silence doused her hysterics. When she dared to look back up, he was staring dispiritedly at the floor. Maddie moved to stand beside him.

"Do you want to talk about it?" she asked, nudging him gently. "Your burdens are my burdens, remember?"

He shook his head and turned to look at her. A grateful smile spread slowly across his lips. "Just knowing you're here and I have you to talk to is making me feel better," he said.

Maddie grinned. She knew exactly what he meant.

CHAPTER NINE

The next few days passed in a blur of work, sleep and Christmas preparation. It was a little late to be putting up the tree, but Maddie and her parents had been busy with preparations for the retreat, planning their travels and learning how to take care of Pigglesworth Snortimer, so a haphazard and rushed effort was all they could manage this year. They left a few branches bare for Benjamin to decorate, much to his delight. Maddie and James found some time one afternoon after school to make paper streamers with him, which he insisted should be wrapped around the banister. He made a paper star at school on the Friday before he broke up, which he placed ceremoniously on top of the tree a mere five days before Christmas.

That same day, Pip came home for the holidays. He barrelled through the front door ahead of his parents, screaming Maddie's name. She was painting the skirting board in the hallway between the kitchen and living room with James. Stevie Licks jumped up from her spot in front of the radiator — where she could snooze and keep an eye on them both — and shot off towards the kitchen, barking as she went. Pip let out an excited little squeal and a barrage of baby-talk, which clearly sent Stevie into a wagging frenzy. They could hear her tail hitting the walls and the clicking of her claws on the floor as she circled this new person excitedly. Since she'd been spending so much time with the Whittles, she was so much better at being without James. It was as though she now knew that her human would always come back to her. It made James happy. Maddie smiled at him. She had warned him that Pip was a bundle of energy, but she wasn't sure he'd understood just what an extrovert her brother was. Pip bellowed so loudly that James started and almost dropped his paintbrush.

"We're in here," Maddie shouted. Pip stalked through the kitchen and into the hallway, holding his arms open for her to run into. She put down her paintbrush and complied. Pip swung her around several times, squeezing her tightly to his tall, slender frame. Maddie loved her entire family, but she absolutely adored her little brother. Because they had both been so busy — Maddie with the retreat and Pip with work — it had been almost three months since she had last seen him. That was part of the reason he'd taken extended leave over Christmas, so he could spend some proper time with his sister and help her with retreat preparations. Maddie was as grateful for the promise of quality time as she was for the offer of help.

She was fairly sure Pip's existence had saved her from years of feeling like an outcast. Just as Ben was not Bowie's, Marley's or Bluebell's father, Emma was not Maddie's biological mother, and she'd felt some pretty big feelings when she'd found that out at the tender age of six — though she hardly ever thought about it now. Because Emma's biological children were so close in age and not technically her real brothers and sister, Maddie had felt suddenly very separate from them — until Pip had come along when she was nine. Her older step siblings had never once treated her differently, or ever referred to her as anything other than their sister, nevertheless, there was something unhealthy there, inside her head. It had caused her to act strangely. She was old enough now and had done enough work on herself to know that she'd felt rejected by her biological mother as a child and had tried to protect herself from pain by 'othering' herself in case Emma decided to leave her too, and take her children with her. She had never understood how Bowie, Marley and Bluebell had avoided this feeling. Their biological father had disappeared from their lives never to be heard from again, and they had just accepted it. They never spoke of him. Never felt rejected by him. The only time Maddie had ever heard them mention their dad was when Marley once referred to him as a 'sperm donor'.

"Now that I'm a dad myself, I'll never understand how that sperm donor could just walk away from his kids and never look back," he'd said. "I doubt he even knows Bowie is dead."

For three years after she'd found out Emma was not her 'real' mother, Maddie had struggled to find her place in their family, but when Pip had come along, suddenly, there was a little baby brother tying her to these people so much more than her dad's marriage to Emma. A living, breathing human being. He was *her* brother and he was *their* brother. They were finally biologically linked. Pip solved everything, and Maddie adored him for it. They didn't speak as much these days, as Pip was so busy in London, but she was utterly devoted to him.

"I've missed you so much." He wrapped his arms around her, enveloping her completely. Maddie squeezed him tight. Pip looked as good as he always did, and Maddie, who had always been proud of her brother, felt even prouder of him today. She felt a warm, fuzzy feeling inside. In just a few days, Bluebell would be home, too. Nothing made her happier than having her family all together. She gently pushed him away so she could get a better look at him, holding him at arm's length. He posed comically for her, grinning. "I'm just the same as always," he said.

She hugged him again. "I'm so glad you're home."

He gave her one last big squish. "Me too, babes." She could tell from his stance and the change in the tone of his voice that he'd spotted James behind her. She couldn't remember whether or not she'd told Pip about James. She was sure she must have, but so much had been going on lately, it was entirely plausible she hadn't.

"Hi," James said, setting down his paintbrush and holding his hand out for Pip to shake. "I'm James."

"Pip," Pip said, turning to Maddie and raising his eyebrows suggestively. Maddie rolled her eyes and biffed him. James glanced between the two of them, confused.

"Ignore him, James, he's a tease," Maddie said, heading for the kitchen. James and Pip followed her dutifully, as she'd known they would.

"I've heard a lot about you," James said. That was entirely true. Maddie had told James all about Pip. James knew that her little brother was communications manager for an LGBTQ+ rights organisation based in London, a campaigner for the Green Party, a civil rights protestor, a social butterfly and all-round good guy. She knew he was seriously considering pursuing a career in politics, something he'd joked about for a really long time. As he'd grown older, his skills in communications and kind heart had led many people to remark that he'd manage candidacy well, but Pip wasn't so sure. He wanted it more than anything, but he'd confessed to having seen a different side to himself after Bowie died and when Marley and Autumn had admitted what they'd done to him. Pip had experienced thoughts dark enough that he wasn't so sure he was a good person at all anymore.

"I've heard absolutely nothing at all about you," Pip remarked. Maddie took two wine glasses out of the cupboard and raised a third towards James in place of a question. It was not simply 'would you like a glass of wine?' it was also 'are you staying over?'. Recently, James had fallen into the habit of drinking with the Whittles in the evenings and making use of the bedroom they had given him, usually because he was too tipsy to walk in a manner that reassured Emma he and Stevie would be safe on dark and slippery winter roads. He thought about it and nodded. Maddie was glad. Pip watched the exchange, then continued, "I'm very disappointed in you, Madison," he said.

"I didn't know your name was Madison," James remarked.

"Did you think it was Madeline?" Pip asked. James nodded. "A common misconception."

"Nobody calls me Madison." Maddie sliced the plastic cover from the top of the bottle with a kitchen knife and flicked it at Pip. He caught it, grinning mischievously. "And they never will."

Pip scoffed and made James laugh. "It suits her, don't you think?" Pip asked.

"Pip," Maddie warned him. Madison was her biological mother's surname. Julianne Madison and Ben Whittle had not been married when Maddie was born, so they'd named her Madison Whittle so that her name was an amalgamation of both of theirs. Pip knew Maddie was technically his half-sister, but he did not know where her moniker had come from, he thought she just hated the name. If she didn't nip this in the bud now, he'd call her it all winter. He stuck out his bottom lip and murmured an apology. Maddie forgave him immediately, handing him a glass of red wine. "Where did Mum and Dad go?" she asked her little brother.

"To take my bags upstairs, I think," he said. Maddie slowly shook her head. "I told them to leave them. It's not my fault."

It was an ongoing joke between Maddie and her siblings that Pip was the favourite child. Because he was the youngest and had been a complete surprise, everything had always been done for him, especially by Bowie and Marley, who were fifteen when he was born and had thoroughly enjoyed having a baby brother. The three boys had been exceedingly close, so Bowie's death and Marley's betrayal devastated him. His brothers had spent Pip's entire life preventing him from experiencing a single ounce of angst, only to cause him more pain and torment than anyone else ever had, albeit for very different reasons.

"Marley texted not long ago. He and Autumn are on their way over with Benjamin," Maddie said. Pip's eyes lit up, though Maddie was sure she saw his eyes flit in the direction of Bowie's old bedroom. She wondered if anyone would ever think about Marley without remembering Bowie, too. She doubted it. She wondered if that ever bothered Marley. "Autumn said you're all Benjamin talks about since she told him you were coming home," Maddie added.

"He's desperate to introduce you to Pigglesworth Snortimer," James concurred. Pip laughed at the name like he always did, shaking his head.

"How's the pig getting on?" Pip asked.

"He's quite well behaved, actually," Maddie said. "He roams around the garden all day with James' dog, Stevie, and he mainly keeps out of trouble. Every now and then he'll misbehave, usually if someone is in the garden and he thinks they have food. He's growing really fast!"

"I can't believe we have a pig now," Pip said with a grin.

"I can," Maddie and James said together.

"You guys are finishing each other's sentences already?" Pip teased, gleefully. "Cute!"

Maddie opened her mouth to tell Pip off, but before she could get out a word, the back door opened and Marley, Autumn and Benjamin announced their arrival with delighted shrieks and arms that beckoned for Pip. He obliged, hugging them all one by one. He started with Benjamin and then went back to him at the end, picking him up and kissing him all over his face. Benjamin giggled.

"I heard there's a pig you want to show me?" Pip said.

"Yes, there's a pig in the garden," Benjamin said.

"Wanna show me now?"

Benjamin nodded, pointing at the back door. Pip hitched his nephew further onto his hip and headed for the garden, reaching out to squeeze Marley's arm as he passed. Maddie saw Marley catch Autumn's eye and beam. Pip and Marley falling out had been so incredibly hard. Pip had been the main slinger of vitriol. He'd said things so terrible Maddie had been sure Marley would never forgive him. But he had, almost instantly, every single time. Maddie wasn't sure exactly when things had righted themselves. Benjamin had helped, she was sure of it. Even when things had been so bad Pip and Marley could not be in the same room together, Marley had been eager to ensure Pip and Benjamin had a relationship, and Pip — despite his anger — had appreciated that. Slowly, over time, her brothers had become cordial, then warm, then friendly, and now it looked like they might almost be back to being loving brothers. Without meaning to, Maddie turned to James and smiled. He caught her eye and smiled back, though she knew he had no idea what they were beaming about.

"I brought my guitar," James told Marley.

"Oh, amazing — I brought mine!" Marley fished his car keys out of his jacket pocket. Maddie and Autumn groaned. "You used to think my guitar playing was sexy," Marley reminded his fiancée.

"That was before you did it several hours a day every day for five years," Autumn said. Maddie laughed.

Marley frowned. "OK, when we get home, I'm burning your books, then." He ducked Autumn's playfully swiping hand and slipped out of the house through the back door. Autumn looked fondly after him, shaking her head.

"Have you seen the wedding altar we've built, Autumn?" James asked, pouring her a glass of wine.

Autumn shook her head. "Not in the flesh. Marley showed me some pictures — it looks so beautiful."

Autumn was saying the right things, but Maddie got the distinct impression she had no real interest in talking about the wedding — she couldn't blame her. It was all anyone wanted to talk about these days. Every time Autumn and Marley were at the house, Emma bombarded them with ideas she'd seen on Pinterest and talk of mood boards. Autumn hadn't said anything, but Maddie knew it was getting on her nerves.

"It is, if I do say so myself," James said.

"How much of it did Marley build?" Autumn asked. "Because he's telling me he contributed a fair bit, which would theoretically mean he's more than capable of putting the TV on the wall in our bedroom, despite his protestations."

Maddie and James laughed, but Autumn was not smiling. She pressed James for an answer by raising her eyebrows. "This feels like it might be a trap," he said.

"The truth will set you free," Autumn said.

The back door opened and Marley re-entered the kitchen, alongside Pip and Benjamin, whose cheeks were tinged pink from the cold. All three were smiling.

"It was too cold to be out there for long, but we gave Pigglesworth an apple," Pip explained.

"Lovely, he likes apples," Maddie said, holding her hands out to take Benjamin.

"His pen is beautiful," Pip said.

"James made it." Maddie nodded at James.

"Nice work," Pip said and James returned his grin. "What are we doing for dinner?" Pip asked Maddie.

Maddie shrugged her shoulders. "I hadn't even thought about it," she admitted.

"Can we have Chinese?" Pip suggested. "I've been dreaming about a Peking Garden for weeks."

"I bloody love the Peking Garden," James said.

Emma and Ben sauntered into the kitchen.

"Me too," Emma said. "Pip, James has your old room now, so we've put you in the back room. It's the one that's most finished."

"Great." Pip nodded, taking out his phone. "What does everyone want from the Chinese? I'll order it. Usuals?"

Everyone nodded except for James, whose eyes darted to Maddie. Maddie knew what he was thinking — he would have no idea what to add to a vegan Chinese takeaway order. She thought about letting him squirm, but it felt mean. True to his word, he hadn't once eaten or worn anything non-vegan in front of her at work. He deserved a little credit — and some help.

126

"Can you add some extra salt-and-pepper tofu to the order and perhaps another portion of rice with curry sauce? We have an extra mouth to feed." Maddie nudged James.

"Oh, yes, no worries." Pip typed the order out on his phone. Maddie already knew what he'd be inputting, because her family had had the same order for years. Three portions of chips, four cartons of curry sauce, three cartons of rice, two portions of vegetable spring rolls, two portions of salt-and-pepper tofu, two portions of sweet-and-sour tofu, and one Chinese broccoli stir-fry. "Are you vegan, James?" Pip asked.

"Vegetarian," James said. Maddie reeled. This was news to her. True, they hadn't spoken about James' diet since she'd banned him from consuming non-vegan food in her family home — they hadn't had cause to. But she'd expected he would tell her if he'd made such a big, relevant decision.

"There's a chance we could convert you then," Pip said.

"How long have you been vegetarian?" Marley asked.

"Since that day Pigglesworth escaped and found his way here," James admitted. "It's hard to see him — to see animals — as food anymore, you know?"

The Whittles nodded.

"Shall we move into the living room?" Maddie suggested. "It's a little chilly in here." She let her family filter out before her so she could hang back and check on James. "You OK?" she asked, squeezing his arm affectionately.

He nodded a yes. They followed through to the living room and found places to perch. Maddie sat in front of the fire with Autumn and Benjamin, while James perched on the arm of the armchair Marley was sitting on over by the window. Emma and Ben had sandwiched Pip between them on the sofa and were firing questions at him about work, his friends and his flat. Pip, as always, was revelling in the attention.

"I heard one of your songs on Spotify the other day," James said to Marley. "It just came on and I thought 'I recognise that voice', and then I realised it was you."

Marley smiled sheepishly.

"It was really good," James said. "I didn't know you had music out there."

"There's quite a bit." Marley nodded. "They're demos Bowie and I made before we lost him. He put them online before he died — the little shit. They bring me a nice bit of income every month. Nothing spectacular, obviously — Autumn is the breadwinner in this family by a mile — but enough considering I haven't done anything with it in years."

"Did you never try to make it?" James asked. "I feel like you could have done really well."

Marley shook his head. "I used to want it so bad. Honestly, it was all I thought about. But when Benjamin arrived, everything changed. I chased it for a little while — met some managers, did some gigs — but it meant being away from home, and that wasn't what I wanted anymore. I had to have some really difficult conversations with myself, and with Autumn, who, it turns out, really wanted to be the girlfriend of a rock star."

Autumn laughed and shook her head. "Tell the truth."

Marley wrinkled his nose affectionately and continued. "I had to let her down really gently. Remind her she was a parent, she couldn't be a groupie, too. Kidding! But in all seriousness, it did come down to the fact we're parents. Pursuing that dream and simultaneously spending time with my family would have meant them coming along with me. It didn't feel fair to drag them around. Plus, Autumn has to be away from home sometimes for book-writing stuff. I wanted her to have the freedom to do that. She deserves her success — she's a role model for little girls with big dreams — it just didn't feel right to jeopardise all of that to chase something I didn't care all that much about anymore."

"Wow," James said, his admiration clear.

"I didn't do anything women don't do for men all the time," Marley protested. Maddie was glad he'd said that, and could tell from the smile on her face that Autumn was, too. "I was a stay-at-home dad until Benjamin went to school and, now, I'm in the show, which I absolutely love — though it does mean being away from home a lot now. I'd quit in a heartbeat if Autumn wasn't happy about it, or if I thought Benjamin was suffering."

"Which is not the case," Autumn said. "So stop worrying about it all the time."

Autumn and Marley locked eyes and smiled at each other. Maddie saw James watching them with intrigue, before his eyes landed on her. She nodded, knowing he too was remembering the night Marley and Autumn had skidded from the road, the night he'd wondered aloud what it must feel like to be loved the way they loved each other. It was the same night she'd told him how their relationship had come to be, how Bowie had become convinced that they were destined to be together and had engineered their relationship despite the pain it caused him to do so. Now they weren't just lovers, they were best friends. They knew each other completely and loved each other implicitly. Maddie had never seen love like it before. It always made her feel a little bit teary, but this was the first time she was seeing someone else bear witness to true love for the first time, and it was another person who — just like her — had never felt anything close to it themselves. She had to turn away from him to stop herself from tearing up even more.

Predictably, Pip shattered the moment. "Is this the first time you've ever met an unselfish straight white man, James?" James straightened his face. "Aside from yourself, of course," Pip added.

"I'm bisexual, actually," James said. Maddie and her family members all turned to look at him, and nobody knew what to say. She was disappointed in herself for being surprised. She and James had never had a conversation about sexuality, and she'd let her bias about how a bisexual person might present keep the notion James might not be straight far from her mind. She had thought herself a better person than that. "I hope that's OK?" he added when nobody spoke.

"I'm fine with you exploring the heterosexual side of your attraction as long as you don't do it in front of my face," Pip quipped. Everyone laughed.

"Bluebell is bisexual, too," Emma said.

"She's not, actually, Mum — she's pansexual," Marley said.

"Well, it's the same thing, really, isn't it?" Emma said. Everyone except for Ben shook their heads. Emma rolled her eyes, gesturing for the bottle of wine Maddie was still holding in her hand. "OK, she's pansexual, James. I don't really give a toss, she's just wonderful, and that's all I care about."

Maddie and Marley smirked at each other. They had tried in vain to educate their mother on various identities and, though she said she understood how important it was to learn about these things, Emma just could not get her head around it all. She often brushed it off and said she didn't care, she just loved everyone and that should be enough, but — as the only two straight siblings — Maddie and Marley had an unspoken pact to persevere in the name of allyship, calling her out whenever she said something ignorant.

"How long ago did we order the Chinese?" Autumn clutched her stomach.

"I don't know, but I'm famished," Ben said.

Pip nodded. "We need a distraction."

"Why don't you play your guitar for us, James?" Emma suggested.

James nodded and stood up, passing Maddie his wine glass to hold while he went to the kitchen to retrieve the instrument. He'd hardly been gone half a second when Pip gestured theatrically after him. "He's the hottest fucking thing I've ever seen," he said.

Everyone laughed except for Maddie. She wasn't sure why she didn't find it funny — she *always* found Pip amusing, especially when he was grossly attracted to someone — but she couldn't raise a smile this time. To make matters worse, she knew Autumn was witnessing her lack of reaction. Maddie tried to keep her gaze away from Autumn's. As her little brother comically fanned his face, gushing over James' face, hair, dress sense, humour, Autumn shuffled closer to Maddie — they now sat side by side.

Autumn knew there was something going on. There was no way she could know the extent of it, but at the very least she knew there were feelings involved, and that made Maddie feel sick. This was not her. She was not used to this. She did not like it and she wanted to run away.

James re-entered the room carrying his guitar, and Maddie planted her gaze on the floor. Autumn, unlike the others, was perceptive enough to notice. As James took his seat on the arm of the armchair, Autumn put her arm around Maddie and squeezed, raising her eyebrows in a knowing manner when Maddie turned to look at her. She waited for James to start playing and singing before she said anything, so that the words they exchanged were just between the two of them. James was a skilled player and had a nice voice. His long, thin fingers were quick and well-practised. He held the guitar the same way Marley did — as though it was an extension of himself.

"Ready to be honest?" she murmured. Maddie watched James, her heart beating wildly at the sight of him. He was always sexy, but holding that guitar and blushing while he sang a love song, and very obviously struggled to keep his eyes off her, Maddie felt breathless with desire.

"Nope," Maddie said, trying and failing to stifle a smile.

"Fair enough." Autumn chuckled. "But I'm here for you, Mads. Whatever has happened and whatever you're feeling, you just let me know when you're ready to talk."

* * *

As it turned out, Maddie was ready to talk much earlier than she'd anticipated. Later that night — slightly drunk and fresh from a night of frolics with her family — Maddie ran into Autumn in the kitchen. She was raiding the Chinese takeout boxes for stray chips. Maddie joined her at the kitchen table, and the two farmed the cartons together in silence for a while. Maddie had just said goodnight to her parents, and everyone else had gone to bed hours ago, so the house was still and quiet. Maddie really didn't want to talk about the way she was feeling, but she knew she needed to.

"He really likes you," Autumn said, dipping a chip into a half-empty carton of curry sauce. Maddie bit into a spring roll and nodded. She knew James liked her, of course she knew. He could hardly keep his gorgeous brown eyes off her. He'd barely been away from Greystones since they'd spent the night at his. He looked for excuses to touch her and was constantly trying to make her laugh. They spent almost every waking moment together.

Maddie wondered if he knew she liked him, too. She had given up trying to argue with herself over this. James was the best part of her day, and that haunted her at night. She'd never wanted any man as much as she wanted him. Each evening, she tormented herself for hours by imagining him kissing every inch of her body. In her head, he had done things to her no man had done before. She'd concocted scenarios that made her blush when she thought of them outside the privacy of her bedroom. She yearned so deeply for the weight of him upon her, one time she had to force herself into a cold shower in the middle of night to prevent herself from bursting into his bedroom and begging him to take her. She had never been so excited. It was torturous. This primal, visceral, soul-crushing attraction to him was ruining her life.

She couldn't let it happen. Her original reasons for not sleeping with him had almost all evaporated — they were drilling through the work they had to do at an exceptionally fast rate and her mental health was miraculously improving now that she had someone helping her, a friend to talk to and laugh with. However, she had a brand-new reason not to give in to her carnal desires. A biggie. She knew, if she did, she would fall in love with him.

James was fast becoming her closest friend. He was funny, smart and sensitive. They liked the same movies and he took note of the books she suggested he read. Most days he was working from 8 a.m. to midnight to get through the tasks they needed to complete for the opening of the recovery retreat and the garden infrastructure for Marley and Autumn's wedding. She was paying him, but he accepted the money begrudgingly, and only because she insisted. She believed him when he said he just wanted to help. He sent her videos and memes he knew she'd find funny, left her notes around the house to make her smile. He said nice things about her to her parents, things he knew would get back to her.

"He's leaving in the spring," she told Autumn. This was the crux of the problem. She could not let her feelings for James drive her actions, because they weren't in the same car. He was in a camper van with Stevie, heading in the opposite direction.

"You could still have a little fun," Autumn said, gleefully holding up a large chip she'd found. Maddie eyed it enviously. Autumn dutifully ripped it in half, passing her the bigger half.

"I don't know if I'm that kind of woman." Maddie dipped her chip. She knew Autumn would understand what she meant. Maddie saw nothing wrong with casual sex, it was just that she'd only ever done it a few times before and she had never really enjoyed it, so she'd sworn she'd never do it again. Plus, she hadn't had sex in years. The idea of going to bed with someone made her feel nervous.

"Fair enough." Autumn nodded, turning to look at her. Maddie tried to straighten her face, but she couldn't. She knew she was in a mess. She'd not taken a single shred of joy from her little brother's jesting about being attracted to James. She'd felt possessive. His joke had made her feel sick. She hadn't wanted to talk to anyone about it because she felt like she might be going crazy. Unfortunately, her feelings of fear had continued to build through the evening, and she needed to tell someone.

Maddie looked right back at Autumn. Autumn sighed. "Something about him being here is bringing you back to life," she whispered. Those words were all it took to tip Maddie over the edge. She started to cry. Autumn held her arms open for her, pulling her into a hug.

Safe in her friend's embrace, Maddie realised Autumn was right. James' presence *was* bringing her back to life. She hadn't even noticed she'd been metaphorically dead until she'd belly-laughed five days ago and realised it was the first time she'd done so in years. She'd started singing again, and become playful. She was thinking about starting yoga once more — a hobby that used to bring her great peace and joy — and she wanted to paint and try wild swimming.

Maddie's curious nature had disappeared several years ago and she had put this down to growing up, but she could see now it wasn't that. When Bowie had died, the innocent part of her, the child within, had died with him. Her sole focus had shifted from caring for her brother to making sure she didn't cause her family any pain or worry. Something about James was bringing her back to herself. Perhaps it was because he understood exactly how she felt. There was no need to hide the deep sadness within her, but also no need to make mourning her entire personality. Maddie could be herself around him, without worrying that seeing her sad or happy might affect him in the way it would her parents and siblings. She felt free to be herself again now that she had a friend. She was deeply enjoying this new phase of her life, and knew there was more to be enjoyed — but she was also very much afraid of the consequences of letting go. James would leave eventually. She would be sad again. Maddie wasn't sure she could bear it.

"I'm so sorry, please don't think I'm daft," Maddie said.

Autumn pulled away and held Maddie at arm's length. "Why would I think you're daft?"

"I don't know, I just feel silly. This might be nothing. Why does it feel like . . . everything?"

Autumn shook her head, smiling knowingly. She looked like she was about to cry herself. For want of anything else to do, Maddie dug through the wrappers until she found another chip and ripped it in half, passing the biggest half to Autumn. Her friend accepted it graciously.

"Bowie did this to me," Autumn said. "Honestly, after our first night together, I felt like I might die if I didn't see him again soon. He was all I could think about. You know me, Mads. Can you ever imagine me simping over a man like that?"

Maddie laughed heartily, because she couldn't imagine it. She said nothing because Autumn hardly ever spoke to her about her romantic relationship with Bowie and she didn't want to interrupt her. She knew Autumn and Marley talked about their feelings for Bowie all the time, though, having permitted themselves to mourn all the ways Bowie had shown up in their lives, as Marley's friend and brother, and Autumn's friend and lover.

"He did something to me nobody else has ever managed to do," Autumn said. "Marley is my soulmate, I believe that now wholeheartedly, but I'd never have been open to the kind of love we have if it hadn't been for Bowie and what we shared. It was . . . It was like . . . I'm a writer, for God's sake, and I can't describe it."

She threw a spring roll across the greasy takeout paper, frustrated. Maddie sighed and grabbed her hand. They sat in silence for a moment.

"Bowie saved me," Autumn continued. "He didn't mean to, but he did. And you know me, Mads, I hate this narrative. I wasn't sitting around waiting for him, he didn't do anything particularly special. It wasn't that my life was without fun or empty of happiness before he appeared, it's just that he was his best self when he was with me, and I was my best self when I was with him. I felt safe and so did he. So, when our worlds collided, it was this beautiful . . . thing. It opened me up to everything I have now and made me the woman I am . . ."

Autumn stared at the table. Maddie watched her friend and felt suddenly very sad. They should be taking time to talk about this stuff more often. She vowed to make clear it was OK for Autumn to come and talk to her about her love for Bowie whenever she wanted to.

"I find explaining it to anyone else really difficult," Autumn said. "Even Marley." Facing Maddie, her eyes glistened with tears. "The only person who will ever know what it felt like is Bowie, and he's gone. And perhaps it felt that way because he was going, I don't know. But I do know that there was magic in it. There had to be magic in it somewhere. You know I never believed in that stuff. I was adamant everything was a fortunate coincidence. Bowie thought the same. Bluebell and I used to argue about it all the time, but, honestly, I've given it years of thought, and concluded there's no other explanation for it."

"I'm scared," Maddie admitted. "I'm scared of that feeling. I've never felt it before and I know it would be wonderful, but what do I do when he leaves me to go travelling? How do I cope then?"

"You just do," Autumn said, shrugging her shoulders. Maddie was frustrated by that. She wanted a clear plan, a strategy, a way of moving forward if she fell in love and had that love ripped away from her, but Autumn — who knew more about this than anyone — couldn't give her one. "If I can survive Bowie dying, Maddie, you can live through James going travelling," she added.

Maddie felt like she was being scolded, and she probably deserved it. She narrowed her eyes comically at Autumn, who grinned in response. "All right, Ms Reality Check," Maddie said. Autumn laughed, and Maddie couldn't help it, she laughed, too.

"Life is too short, Mads," Autumn continued. "Honestly, it really is. And even if it isn't, and we're lucky enough to be rattling around here when we're ninety, do you really think you'll look back on your life and think, 'Gosh, I'm so glad I didn't shag that really funny, sweet, good-looking man when

I was thirty-three. Thank God I protected myself from having my heart broken'. No. You'll look back and think, 'I wish I'd let that sexy bastard give me a good seeing to'."

Maddie giggled, blushing. "You're disgusting," she said, shaking her head.

"I'm right, though, aren't I?"

Maddie nodded with a sigh. "Yeah," she conceded. "You're right."

CHAPTER TEN

Maddie knew what she wanted, but that didn't mean she had the nerve to do it. Over the next few days, she tried to increase the flirty banter and instances of prolonged eye contact between her and James, but he either wasn't taking the hint or was waiting for a stronger indication of consent.

One afternoon, the day before Bluebell was due home, three days before Christmas, he took her to get a tattoo to commemorate Bowie, and she was absolutely certain something would happen. They'd agreed to take a day off work and drive to Norfolk, where they'd spend the day on the beach in Hunstanton, a pretty little town with a big, beautiful coastline. James insisted it was home to the world's greatest tattoo artist, a man he had gone to university with, called Ryan. He promised her Ryan would do her tattoo idea justice and do everything he could to make her feel comfortable, so he was well worth a four-hour round trip.

"Plus, we can rent out a beach hut and stroll by the stripy red cliffs. There's a café on the beach, and I know for a fact they sell vegan cakes because I googled it."

Maddie was already sold on the idea, but she enjoyed James' enthusiasm, so pretended to falter.

"Please come to Hunstanton with me and get a tattoo from Ryan," he begged. "It'll be the best day ever, I swear."

"Fine." She grinned. "But I need you to actually book a beach hut, as I have never been in one — and there better actually be vegan cake."

The day was cold and the air was crisp. They set off early in the morning, stopping for coffee and pastries on the way. Maddie was driving, so James was in charge of the music. He spent the entire journey searching for songs she would remember from her teenage years. They started with the indie tracks they'd danced to at university, then moved onto 00s movie soundtracks, then boy bands. He monitored her reaction to each song and followed the thread of her excitement, until they ended up at the Spice Girls.

"Which Spice Girl were you?" James asked.

"Geri," Maddie said. "How about you?"

"Posh Spice." He didn't miss a beat. Maddie laughed so hard she spat her coffee on the dashboard. James grinned at her reaction, pouting his lips in imitation. Maddie shook her head.

"You're a goof," she said.

"I am when I'm around you." He turned back to his phone, presumably to choose another song. Maddie knew she should say something, but she was afraid to. After her conversation with Autumn, she'd been sure pursuing James was the right thing to do, but now she'd lost her confidence again, frustratingly. It wasn't because she didn't think it was a good idea — he was a distraction from her troubles, which had to be a good thing. Yes, he'd be leaving, but Autumn had embarked on a relationship with Bowie when she'd known he was dying, and she said it was the best thing she'd ever done. It wasn't because she thought he might reject her, either. She knew with one-hundred-per-cent certainty he wouldn't. It was actually because she worried she was messing him about. She'd given him permission to kiss her then told him they couldn't be anything more than friends. Now, just a week later, she was changing her mind again. She knew there was a good chance he'd ask her why the sudden change of heart — the issues she'd presented as excuses were still there — and she'd have no answer to that, except that her feelings for him had grown stronger since that morning in the kitchen. Back then, he'd been an irritatingly attractive man who worked for her. Now, he was the first thing she thought about when she opened her eyes in the morning, and the last thing she thought about at night. Just looking at him made her lips tingle. He wanted her, and she liked him too much to resist him any longer. She wasn't sure how he'd react if she told him all that. He might think her too complicated for him, that it had been fine when there'd been no feelings present but that now it would be silly to take the next step. He might say he couldn't bear to potentially lose her as a friend, or that he didn't want to hurt her, or use any one of the countless other excuses men often use when women propose anything besides mindless fucking.

She didn't want to be rejected like that. She'd be irreparably disappointed he did, in fact, turn out to be no different from any other man she'd ever met. The whole thing was a giant mess and Maddie wished she could get out of her own head, but this stuff didn't come naturally to her. There was no way for her to control everything to the best of her abilities if she wasn't perpetually trying to figure everything out. And Maddie really wanted to control all things. It kept her safe.

They arrived just before midday. The skies were a moody grey and promising rain, but they didn't let that dampen their spirits. They parked a fifteen-minute walk from the beach, five minutes from Ryan's tattoo shop. He was expecting them, but still reacted as though seeing James was a complete surprise. The two men marched into each other's arms, holding each other tightly.

"I've missed you, man," Ryan said.

"This is Maddie," James said, breaking their embrace. Ryan held out his hand, seemingly thrilled to meet her.

"Hi," Maddie said, accepting his greeting.

"It's lovely to meet you. James has told me so much about you."

Maddie was surprised at that. James was in a group chat with a bunch of lads he'd known since he was young — she often saw him laughing away to himself as he typed a reply out on his phone — but she hadn't anticipated he might have mentioned her name in such a conversation, let alone told his friends about her. She was secretly thrilled.

Ryan, who looked to be almost seven feet tall, led the way from the foyer of his little shop into a room at the back. The space was clinically white and spotlessly clean. The walls were covered in photographs of incredible tattoos — entire sleeves stitched together from individual artworks, giant back tattoos, birds, flowers, portraits and landscapes of all shapes, sizes and colours. Maddie and James spent a couple of minutes admiring Ryan's portfolio. He stood back and watched them, visibly proud.

"These are amazing," Maddie said.

"Thank you very much." Ryan grinned.

"I almost feel bad asking you to tattoo me with my simple little design," Maddie confessed.

"What is it?" Ryan made his way over to her. James nodded reassuringly when she caught his eye. She fished the note out of her bag and laid it carefully on the table. Bowie had written it for his family just a few days before he'd died. James and Ryan took a moment to read it.

> *My Loves. Autumn has taken me to London for the day. We needed to get out. I know it will give you no comfort to know we've taken every precaution we can. Please, try not to worry. We'll be in touch later today.*
> *Forever yours, with infinite love, Bowie x*

"My brother Bowie wrote this," Maddie explained to Ryan. "He passed away not long after. I'd love you to tattoo that last part — *Forever yours, with infinite love, Bowie x* — in his handwriting, if you wouldn't mind?"

Ryan carefully picked up the note and admired Bowie's penmanship. "What a lovely way to sign off a note," he said.

Maddie smiled. "Bowie was a real poet. A songwriter, actually."

"Same thing." Ryan nodded.

"Yes, well, this note was beautiful, but all of his notes were beautiful. This one is unusual only because it was the last he ever wrote . . ." Maddie's words caught in her throat. That wasn't strictly true. Before she'd helped him take his own life, she'd asked Bowie to write a suicide note for his family.

Loves. I'm so sorry, I can't stay.
Yours evermore, Bowie x

To avoid an inquest and prevent Bowie's cause of death being registered as 'suicide' — when it was undoubtedly lymphoma and its terrible symptoms that had in fact ultimately killed him — Maddie had suggested they shouldn't disclose the note to anyone official. None the wiser, the doctor had signed off Bowie's death as being due to his terminal illness. Less than an hour after his body had been collected — while her family were drowning in grief — Maddie had clutched the note to her heart and taken it into the garden. She'd lit the firepit, read it one last time, then tossed it into the flames, collapsing in a heap as it burned.

Remembering the extent of her grief, tears streamed down her cheeks afresh.

"Hey." James was bursting with concern. He put his arms lovingly around her and pulled her into his chest.

Maddie was embarrassed. She hated crying in front of other people, but she couldn't help herself. She felt Ryan move away from them and heard him leave the room. She was so grateful to him. Maddie buried her face in James' sweatshirt and sighed. He squeezed her tightly to him, rocking her gently. "Take your time," he murmured. Maddie wound her hands in the fabric of his jumper and nodded, resigned to giving herself a few minutes to collect herself.

"I'm so sorry," she said eventually, pulling away. James was shaking his head. "I don't know what came over me."

"Maddie, you don't have to explain this to me of all people," he said. Maddie gazed up at him, but didn't let go of his clothing. She felt warm and safe. She saw his eyes flit to her lips and knew he was stopping himself from kissing her. Her mouth twitched tellingly. James shook his head, amused.

"What is this thing we have about kissing whenever one of us is crying?" he said.

Maddie stood up on her tiptoes, resting just three or four inches from his mouth. "We should perhaps psychoanalyse that later," she whispered. Her lips met his and her senses flooded with the memory of their last intimate encounter — the way he'd smelled, the way he'd felt against her, how her body had pined for him, and still did now. His hands found her face, then spread out to cup the back of her head, dislodging her headband. He wound his fingers in her hair and pulled gently, pressing himself against her with a frustrated moan. It was quiet, but loud enough to shock her into stopping as she remembered where they were. She pulled away, her eyes wide with worry.

"Please don't change your mind again," James begged.

Maddie smiled at that. "I won't." She shook her head. "It's just, we're in public."

"Oh, I'm sorry, did you not want to do this in front of strangers?" James quipped.

Maddie pulled back, balling her hand into a fist and thumping him jovially on the chest.

"But you're such an extrovert," he continued, teasing her. "I have clearly very grossly misunderstood." He dragged her back into a hug.

"You guys all right in there?" Ryan called from the foyer.

"We're all good," James shouted back. Ryan poked his head around the door.

"Sorry, Ryan, you can come back in," Maddie said, dropping James and straightening her headband. She wondered if she looked as flustered as she felt. James was looking her up and down. She caught his eye and he winked at her. She was fairly sure by this point he could read her mind, so took this as wordless confirmation that she looked OK. With her permission, Ryan picked up Bowie's note and traced his handwriting onto a separate piece of paper, before carefully handing it back to her. Maddie gently folded it and put it back in her bag.

"So, where do we want it?" Ryan asked. Maddie looked to James. She hadn't discussed wanting her brother's commemoration tattoo in the same place he had his, but knew, somehow, he would be OK with it. It was such a lovely idea, to tattoo something so sentimental across your heart. Maddie hoped he *was* all right with it because she could not imagine having the tattoo anywhere else. James knew what she was asking.

"Across her heart," he said to Ryan, not taking his eyes from Maddie's.

"Are you sure that's OK?" Maddie asked quietly.

"Of course it fucking is!" James couldn't sound any more certain. "I'd be honoured to have matching brother tattoos across our hearts."

They grinned at each other, and Maddie found herself wondering how she'd gotten so lucky. She had never in a million years expected to meet someone she felt so safe with. Never mind in her very own village.

Ryan nodded, tapping the reclining chair before him. "Pop up on the chair, then, Maddie, and let's get this show on the road."

* * *

"It didn't hurt nearly as much as I thought it would," Maddie babbled. "A couple of little scratches and that was it. Like a nettle sting, or a friction burn. It didn't go as red as I thought it would, either. It might go red later, I guess. I can't believe I've done it. I've been contemplating it for so long! It's most unlike me to make a decision like this. Sorry, I'm talking too much, aren't I? I'll stop."

Maddie and James strolled gloved hand in gloved hand towards the beach. He was watching her chatter away, visibly amused by her frivolity. Every now and then, Maddie would hold her hand to the spot on her chest where Bowie's words were now etched into her skin. Her brother hadn't had any tattoos, but she knew he would have adored this one, because Bowie had loved grand gestures. She already knew she'd never, ever regret getting it.

"Don't stop," James said, squeezing her hand. She wasn't sure when they'd started holding hands, but it had certainly been at least five minutes ago, and it felt so natural she hadn't noticed until now. "It's nice to hear you so excited about something," he said.

Maddie thought about that. There were lots of things she was excited about, but she supposed she hardly ever talked about them. She was excited about the recovery retreat — it had long been a dream of hers to own her own establishment, to take all of the best things she'd learned about caring for people and help as many people as she possibly could. She was thrilled to have Pip back and that Bluebell was coming home. She was ecstatic about Marley's and Autumn's wedding — whenever she remembered it was happening, that is. She was obsessed with whatever was happening between her and James. She made a mental note to talk about the things that made her happy more often in front of James and other people she cared about. She didn't want them to think she was a bore.

They reached the beach and took a left, pausing for a moment to admire a bride and groom getting their photograph taken amid a crowd of wedding guests. The photographer was counting down from three and the group were trying to jump at the exact right time, but a few of the guests kept jumping too early or too late. From their position behind the camera, Maddie and James could see that the photographer had given up on capturing the jumping photograph and was instead focusing on the laughing faces of the bride, groom and guests every time they tried and failed to nail it. She captured the most beautiful picture of the bride, who was wearing a floor-length lace, emerald-green gown. Every jump revealed a glimpse of her black Dr Martens, and she had to hold the gold crown on her head to stop it flying off.

"She looks amazing," Maddie said.

"Do you think Autumn will wear something like that?" James asked.

Maddie laughed. She and Autumn had talked dresses on a couple of occasions, but Autumn hadn't bought anything yet. She was waiting for Bluebell to come home so they could all go shopping together. Maddie wasn't sure what Autumn would choose, but she was almost certain it wouldn't be green. "I think she'll wear something quite traditional."

James nodded thoughtfully, tugging gently on her hand and pulling her towards the café he'd used to bribe her to come today. It was right on the beach, a large wooden hut with pretty bay windows. Through them, Maddie could see bookshelves lining the walls, glass cabinets bursting with cakes, floral wallpaper and scented candles. She caught him checking her reaction, proudly admiring her awe. "Isn't it lovely?" he asked. "I thought we could have lunch, then maybe take some coffees and cakes to the beach hut for a couple of hours?"

"Sounds like a plan," Maddie said. They made their way inside and James joined the queue, while Maddie said hello to a French bulldog sitting in the corner. When James was almost at the front, she joined him, browsing the shelves of cakes and scones. She wasn't used to having this much choice. There was an incredible vegan selection to choose from — lemon cake, banana cake and ginger cake, blueberry muffins, croissants, vegan cheese scones, plain scones, several types of homemade biscuits and half-a-dozen sandwiches. In the end, she passed the decision on to James, who chose a selection of sweet and savoury snacks for them to take away, and ordered them a chip butty each to have now, as well as a pot of tea for two and a couple of bottles of dandelion and burdock.

He let Maddie choose where they sat. She led him to a window seat facing the ocean. Maddie ran her hand across the soft wood of the table, leaned forward to draw in the scent of the nearest candle and leafed through a pile of books on the windowsill. She felt truly present for the first time in a long time. When she turned her attention back to James, he was watching her. He caught her eye and smiled.

"I'm having a really nice time," Maddie said. His smile widened.

"Me too," he said.

"We should have brought Stevie," she said, admiring another dog, a chocolate-coloured Labrador.

"She hates being left in the car, and I really wanted to be inside with you when you got your tattoo," James said.

Maddie nodded, her eyes wandering around the room again. She'd hardly been out in six years, and had forgotten how much she enjoyed a nice atmosphere, a good coffee, and a talkative friend. She reached across the table and grabbed James' hands. He lifted hers to his mouth and kissed her fingers, his big brown eyes sparkling with promise. Maddie enjoyed his gaze upon her, but she wanted to tell him to look away. The expression on his face — excited but trepidatious — thrilled and frightened her all at once. They both knew that they were at a fork in their relationship. From here, they would go one way or the other. One path led to boredom at worst and contentment at best, but was absent of the thrill that came with a risk. The other forked off again at some point in the near future, and the choice of destination from that point on was unclear.

"The beach hut thing . . ." he said, scratching at the table with his fingernail. "We don't have to do that if you don't want to."

Maddie planted her eyes on him. "Why wouldn't I want to?" she asked. He shrugged, and she knew he was giving her an out, in case she needed one. The tension between them was palpable, and any private time spent together was likely headed in only one direction. She poured herself and James a cup of tea each and avoided his gaze. She wished, not for the first time, that she was more like Bluebell — fearlessly sexual and unabashed. James was a man with experience. He knew her well enough not to be expecting theatrics, but she still wished she was a little more forward. Mainly because it would help her confidence. She picked up her teacup with one hand and grabbed his hand again with the other. "I think it's pretty obvious I've changed my mind." She ran her thumb across the back of his hand. She thought she felt him shudder at her touch, but she couldn't be sure she wasn't the one shaking. James had not changed his stance — he looked anticipatory but relaxed, like he was waiting for an important meeting. But his breathing belied his composure. He was nervous or excited, she couldn't figure out which.

"I want you to be comfortable," he said.

"I am."

He stared into her eyes and she stared right back, nodding reassuringly. His expression changed almost instantly from one of caution to lust.

* * *

Twenty minutes later, James was pressing a passcode into the keypad of a mint-green beach hut on stilts. He pulled open the wooden barn door to reveal a teeny-tiny space. The hut was no more than twelve feet long and six feet wide. It had a small tea-making station on the back wall, complete with a bright orange kettle that sat on a gas stove. There was a pretty patterned rug on the floor and a bench along one wall, covered in fluffy scatter cushions. The owners had made some attempt at decorating for Christmas by placing a small Christmas tree on a shelf on one wall and hanging several paper snowflakes from the roof. James closed the door, set down their bag of goodies and opened the shutters to let in the light. They took off their coats and stood side by side for a moment, admiring the view. The horizon was heavy with rain clouds, the waves violent, the sea a murky grey. Maddie shuddered involuntarily. The movement prompted James to look at her.

"Cold?" he asked, closing the shutters.

"A little," she said, eyeing him. She thought he'd come for her the second they were enveloped in privacy, but he didn't. Instead, he used a bottle of water to fill the kettle and lit the gas ring. He appeared to be avoiding her gaze. Maddie didn't know how to take that or what to do about it, so she just stood there, staring at him as he made them each another cup of tea. He passed her a cup and then perched on the bench, his eyes roving over the shack's shabby-chic walls and rugged edges.

"I reckon I could make one of these," he said. Maddie didn't doubt it, but she didn't say anything. Small talk was so far from what she wanted from him right now, she couldn't bring herself to participate in it. She stared at him instead. "Bit of wood, a few nails," he said, knocking the bench with his fist. Still, Maddie stood there, her heart beating madly, her mind drilling through potential next steps at a million miles an hour. She'd expected them to jump on each other, and had prepared herself for it. Her nervous system was not reacting well to this deviation from proposed events. She could feel herself getting flustered, feeling weak. Because she hadn't imagined them doing anything in here except attaching themselves to one another, she didn't know what to do next, and her body — which had admittedly been privy only to almost exclusively predictable things for six years — was panicking accordingly. For want of anything else to do, she put down her mug. "It's not very big, is it?" James said, still avoiding looking at her.

"James," Maddie heard herself say. He stopped talking and finally met her gaze, looking not unlike a deer caught in headlights. Maddie felt a lump rise in her throat, and wondered what she had done or said to mess things up between the café and the beach hut. "Have you changed your mind?" she asked, before she could stop herself.

James snapped to attention and planted his eyes on her. He put down his cup, stood up and marched towards her. She thought he was going to grab her, but he didn't. Instead he stood right before her. "Maddie, I have never once for a single moment since the first time I laid eyes on you not wanted this." He reached for her hand as he closed the gap between them. Every bit of him was now pressed against every part of her. He deftly swept her into his arms, and before she had time to say anything else he was kissing her. Maddie felt like she might lose her footing, so she wrapped her arms around his neck and leaned in. That was all the encouragement he needed to pick her up and carry her towards the bench. He sat her upon it, urging her thighs apart with his knee and setting himself between them. He removed his mouth from hers, cupping her face and urging her to look at him when she chased his lips with her own.

"I really like you," he whispered. His confession gave her the confidence she needed to participate beyond doing what his actions told her to. She ran her hands down his chest to the bottom of his T-shirt and touched the skin of his torso, right beside the button of his jeans. He watched her, his breathing heavy with desire. She spread her hand across his erection. "We can take this as slow as you need to," he said.

"I know." But they couldn't. With the power of what was happening between them, it would be virtually impossible for them to do anything except go all the way. And she needed them to go all the way. Then he was kissing her again, her mouth, her neck, her mouth again. Maddie pulled his T-shirt up over his head and dragged him towards her by the belt loops on his jeans so that she could feel his skin pressed against her. He wrapped his arms around her waist and kissed her harder. Maddie moaned and hitched her legs around him, urging him to move rhythmically against her. He complied, groaning as though he was actually fucking her. She briefly thought she might go mad. Suddenly, he pulled away and stared down at her, drinking in her reaction to the pleasure, the torture, the yearning. He set about unhooking the straps on her dungarees, pulling them down to her waist. His hand slipped up under her T-shirt and landed on the cup of her thin, satin bra. Carefully avoiding her new tattoo, he trapped her nipple between his fingers and kneaded. Maddie gasped, tossing her head back, exposing her neck once more to his tongue and teeth. He leaned over her, hooking his arm around her back and pulling her upwards so that her dungarees fell to the floor. That took the layers of material between them from four to three. Maddie grappled with the button on his jeans and pushed them down with her feet. As she did, she put her hand down the front of his boxers and grabbed him. He moaned and stopped kissing her, his legs buckling slightly so that he was leaning heavily against her.

"Floor?" she suggested. He nodded and picked her up, holding her with one hand and using the other to throw down the scatter cushions. He kicked them until they formed a sort of bed, then lowered her onto them, following her body with his own so that he was never not between her legs. Desperate for more of him, Maddie pulled her own top over her head and tossed it. James put some space between their bodies, sitting up on his haunches. His eyes travelled from her face all the way down her form and back up again. Maddie blushed, suddenly shy.

"You're the most beautiful woman I've ever seen," he said. Maddie resisted the urge to laugh off his compliment. Nobody had ever said anything like that to her before. She knew if any other man had spoken those words to her she wouldn't have believed them — they might, in fact, have given her the 'ick' — but there was something about the way he said it. She reached her hands out towards him, grabbing the air playfully until he complied and set himself back between her legs. He kissed her deeply, his tongue against hers. She grasped his back and tensed her hands, running her fingernails gently from his shoulder blades to the small of his back. He groaned, tearing his lips from hers and kissing her breasts, then her stomach, then her thighs, using his fingers to pleasure her through the thin fabric of her underwear as he did. When his fingers searched to move the fabric to one side, Maddie must have visibly tensed, because he stopped and crawled back up her body so they were face to face again.

"I'm sorry," she said.

"Do not apologise." He shook his head, kissing her sweetly on the lips.

"Nobody's ever done . . . that to me before." She gestured with her eyes. He gazed at her, quizzically. She shook her head in confirmation.

"I apologise on behalf of men everywhere." He sounded so earnest that it made Maddie laugh. "Seriously," he continued. "I bet you have some skanky ex-boyfriend somewhere who let you suck his dick but never went down on you, am I right?"

Maddie nodded solemnly.

"For fuck's sake," he muttered. "Well, I would *love* to be your first. But I totally understand if you would rather not."

Maddie stared up at him thoughtfully. She wanted to be brave enough to do it, but she couldn't imagine a sexual act that made her feel more vulnerable. She had never fully understood the appeal, had never been able to fathom how women could relax enough to enjoy having a man's head so close to their most intimate parts.

"I'm excellent at it, just so you know," James continued, making her smile again. "I'm not being big-headed. I just want you to understand what you're getting yourself into. Satisfaction is guaranteed. You *will* come harder than you have ever come with any man ever."

"No man has ever made me come," Maddie said. James' eyes widened and his mouth fell comically agape.

"You're lying," he challenged her. Maddie shook her head. James sat back up on his haunches, shaking his head in disbelief. Maddie propped herself up on her elbows. "You have come, though, right?"

"Of course!" Maddie said. "I've always been on my own, though. Except for one time, when I was so unsatisfied after sex I finished myself off. That did not go down well. He felt inadequate."

"He fucking was inadequate!" James said, shaking his head again. "Who the fuck are these men?"

"We were young," Maddie said. "It's been almost five years . . ."

James snapped back to attention again. "You haven't been with a man for five years?" Maddie nodded. He eyeballed her curves, constrained only by the teal satin bra and knicker set she'd dug out especially for today. "How is that even possible?" He crawled back towards her, kissing her hard on the mouth. This time he did not climb on top of her. Instead he encouraged her back onto her back and lay on his side next to her, stroking her hair with one hand and letting the other wander across her breasts, tummy and torso, so gently at times she wasn't sure if he'd stopped. Every now and then he'd tug her hair and force her head back until she felt gloriously constrained by him.

"Can I touch you?" he whispered after a while. Maddie did not open her eyes, but nodded a yes. "Are you sure?" he checked. She found his hand and pushed it lower, guiding his fingers beneath the elastic of her knickers. He rubbed her gently, slipping his middle finger inside of her as he did. Maddie gasped and arched her back, but before she could move against his hand, the ball of which was artfully resting against her clitoris, he'd removed it. She opened her eyes to demand he replace it immediately, and found him smiling lasciviously at her.

"I'll kill you," she said. He laughed, low and wicked. Maddie reached out to touch his face and he kissed her palm, then bit the tips of her fingers one by one, flicking them with his tongue. At the same time, his hand was tormenting her once more by circling teasingly close to where she wanted him — needed him — to go. Maddie groaned and arched her back again, desperate for him. He obliged, filling her up once more. He proceeded to pleasure her at a frustratingly slow pace for a really long time, until Maddie's whole body tingled with desire. She was shaking with desperation and knew if he increased the tempo even slightly just for a little bit she would climax in a few short seconds. She was devastatingly close and yet felt so far away, and she knew he was doing it on purpose.

"Please," she gasped eventually. James slowed his pace even further, so that he had almost stopped. "No!" she begged, grabbing his forearm and moving against him. He tested her determination by trying to remove his hand, but she clawed at him and begged. "Please. Please. Please."

"Patience is a virtue," he murmured, stopping completely. Maddie almost screamed in frustration. Before she knew what she was doing, she was reaching to pleasure herself, but James grabbed her wrist. "Please, let me do it," he whispered. Maddie nodded. He forced her legs wide open by hooking his own leg over hers, then pleasured her with his fingers, turning them in circles, hard and fast, until she came against his hand. He gave her less than a minute to recover before he brought her to climax in the same manner again.

Not yet satisfied and drunk on endorphins, Maddie pulled him on top of her, grappling with his boxers until they were off. He produced a condom from somewhere and deftly put it on, then settled himself back between her legs and pushed himself inside of her, moaning with obvious relief. She urged him to take her harder. He complied, alternating between gentle lovemaking and frantic, determined pulses, until she shuddered through an orgasm and tipped him over the edge. Afterwards, she lay beneath him, wondering if she'd ever get enough of him. He hoisted himself up on his elbows to look at her, still inside her.

"So we really just went from zero to one hundred, huh?" he said.

"Don't blame me, you're in charge here," she teased.

"In principle, but most certainly not in practice." She used her gaze to question him. "I have absolutely no say over any part of my body, my dick specifically, when it comes to you."

Maddie grinned, because his desire for her was obvious and it had done wonders for her confidence. She was red and sweaty, but had no qualms about him looking so intently at her from such a close distance. She cocked her head to one side, inviting him to kiss her. He withdrew from her as he did so. Maddie felt empty. He rolled off her. She turned onto her side and surveyed him naked, in full form, for the first time. She was certain she could happily remain naked in this beach hut with him to the exclusion of everything else for months and still would not manage to get her fill of him. He watched her watching him, his face bursting with mischief.

"What?" she asked.

"Sometimes, just for fun, I like to go back in my mind to something I've lived through and watch the past version of myself do his thing without any idea of what's coming next. I just went back and rewatched our first conversation."

Maddie smiled and shook her head. "You goof," she teased, running her hand across his torso. She spread her fingers out and ran her palm across the ridges on his stomach. He watched her, silent and hard.

"Can I touch you?" she whispered. He nodded, closing his eyes.

"You can do literally whatever you want to me," he said.

"You might regret saying that," she warned him.

He put his hands behind his head and braced himself. "Unlikely," he sighed.

CHAPTER ELEVEN

Maddie walked through the kitchen door and into the arms of Bluebell, which should have been impossible, since her sister's flight wasn't due in until tomorrow.

"Oh, my God!" Maddie cried, holding her sister at arm's length. She stared into her face as though checking she was real. Bluebell beamed at her, poised to jump back into Maddie's arms. "What are you doing here?" Maddie said, pulling her sister back into a hug.

"Surprise!" Bluebell grinned.

"I was picking you up tomorrow, wasn't I?" Maddie squeezed her sister tightly, drinking in her scent and enjoying the feel of her hot skin against her own freezing cheek. Bluebell held her right back. "The day before Christmas Eve, you said, I'm sure?"

"I wanted to surprise you," she said. "I had no idea you'd be out gallivanting, of course."

Maddie had almost forgotten that James was standing behind her. She dropped her sister and stepped back so that Bluebell could see him and he could see her.

"Bluebell, this is James. James, this is my sister, Bluebell."

"Pleasure," James said, shaking Bluebell's hand.

"Nice to meet you in person, James," Bluebell said, her eyes bright with what Maddie knew was approval. Maddie's heart lurched, and she quickly had to remind herself that James was quite clearly crazy about her. He'd told her plenty of times this afternoon, with his words and with his actions. Yes, her sister was beautiful, but he was hardly going to run off with her, was he? She felt vaguely disappointed in her visceral reaction. She had considered these insecurities dead and buried, but here they were, ruining what should be a happy reunion.

"Mum said you went to get a tattoo," Bluebell said. Maddie nodded, putting down her handbag and taking off her coat. She pulled her top down at the collar and showed Bluebell the tattoo, which was safely encased behind a clear, sticky plaster. Bluebell read the words with wide eyes, theatrically sticking out her bottom lip as she did. "That's so gorgeous," she said, squeezing Maddie's arm. "Bowie would love it."

"He would," Maddie agreed, going to fill the kettle. "Where is everyone?"

"They're in the front room with Marley, Autumn and Benjamin," Bluebell said.

"I'm going to head off, I think," James said from where he was standing awkwardly by the door. He reached down to greet Stevie, who had finally realised James was back and come to say hello. He clipped her lead to her collar and readied himself by zipping up his jacket. Maddie's heart sank with disappointment. She had hoped he might stay over in the spare room, so that she could sneak across the hall when everyone was in bed and they could rerun the fun they'd had earlier. She knew James was trying to do her a favour by leaving her to spend time with her family, but at that moment she felt quite sure any distance at all between them was entirely too much.

"Oh, are you leaving?" Bluebell said, visibly surprised. "I thought you practically lived here now? Mum and Dad said you're basically part of the family."

James caught Maddie's eye, and a wordless communication passed between the two of them. This was exactly why they couldn't tell anyone that there was anything happening between them. Her parents adored him already, Marley and Autumn were well on their way to feeling platonic love towards him, Bluebell and Pip would follow suit, and Maddie and James knew there was a good chance this situationship would be hijacked by the people they cared about and overcomplicated. They liked each other and they had limited time together, so they planned on spending as much of that time with each other as they possibly could. This did not need to be made any more convoluted than that.

"Honestly, I haven't been home in a few days," James said. "I should really check on Mum."

Bluebell shrugged, throwing him a little wave. He waved back, catching Maddie's eye as he did. She had to work hard to keep her face straight, and to stop herself from marching over to him and giving him a hearty kiss goodbye. Instead, she somehow mustered the energy to nod in a nonchalant, unconcerned, 'we're definitely not sleeping together' type manner. He nodded in response, opened the back door, called a cheery 'goodbye', and was gone.

Bluebell turned to her. "Oh my God, you're fucking him!"

Maddie reeled, her mouth agape in disbelief. There was no point in lying about it, Bluebell knew her better than anyone in the world. That composed performance had been Maddie's very best attempt at indifference. If she hadn't managed to convince Bluebell with that, then she had no chance of doing it across an entire winter.

"Shush," Maddie demanded.

"Finally, the drought is over." Bluebell put her hand over her mouth and stifled a giggle. "Tell me all about it. Immediately." She was whispering, but clearly enthralled. If anyone were to walk in the kitchen, especially Autumn, there would be absolutely no hiding the fact they were talking about something juicy and secretive. Maddie kept an eye on the doorway.

"Later." She gestured towards the living room.

Bluebell gasped. "Is it a secret? Am I the only one who knows? Oh my God, this is so fucking hot."

"Stop." Maddie groaned, exasperated.

"I'm sorry, I can't." Bluebell reached theatrically into the air, as though she was performing a monologue. "This is so exciting. A winter love story. My sister and the stable boy . . ."

"We don't have any stables," Maddie pointed out.

"We do for the purposes of this dramatic retelling."

"Stop," Maddie begged, though she couldn't hide her smile.

"Promise me you'll tell me every single detail later," Bluebell said, earnestly.

Maddie nodded fervently, pouring herself a cup of tea. She gestured to ask Bluebell if she wanted one, but her sister was heading for the wine cupboard. Bluebell was a walking party. She was also a terrible influence on Autumn. The two of them together were borderline hysterical ninety per cent of the time. Maddie thoroughly enjoyed seeing them so happy, but her introverted personality meant she often found it overwhelming. She braced herself, then followed Bluebell into the living room.

Emma, Ben, Autumn and Marley were sitting on the sofas. They smiled warmly at Maddie and Bluebell, shuffling up to make room for them both. Benjamin was sitting on the floor by the fire, drawing pictures.

"How was your day, love?" Emma asked, then, without waiting for an answer, she said, "Show us your tattoo!"

Maddie put down her teacup and adjusted her collar so her family could see Bowie's beautiful words inked permanently across her chest. They were copied exactly as Bowie had written them and were about the length of a forefinger. It was perfect. Ryan had done a spectacular job. Their eyes filled with tears, as Maddie had known they would, but something had been shifting recently, and this time she was sure that even Marley's tears were happy tears. They were all terribly sad, of course, but they were also glad. They had once had their very own Bowie, and he had loved them. He was gone — and that had taken time for them all to come to terms with — but Maddie felt like they might finally be doing that in the midst of everything else they had going on. She felt like they'd been stuck in time, focused only on getting through each day, but it looked like happiness might be on the horizon. So, while Maddie knew that any mention of Bowie would most likely always bring tears to their eyes, something had shifted. Just like the tears she had shed in the tattoo parlour that morning, these were not tears of desperation and despair. They were tears of fondness and remembrance. They were tears of gratitude.

* * *

Pip had gone out with some old school friends, which was a shame, as it had been a while since Maddie had been in the same room as her entire family. She'd have enjoyed that immensely. Still, she was thoroughly satisfied to sit on the rug before the fire with Benjamin on her lap, Bluebell on one side and Autumn on the other. Bluebell did most of the talking, regaling them with tales of her travels, men and women she had met, animals she'd saved. Maddie and Autumn knew most of these stories already, having kept in constant contact with Bluebell while she'd been globe-trotting, but they never tired of hearing about Bluebell's adventures. Her sister had such a funny way of describing things, so they were as riveted by her ramblings this evening as they always were.

"You really should start a podcast," Autumn said, pointedly sipping her wine.

Maddie nodded in agreement. "We've been saying this for years."

"Nobody wants to listen to this." Bluebell rolled her eyes.

"I do!" Maddie and Autumn said together. Bluebell laughed, shaking her head.

"You underestimate yourself," Maddie insisted. "You are really, really good at this. You're funny, interesting, intelligent and adventurous. You have so many stories to tell. Honestly, Bluebell, you should do it."

Autumn and Bluebell were eyeballing Maddie. Their eyes flitted to each other, then back to her. They were smirking knowingly, their gazes laden with mischief. Maddie tried to straighten her face, but it was too late. She'd been smiling like an idiot. She worked hard to present herself as a person who was generally content, but she very rarely displayed any real enthusiasm for anything. She certainly never beamed, which is what she'd been doing just then. This was unnatural behaviour for her. Bluebell, who already knew why Maddie was so happy, was grinning because she was enjoying Maddie's giddiness. Autumn was smirking because she was suspicious, though Maddie was almost certain her sister's reaction had quietly confirmed what Autumn had already guessed.

"Benjamin, could you go and sit with Daddy for a minute? I think he's lonely," Autumn said. Benjamin obligingly picked up the book he was reading and clambered onto Marley's lap. Autumn checked that Emma and Ben were fully engaged in conversation with their son before raising her eyebrows knowingly at Maddie, nudging Bluebell for backup as she did. "Tell me," she whispered. "Right now."

"Tell you what?" Maddie shrugged.

"Don't give me that . . . nonchalance," Autumn hissed, gesticulating wildly into the air. "You are not a nonchalant person generally. You are the opposite. Extremely the opposite. You're chalant. Extremely chalant. Tell me. Right now."

Bluebell put her hand over her mouth to stifle a laugh and Maddie, to her surprise, found herself quite enjoying attention for once. This was most unlike her, but then she'd never had a happy romantic situation to discuss heartily with her friends. It was nice. Autumn and Bluebell leaned in closer, their eyes wide with anticipation, their necks craned towards her, ears poised for gossip. Maddie drew out the revelation, sighing and shaking her head.

"James and I . . . did something," she murmured, covering her face with her hands. Autumn shrieked so dramatically she made Maddie and Bluebell jump. She also immediately drew the attention of Emma, Ben, Marley and Benjamin, who stopped the conversation they were having to watch them giggling girlishly on the floor.

"What on Earth is going on?" Marley asked.

"Nothing," they said together, laughing harder.

"Bluebell said something outrageous," Maddie said, trying to appease her curious brother.

"What else is new?" He shrugged.

"Exactly," Bluebell said, shooing him with her hand. "Nothing to see here, go back to your business."

Ben, Emma and Marley returned to their conversation, but Maddie knew she was not the only one who could see her brother watching them out of the corner of his eye. She subtly shook her head at her two favourite women. She was happy to divulge what was happening between her and James to them, but she'd really rather nobody else knew. They'd make a fuss, then it would become a big deal and she'd be left confused. She needed some time.

"I'll sleep in your room and you can tell me then," Bluebell muttered.

Autumn gasped. "What about me?"

"Stay," Maddie said. Autumn's eyes lit up and she nodded, turning towards her partner and parents.

"Marley my sweetheart, my darling, my love," she called. Marley stopped talking again to give Autumn his full attention. He looked expectant and mildly amused. "You're on bedtime duty, tonight." She grinned. "I'm having a sleepover with your sisters."

* * *

"It's been years since we did this," Bluebell said, crawling drunkenly into Maddie's bed. Maddie tapped the empty space beside her, scooching as close to her sister as she could, once Bluebell was safely beneath the covers. They both sighed happily. "What's Autumn doing in that bathroom?" Bluebell muttered.

"Autumn, hurry up," Maddie demanded. Autumn didn't reply, but they heard her electric toothbrush whizz to life behind the bathroom door. She'd asked Marley to go home and retrieve it and — though they had once made fun of her obsessive approach to oral hygiene — they now left her alone about it, well aware that Autumn was very particular about brushing her teeth because her mother had never insisted she do it. That had led to expensive and complicated issues with her mouth, teeth and gums.

"You look different, Mads," Bluebell said, staring into her sister's face. Maddie's eyes roamed questioningly over her sister's perfect features in the light of the bedside lamp. "In a really, really good way."

Maddie smiled. "I'm happy," she said. "For the first time in ages. It's taken such a long time. I feel like I've been climbing up a really big hill. Like I've reached a tipping point of some sort."

Bluebell nodded wistfully. "I remember something similar. A watershed. I was sitting on a beach in Greece watching loggerhead turtles hatch. In that moment, I realised I hadn't thought about Bowie dying for days. I'd thought about him, but not about those last few weeks. It felt like life was finally about something else. I felt guilty for a bit, I even said sorry to him, but then I remembered how much he loved us, and I swear, Mads, you'll think I'm mad, but I heard his voice in my head telling me to get a fucking grip. He was laughing when he said it and it made me laugh out loud. I was just sitting there, staring at these baby turtle eggs, crying and laughing like a weirdo."

Maddie laughed and gave her a hug. Autumn, having finished her tooth-cleaning routine, was climbing into bed on the other side of her. It was a double bed and so not quite big enough for three. They'd be snug, but Maddie didn't mind. She was just glad to have her two best friends back beside her.

"What are we talking about?" Autumn asked.

"Bowie," Maddie and Bluebell said together. Autumn nodded and sighed. She buried her head into the pillow a little bit. Her friend did this often, and Maddie knew it was because Autumn never quite knew how to react to Bowie's sisters talking about him. As Bowie's former lover and Marley's soulmate, her grief was much more complicated and entirely different. Maddie grabbed her hand and squeezed, a declaration of reassurance. Autumn squeezed back.

"Tell us about this shag." Bluebell changed the subject. Autumn laughed and Maddie groaned, covering her face with the duvet. They waited patiently for her to gather herself, then Bluebell nudged her pointedly.

"It was amazing," Maddie said.

"Did you . . . you know?" Bluebell asked. Maddie squeaked a yes, bracing herself for the giddiness she knew would come, and it did. Autumn and Bluebell hooted and hollered, playfully hitting the duvet and pillows in celebration "Finally!" Bluebell said. "Well done, James."

"I felt really comfortable and he knew what he was doing."

"A fantastic combination," Autumn said.

"He was excellent at it, actually."

"How wonderful," Bluebell said.

"I think it's because I got to know him first. We didn't like each other at all when we first met, then we became friends, then I liked him, but it all felt so complicated. It felt overwhelming, so I tried to stop it, to stay away from him, but in the end I just couldn't."

"How do you feel about him now?" Autumn asked. Though Maddie had known this question was coming all evening, she didn't feel remotely equipped to answer it. She liked him, that much she knew. She was immensely attracted to him, he took care of her and made her laugh. She thoroughly enjoyed having him around. In fact, if it were up to her, she'd spend most of the next few weeks trapped between James and a mattress. Or a wall. Or the floor. Whatever and wherever, really, as long as he was attached to her. But it was much more complicated than that. He had spoken to her at length about how much he hated being at home, how everything reminded him of Harry, how being around his mum made him sad, how travel set his soul on fire, how he never really felt like himself unless he was travelling a stretch of road towards an unknown destination. Maddie knew how he felt because she felt the same way about caring for people. Even before Bowie had died and left her the inheritance she was using to open the recovery retreat, Maddie had always intended on going back to work in social care. It was her life's purpose, something she'd known since she was a teenager. They were on different paths, heading in different directions. She didn't know how she felt because she didn't think it was wise to let herself feel any feelings she had for James too deeply. He would be leaving soon, and she was staying here. She didn't regret what had happened between them today, but she was smart enough to know it wasn't the best decision she'd ever made. She just hadn't been able to help herself.

"I don't know." She sighed.

"I think you do," Autumn said.

"Don't worry about anything, Mads," Bluebell said. "Just enjoy yourself as much as you can for as long as you can, and sort the rest out later."

"I literally couldn't do anything else even if I wanted to," Maddie confessed. "He lives rent-free in my head now."

"Oh, God, I remember that feeling," Autumn said. "I don't envy you, Mads. It's like torture."

"You feel it right here." Bluebell pointed to her chest. "A yearning, a pining you can't quench."

"Even when you're with them, it's still there," Autumn agreed. "You feel like you'll never get enough of them."

"You question your own sanity," Bluebell said. "There have been times when I have fundamentally questioned whether I know anything at all about myself, given how silly I'm acting over the mere existence of a person and their proximity to me."

"Does it die down eventually?" Maddie asked, feeling overwhelmed. Autumn and Bluebell were not only sensible women, they had both been staunchly anti-monogamy for periods of their lives. Bluebell still had no plans to enter a traditional relationship, and Autumn hadn't had any desire for a boyfriend until she'd met Bowie at age thirty-two. If even they had been swept up by the borderline hysterical level of desire Maddie felt like she might be tipping towards, there was absolutely no hope for her. The two women were silent for a moment.

"I'm pretty sure she's talking to you," Bluebell prompted Autumn. Autumn laughed softly. Maddie knew she didn't know how to answer the question.

"You really want me to talk like this about your brother?" she asked. Maddie and Bluebell nodded.

"Just, you know . . ." Bluebell said. "The PG version."

Autumn chuckled, repositioning herself so that she was propped up by her elbows. "Honestly, when Marley and I finally gave in and first got together, I genuinely thought I would never get enough of him. We were obsessed with each other. He could put his hands on me absolutely anywhere and I'd succumb. We were like that for months, maybe years. I never thought it would fade away, but it did, eventually. Life gets in the way. Everything becomes familiar."

Autumn lay back down.

"But honestly, guys, what we have now is so much better. Now that the fog of lust has gone, I can see what we have besides it, and it's *a lot*. Marley is my best friend, my biggest cheerleader, my protector. Nobody makes me laugh like he does. He takes his position as a member of this team we've created extremely seriously. I'm not naive, I know that's rare."

Maddie smiled. Her brother had made mistakes in his past, but he was a wonderful man now, she knew that. Autumn had undoubtedly influenced him. He was humble, less self-absorbed, more empathetic.

"We're crazy about each other," Autumn continued. "I say that with every shred of conviction within me. I would die for him, he'd die for me. I truly believe there is no greater living man anywhere on this planet, and, while we're at it, he got out of the shower this morning and his hair was all wet and he was all shiny, and I knew in that moment I could go up against anyone and compellingly make the case he's the sexiest man in existence."

"You're straying into non-PG territory here," Bluebell warned.

"I *never* get to talk about sex with you anymore, it's so unfair!" Autumn whined.

"No, you do not," Maddie said, warningly. Autumn laughed. They fell into a comfortable silence, and Maddie wasn't sure if the other two had fallen asleep. She let her mind wander to James and their tryst that afternoon. She marvelled at how incredibly comfortable and present she'd felt, how satisfied and happy. Afterwards, they'd lain side by side, her head on his chest, his hand stroking her hair, talking for two or three hours about all sorts. She couldn't remember what exactly, but they had barely taken a breath. They'd only stopped talking to kiss. They'd contemplated renting somewhere and staying overnight, but Maddie had known such a gesture would cause speculation she'd rather avoid, so they'd trudged begrudgingly back to the car and moseyed on home. James had hardly left her mind since. She couldn't wait to see him again.

"Do what makes you happy," Autumn murmured, so gently Maddie wasn't sure she'd heard her right. She turned to her friend. "Bowie's rules, remember? Do what makes you happy was rule number six."

Maddie did remember. Bowie and Autumn had compiled a list of rules throughout their relationship to help keep them on course. *Do what makes you happy* was born from a conversation they'd had not long before he had died, in which he'd told her Marley was falling in love with her. He had implored her to do whatever made her happy when he was gone. His words — which he had written on a piece of paper and left in a box before he'd died, trusting Bluebell would give it to

Autumn at exactly the right time — had provided the strength she'd needed to admit her feelings for Marley.

"Do what makes you happy," Bluebell repeated the words. Maddie smiled and snuggled closer to her sister, dragging Autumn with her. The three women quickly fell asleep.

* * *

Maddie slept in longer than Autumn and Bluebell, and woke up in bed alone. It was early, not yet 8 a.m. She contemplated closing her eyes and catching another couple of hours, but she had too much to do, so she forced herself out of bed and into the shower, smiling goofily as she washed over the scratches carved passionately into her upper arms through James' expressions of ecstasy. She couldn't wait to see him today.

She pulled on gold corduroys and a loose grey sweater, swept her hair into a messy bun and slathered sun cream and tinted moisturiser on her face, then headed for the kitchen. Bluebell, Autumn and her mother were grouped around the stove, stepping enthusiastically from side to side as they cooked what smelled like scrambled tofu. Autumn and Bluebell had their arms in the air, as though they were dancing. Emma was jumping enthusiastically from foot-to-foot. Ben sat at the kitchen table, nursing a coffee and watched them, clearly amused.

"What are you doing?" Maddie asked.

"Getting our ten-thousand steps in," Bluebell said.

"Why?" Maddie asked.

"Bluebell says it's good for your heart," Emma said, shaking her hips. Maddie laughed and poured herself a coffee, sitting beside her father.

"Join in!" Autumn encouraged Maddie. "It's putting me in a tremendous mood."

"I do plenty of steps every day walking to and fro around here, thank you very much," Maddie said.

"That's not the same," Bluebell said. She was hopping from side to side and turning around in a circle, staring at the ceiling. "They taught us about this in Bali. You have to be intentional in your movements. You have to do it while lovingly focusing on the fact you're doing it as a treat for your body. That's how you get the best results."

"Who taught you that?" Maddie challenged.

"Some guy," Bluebell said.

"Did he also tell you that you have to be weird while you're doing it?" Maddie asked. Ben chuckled, shaking his head.

"You don't know what you're missing," Bluebell sang, jumping vigorously up and down. Just then the back door opened and Marley, Benjamin and James stepped into the kitchen. They froze by the coat stand, as they took in the scene before them. James bent his head to one side, like a curious cocker spaniel. Though he had barely left her mind since yesterday, Maddie had almost forgotten how gorgeous he was. Now that she could see him, she could remember the feel of his lips, the sounds he made, the loving way he'd watched her caress him in such striking detail it made her stomach flip.

"What are you doing?" Marley said, dumbly.

"Ten-thousand steps," Emma answered, stirring the scramble and gesturing for Autumn to check on the bread toasting under the grill. Autumn danced to the cooker. Bluebell checked the step counter on her watch.

"We have about two-thousand steps left to do, if you guys want to join in," she said. To Maddie's surprise, James immediately started jigging from side to side, clicking his fingers enthusiastically with each step he took, and made his way towards the dancing women. Her family burst into laughter and cheered. Their approval made Maddie blush inexplicably.

"Can I do it?" Benjamin asked.

"Go for it, darling," Marley said, bending to take off his coat. Benjamin ran to the group, skipping happily, a wide grin on his face. Maddie could see the top of his little blond head over the countertop each time he jumped high enough. Spurred on by his son, Marley joined in too, comically sidestepping his way through the group until he reached Autumn. She stopped dancing for a second to kiss him sweetly. Maddie cradled her coffee and watched them jig, giggling and mimicking each other until they were hysterically counting down the last few hundred steps. Marley picked up Benjamin and held out his hand to twirl Autumn around and in that exact moment — watching her blissfully happy friend melt into the arms of her brother and nephew — Maddie gained a clarity she'd never had before about what she really wanted. She wanted a beautiful, wholesome, unashamedly devoted kind of love. A love that was certain and steady. A love that was bursting with promises of a future full of fun — of jumping, joyful children, and bread left to burn in favour of dancing in the kitchen.

Without meaning to, she caught James' eye. He was watching her, a mischievous grin on his face, his floppy curls bouncing to the invisible beat Bluebell was dictating. He gestured for her to join them. She smiled shyly, shaking her head, but he held out his hand towards her, insistent. Despite her better judgement — caught up in the frivolity and driven by the momentous conclusion she'd just come to terms with — Maddie relented, pointedly draining her coffee before standing and making her way to him. He grabbed her hands and encouraged her to dance, gesticulating wildly in what was, she knew, an attempt to make himself look ridiculous. He was trying to take the attention off her and she appreciated it, though she knew her family was still looking. Still smiling. Still nodding their heads knowingly, catching each other's eyes, daring to dream and full of hope that mournful, marooned Maddie might finally feel brave enough to cast her sails and steer herself in a new direction.

She kept her eyes on James' and felt warm and fuzzy. She was sincerely hopeful that she might feel brave enough, too.

CHAPTER TWELVE

It was Christmas Eve 'Eve', as Emma liked to call it, and there was a lot to be done. The Whittles didn't give each other gifts, they bought presents only for Benjamin, preferring instead to spend money on sharing experiences with one another throughout the year, but they did still enjoy several Christmas traditions, including a very hearty lunch. There were many vegetables that needed to be prepped and, even though they were in the middle of renovations, Emma was insisting that the house must be spick and span, so Maddie agreed that she and James would focus on sorting out the upstairs rooms and let Emma and Ben tidy the downstairs rooms today.

"What are you doing on Christmas Day, James?" Emma asked, clearing away his breakfast plate.

"Not much." He sounded perfectly normal when he said it, but Maddie thought she saw a shadow of sadness pass across his features. She squeezed his thigh under the table.

"Why don't you come up here?" Emma suggested. "Stay tomorrow night and celebrate Christmas with us."

"I feel bad leaving Mum," he said. "It's always been her and Nan at Christmas. This is her first Christmas without her."

"Bring her!" Emma said. "There's plenty of space! Autumn's mum and sister are coming. They're bringing Autumn's new baby niece to meet us all. The more the merrier, honestly."

James nodded gratefully. "I'll ask her. Christmas is . . . a funny time in our house. I'm sure you understand."

Emma nodded knowingly and sighed. "Oh yes," she said. "I know exactly what you mean."

Maddie and James made fresh coffees and took them upstairs to the back bedroom, which was the last room they needed to paint. Between Christmas and New Year, the first lot of new furniture would be arriving and it would all need putting together, so it was really important they finish the painting today. They were keeping some of the old stuff, the rest of it they were donating to charity. They still needed to fix the orangery after Pigglesworth had ruined it — some of the stone flower beds needed to be rebuilt. They had so much to do to the outside of the house, too. The porch needed sanding and painting, as did all of the wicker furniture. They needed to lay the groundwork for several outdoor areas and dig foundations for a pond. Maddie still had no idea what they were going to do with Bowie's old room, while her bedroom remained a clutter-filled disaster. And then there was everything that needed doing for Marley and Autumn's wedding. Her to-do list felt never-ending. She was stressed to say the least.

Luckily, James was on hand to distract her. He took her coffee and set it down on a paint pot, then closed the bedroom door and pulled her to him, kissing her deeply. She groaned and wrapped her arms around his neck, her woes instantly fleeing her mind. She deserved a few minutes to indulge in the sweet torture that came with this feeling, she reasoned. She hitched a leg around his waist, encouraging him to lift her up. He obliged, pressing her back against the bedroom wall.

"I've missed you so much," he said, gazing up at her.

"You saw me yesterday," she teased.

"After what we got up to yesterday afternoon, that night apart felt like a lifetime," he whispered. She nodded because she agreed. "Although, I had excellent fun reliving it on my own last night," he murmured, raising his eyebrows suggestively. Maddie whimpered and it made him smile. He kissed her deeply again, grabbing at her waist and driving their bodies together in what she knew was an indication of frustration. She groaned into his mouth.

He kissed her for a couple of minutes, before pulling away to look at her. "We have to stop this. We have work to do."

"Agreed," she said, enjoying the fact he had not yet put her down.

"Where shall we start?" he asked, pressing his lips to her neck. His breath against her skin made her shudder. Maddie moaned, winding her hand in his hair to hold him in place.

"I can do the cutting if you want to do the rolling?" she murmured. He nodded, biting her ear seductively and grinding himself against her once more. Maddie sighed, wondering with glee how people in lust ever got anything done.

* * *

It took most of the morning to complete the first coat. While they waited for lunch, they talked through plans for the bedrooms. The master bedroom, which had once belonged to Emma and Ben and was still partly inhabited by them, had been split into three smaller rooms. Bluebell's bedroom, which had been almost as big as her parents' room, had been split into two good-sized bedrooms. Her bedroom and Pip's old room, where James now slept, were the smallest rooms and were staying the same. Maddie would keep her room and the other would be used by staff. That meant there were five bedrooms for guests to sleep in. Maddie wasn't sure that was enough.

"I want to help as many people as I can," she said. "But I don't want so many people here that we can't give everyone the attention they need."

"What about Bowie's old bedroom?" James asked, gently. "You could fit another couple of rooms in there?"

Maddie shook her head. She didn't know what she wanted to do with that room, but she knew she didn't want strangers sleeping in it. She might change her mind about that once the retreat was open and her guests started to feel like friends and family, but at the moment they were strangers to her. She didn't want to leave the room empty, but Bowie's old bedroom felt too special for anything her imagination could concoct.

"Why don't you leave that room to me?" James had read her mind. Maddie moved to say no, but James shuffled closer to her and stared straight into her eyes. "It's a beautiful room and it should be used for something. Bowie wouldn't want it to go to waste. I swear I'll be respectful. I know it's hard, but I really feel like you need to take the leap."

Maddie watched him thoughtfully. He was right and she wanted to say yes, but she was afraid to. She never felt closer to Bowie than she did when she was in that room. It was where she went when she was really missing him. What if she let James renovate the room and it lost its comforting qualities? She didn't know what those qualities were, exactly. The room was empty and had been for months, so she couldn't ask him to preserve them.

"I've been sleeping in my bedroom when I'm at home," James said. "Ever since that night we spent in there together. I haven't slept on the sofa once. I just needed a little push. You gave that to me without meaning to. Let me give this to you?"

Maddie couldn't help but smile at that. She was glad their impromptu sleepover had helped him overcome a personal demon and that he was back in the bedroom he'd shared with his brother.

"That night reframed the bedroom in my mind," he continued. "I remembered how much fun I used to have in there with Harry, playing with our toys, talking about girls, bickering about chores. I'd forgotten all of that. I'd let our bedroom become a sad place, when there was so much happiness alchemised in it. It looks different, sure, but it's still the same little square of Earth I once shared with my brother. Some of the best laughs I ever had in my entire life were in that room."

Maddie smiled, remembering with fondness a night her entire family had spent in Bowie's bedroom not long before he had passed away. They'd been dressed for a summer ball they'd never made it to. Bowie had been too poorly to go, so they'd stayed at home with him, talking and laughing until the early hours of the morning.

"OK," she said, nodding her head. James looked surprised, as though he really hadn't been expecting her to say yes. "We need to sort out the other stuff first, but as long as it doesn't take away from what we need to do for the retreat, or what you've promised Marley and Autumn you'll help them with for the wedding, or the stuff I'm expecting you to do to me most if not every single night, then go for it."

He raised his eyebrows at that last bit, chuckling heartily. "I'm going to need more information on what it is you're expecting me to do to you most if not every single night," he said.

Maddie motioned with her finger for him to come closer. "Come here and I'll show you," she said.

* * *

They fooled around on the bedroom floor for a little while. They were quite clearly desperate for one another, but there seemed to be an unspoken consensus that they were not going to have sex on the floor in the middle of the day while her family were in the house, so they stuck to kissing and over-clothes action, playfully battling for dominant positions until they were all wound up and their lips were sore.

"We need to stop," James said eventually. His voice was breathless with lust. "I can't do this anymore, I'll die."

Maddie laughed at the dramatic way he said it, but concurred. She released his wrists from where she was holding them beside his head and climbed off him, taking a moment to straighten her topknot and correct the positioning of her jumper. She knew she was flustered. James was, too. They needed a few moments to settle down before they went downstairs for lunch, so they stood side by side before the window, watching Pip play with Benjamin, Pigglesworth and Stevie in the garden. Pip and Benjamin were taking it in turns to throw the ball across the lawn for Stevie and Pigglesworth to chase. Stevie won every time, of course, but that didn't stop Pigglesworth from chasing it with gusto. Maddie smiled at the scene, so unusual in theory, but so normal to them now because it was part of their every day. She hadn't had much time to spend with Pigglesworth personally, but James and her mum and dad loved him implicitly, and between them they were taking very good care of him. He was growing at a rapid rate and was almost certainly going to be a very large pig. His snout was long and his snorts were loud. His ears were also particularly humorous, as they appeared much too big for his head. He was curious and friendly, a real joy to be around. He was also undeniably spoiled. They'd tried him out with several brands of special food to determine which he liked best and they absolutely hated locking him away in his pen. He now had almost as many toys and boredom busters as Benjamin. Maddie watched him chasing Stevie and, though she couldn't hear him from where she was sitting, she knew he was squawking excitedly. She smiled. Pigglesworth was a very loved and very lucky pig.

"Pigs are so cool," James said. "They're just like dogs, really, aren't they?"

Maddie nodded and didn't say anything, because watching safe and happy farm animals always made her sad for the ones that weren't saved. She thought she might cry.

"His friends are all long gone now," James said, his voice laden with regret. "I can't believe I ever ate them." He shook his head. Taking a deep breath he turned to her. "Shall we go and get some lunch?" He held out his hand for her to take. Maddie grinned, slid her hand into his, and followed him downstairs.

They took their time strolling through the house, prolonging their physical display of affection for as long as possible. They were careful, checking the corridors were empty before they rounded any corners. James' method of checking grew more and more pronounced as they got closer to the kitchen. He was riding off her giggles, she knew that. It was obvious he very much enjoyed making her laugh.

They broke apart as they entered the kitchen. Everyone was there, including Pip and Benjamin, who were sporting very red, wintry cheeks.

"Hey guys," Bluebell said. "You're looking very 'chalant', today, what have you been up to?"

Maddie saw Autumn stifle a laugh and had to stop herself from laughing herself, especially when she turned and saw confusion written across James' features. He caught her eye. Suddenly, he was blushing. He knew she'd told her sister and friend about their fun yesterday. Maddie felt a little guilty for that, though didn't think he'd mind. He knew Maddie's relationship with the two women was special — that they were her biggest cheerleaders — and that Maddie told them everything because she could guarantee they wanted only what was best for her and would give her sound advice. She had told him this many times through various anecdotes. This was the biggest thing that had happened to her in ages, so prevailing common sense would have her telling the women closest to her about her recent sexual adventures. She reassured herself, and then she faltered and started to worry, but just as she started to doubt herself, James caught her eye and winked. His cheeks were still tinged with pink, but his gesture was a definite wordless communication. He was fine, and he wanted her to know it.

"Falafel and hummus bagel?" Marley asked, nodding to the stack of food in the middle of the table.

"Yes, please," James said, sitting beside Emma. Maddie chose the seat right next to him, convinced she'd arouse suspicion if she made a point of sitting elsewhere. James plated her up a bagel before helping himself to one, and they joined her family in comfortable, satiating silence. Maddie amused herself by glancing around the table, basking in the joy of having everyone she loved in one room.

"We have some news about Benjamin." Autumn interrupted her reverie. The entire table snapped to attention. Autumn hurried to calm them. "Jeez, calm down, it's nothing bad."

"Don't do that to us," Bluebell said, grabbing a second bagel.

"And here I was thinking we were about ready to move past this catastrophising," Marley said, pointedly.

"You're right, son," Emma said. "Go on, Autumn."

She nodded, side-eyed Marley, then sighed in what appeared to be a preparatory manner. "We have decided to let Benjamin audition for that part in Peter Ross's play." Everyone was silent and still except for Bluebell, who put down her bagel and stared at her brother.

"Don't catastrophise!" Marley warned her, gesturing to Benjamin.

"I won't say it aloud, but only because I don't need to tell you what I think about this," she said.

"No, you don't," Marley said. "Not only because I already know, but also because you're not Benjamin's parent."

His words were not tossed directly at Maddie, but they stung anyway because she knew they were for her as much as they were for everyone else at the table. Still, regardless of her feelings on the matter, Marley was right. They were not Benjamin's parents, and Maddie couldn't say she was surprised Autumn and Marley had come to a point where they were fundamentally rejecting their family's input. Her parents and siblings were constantly offering suggestions on how Autumn and Marley should raise Benjamin, how they should discipline him, how they should foster his passions. To be honest, Maddie thought they had been incredibly tolerant. This was bound to happen eventually. Bluebell was typically less understanding, especially when it came to this particular topic, so Maddie braced herself for an argument, but, to her surprise, her sister looked only mildly upset by the comment. Bluebell recoiled, then softened, then nodded her head.

Autumn continued. "I wasn't overly keen on the idea myself, but we have a plan. Marley is going to give up work."

Emma gasped. She stared across the table at her son, her displeasure plain to see. Maddie saw her father reach to squeeze Emma's leg and knew he was warning her not to over-react. Maddie smiled at that. Emma loved her children and wanted what was best for them, but she also often thought she was right when she wasn't. Maddie's father was the only one who could talk any sense into her and, right now, he was curbing her response. Such loving gestures and wordless communications were so rehearsed they were like a dance they'd done many times — lacklustre and predictable. Marley threw his father a grateful nod, then turned his attention back to his mother, fixing his gaze on hers as though daring her.

"You love work," she tried.

"I love Benjamin more," Marley countered. "Autumn is worried because she doesn't want Benjamin being chaperoned by strangers, which I think is absolutely fair enough, given what she's been through and what happened to Bluebell. I don't think I'd be comfortable with that either, to be honest. But Benjamin really wants to do it, don't you, son?" Benjamin took a huge bite of falafel and nodded. Marley smiled and refocused on the adults at the table. "It's not feasible for Autumn to give up work, she's the breadwinner. She *also* really loves her job. She's never going to be comfortable letting him chase his dreams unless one of us is there with him, and it makes sense that it would be me. I know you're not going to like it, but we've talked about it at length as a family and this is what we've decided is best for the three of us. Yes, I love my job. I'd do it for ever if I could, but I'm not going to do it if what is best for these two is something else. They mean more to me than anything else in the world. So, please, try to understand."

There was nothing much anyone could say to that, so they nodded and carried on eating their bagels in silence. Maddie took the opportunity to admire her brother and the man he'd become. There had been times when she had considered Marley exceedingly selfish. When they had been younger, he'd insisted on moving to New York, despite knowing an ailing Bowie would follow him. He had lived off an allowance their parents had given him for many years, blowing every penny of it on alcohol and partying while he'd chased his dream of becoming famous for something, *anything*. He'd been driven by an insatiable need to stick it to the industry that had turned its back on him and protected an abuser. When Marley had been nineteen, he'd walked in on a powerful family friend of the Whittles — a middle-aged, married man named Vincent who'd been grooming Bluebell for years — having sex with his sister in a dressing room and had beaten him up. Marley, who had been acting in a professional production, funded by Vincent's company at the time, had been arrested and lost his job. He had been blacklisted from the industry, as most of his co-workers had been too afraid to confront Vincent and take Marley's side. Things hadn't changed until the #MeToo movement had shifted the narrative.

Finally, the world of theatre had been ready to welcome back Maddie's undeniably talented brother. Marley was an incredible songwriter and an organically creative person. He loved to play guitar and sing, enjoyed people watching him and basked in their compliments. He was a natural extrovert. Since he'd been back on stage, Marley was happier than Maddie had ever seen him. He had Autumn and Benjamin, his work and his family — the only thing he was missing was Bowie. That last part was the important part. Losing Bowie had reset Marley's priorities. Autumn and Benjamin came before absolutely everything else. He knew better than anyone that a future together was not guaranteed, and would never put anything above the people he loved ever again. If something he was doing was not what was best for them, he would give it up. He loved the stage, but he was happiest when the people he loved were happy. They were not his, he was theirs. Everything he did was to make their lives better. She was so incredibly proud of him, of his integrity, his caring nature and his drive to love everyone around him wholeheartedly. He'd become an incredible man.

Maddie didn't realise she was staring at her brother until he caught her eye and winked reassuringly. Maddie smiled and threw him a subtle nod, turning back to her bagel.

* * *

When they were done with lunch, Maddie and James headed back to the bedroom to apply more paint to the parts of the wall that were looking dry enough. They sang along to Christmas songs as they did so and chatted the afternoon away. James told her about his travel plans. For a long time he'd been touring Europe in search of adventure, finding work wherever he could in exchange for very little cash in hand, often just bed and board, and living day by day, but he'd recently decided he wanted to make this a more permanent lifestyle. Money was the primary obstacle. Work was seasonal and not always guaranteed, and since running out of cash had forced him home after a three-year stint away this winter, he recognised that this was the issue he needed to resolve if he wanted to stay abroad. He'd signed up with a couple of agencies he hoped might offer him more permanent opportunities, which would solve those annoying visa restrictions that currently meant he needed to leave Europe every ninety days and stay away for three months before he'd be allowed to return. If he could manage that, he would get Stevie a European passport from a vet in France, which would mean she could stay, too. Previously he'd had to bring her home periodically to get an Animal Health Certificate to verify she was safe to travel. He didn't need much and was happy to rough it, but he did need sponsorship, guaranteed income and security for Stevie. Finding that without restricting his movement — the key thing he loved about living this kind of life — was proving difficult.

Maddie was enthralled by his stories and impressed by his drive to chase something he really wanted with such heart. She told him so.

"What else is there?" He shrugged. "If there's any silver lining to losing Harry, it taught me the future is not guaranteed. Life is short. I intend to live as much of it as I possibly can doing things that make me happy."

Maddie felt a little boring, so she spent the next hour or so regaling James with happy stories about her childhood, emphasising how fulfilled her family made her feel, how happy she was at home, and how much contentment she derived from caring for people. James listened intently, nodding in all the right places. When she was done, he grinned.

"We're the same, you and me," he said.

"Are we?" She was confused. His life seemed so glamorously bohemian. He was spontaneous and liked new things. He thrived without plans. Maddie was the opposite.

James nodded. "Yeah. We both know what we want and we're determined to get it. Your family is the same, your parents have always fostered that way of thinking so perhaps you don't see it as much, but not everyone is out there chasing happiness. Most people don't even know what it is they want. They've been told to work, buy a house, get married, have kids — and they haven't deviated from that plan. Most people never stop to consider if they've changed their mind, or if they even want what they're chasing in the first place."

Maddie thought about that and concluded he was right. They wanted different things, but their approach to determining what it was they wanted was very similar.

"Marley is really good at that, isn't he?" James said. "What he said at lunch really floored me. Being able to compartmentalise the things that are important to you in that way, it can't be easy, especially when you have the welfare of a little one to consider."

Maddie nodded. "He's been through so much, too . . ."

Maddie told James about Marley's history with Bluebell and Vincent, explaining how Marley had fallen into a deep depression because of it and — though he was ashamed of it now — had resented Bluebell, who had been blinded by the grooming and thought Vincent was in love with her. For many years afterwards, convinced he would come back to her eventually, she had maintained that the much older man hadn't had sex with her until she was over the age of consent.

"What a shitshow," James said. Maddie nodded. "Are they all right now?"

"Oh, yeah," Maddie said. "Autumn helped, I think. She talked a lot of it through with Marley when they first got together. Explained the psychology behind it."

James pondered for a moment. "What a lovely little family those three are," he said.

"Gorgeous, aren't they?" Maddie concurred.

James nodded, thoughtful. "You know, I'd never given much thought to what I want family-wise until recently. *Very* recently. But I honestly think I want what they have. Best friends in love and a little cool dude to boot? Sounds cracking."

Maddie smiled. As someone who was 'involved' with James — someone he'd just shared his detailed travel plans with — she wasn't sure what she was supposed to say to that, so she thought it best if she didn't say anything. James had other ideas.

"Do you want kids?" he asked.

"Yeah," Maddie said, suddenly certain. "I never gave it much thought either, really. Life was too busy and I was so unsettled. Plus, I'd never been around a baby, not until Benjamin arrived. He changed my mind completely. I love him so much. It's probably not a very feminist thing to say, but yes, I'd like a husband and children."

"I think it is quite feminist, actually. Feminism is about choice, and that's *your* choice, isn't it? It's not like you've come

183

to the conclusion without considering it properly, is it? You've seen a sterling example and decided you want it."

Maddie blinked at him. "You're not mansplaining feminism to me, are you?" she teased.

"No!" He laughed. "I mean, maybe I was, actually. Sorry."

Maddie shook her head. "You're right, to a point. The principle of a husband and family isn't very feminist, but only because that idea traps most women in a patriarchal nightmare. If I were to get married, it would need to be nothing like that. It would have to look something like what Marley and Autumn have. And Mum and Dad, for that matter."

"Makes sense," he said, stepping suggestively towards her and closing the gap between them. He wrapped his arms around her waist and kissed her. They indulged heartily in each other for a moment.

"Are you staying over tonight?" she asked when they broke away.

"Does a one-legged duck swim in circles?" She laughed at his words. "I did tell Marley I would help him build some wooden planters for the wedding, though. And by 'help him build some planters' I mean build them myself while he watches."

Maddie nodded knowingly. "That's fine. Autumn has a deadline, so Bluebell and I told her she could come over and we would watch Benjamin while she works. And by 'watch him while she works' I mean distract her with frivolity."

James tittered, but his expression was suddenly serious. "I'll see you later, though?" His voice was low and suggestive. She gazed up at him.

"Does a one-legged duck swim in circles?"

* * *

Things went exactly as predicted. Marley sat on a bench on the porch watching James make wooden planters from scratch and talking his ear off about politics and musical theatre.

Every now and then, the women — who were successfully distracting Autumn by giving her wine and chatting about anything and everything while they simultaneously kept an eye on Benjamin — would hear the two men laugh heartily with each other.

When they were done building, James and Marley sat on the porch together and played their guitars, singing softly into the winter wind. Nobody acknowledged that Bowie and Marley used to do that together, or mentioned the fact Marley hadn't done it since they'd lost his twin brother. Instead, Autumn and Bluebell commented several times on how incredibly wonderful it was that Marley and James got on so well. Maddie avoided their pointed tones, burying her face in her wine each time. They were well meaning, but they'd not been there when James had talked so passionately about travelling. The new experiences. The lack of routine. The new people. Picking up and moving on with barely a moment's notice. He'd told her once that he yearned only for adventure, unpredictability and the open road. He had talked about settling down today, but she wasn't inclined to believe he meant it. Not yet, at least. She was sure he was just swept up in the emotion of what was going on between them and impressed by Marley and Autumn. It all felt so complicated and confusing.

They put Benjamin to bed at 8 p.m. and, before Maddie knew it, she'd buried her face in her wine enough times that she was unsteady on her feet. Between them, the three women drank copious amounts of Merlot.

By the time they heard Marley and James finishing up outside it was almost midnight, and the three women were not making much sense at all.

"Marley!" Autumn threw her hands in the air when she saw him, as though she hadn't seen him for months. Marley side-eyed Bluebell, who laughed and shrugged. "Come here, you sexy bastard." Autumn threw herself into his arms.

"Have you had a good night, darling?" he asked.

Autumn nodded, running her hand across his chest. "Let's go to bed. I have a present for you," she tried to whisper, but failed.

Marley raised his eyebrows and laughed. James caught Maddie's eye and she thought she saw him blush. She held onto the counter to steady herself, embarrassed by how drunk she felt and hoping she was hiding it well.

"Gross," Bluebell said.

Marley looked at her. "Why is she only ever this wankered when she's with you?"

Bluebell thought about that. "Because I'm a vibe?" she suggested.

"That's one way of putting it," Marley muttered, clutching Autumn tighter to him. "Where is my child?"

"Mum and Dad put him to bed in the back bedroom with Stevie Licks," Maddie said.

James smiled and shook his head. "She bloody loves your kid," he said to Marley. "He's cured her of her fear of being without me. When we arrive in the morning she goes looking for him straight away."

Marley chuckled. "I'm surprised he hasn't asked us to get a dog. Though I think it's her specifically he loves. So as long as she's around he'll be happy. Not planning on going anywhere, are you, James?"

James laughed awkwardly and shrugged, but he didn't say no. That was all the confirmation Maddie needed. Far from feeling perturbed, she felt relieved. She knew where she stood, even if James didn't.

* * *

As Marley put Autumn to bed in one of the partly decorated bedrooms, Maddie said goodnight to Bluebell, then made her way clumsily to her own bedroom to brush her teeth and check her appearance. She was eager, so she rushed, marvelling at how secure James had made her feel. It didn't matter that her hair was a mess, she was covered in paint and had no make-up on. This man was driven wild by her and had made it so clear that she didn't care a jot.

She knocked on his bedroom door and he opened it immediately. He must have been standing right by the door. He pulled her into the room and kissed her deeply, shoving his tongue against hers. She was about to push him back towards the bed when he stopped and stepped away, holding both of her hands in his.

"Are you drunk, Mads?" he asked. Maddie somehow knew the gravity of the question and the consequences of saying yes. She really wanted to lie, but knew he'd be able to tell. She wasn't sure what had tipped him off, she'd thought she was hiding it well, but it was likely she'd done a terrible job. She smiled sheepishly.

"Ah, Maddie, we can't do this if you're drunk," he said, shaking his head. Maddie gazed up at him. Her mouth was open, but her disappointment had rendered her voiceless. "Please don't look at me like that," he said, his mouth twitching in what she knew was the start of a smile.

"But I want to," Maddie said. His stance softened, but she knew the answer was still no.

He shook his head. "Not when it's all so new."

"It's not the first time," she said, pointedly.

"It's still new," he said, squeezing her hand and then opening his arms to receive her. He kept his lower body away from hers. He was not relenting. He clutched her face in his hands and planted kisses on her lips, nose, cheeks and forehead, then wrapped his arms around her and pulled her into a hug. Maddie could feel his erection pressed against her stomach and his heart beating wildly against her temple. "I want to," she whispered again.

"I want to, too," he said, pulling away to stare into her face. "But we can't."

Maddie stuck out her bottom lip and stomped her foot a little bit. That made him laugh. "You can still stay with me," he suggested. His tone was gentle but laden with warning. "But no funny business, Maddie, or I'll leave."

She agreed to the terms of his suggestion and climbed under the duvet, waiting until he was settled beside her before she found a place to rest her head. He pulled her as close to him as she could possibly be, so that she was straddling his hip, then turned and kissed her gently on the mouth for the longest time. They were holding each other by the face as though they were each afraid the other might stop. While Maddie was appreciative of the thought and care he was putting into this, she was unbelievably frustrated. She told him so.

"This isn't about me protecting myself from any sort of false allegation, it's just about doing the right thing," he said. "Drunk sex is great when everyone's drunk and you've been together an age, but I think it should be left out of anything new. Alcohol makes everyone feel different. Nobody should be having sex with you if you're not your normal self."

He rolled onto his side and Maddie took her opportunity to turn away from him so that her back was pressed into his chest and he was spooning her. His big arms enveloped her and he tossed his leg across hers and pinned her bottom half to his. His skin was hot and soft, and there was a musky smell present that she'd come to associate with him, a cologne or a shampoo perhaps. She could hear his heart beating gently against her back. She was sure she'd never felt this relaxed her entire life. He nuzzled into her hair, inhaling deeply. Maddie backed up a little bit, pressing herself against him.

"Stop it," he said.

"Stop what?" she asked, innocently.

"You know what," he said, squeezing her tightly to him. Maddie laughed softly, stroking his forearms with her fingers until he was breathing deeply and she was sure he was asleep. She was very tired and had been all evening, but she wasn't ready to surrender to sleep. She wanted to enjoy the moment. She forced herself to stay awake and be present for a while. She realised with a jolt that this was the happiest she had ever been, and immediately felt guilty. Though she knew Bowie would want her to be happy — her brother had wanted *everyone* to be happy, that's part of what had been so wonderful about him — she felt bad for acknowledging that the most joyful part of her life so far was a time in which he no longer existed. It made her feel terrible. She was suddenly wide awake, and wished she had let herself fall asleep earlier. She sighed, anticipating a restless night.

"You OK?" James asked, sluggishly. Maddie nodded but didn't answer aloud. She was afraid she would cry again. She was fairly certain this man must be sick of her teary displays. "Do you want me to tell you a story?" he asked, sounding slightly more awake. Maddie giggled and nodded. "All right," he said. "Once upon a time there was a dragon named Dragonsworth Roariter . . . He escaped from a giant, green ogre of a dragon killer and made his way to a big, beautiful castle. In the castle lived a princess called . . . Margaret. She was the most beautiful woman the giant, green ogre of a dragon killer had ever seen."

Maddie laughed, snuggling closer to him. Suddenly, it felt very OK to feel happy again.

CHAPTER THIRTEEN

Maddie crept back to her bedroom and slipped giddily into the shower. She set the water to a lukewarm temperature in an attempt to freeze the flush from her cheeks. She could hear her mother humming somewhere in the house, presumably the kitchen. The air was bursting with her favourite smells — cinnamon and hot wine, spiced orange, sugary biscuits and baking bread. For as long as she could remember, Emma and Ben had put an enormous amount of effort into making Christmas magical for their children. They were grown now, but nothing had changed. It was, without a doubt, Maddie's favourite time of year. She felt as though she'd hardly had time to get ready for it this year, she'd been too busy worrying about the retreat, so it felt like the festivities were hitting her like a Santa-shaped brick to the face. She readied herself quickly, desperate to join her family for breakfast.

She was the last person to arrive, but someone had scooped a ladle of piping-hot porridge into a bowl and set it out for her already. Maddie thanked the table gratefully, tipped banana, raisins, apple chunks and a teaspoon of maple syrup on top and dug in. She chatted excitedly with Benjamin about Santa Claus and what he might have brought him in exchange for being a good boy all year. He told her what he'd bought for Stevie Licks — a basket full of toys and a new ball to play with. He whispered it in her ear, in case the dog heard. Stevie was splitting her time between sitting beside James with her head on his lap and staring hopefully up at Benjamin's bowl. James warned him not to give her any raisins, but said she could have a couple of slices of banana if she was behaving herself, though she wasn't to beg, or to have too much. Every now and then, Stevie's nose would stray a little too close to Benjamin's plate and James would command her to stop. His warning tone would return the dog dutifully to his side, where she would stay until she was sure he'd forgotten all about her bad behaviour, then she'd slip back under the table to sit once more beside Benjamin.

When they were done with breakfast, Maddie followed her mother upstairs to fulfil her promise to help her clean the bedrooms. There wasn't a great deal they could do — the rooms were practically upside down and would have to stay that way for the moment, but they worked hard to make up a room for Autumn's mum, sister and niece, and Bluebell's room for James' mum, in case she chose to come, in which case Bluebell would sleep with Maddie. James had reiterated over breakfast that he was doubtful, but had returned home to ask her anyway. He'd be back either way, he promised, but if Jennifer didn't want to accompany him then he'd return home in the evening. Maddie knew it was the right thing to do — it would be his mum's first Christmas without his nan — but she desperately wanted him here for Christmas Day and hoped wholeheartedly his mother would agree to join them for the festivities. She played her anxiety down in front of her own mum, of course.

They'd just finished cleaning upstairs and were joining Bluebell and Benjamin to watch Christmas movies in the living room when Autumn's mum, Katherine, and sister, Lilly, arrived in the early afternoon, much sooner than expected. They always stayed at the big house when they visited since there was much more room here than there was in Autumn's and Marley's cottage, so it was much more comfortable for everyone. Maddie went with her mum and dad to meet them at the front door, hugging them briskly and taking their cases.

"Sorry, Emma," Katherine said, looking flustered. "We set off early because we thought we'd run into traffic, but the roads were all clear, so we had a really good run down. I tried to call Autumn, but she isn't answering her phone."

"Oh, don't worry about a thing," Emma said. "She and Marley are at home getting their things together. They left Benjamin with us. He's in the front room with Bluebell."

"Where's my favourite grandson?" Katherine called, heading for the living room. Lilly rolled her eyes at Maddie, who smiled politely. She'd tried to force herself to like Autumn's mum, but it was no use, she really didn't. She knew too much about how Katherine had failed Autumn and Lilly when they were young. She'd left them without food and heating, prioritised relationships with men over their safety, made them feel unloved and unwanted. Still, she was trying to make amends for it now and Autumn had invited her to do so. It really wasn't any of Maddie's business. She would swallow her disdain and be polite, as always. She pulled the suitcases into the house and handed them to an eager-looking Pip, who she suspected had vacated the living room when Katherine had arrived. Her brother was not a fan of Autumn's mum, either.

"How are you, Lilly?" Pip greeted Autumn's sister with a kiss on the cheek. "Who's this little beauty?" He gestured to the pink bundle in Lilly's arms.

"This is Daisy," Lilly said, proudly twisting her arms so that Maddie, Pip, Emma and Ben could admire her baby daughter. She was four months old and full of smiles. Maddie and her family cooed, and Daisy rewarded them with a grin and a giggle.

"She's gorgeous," Maddie said. "Nice work, Lils."

"Thank you," Lilly said. "I need a wee. Do you want a squidge?"

Maddie squealed excitedly, holding out her arms to take the baby. She carried Daisy into the living room, where she laid her on a pouffe and freed her from her giant snow suit, singing happily as she removed the baby's hat and mittens. Daisy was a calm, courteous baby. She fixed her eyes on Maddie's face and let her take off the garments without any fussing or fighting. Maddie was glad. She'd loved her time with Benjamin as a baby, but he had been well behaved. She wasn't sure what she'd do if Daisy started crying. She was almost done straightening the baby's floral playsuit when Benjamin caught sight of them. He immediately lost interest in whatever he was doing with Katherine and made his way over.

"What's her name?" he asked, watching Maddie intently.

"This is your cousin, Daisy," Maddie said.

"Daisy is a flower name, like Aunty Lilly's," Benjamin said. Maddie, who had not noticed the name theme until now, nodded enthusiastically. "What's a cousin?" he asked.

Maddie explained. "If your mummy's or daddy's brothers or sisters have babies, those are your cousins. Aunty Lilly is your mummy's sister, so Daisy is your cousin. If Aunty Bluebell or Uncle Pip had a baby, they would be your cousins, too."

Benjamin nodded thoughtfully. He watched Maddie pick up Daisy and gently bounce the baby on her knee. Daisy squealed happily. Benjamin reached out and took the tot's hand in his own. He eyed her with extreme curiosity and Maddie realised in that moment he had little experience of babies, and had certainly never seen her holding one. She wondered if he was feeling a little jealous. "Are you going to have a baby, Aunty Maddie?" he asked.

"Maybe one day," Maddie said.

"With James?" The question took her completely by surprise.

"Why would you think that?" she asked. She tried to sound unfazed, but was worried he'd seen or heard something, perhaps caught her and James kissing or — God forbid — worse. She could not imagine anything more awful than being responsible for poisoning the innocent mind of Autumn's and Marley's child. She knew she didn't *look* unfazed in the slightest.

"Because he loves you," Benjamin said. He spoke the words as though they meant nothing, as if he was telling her what he'd had for breakfast.

Maddie reeled. "He's my friend," she said, her voice high and squeaky. She was glad none of her family members were in the room to hear this exchange. Her brothers and her parents knew her very, very well. They would know instantly from her reaction that Benjamin had taken aim and hit a nail on the head.

"He looks at you all the time," Benjamin said, dropping Daisy's hand and standing on his tiptoes to stroke the baby's hair. He gazed up at her as he did so, and Maddie saw Bowie looking back at her. It wasn't just that he had Marley's hair, blue eyes and skin tone — and therefore naturally looked like his father's twin brother — there was something in the way he held himself. The sparkle in his eyes and the tilt of his head. They were such Bowie-like gestures they rendered her speechless for a moment.

"He's my friend," Maddie tried again.

Benjamin shrugged. "If you say so." He turned his attention back to Daisy. Maddie had never heard him say something like this — questioning, a little mocking, disbelieving — and it took her by surprise. She made a mental note to ask Autumn if he'd ever said it before. Benjamin would often hear things when he was watching cartoons or movies and then repeat them. That was all this was, Maddie reassured herself. She shook her head, urging herself to get a grip.

"Who's James?" Katherine asked. She'd been sitting in the corner looking at her phone, but quite clearly listening to their conversation. Maddie had been hoping she wouldn't insert herself.

"He works here," Maddie said, pausing to coo at Daisy. "He's helping me with renovations. We're friends, that's all."

Benjamin stared up at Maddie, his eyes wide with mischief. "If you say so," he said again.

* * *

Autumn and Marley arrived shortly afterwards and Daisy was taken from Maddie almost immediately. Marley loved babies and hadn't yet met Daisy, so he was desperate for a cuddle. Maddie protested playfully, but her brother was so eager and it was so cute that, with Lilly's approval, she relented quickly. Marley sat back on the couch and rocked little Daisy slowly to sleep, reassuring a rather jealous-looking Benjamin as he did so. He invited his son to sit beside them on the couch, but firmly requested Benjamin give the baby space.

"Daddy is cuddling Daisy right now," Marley said, gently. "I'll be done soon and then I'm all yours again, but for now you need to share me, OK?"

Benjamin nodded, but looked disheartened. Maddie wasn't surprised he was feeling envious. He had been the centre of everyone's universe for so long. Maddie had experienced this, and she remembered the feeling well. She had been the youngest until Pip arrived and she'd found it horrendously difficult sharing her parents and siblings with a new bundle of joy. She'd been nine years old, which meant she was easier to reason with than Benjamin was right now, but it also meant she had been the baby for much longer. Her parents had done everything they could to stop her feeling neglected, but thirteen-year-old Bluebell and fifteen-year-olds Bowie and Marley had all been obsessed with their new baby brother. Maddie had been heartbroken about it. Even now when she thought about it, the feeling of rejection was raw. She desperately wanted to swoop Benjamin out of the room and distract him, but she knew Marley was using this as a teachable moment.

Given how ardently he'd recently insisted they remove them-selves from his choices when it came to parenting, she didn't want to intrude.

* * *

Two hours later, they were all gathered in the living room nursing glasses of mulled wine when James arrived with Stevie and his mother in tow. Maddie — who had given up any hope of him returning — had to work hard to make sure her reaction was measured and ordinary, especially now she knew Benjamin and Katherine were watching her. She let her mother and father be the ones who went to the kitchen to greet them, preoccupying herself by talking to Autumn and Bluebell, both of whom, she knew, were humouring her. After what felt like an age, James brought an anxious-looking Jennifer into the living room and introduced her.

"Everyone, this is my mum, Jennifer. Mum, this is Maddie, Autumn, Marley, Benjamin, Pip and . . . I'm sorry, I don't know you guys."

"I'm Katherine, Autumn's mum. This is Lilly, Autumn's sister, and that's Daisy, Autumn's niece."

"Lovely to meet you," James said, shaking Katherine's hand. He waved at Lilly, who was sitting in an armchair feed-ing the baby. There was a moment of silence while everyone reset themselves. Emma took Jennifer's coat and passed it to Ben, gesturing to a chair by the fire. Maddie, who was sitting on the rug nearby, threw Jennifer a hearty wave. She nodded in recognition, and Maddie thought she caught a hint of a smile, but she couldn't be sure. By then everyone had resumed their conversations. James joined Marley and Pip by the win-dow, where they'd been talking about bands for over an hour.

Emma perched on the arm of Jennifer's armchair. "We have met before, Jennifer, many years ago, when the kids were at school. I'm so glad you're here. Would you like a glass of mulled wine? I made it myself."

"By 'made it herself' she means she poured it into a pan and added oranges and cinnamon to it," Marley said, laughing. "She didn't squish the grapes or anything."

"That's more than you've done round here today," Emma said, pointedly.

"Fair play." Marley nodded. "I'll get this round in. One for Jennifer. Who wants a top up?" One by one, every person in the room held up their glass, even those who still had wine left. Marley glared comically at them. "You're all dickheads," he said.

"Marley," Autumn scolded, nodding pointedly towards Benjamin.

"Sorry. You're all . . ."

Autumn put her hand over his mouth, pushing him towards the door. "We don't call people names, remember?" she said, following him out of the room. "We'll bring a jug of wine in," she called back to them. Benjamin jumped off the couch and tore after them. Maddie knew he was seizing his opportunity to bask in their undivided attention. He wanted a few moments with his parents alone. Maddie couldn't say she blamed him. Stevie was hot on their heels.

"I think your dog might not be your dog anymore," Bluebell said to James. He laughed.

"Nonsense," Emma said. "I've never seen a dog love a human like that dog loves James. She just knows Benjamin drops food on the floor all the time."

"I think the truth is somewhere in the middle," James said. "She's my dog, but she certainly views you all as family now."

"Well, that's grand," Ben said. "Because we very much view you as family, too."

James smiled gratefully. Maddie took her opportunity to steal a glance at Jennifer, who looked surprised by Ben's declaration of fondness for her son. Maddie felt James' eyes upon her, but she made a point of ignoring him. There were too many people in the room, too many opportunities for them to be discovered. It was nearly impossible, of course. She was desperate to stare at his beautiful face. But the rate at which people were figuring out there was more to their relationship than they were letting on was alarming her. She picked at her fingernails until she was sure he'd gone back to talking to Marley and Pip. When she looked up, Jennifer was watching her son joking with the two men, insisting he had not abstained from buying them gifts because of the 'no gift' rule, but because he wasn't being paid enough to buy gifts and they were jovially calling his boss — her — a real tight arse. Jennifer was looking at James like it was the first time she'd ever seen him. Perhaps it was, Maddie thought. James said Jennifer had been permanently distracted since Harry had died two decades ago. She never went out and socialised and hardly spent any time with James when he was home. Maybe this was the first time she'd seen him properly as a grown adult. Maddie wondered if she was proud. She didn't look it. She appeared irritated, if anything. Maybe she was angry she'd missed out on so many fabulous times with such a wonderful young man.

"Can we play Carrot in a Box?" James was asking.

"What's that?" Bluebell asked.

"It's a two-player game. Each person has a box. There's a carrot in one of them and the other one is empty. At the start of the game, one person gets to look in their box, so that person will know which box has a carrot in it. The other player, the one who doesn't know, gets to choose whether they switch boxes or keep their own. The person who knows where the carrot is has to persuade or dissuade them from swapping. The winner is the person who has a carrot in their box at the end. It's great fun."

"Sounds really easy," Pip said.

James laughed knowingly. "It's not." He sold the idea to Autumn and Marley when they returned with the jugs of mulled wine, then insisted he and Maddie be the ones to retrieve boxes from the recycling bin and a carrot from the pantry.

"We're being really obvious," Maddie said, closing the pantry door behind them.

"I do not care," James said, pulling her towards him and pressing his lips against hers. They only had a few minutes before they'd arouse suspicion, so Maddie fully understood the urgency. She ran her hands all over him and they kissed like they might never see each other again, before breaking apart as though nothing had happened.

"I'm drinking today," Maddie said, looking for carrots while James pulled two boxes out of the recycling bin. He eyed her, quizzically. "So I am telling you now, while I am of sound mind, that I want to have sex with you later," she explained. "Do not reject me. Unless you don't want to, of course."

James chuckled. "OK, just don't get *too* drunk," he said. Maddie nodded.

They'd overdone it and taken far too much time, so they hurried back to her family without defining the conditions further. Maddie saw Autumn and Bluebell side-eye each other knowingly, but she was relieved to see everyone else seemed none the wiser.

Pip pointed to the broccoli Maddie was carrying. "That's not a carrot," he said.

"All of the carrots have already succumbed to the pot, so this was the best I could do," Maddie said.

"Can you play Carrot in a Box with broccoli, James?" Pip asked, downing the rest of his mulled wine.

"You can play it with anything," James said, setting the boxes on the floor in front of the fire, where everyone would have a good view of them. He framed them with cushions, gesturing to Maddie for the broccoli. She tossed it to him. "Who's going first?" he asked. Pip and Bluebell raised their hands, glaring comically at each other. Maddie, Marley and their parents laughed. Bluebell and Pip were the Whittle's most competitive family members. When they were younger, their mother had once hidden a games console they'd been given on Christmas morning part-way through the afternoon because they were arguing over it with such volatility. Unaware of their competitiveness, James told them both to turn around, checked they weren't looking in any reflective surfaces, then put the broccoli in the box on the right, the one Bluebell went to when they were told to take their seats. She offered to be the one who looked inside the box, took a peep, then slammed the box shut theatrically.

"I'll keep this box," she said.

"Are you sure?" James asked.

"Yes, it has broccoli in it," she said. Pip narrowed his eyes at her. Bluebell avoided his gaze, sipping her wine.

"She's bluffing," Pip said, surveying the room for clues. "There's no broccoli in that box."

"There is," Bluebell said.

"I don't believe you."

"Swap me, then?" Bluebell said, smirking. Pip faltered. Her reaction had thrown him.

"Are you double-bluffing me?" he asked. Bluebell shrugged, tapping her wine glass with her fingernails. Maddie tried to keep her face straight as she admired her sister's ability to bluff. If Pip tried too hard to figure out what she was up to, Maddie was fairly certain Bluebell would win the game. His absolute best chance was to guess. "Oh, God! Maybe there *isn't* broccoli in the box," Pip said.

"Don't swap me then," Bluebell said, in the same indifferent tone.

Pip eyed her suspiciously. "You blinked funny that time. I think you *do* have the broccoli in the box. I want to swap."

"Are you sure?" James asked.

"No!" Pip shouted. Everyone laughed.

"You should swap with me," Bluebell said. "There's broccoli in my box."

"I don't believe you," Pip said.

"Would I lie to you?" Bluebell asked.

"One-hundred-fucking per cent you would."

"Pip," Marley warned, nodding at Benjamin.

200

"Sorry," Pip said. "Don't say that word, Benjamin, it's naughty."

"Are we swapping boxes or not?" Bluebell asked.

"Yes! No! Yes! Yes, swap boxes with me."

"Are you sure?" James checked.

"Yes! No, I'm not." Pip paused, clearly thinking hard. He stared at Bluebell's box, as though trying to see through the cardboard. Maddie, who really didn't care who won, was thoroughly enjoying watching her siblings behaving so seriously over something so trivial. There had been a time when there'd been no room for frivolity in this house. For so many years every shred of the time and space within it had been taken up by fretting, then by grief. She stared around the living room at the people she loved most in the world, realising she was grinning goofily and had been for some time. She did not correct her face. Instead, she reached for her mother's hand and squeezed. Emma turned to look at her, and Maddie saw tears in her eyes and a small smile on her lips. She knew they were having the same thought.

"How lucky we are," Emma said. Maddie nodded, squeezing her mother's hand once more.

Pip's protests interrupted their moment. "I'm not swapping the box. Bluebell is a liar, there is no broccoli in the box."

"Are you sure?" James asked.

"Stop asking me that," Pip said irritably. "I'm bloody sure. I'm keeping my box because my box has broccoli in it."

"All right, Pip! Open your box and reveal the broccoli."

Pip dramatically whipped his box lid open to reveal the vast emptiness within. Before it was even part-way open, Bluebell had jumped in the air, victorious. "No!" Pip shrieked, throwing himself to the floor. He rolled onto his back and closed his eyes in what Maddie knew was an attempt to shield himself from Bluebell's gloating. Her sister was jumping excitedly up and down, waving her hands in the air with glee.

"Rematch!" Pip demanded.

"No, sorry," James said. "Pip, you're out. Emma and Ben, you're up next! Once everyone has had a go we'll start the next round. Winners play winners, until one person emerges victorious. It'll be me, obviously. Let's go!"

* * *

There was an odd number of adults, so Jennifer offered not to play. Instead she perched on the edge of the couch, positioned as though she were about to bolt at any moment. Emma kept trying to engage her in polite conversation, but Jennifer would reply with just one or two words, doing just enough to not seem rude, but plenty to make it clear she was not fully comfortable being here.

The winners of the first round were Bluebell, Ben, Autumn, James and Lilly. Ben beat Emma, Autumn beat Marley, James beat Maddie and Lilly beat Katherine. The second round saw Ben beat Bluebell, James beat Lilly and then — because they were odd again — they voted Autumn should play Pip, since he was most desperate to carry on playing. She beat him, much to his dismay. That left three people in the final: Ben, Autumn and James. They agreed everyone would play everyone and then they'd go from there, but since James was the only one who won both of his games, he was crowned victorious. He was not a gracious winner.

"You're all speechless, I know," James said. "I am actually the Carrot in a Box' undefeated world champion and now I've aced 'Broccoli in a Box' as well, so clearly I'm a legend at this."

"Nobody likes a bragger," Autumn said.

"Spoken like a true loser," James said.

Autumn reeled comically. "Marley, defend my honour immediately."

Marley looked between the two of them. "James, you take that back right now, or else," he said, in a tipsy and lacklustre manner. Everyone laughed, including Jennifer. She covered her mouth as though she was trying not to be amused. That made Maddie smile. Autumn rolled her eyes at Marley, who shrugged. "I really like James."

202

The living room burst into lively chatter among groups while everyone stretched their legs and replenished their drinks. Emma left the room to plate up some spicy roast potatoes she'd put in the oven, returning ten minutes later with several plates of snacks balanced precariously on her out-stretched arms and in her hands. Maddie and Jennifer rushed to unburden her.

"Thank you, ladies," Emma said, inviting them to take a plate each. Maddie loaded hers up, topping it with a dollop of red-pepper hummus. Jennifer took hardly anything. They sat down on the sofa. "What are your plans for tomorrow?" Emma asked Jennifer. It was the first question Emma had asked that hadn't made Jennifer wince. Maddie's mother was wearing her down with mulled wine and cheery chatter. The two women were sitting so close to each other a stranger might think they'd been friends for years. Maddie loved this side of her mother. Emma was a genuinely good person — she wanted everyone around her to feel as comfortable as possible and would go out of her way to make sure it happened. She was a first-class charmer and an immensely perceptive woman. She knew exactly what an individual needed in any given situation — affection, attention, someone to listen, someone to agree — and would make sure she became it in order to bring out the best in them.

"We don't have any plans," Jennifer said. "I have no real interest in Christmas. James has been away travelling for years, so it was always just Mum and me, but I lost her this year, so I have no real idea of what Christmas looks like from now on."

Emma nodded. "I'm sure James has already told you, but you're very welcome to celebrate here with us," she said. "There's plenty of room for you to stay the night. We don't do a great deal on Christmas Day. We eat, drink and play games, just like we have tonight. We would love to have you, honestly."

Jennifer looked a little sheepish. "I get a bit wallowy at Christmas," she said.

"So do I," Emma said. "We can wallow together. Please, think about it. I think James really wants to be here — he's struck up quite a friendship with Marley, Maddie, Autumn and Bluebell — but I know he's reluctant to leave you alone."

Jennifer looked surprised at that. She blinked pointedly at Emma, her eyes darting between Maddie and her son, who was now chatting animatedly with Lilly and Katherine. "Did he say that?" she asked. Emma nodded. Jennifer's gaze found Maddie, who smiled gently and nodded. "I'm shocked," she said, holding her hand to her chest. "We have a . . . strained relationship."

"Oh," Emma said, as though she had not known that. "Well, that is a shame. I'm very sad to hear it. But I promise, I'm not lying to you. James was adamant he would only celebrate with us if you agreed to come too because he didn't want you to be alone at Christmas."

Jennifer shuffled in her seat and took a sip of her drink. Maddie thought she could see tears in her eyes, but she couldn't be certain. Because she'd been told Jennifer was cold and avoidant, she expected James' mother to make excuses and leave the conversation, but she didn't. Instead she composed herself, cleared her throat, and spoke in a tone that sounded both uncertain and eager all at once. Maddie could tell she was desperate to get what she was saying off her chest, but she was also very worried about doing so.

"When we lost Harry, James said the vilest things to me, and I'm ashamed to admit I said some horrible things back to him. He heard rumours I was drunk when I crashed the car. Believed them, I think. I wasn't in the headspace to deal with that accusation, and I responded in the worst way possible. I can't bring myself to tell you what I said. It was truly terrible stuff. James ran away from home as soon as he could. He stayed away for years, only coming back when he absolutely had to. We've never gotten over it. We never had time."

Emma nodded sympathetically, absently holding her glass towards Ben, who'd called out to ask if anyone wanted a refill. His shout garnered the attention of everyone in the room and broke James' concentration. Maddie saw his eyes seek her out. He fixed his gaze on hers and smiled warmly. She beamed back.

"I've never seen him so happy," Jennifer said, drawing Maddie back into their conversation. "Though, admittedly, we haven't spent much time together since he was a child. He's all grown up now and I . . . I don't really know him. I only just realised that's why we haven't sorted things out. It's not because he's been away all this time, it's because I don't know where to start."

Emma sat back and admired James, her expression thoughtful. Maddie knew her mother would be thinking very carefully about what to say next. She was a fixer, especially when it came to families. Emma would be distressed that James might not have a parental figure in his life and heartbroken by the idea a mother might become avoidably estranged from her son. Maddie and her siblings had long since given up advising Emma to keep her nose out of other people's business. She never listened. Luckily, she was quite good at achieving her objective of making things better.

"You know—" she said, lowering her voice so it was barely above a whisper — "Pip said some truly terrible things to Marley after Bowie died. Awful things I wouldn't do him the indignity of repeating. We never, ever thought they would get over it, did we, Maddie?" Maddie dutifully shook her head. Emma sighed. "But they did. It wasn't easy. They each had to take responsibility for what had happened, they both had to apologise sincerely, they had to be raw and real with one another about how they felt and who was in the wrong and for what. But they made it through. There are still moments, I think, where things are a little awkward between the two of them, but they're mostly OK. Better than OK, actually."

"I do want to talk to James," Jennifer admitted. "But I'm afraid he doesn't want to talk to me. I'm scared he'll reject me, that he might repeat those horrible things he said years ago and it will ruin our relationship for ever."

"Ah, see, that's your problem, right there," Emma said. "You want to apologise for the things you know you did wrong, but you're only willing to do it if you can guarantee James will be receptive, and that he'll apologise in return for the things *he* did. Your ultimate goal is mending the relationship, instead of just making the things *you* did wrong right. Actually, if you're going to say sorry, you need to apologise just because you know it's the right thing to do, regardless of the outcome."

Maddie winced. She was worried Jennifer might react badly to that, but the other woman tensed, looked thoughtful, then shook her head with a sigh.

"You're right," she said. "I know you're right."

"When Pip apologised to Marley, he said sorry despite the fact he was still angry at him, and even though he knew Marley might shun his apology. He said sorry because he knew the things he'd said were far too harsh."

Jennifer nodded, her expression sad, with resigned foreboding.

Emma reached out her hand and squeezed Jennifer's shoulder affectionately. Emma continued. "If he didn't love you, Jennifer, he wouldn't have given a hoot about leaving you home alone on Christmas Day. He wouldn't, would he, Maddie? You know him better than me, love. What do you think?"

Maddie did not feel comfortable being part of this conversation, so at first she shrugged and shook her head, glaring a little at her mother for dragging her into this. But then she saw Jennifer's face fall, and she couldn't help herself — she felt sorry for James' mum. Relations were frosty between James and his mother — and Maddie's instinct was to protect him and internally demonise her — but there was a vulnerable side to Jennifer that Maddie hadn't seen when they'd met before. This woman wasn't dissimilar from her own mother. Emma and Jennifer both moved about the world with part of their hearts buried beneath the ground. She'd said terrible things and she'd isolated herself from her surviving son, but she was also a grieving mother. Maddie had lived with one of those for six years now, and knew how fragile they really were. "I can't speak for him," she said. "But if you love him and you accept there are things you did wrong, you should apologise and see what happens. It could end with the worst-case scenario, but it could also be the absolute best."

Jennifer nodded, swallowing audibly. "We will stay tonight, Emma," she said. "If it's all right with you? I think it will do me good. Both of us, actually. James loves being here, that's clear to see. It makes me feel a bit better, actually. I thought he was avoiding home because he didn't want to be around me, but I can see it's also because he enjoys spending time with your lovely family."

Maddie smiled at that, not only because Jennifer was taking steps to make things better between her and her son, but also because it meant she got to spend another night with James. That would top off a lovely evening, and create a thoroughly perfect Christmas morning.

* * *

At 10 p.m. they put out a tray of vegetables for Rudolph and bid Benjamin goodnight. Marley put him to bed, then rejoined the frivolity. They stayed up past midnight, wished each other a Merry Christmas, then all headed up to bed together. Maddie went to her own room at first. She changed into her nightie, then listened intently at the door until she was sure Emma and Ben had finished settling Jennifer in Bluebell's room and had gone to their own bedroom. When she was certain, she bid a dozing Bluebell goodbye. She tried to be quiet, but every step she took solicited the woody creak of a floorboard. As she shut her door behind her, the sound seemed to bounce off every hard surface in the house. She froze, listening intently, but heard nothing. Mercifully, she found James' door slightly ajar, artfully propped open with a slipper. James was in bed.

She could tell by the way he raised his head as she entered, his eyes half shut and mouth slightly agape, that he'd been asleep.

"Hey," she said. He held out his hand towards her, stifling a yawn. Maddie closed the bedroom door gently behind her and crawled into bed beside him. He turned onto his side to face her, kissing her gently on her nose. He could hardly keep his eyes open, so Maddie stroked his hair back from his face until he fell asleep, basking in how gloriously ordinary it felt to have this man gaze lovingly at her as he slipped into slumber. She tried to nudge aside the intrusive thought that this was fate, that she was meant to be here. That was not possible. He was leaving soon. Both enthralled and terrified by the strength of her growing feelings, she knew she had to do something to protect herself, to calm herself down. She just wasn't sure that she wanted to.

* * *

At six in the morning, James kissed her gently awake. "If you want to keep this a secret, you should probably go back to your own bedroom," he said. Maddie nodded and sat up, stifling a yawn. He gazed up at her, his eyes droopy with exhaustion. Maddie ruffled his hair affectionately. He threw her a sleepy smile.

"Before you go, I got you a Christmas present," he said. Maddie reeled. They had expressly agreed not to buy each other presents. "Chill out, it's not that deep," he said, rolling to the side of the bed and opening his bedside table drawer.

"I didn't get you anything!" she whined.

"Oh, shush," he said, handing her a small box. Maddie stared at it, overwhelmed and even a little bit annoyed. She wished he had stuck to their agreement not to buy anything. She knew he hadn't meant to make her feel this way, but she felt cheap and unthoughtful. "Stop it," he said, nudging the box and gesturing with his head for her to open it. She sighed and did so. Inside were two dainty gold studs shaped like suns, each with a grey stone in their centre.

Maddie ran her thumb across their shiny surface. "They're lovely."

"Take one out and have a closer look at that stone in the centre," he said. Maddie did as she was told. Nothing came into focus at first, but eventually she could make out the overcast view they'd admired together from the window of the beach hut on the day they'd spent in Hunstanton together. Maddie gasped. "Do you like them?" he asked.

"I love them," Maddie said, removing one of several studs in her right ear and replacing it with one of the earrings. She was overwhelmed by how thoughtful a gift they were. Maddie loved jewellery shaped like the sun, moon and stars, and although they had never spoken about that, he had obviously deduced it on his own. To anyone else, the earring would look just like something generic Maddie would wear, but she and James would know the earring was a secret nod to the day things became serious between them. Suddenly, she had an idea. She took out the second earring and held it out for him to take. His eyes roamed her face for answers.

"If you put this in your helix piercing, nobody will be able to see it because your hair will cover it, but I'll know it's there," she explained. He smiled and held out his hand, but she pushed it softly away and leaned over him, brushing his hair gently to one side and taking out the earring he currently had in the hole at the top of his ear. She replaced it with the new one, patted his hair down to cover it, then sat back to admire her work. James was grinning at her.

"There you go," he said. "Now you have given me something."

"It's hardly the same," Maddie tutted, stroking his hair away from his ear to admire the earring once more.

"I'm not talking about the earring," he said, clutching his chest. "I'm talking about that warm fuzzy feeling in here."

"Loser," Maddie teased him, hitting his arm playfully. He laughed, and pulled her close.

CHAPTER FOURTEEN

Christmas Day passed in a blur of delicious food, festive drinks and silly games. Benjamin had the whole house awake by 7.30 a.m. and Emma was serving vegan sausage sandwiches to a room full of yawning but excited individuals by half eight. They drank coffee and watched Benjamin open his gifts: a new bike from Autumn and Marley, a Scalextric set from Maddie, go-karting vouchers from Pip, and a three-day trip to Disneyland Paris over New Year's Eve from Emma and Ben. Maddie knew her parents had been desperate to give him this gift and that they'd been locked in negotiations with Autumn and Marley about it since October. From the look on her brother's face, she could tell that they'd given permission, but that Marley really wasn't happy about it.

"We've accepted the park tickets, but we're paying our own accommodation costs, flights and spending money," he clarified for the group. Later, over coffee in the kitchen, he explained his reservations to Maddie and James. "It's lovely they want to spoil him and I don't take it for granted they can afford to, but have you ever tried to raise a child who can have whatever they want? I'm terrified he'll grow into a terrible person. I'm also worried they'll try to outdo themselves every year."

"How do you outdo Disneyland Paris?" James asked.

"Disneyland Florida," Maddie and Marley said together. James laughed.

"I hope you don't mind, but I bought the little dude something, too. It's in my room," he said, sheepishly.

Marley was visibly surprised. "You didn't have to do that," he said.

"I know, but I wanted to. It's only a silly thing. It's a mini toolbox. He's always following me around, trying to help. It has a tape measure, with no sharp edges, and a screwdriver. I think there are some cardboard things to build. I can take it back if you'd rather I didn't give it to him."

Marley smiled and shook his head. "No, mate, that's lovely. Thank you. He'll love it."

They spent the morning playing Who Am I? Everyone chose a character or famous person for the person to their left and wrote it on a sticky note for the other person to guess via yes or no questions. James and Marley set up Benjamin's Scalextric set and arranged a tournament, which they all let Benjamin win. At midday, they switched from coffee to wine and beer. By the time lunch was ready, at two o'clock, they were on their way to being very merry indeed.

After lunch, everyone split up to clear the table and tidy the living room. Safe in the knowledge that things were so hectic there was very little chance anyone would notice they were missing, Maddie and James sneaked off to his bedroom for some time alone. Before they rejoined the others, he pulled her close and kissed her deeply. She could feel him smiling as he did so. It made her really happy.

James gazed upon her, his eyes soft. "I'm having the best Christmas of my life," he said.

Maddie nodded her agreement. She marvelled at how quickly things had changed, how different everything was now compared to just a few weeks ago. If the Maddie she had been in November had been told about her situation now, she wouldn't have believed it. She had dreaded Christmas Day for years and had never had any real desire to find some-one. Maddie had never considered those two things might be interlinked, that someone could come along and everything that had once felt grey would suddenly burst into colour. Ironically, that was something the source of her annual sadness, Bowie, had known all too well. Maddie thought of him now, of how he'd raise his eyebrows in a silent expression of *I told you so* if he could, and it made her smile.

* * *

As the sun began to set, snow started falling. Maddie stood with her family and friends before the large bay window in the living room and watched it cover the garden. To her right, James and Jennifer were standing side by side. Maddie saw them look at each other and smile. After a moment or two, Jennifer gestured with her head for the two of them to leave the group. James nodded, following her to the kitchen. Maddie watched them go, crossing her fingers with hope that they would find the strength and humility she knew they both needed in order to repair their relationship. It was what they both wanted, that much was obvious. Over the last twenty-four hours, Maddie had caught them watching each other on a number of occasions. Each time, Jennifer looked thoughtful and proud, while James looked lost and apprehensive. It was clear to absolutely everyone that they wanted to be all right again and — bit by bit, hour by hour — they were visibly accepting that truth for themselves. The awkwardness was dissipating from their shoulders, they had laughed together and teased each other. Maddie watched their retreating backs fully understanding James' apprehension, but then she heard Autumn laugh at something Katherine had said, and, when she turned around, she saw that Marley and Pip had their arms slung around each other — they were all grinning like goofballs.

Faced with the living proof it could be done if everyone worked hard enough, Maddie felt much better.

* * *

James and Jennifer were gone for almost an hour. Nobody asked where they were — everyone seemed to know, and the kitchen became temporarily out of bounds. When they returned, it was obvious they had both been crying, but nobody said anything about that, either. To Maddie's relief, despite their teary eyes, they both looked happy. James sought Maddie out right away. He threw her his trademark smile and she knew he was trying to reassure her that he was OK. She locked her gaze on his and he nodded, but she saw him swallow hard. He looked consumed and overwhelmed, not at all ready to return to the group. Maddie had to stop herself from going to him. Luckily, Emma was on hand to give him a long, loving hug. When she was done, Marley asked James if he wanted to help him replenish everyone's drinks, and Maddie found herself feeling grateful for her brother's perceptiveness and his growing friendship with James, who accepted the request, looking relieved. They were gone so long that Autumn and Emma gave in and replenished everyone's drinks instead, but nobody complained. Everybody seemed to know that the two men were talking about something important, even Jennifer, who spent a good hour sitting in the window seat with Emma, hashing out the conversation she'd had with her son.

To her dismay, Maddie didn't get a chance to talk to James personally until they were in bed together later that evening. They kissed a little bit, but conceded they were both too tired to do anything but talk. James told Maddie that Jennifer had apologised wholeheartedly for the things she'd said to him when he was young and the way she'd acted towards him in the years since. She'd made no excuses and asked for no sympathy, she'd simply said sorry. In return, James had done the same, then they'd hugged and hugged and hugged some more.

"We literally said about a dozen words to each other and spent the rest of the time hugging and crying," he said. "I don't know what happened. She pulled me into a cuddle and I was flooded with sadness and love. I literally felt it rush around my body. I cried like a little boy, Maddie. We have a lot of work to do, we both know that, but I feel like we've taken a massive step forward."

Maddie stroked his hair back from his face, happy to let him talk.

"Thank you," he said. She questioned him with her gaze, confused. "I know you spoke to her last night," he explained.

"That wasn't me, it was Mum," she said.

"Well, she said it was both of you, so whatever you said to her, you really made her see sense. She's been watching your mother these past couple days, too, I think. The way she is with you all, with all of us, actually. Mum wants that. She's always wanted that, and now she knows she can have it. She's finally getting out of her own way, we both are. This family . . . you people. I've never known anything like it."

Maddie smiled and kissed him tenderly, noting the absence of a layer of tension she hadn't realised had been part of his everyday form before. It was as though the weight of the world had been removed from his shoulders, like he was finally free from a set of mental shackles she hadn't known had been holding him back. He pulled away to gaze at her, his pretty eyes glinting like shiny pennies in the moonlight. She stared straight back at him. She'd never felt luckier. Suddenly, she felt obliged to shatter the moment.

"Don't," she whispered. It worked — he blinked, visibly confused. "Don't look at me like that. It scares me," she said.

She was worried he was going to say he loved her, or ask her to be his girlfriend, or do something else that would verbalise the seriousness of what they were doing and how they were feeling. She wasn't ready for any of that. There was still so much to do around here, she couldn't add someone else's happiness to her list of things to maintain, to sort out. His face softened and he nodded, kissing her gently.

* * *

Christmas rolled towards New Year and, one by one, everyone left. Jennifer bid them goodbye on Boxing Day morning. She was clearly still not completely comfortable with general social interaction, but she was much warmer than she had been. She gave Maddie a fleeting hug and James a bigger one. Katherine, Lilly and Daisy went home the day after, and Pip left for London the day after that. Ben, Emma, Bluebell, Autumn, Marley and Benjamin left for Paris the day before New Year's Eve. Although it was not originally part of their plan to take Bluebell, she and Autumn were eager for some 'best-friend time', so the rest of the group agreed she could join them. In secret, she told Maddie that was not the real reason she was going. Instead, she said she and Autumn had conspired to do Maddie and James a favour.

"You'll have the house to yourself, so you can shag all day and all over the place. No sneaking around, no rushing, no silent sex for three whole days. You're welcome."

Maddie laughed and rolled her eyes, but she was secretly thrilled and so was James. He stood dutifully on the steps beside her, waving her departing family goodbye. The moment they were out of sight, he dragged her into the living room, where he took his time undressing her, kissing every part of her body as he did so. That night they had sex for hours, pausing only to drag James' duvet from the bedroom to the living room. They slept by the fire, their naked bodies tangled together in a way that felt like art.

* * *

Over the next few days, they got through twice as much work as they usually did, despite having significantly more sex than they were typically able to. Spurred on by the desire for free time to spend together, they worked as quickly as they possibly could.

"I will never get enough of you," James told her very frequently. "You're the sexiest, best-smelling woman I've ever met in my entire life."

Maddie wasn't sure how to accept these compliments, so she would typically giggle and say something nice back. Now that there was no need for him to rush the things he said or whisper them in passing, it wasn't long before he realised she was essentially rejecting his words. The third time she did it, he stopped her.

"What's going on, Mads?" he asked. He grabbed her wrist to stop her from pulling on her jumper dress over her underwear, his eyes greedily drinking her in. "You do know how gorgeous you are, don't you?" He held her hand in the air and encouraged her to turn on the spot, straining to view every inch of her as he did. When she reached the starting point, he made a funny little noise, as though he'd just taken a bite of something delicious.

"Stop," Maddie whined, stepping towards him in what was a subtle attempt to cover herself with part of his body. She moved to kiss him — when he was kissing her he wasn't looking too closely at her and she felt better about herself — but he stepped away and came up behind her, wrapping his arms around her and encouraging her to look at herself in the full-length mirror before them. His groin, hard with desire, was pressed against her bum.

"Look at those curves, that skin, those eyes, your hair. You're incredible."

Maddie didn't say anything because she didn't know what to say. She was nowhere near as insecure as she had once been, but she hardly ever felt gorgeous. She was ashamed to acknowledge that she did feel prettier since James had been in her life, which meant a little bit of her self-worth was tied to what handsome men thought of her, and that irked her. She was also embarrassed to admit that — despite how obviously he desired her, how obsessed he was with looking at her, touching her, taking her to bed — she was convinced he would prefer her shorter and slimmer, which felt like a silly thing to admit.

Maddie hated these stupid notions. She hated the fact that society's beauty standards for women were so incredibly limited. She had learned through personal experience that it didn't matter what most individuals really liked, skinny was always in. It was hard to shake the thought that James would feel like that, too. She knew he liked her, but she was worried he secretly felt like they'd be better suited and more palatable to everyone else if she'd just comply and lose a few pounds, even though he had never — not once — given her any reason to believe that was how he felt. She wanted to tell him the truth about why she kept rejecting the nice things he said to her, but she struggled even to explain it to a woman who wasn't in the same situation, so she wasn't sure she'd ever feel safe saying these things to a man. She'd tried before, but generally men just brushed off her concerns, even when, like now, she'd been asked to explain herself.

When she wasn't forthcoming, James took it upon himself to continue. "The moment I saw you, I was, like, 'that is the most beautiful woman I have ever seen'. Then you smiled in front of me, like, a week later, because of something Marley said to you, I think, and I was, like, 'I might die if she doesn't smile like that at me one day'."

Maddie smiled now, involuntarily.

"Tell me you know how gorgeous you are," he whispered in her ear. "I couldn't bear it if you didn't."

She didn't say anything, instead she stared at herself in the mirror and wished she could say what she wanted to. He watched her reflection, his features shifting slowly, heavy with sadness. Maddie smiled sympathetically.

"Patriarchy did a number on curvy feminists," she said. "My punishment for 'eating too much' is feeling shitty about myself for ever, for refusing to starve myself, and feeling like a bad feminist every time a man like you tells me you find me attractive and it makes me feel good."

"Fucking hell." He groaned, burying his face in her neck.

"I appreciate you telling me you think I'm gorgeous and I believe you do, by the way. But it's very unfeminist to tie my self-worth to you. At the same time, society keeps telling me

I'm undesirable, and it's really hard to miss that messaging, no matter how hard you try. I'm not always strong enough to reject it. So, it's a never-ending cycle of shit, you see. I'm a bad woman for not being skinny, then a bad feminist for feeling desirable when a man like you tells me I am."

James rested his chin on her shoulder, watching her once more in the mirror.

"I don't know what to say," he admitted. "Women are the best. You, individually, are the best. I want to tell you you're gorgeous twenty times a day and I want you to believe it without feeling guilty because I'm a man and I said it, and without worrying that it isn't true because people, generally, are shits."

Maddie laughed softly, reaching up to wind her fingers tightly in his hair. He smiled against the skin on her neck, kissing her suggestively. She watched him in the mirror, his hands roaming over the curves she knew he loved. This man was beautiful, sweet and funny, and she drove him wild. That made her feel proud and sexy. For the first time, she forced herself to feel those things without a hint of guilt.

* * *

They greeted the New Year on the porch, wrapped in blankets and bathed in candlelight. They were so absorbed in conversation they were momentarily confused by the popping of fireworks in the distance, having not noticed midnight was approaching.

It was the freedom to be consumed with each other Maddie missed most when her family returned. She was glad to see them, but she'd have been grateful for a few more days alone with James. She didn't want to go back to hiding their relationship, but when he broached the idea of telling people their secret, Maddie didn't want to do that, either. She was relieved he didn't ask her for an explanation, because she knew he wouldn't accept the only one she had as a valid reason to keep things a secret. James hadn't mentioned travelling for a while, but she was convinced he still wanted to go, and she knew her parents would be worried she'd be hurt by his impending departure if they found out about their relationship. They would almost certainly say or do things to try and sway his decision towards staying with Maddie. She cared too much about him to let that happen. She also didn't want to feel like he'd only stayed because he liked the Whittles and wanted to make them happy. If he stayed, she wanted that to be because he really wanted to be with her. So, for now, they needed to keep their secret. That meant endlessly yearning for hand-holding over the breakfast table, spontaneous kisses and moonlit walks in the garden together. Maddie missed cooking for him exclusively, sharing showers, snuggling up on the sofa. She could tell from the look in his eyes he missed these things, too.

"God, he's like a love-struck teenager," Bluebell remarked, two days after their return. "Moping around here, gazing longingly at you every five seconds. How Mum, Dad and Marley haven't figured you two out yet, I'll never know."

"Are you sure they haven't?" Maddie asked, nervously.

"They never mentioned it when we were away," Bluebell said. "You know what Marley is like, Mads. If he knew, he would say something."

"I can't believe Autumn hasn't told him," Maddie remarked.

"I can," Bluebell said. "She's a solid friend, that one. What's between her and us stays between her and us. She's a fucking legend."

Maddie changed the subject. "I'm so excited to go dress shopping with her and Mum tomorrow. Does she have any idea what she wants?"

Bluebell shook her head. "Something classy as fuck, knowing Autumn. She said she wants something understated, but when has she ever been that? She couldn't underplay herself if she tried. She could put a bloody bin bag on and still be the hottest woman in the room."

"What about bridesmaid's dresses, has she mentioned them?"

The thought of being promenaded in front of a crowd, even one that was relatively small, made Maddie feel anxious. She did not like being the centre of attention even for a moment. Sure, most eyes would be on Autumn, of course, but that didn't make her feel any better.

Bluebell shook her head. "She'll put us in something gorgeous, though. Something simple and chill. Something we really want to wear. I know you hate being paraded, Mads, but you'll have nothing to worry about. Autumn hates attention, too. She knows how you feel. She'll make sure you're comfortable."

CHAPTER FIFTEEN

The following morning, on their way to the bridal boutique, Autumn confirmed Bluebell's sentiments. She told them she'd like them both to wear floor-length gowns in black — because that was the colour Benjamin had chosen when she'd asked him what suited his aunties best — but they could choose whatever style they wanted, and they didn't have to match. Emma could wear whatever she liked. Autumn had no idea what she personally wanted in a wedding dress. Something full-length. Not bright white. Something plain.

"It's your wedding day!" Bluebell said. "You only get to do this twice, maybe three times, maximum. You should wear something a bit different."

Autumn ignored the joke, shaking her head. "I'm not sure I give off traditional bride vibes. I think I'll feel uncomfortable."

"Nonsense," Emma said, rolling her eyes. "You're a bride, therefore you *are* bridal vibes. Just try the dresses on, Autumn. Humour us, would you? We can have a little fashion show."

"Not this again," Autumn groaned. Emma, Maddie and Bluebell giggled. Despite her protestations, Maddie knew it was important to Autumn that the three women were with her because her own mother and sister were unable to make it due to an appointment they had to keep for Daisy. She had been born prematurely and had to be checked routinely for developmental delays. Autumn could have come alone, but she had chosen not to, despite the fact she'd known she'd be expected to put on a display. "All right, fine. I'll try the bloody dresses on," she said. "But only because it's been six years since you last made me do this — for that ball we almost attended that summer with Bowie — and that's an acceptable amount of time between humiliation events."

Emma grinned. "Excellent," she said.

The bridal boutique was located at the top of the high street, so they parked up, pit-stopped at a coffee shop for a takeaway, then headed straight there, arriving five minutes before their allotted appointment time. The shop was cosy and warmly lit. The air smelled of orange and cinnamon. Maddie inhaled it deeply. She'd never get enough of that smell.

"Hello!" Emma called, a little cautiously, into the void. There was no sign of anyone.

"Just a minute," someone shouted from the back. "Feel free to start looking!"

Maddie was desperate to drill through the frocks lining every wall, but it felt rude to do so when Autumn wasn't moving, so she stood dutifully by her friend's side, instead. Autumn was looking from rail to rail, her shoulders pitched high, her stance mildly panicked. "I don't know where to start," she said.

"At the beginning," Emma said, squeezing her arm reassuringly. She pointed to a nearby mannequin, cloaked in a giant gown made from candy-floss-coloured lace. "What do you think of that?" she asked. Autumn glared at her. Maddie and Bluebell laughed. "What?" Emma asked, innocently. "You've given us no direction, so absolutely everything is still on the table."

"I said plain," Autumn reminded her.

"Ah, yes, so you did." Emma nodded, grinning mischievously. "What about that one, then?" She pointed to a dress in the window. It was floor length, satin crêpe, with a sweetheart neckline and dainty, loose-fitting, off-shoulder sleeves. It had a small train and buttons all down the back, dozens of them, from the very top to the very bottom. It was ruched to one side at the front, tighter around the bosom, waist and bottom, then floaty to the floor. The gown was perfected by a slit that went thigh-high. Maddie loved it. It was exactly what she would have chosen to try on if she'd been shopping for herself.

"That's more like it," Autumn said, reaching out to touch the material.

Suddenly, a very small woman with very big hair was unbuttoning the dress and tearing it from the mannequin, nodding enthusiastically. "Something simple and elegant," she said. "I'm Moira Violet, owner of Moira Violet's Bridal Boutique. It's lovely to meet you. Would you like some champagne?"

"I'd love some," Autumn said. Moira put the dress on a hanger and took it to the changing room, which was actually a pair of silk curtains suspended to give brides privacy in one corner of the room.

"Excellent. When are you getting married?" Moira asked.

"March fifteenth," Autumn said.

"Lovely. What's your wedding theme?"

Autumn looked confused. "Generic wedding," she said.

"They're having an informal ceremony with a few dozen guests in our garden on March fifteenth, which is what the dress is for, then getting married — just the two of them and a couple of witnesses — in a registry office the following Monday morning," Emma said. "Lots of flowers, lots of candles, twinkling lights in the evening. Alcohol, dancing, a big party bursting with friends."

"Romantic and intimate," Moira said, nodding.

"Exactly!" Emma said.

"Lovely." Moira clapped her hands together. "So, based on the theme and the dress you've just pointed at, I'm going to pull a few options from the rails. I suggest you ladies do the same. Have a look at everything and try on as much as you want. Have fun. I'll get the champagne."

Emma squealed excitedly, diving towards the nearest dress. Bluebell rolled her eyes at Autumn and followed their mother. Maddie met her friend's gaze and smiled, but Autumn was not smiling back. Instead, she looked completely overwhelmed. She was twisting her engagement ring around and around on her finger, her eyebrows set in a frown.

"Are you OK?" Maddie mouthed. Autumn quickly corrected her face, her lips curled up into a dutiful smile. She nodded with absolute purpose, but Maddie saw her swallow hard. Maddie opened her mouth to say something else, but was interrupted by Emma calling Autumn over, convinced she'd found her the perfect dress. Autumn tore her eyes from Maddie's and turned away, striding towards her future mother-in-law. Confused, Maddie watched them for a moment. There was no hint of apprehension from Autumn now, but Maddie knew she hadn't imagined it. Something was wrong.

* * *

They spent the next forty-five minutes working their way through every dress in the shop, desperately searching for a gown that would make Autumn gasp. To Maddie's dismay, she didn't seem overly keen on any of them. Still, they pulled out ten for her to try on. They were all satin or chiffon, all floor length, some were floaty and others were tight, some had sleeves and some didn't, but they would all almost certainly look lovely on Autumn. By the time they were ready for her to start trying things on, the women had sunk three glasses of champagne each and Bluebell had talked Moira into joining them for a drink.

They started with the dress from the mannequin, the first one Autumn had approved. Moira helped her into it behind the set of silk curtains, theatrically drawing them back to reveal an apprehensive-looking Autumn standing on a podium. She was clipped into the dress because it was too big, but she looked more beautiful than Maddie had ever seen her. The three women cooed, then fell silent and stared. Suddenly — and entirely predictably — Emma burst into tears.

"Oh, for God's sake," Autumn said, trying and failing to hide a smile. She turned to look at herself in the mirror.

"I'm so sorry. It's just that you look so lovely," Emma said.

"There are tissues in front of you." Moira gestured to the coffee table, her voice tinged with mild concern. Maddie wasn't surprised. Her mother had always been a very dramatic crier.

"She does this all the time. She's fine," Bluebell said.

Autumn turned to face the mirror. Emma wailed louder, resting her head on Maddie's shoulder and patting Bluebell's lap, searching for her daughter's hand. She found it and clutched it to her chest.

"Oh, it's not too bad, actually," Autumn said, as though nothing at all was happening behind her. Maddie smiled. Autumn had been part of this family for so long Maddie could hardly remember a time without her, but even after all these years, she knew her friend would never, ever be comfortable with such public displays of emotion.

"You look amazing," Emma sobbed into a tissue. "I can't believe you're getting married. I'm so happy and proud."

"Calm down, would you, Mum?" Bluebell said. "It's just a wedding."

"It is *not* just a wedding, it's Autumn's and Marley's wedding," Emma said. "*Autumn and Marley!* Two people who never showed a sliver of interest in monogamy before, let alone getting *married*, who fate brought together, who have been through *so much*, who I never thought would commit to doing something so romantic. I'm sorry, I'm quite overcome."

"That's not like you at all," Autumn teased. Maddie watched her friend carefully. Autumn was forcing herself to be jovial, Maddie was sure of it. Beneath the surface, this was irritating her. Maddie could tell from the frown etched on Autumn's face that this was taking a monumental amount of effort. Autumn was hiding something. Right on cue, she sighed, shaking her head at Emma's reflection. "I was always going to spend the rest of my life with him. This'll just be . . . another day."

"It is not just another day," Emma said. "It's your *wedding* day."

Autumn didn't answer, instead she turned from left to right, looking herself up and down. Something had shifted. The mood had changed, had sunk even further. Autumn looked tense. Maddie found Bluebell's gaze. Her eyes were wide with concern. "I'll take it," Autumn said, suddenly. The other women, including Moira, gasped.

"What do you mean?" Emma asked, aghast. "There are another nine wedding dresses waiting in there to be tried on."

Autumn shook her head. "What's the point? I need a dress, I found a dress. I feel lovely. Trying on a million is a total waste of time."

"But . . ." Emma tried.

Autumn held up her hand. Emma dutifully stopped pressing. Bluebell and Maddie side-eyed one another once more. It was not at all like Autumn to cut Emma off like that. They sat in silence watching Autumn, who was frozen and staring at the ground.

"I just want to marry Marley," she said. "That's all I care about, honestly. If it weren't for all of you, I would marry him in a pair of jeans and a baggy jumper at the registry office and be done with it. I'm sorry for snapping, it's just that . . . All of this is lovely, but it isn't us. Marley and me, I mean . . ."

She stopped, raising her head to stare at herself in the mirror. She gestured at the dress, then at the shop more generally.

"This is what we would be doing if I was marrying Bowie," she said. Emma opened her mouth to speak, but Autumn's comment had rendered her speechless. Autumn seized her opportunity to elaborate, speaking quickly, her voice laden with sadness. "He was the romantic one, wasn't he? Getting married in the garden, surrounded by candles, loads of people there, a floaty, almost-white wedding dress, those are very Bowie-like things. If we hadn't lost him and he and I had lasted, if our conventional, love-at-first-sight fairy-tale had made it this far, this is the type of wedding he'd have talked me into. Marley and I, we want to make you all happy, but I'm really scared we're sleepwalking into a wedding we, as a couple, don't really want, so that we can give you the day Bowie and I would have given you had things been different. Getting married in the garden is the only part of this we really want, the rest of it, the fancy altar, the planters, the proper dress, all the people . . . we don't care about any of it."

So much became suddenly clear to Maddie. Autumn's general lack of interest in the wedding, her calm compo-sure despite having almost nothing organised, the way she shrugged every time Maddie or James asked her a question about the positioning of the altar or where she'd like them to place a wooden planter. Autumn couldn't care less. If Maddie had to guess, she'd say that it was in equal parts because she felt bad that she was organising Bowie's dream wedding with someone who was not Bowie, but also because it wasn't her vibe — and it wasn't Marley's vibe, either. The two of them had been through so much to get where they were. Surviving had required knowing wholeheartedly who they were, as indi-viduals and as a couple. Maddie and Autumn rarely talked about it, but Marley and Autumn had been forced to navigate incredibly difficult conversations over the past few years about how they were feeling and what they were thinking. They'd sailed the stormy current of their grief together and come through the fog of sadness stronger and united, despite the odds being stacked against them. They absolutely knew what they wanted and what they didn't. But they also loved their family very much — knew that these people were still grieving a man they'd lost and a wedding he would never have — and had tried to find a comfortable medium because of it. Maddie locked her eyes on Autumn and winced. The woman before her looked the exact opposite of comfortable.

"Marley will go mad when he finds out I've told you this," she said, her eyes on the three Whittle women. "It's literally the first time I've been alone with you for wedding-related stuff and I've just blurted it all out."

"He doesn't have to know," Bluebell said.

"I can't keep it from him, we don't have secrets." Autumn shook her head, sadly. She turned back to the mirror to look at herself. Her eyes roamed over her reflection. "It really is a beautiful dress," she said. "I think I could get onboard with wearing it. It's just the rest of it. An aisle, all those eyes on me, fixed hours, expectations, a day of small talk. I'm dreading it."

"Then don't do it," Emma said.

Autumn snapped to attention, her eyes full of hope. "But everyone . . ."

"Naff everyone," Emma hissed, waving her hand theatrically. "My love, I can absolutely promise you that none of us want to do this if you and Marley don't want to do it. Yes, we love a party. Yes, we'd like a big wedding. But only if it's what you want."

Emma stood up and stepped towards Autumn, holding out her hands for her to take.

"Thank goodness you've told us. My God, if you'd gone through with this and I'd found out afterwards that you'd hated every second of it, I'd be devastated, and so would everyone else."

Maddie and Bluebell nodded their agreement.

"I know we can be a lot," Emma said. Bluebell shuffled pointedly. Emma rolled her eyes, sighed, and continued. "I, specifically, can be a lot. I know it's taken you a really long time to get used to that. But Autumn, I love you. I only ever want you to be happy. I'm so sorry you've felt like you have to go along with this. I never meant to make you feel that way. I know where I've gone wrong, and I should have stopped when I felt a hint of resistance. Will you accept my apology?"

Autumn had already softened. "Of course, Emma. I don't want you to feel bad. This thing we're planning, it's what most people want. It's just . . ."

"Not you," Emma interrupted, nodding her head. "I get it. And it's *your* day, yours and Marley's, so every inch of it should be you. Marley will twist when we tell him we know, only because he doesn't want to disappoint us, but we'll explain everything and he'll understand it's for the best. If he gives you any stick, you send him to me. I'll straighten his face for him."

Autumn laughed a little and the atmosphere in the bridal boutique thawed. Maddie's shoulders, which had at some point risen towards her ears, dropped to their usual position. She unclenched her jaw and unballed her fists, relieved on Autumn's behalf. Bluebell hurled herself out of the sofa and cast herself into Autumn's arms, mumbling supportive statements and squeezing her tight. Emma caught Maddie's eye, and the two women smiled, resigned. Maddie felt sad. She didn't care what Autumn and Marley did, but Emma was very obviously disappointed. Maddie was proud of her mother for shunting her own feelings to one side to put Marley and Autumn first. Not all parents were capable of such maturity.

"So," Moira said, shattering the moment. She had slowly backed away from the group and was perched on a stool as far away from the troop as she could get. Maddie knew she'd be incredibly confused, though she doubted this was the weirdest thing that had ever happened in her shop, hence the pointed retreating. "Are you buying the dress?" she asked.

Autumn stepped away from Bluebell and turned back to the mirror, admiring herself once more. "It really is beautiful," she said.

"It is," Maddie concurred.

"Buy it, Autumn!" Emma said, correcting her tone immediately. "If you want to, I mean."

"There's no rule that says you can't wear a big, beautiful dress to a small wedding," Bluebell agreed.

"There isn't, is there?" Autumn asked. The Whittle women shook their heads. Maddie was sure Autumn was about to say yes, but she sighed and turned away from her reflection. "No, I'm not going to buy it," she said. "Help me out of it, will you?"

Moira did a great job of pretending she wasn't annoyed by how colossally they had wasted her time, but Maddie could still tell she was. She waited until the shop owner had helped Autumn out of her dress and left her alone behind the curtain to put her clothes back on, then approached her to apologise quietly. Moira straightened her face and threw Maddie a smile, sighing thoughtfully. "Do you know how many women have passed through these doors who I can tell don't want to get married, or don't want a particular dress, or aren't happy with the venue or the wedding more generally, but they're pressured into going ahead with it anyway? I wish Autumn's answer had been different, of course I do — I'm here to sell dresses — but I found that entire conversation very refreshing, to be honest with you."

Maddie wasn't entirely sure she believed her, but nodded appreciatively anyway.

* * *

That afternoon, Maddie chased James out into the garden. He was heading to the sofa on the porch with his guitar, where he often spent a half hour or so playing songs and singing softly to himself. It was a form of meditation, he'd told her once, a way to reset himself and clear his head. She informed him he no longer needed to prepare the garden as formally as they had planned for the wedding, since the idea of doing so was overwhelming Autumn. Now the only people who would be there would be the Whittles, Autumn's family and exceedingly close friends. She was happy to keep the altar and for them to put out some pretty decorations in the form of lights, planters and flowers, but she didn't want hordes of people or a huge fuss. She wanted the people closest to her present for a blessing and their friends could come later for a party.

James blinked at her. "I'm confused."

Maddie shrugged. "It's just not them. The big, fancy wedding thing was never their vibe," she explained. "They were going along with it because they wanted to make everyone else happy."

"Right," James said, sounding uncertain. "Well, at least I'll have more time to work on Bowie's old bedroom."

Maddie was relieved by the change of subject. "What are you doing in there, exactly?" she asked, narrowing her eyes at him playfully. She'd seen him carrying materials in and out of the room — he'd spent several hours in there since she'd agreed to let him renovate it — but she had no idea what he was up to. Plus, to her surprise, she realised she trusted him. She knew whatever he was doing would be carefully thought through and sensitively executed, so she focused instead on the fact they only had a few months until the retreat opened. Maddie was too busy updating her website and social media sites and taking her first bookings to pay much attention to anything else. She had three guests so far, they had both been sent to her by charities, who were paying for them to stay. They were a woman with breast cancer, a woman with leukaemia and a man with lymphoma. That last one scared Maddie a little bit, as having him here would bring back so many painful memories of Bowie's last days, but she reminded herself this was what she was here to do.

"Never you mind," James interrupted her ruminating, stepping towards her. Before she could stop herself, Maddie backed away, searching around self-consciously. When she looked back at James, his features were heavy with rejection, and she could tell her action had flooded his heart with sadness. He tried to correct himself, but she never, ever wanted to make him feel like that.

"I'm sorry," she said. "I just don't want anyone to see."

James nodded, but his jaw was tense and he averted his gaze. Maddie was taken aback. This was the first time he'd shown any hint of irritation at their situation and the first time in weeks there had been any friction between the two of them. It made Maddie want to cry. She bit her lip and lowered her head, her eyes filling with tears. She was failing in her mission not to hurt someone she cared about.

Behind him, perched on the wooden porch railing, Maddie caught sight of the robin. It was standing stock-still and staring at her, as though trying to communicate. Bowie entered her mind the way he always did whenever she saw a robin, and that made her want to cry harder. She really wished he was here to talk this through with. Right on cue, the bird skipped across the railing so that it was closer to her. It was watching her in a way that felt rather pointed. Maddie wiped her eyes. Perhaps he was here, after all.

"Hey," James whispered. "Please don't get upset. I am so sorry, I didn't mean to make you sad."

"I'm being stupid." Maddie wiped her eyes and tried to look at him, but they filled once more. James stepped towards her, shaking his head.

"Please don't," he pleaded. "If you cry I'm going to have to hug you, and then everyone will know."

Maddie couldn't help it and laughed at that. Something about the way he said it made her feel comfortably ridiculous. She knew she was being silly. James was her friend, so those who didn't know there was anything romantic between them wouldn't be tipped off by him hugging her when she was upset, and there was much to be upset about at the moment. She was being overly cautious, she knew that.

"I'm sorry," she said. He was standing so close to her now she could smell the citrus shampoo he used in his hair and the shaving foam that haunted his skin. He opened his arms to receive her.

"Come here immediately," he said. She cast herself into his embrace, burying her head in his chest. She let him rock her from side to side for a few minutes, enjoying the heat of his body and the thumping of his heart against her temple. In that moment, she was scared of the power of her feelings for this man. It took very little effort from him to turn her mood right around. The mere sight of him lifted her spirits and lightened her heart. She was never happier than when he was beside her.

"I need to talk to you," he said, bang on time. "About us. What we're doing and where we're going. It's nothing to worry about, but I do think we need to have a conversation. I'll take you for dinner?"

Maddie couldn't help it, she beamed at that. "I haven't been taken out for dinner by a man in for ever."

James shook his head. "A fucking travesty," he said.

CHAPTER SIXTEEN

The moment Bluebell got wind of the fact Maddie had been invited out to dinner with James, she set about figuring out how they could make it an entire weekend.

"We can say we're going to Autumn's for a girls' night, you can get ready there, then fuck off out with James. You can say you're staying the night, then the two of you can get a hotel! That's what I would do."

"An excellent idea, but how do we get around Marley being there?" Maddie asked.

That stumped Bluebell. "Autumn will have the answer to that question," she said.

Bluebell was right. Autumn did have the answer. "He's desperate for a night out with his theatre friends, so I'll tell him we're having a girls' night and send him off to London for the evening. He'll get smashed, and either stay over or be back so late and so drunk he won't know who's in the house and who isn't."

"Sounds like a plan," Bluebell said. "Can we orchestrate it for this weekend?"

"Abso-fucking-lutely we can," Autumn said. "I'll come back to you this afternoon, but consider it on for tomorrow night. I know for a fact he'll jump at the chance."

As promised, Autumn delivered. It turned out Marley — who had worked his notice period and had hardly left the village since — really was desperate for a night to blow off steam. Now that their wedding was significantly slimmed down — which Marley was relieved about, despite being a little bit annoyed about how their true feelings had come out to his family — he was no longer feeling the pressure of helping organise it, but he was immensely stressed at the responsibility that came with being a stay-at-home parent. He loved Benjamin, but maybe needed some time away from him. He jumped on the idea the moment Autumn suggested it, calling his friends and excitedly planning a pub crawl around Borough Market.

"Absolutely everyone is up for it," he told Maddie enthusiastically. "All the old crew are going to be there. We're going to see a show first. I'm not sure which one yet, then we'll head out for dinner and then out for the evening. I can't wait."

"Sounds like fun," she said. "We'll be drinking cheap Prosecco and scranning Chinese food at yours."

"Booze, good food, great company," Marley said. "Sounds the same, just different."

In fact, Maddie had no idea what she would be eating, as James handled the specifics. She only knew she needed to dress nicely and bring an overnight bag, which he told her via a note attached to a bunch of flowers he left in a vase by her bed the night before they were due to go away. She discovered them with Bluebell, who had taken to sleeping in Maddie's room with her whenever James wasn't staying over, so that she could get a full update on how things were progressing. Maddie hadn't thought her sister could love James more than she already did, but she was wrong.

"I swear to fuck, if you don't marry him, I will," she said.

Maddie rolled her eyes. "You don't even believe in marriage," she pointed out.

"I might, if I had a man like that," Bluebell said.

* * *

Maddie and Bluebell made their way to Autumn's and Marley's house early Saturday afternoon, just as Marley was about to leave to catch his train. He looked smart in a pair of emerald-green, corduroy trousers and a crisp white shirt. He'd swapped out the studs he wore in his ears for a couple of dangly earrings and put on a chain. He looked younger, somehow, like the Marley of old times.

"Sisters," he greeted them at the door, hugging them one by one. "Can't stay. I'm meeting Pip at King's Cross for a swift one before I meet everyone else."

"Tell him we love him," Bluebell said.

Marley nodded, putting on his coat. "He already knows that, but I will. Goodbye, my love."

"Bye," Autumn kissed him. "Don't talk to any strange women."

"Ha!" Marley barked a laugh. "Bye, Benjamin!"

"Bye, Daddy!" Benjamin called from inside. Marley skipped through the front door and headed down the street towards the train station. Maddie and Bluebell watched him turn the corner, then stepped into Autumn's and Marley's teeny-tiny home, basking in the heat from their log fire.

"I love this house," Maddie said, taking off her shoes. Autumn smiled gratefully, urging them both further inside. The house was detached, with a garden that wrapped all the way around it. It was built from grey stone and covered in ivy. The front door opened directly into their living room, which had original flagstone flooring and stained beams lining the walls and roof. They had a giant, emerald-green, velvet sofa in the centre of the room, perched atop a giant rug, and the walls were lined with shelves and bookcases stuffed with ornaments and novels. There were cushions and blankets everywhere, pictures Benjamin had drawn tacked to the walls, and bunches of flowers on every available surface. Autumn and Marley could afford something bigger, but they loved the house's character. Since they didn't plan on having any more children, it was all they needed.

Benjamin was sitting on the couch, eating an apple and watching cartoons. He barely looked up as they entered.

"Oi," Autumn chastised him. "Say hello to your aunties."

"Hi, Aunties," he said, his eyes flitting to them briefly and then settling back on the television.

"Sorry," Autumn said. "He's obsessed with television at the moment. I'm trying to get him out of it, but to no avail. It'll probably work to our benefit tonight, though."

"Worst mother ever," Bluebell teased.

"Don't," Autumn said. "I feel terrible about it. I had all these ideals when he was a baby. We were going to restrict TV and only buy educational toys and spend our weekends making crafts and baking cookies, but it just doesn't work out like that in reality. I do try, but he's happiest when he's watching brightly coloured, addictive crap on the television."

"It never did us any harm," Maddie said, pulling a bottle of Prosecco out of the bag she was carrying. Autumn received it gratefully, leading the way to the galley kitchen — long, thin and tastefully decorated. The walls were panelled and painted sapphire blue to match the vintage aga stove. Autumn and Marley displayed their wine glasses artfully on a mounted bar. Maddie got three down while Autumn retrieved a bottle of wine from the cooler.

"Thanks, Mads," Autumn said, popping open the Prosecco. "What are you wearing tonight?"

"It's a toss-up," Maddie said, passing her the glasses one by one. "Jeans and a nice top, or a little black dress. It's hard to know what to pick when I don't know where we're going."

"You'll look gorgeous in either," Bluebell said, sighing and taking a seat. "Is Marley coming back tonight, Autumn?"

Autumn chuckled. "Is he shite. He's rented an Airbnb somewhere near London Bridge."

"I'll look forward to a drunk dial from him later, then," Bluebell said. "He's an absolute nuisance when he's pissed."

"He just wants to make sure you all know he loves you," Autumn said, defensively.

"Did he used to do it this much before Bowie died, or did it start after, I can't remember?" Bluebell asked, visibly thoughtful. Maddie shrugged. She couldn't remember, but she had a feeling Marley had perhaps transferred his habit of drunk-dialling Bowie onto them when they'd lost him. He certainly did it more often these days, almost every single time he was drunk. She'd be lying if she said she minded. She'd never tire of hearing how much her family loved her, of being reminded they thought of her often.

"What do we do when he calls later and asks to talk to Maddie?" Autumn said.

Maddie pondered. "Tell him I got pissed and went to bed."

Autumn and Bluebell nodded, sipping their wine. "I mean, you'll likely be in bed anyway, so it's not like we'll be lying," Bluebell said. Maddie raised her eyebrows suggestively. Her sister laughed.

"I bloody love those early days," Autumn said. "When you can't get enough of each other. It's the best. But still, I love where Marley and I are now. There's something nice about us being a long-standing unit, you know. Not a new couple, just . . . Autumn and Marley. Our life is repetitive and predictable, but it's happy and calm. It's peaceful and safe. I love what we've built."

Maddie knew what Autumn meant, especially about being consumed with each other. It felt like every time she and James met, they had to have sex before they did absolutely anything else, or they would explode. It was thrillingly addictive, but it was also frustrating, and that was both a blessing and a curse. Maddie loved their time together, but they were also busy. Between going to bed together and working hard to get the house ready for opening, there was little time for anything else. Maddie wasn't sure what 'anything else' was, exactly, she hadn't had time to give it much thought. She just knew she wanted it. She loved their connection, but Autumn had summed it up for her, there was something to be said for the beautiful normalcy couples shared once they'd settled into things. Autumn and Marley had it, as did her mum and dad. Maddie was starting to feel like it was high time she had it, too.

She felt her stomach flip and, despite the fact James had told her not to worry, she realised she was nervous about their conversation tonight. She felt certain he was going to tell her he wanted to be with her — it was unfathomable that he would choose to leave her, given the strength of their bond, and that was exactly what was scaring her. What if he completely blindsided her and announced that he was, in fact, going away, that he wanted to take a break while he was gone, or to break up completely? What if he said he was going away but he wanted to stay together? That would be better than the other two options, but it still wasn't ideal. Maddie felt sick.

* * *

She successfully managed to push her impending conversation with James out of her mind and be fully present for her afternoon with Autumn, Bluebell and Benjamin. They migrated to the living room to watch cartoons, eat chocolates, drink wine and chat the afternoon away. At five o'clock, Maddie went upstairs to shower and start getting ready. At half five, Bluebell and Autumn came upstairs to help her with her hair and make-up. Maddie tried on both outfits for them and, though she loved the little black dress, she didn't quite feel confident enough to wear it, so she settled on the jeans and nice top combination that made her feel safe. She could dress the outfit up with heels or down with boots.

The jeans were light-blue denim and the top a black bodysuit with a sweetheart neckline and sheer sleeves. She put in a set of dangling earrings and Bluebell added some texture to her hair with a straightening iron, then helped her position a velvet headband. She took one last look at herself, added a smidge of red lipstick for colour and decided boots would be best. Then she waited until Autumn had put Benjamin in the bath before she sneaked downstairs and out of the front door. When he asked where she was, Autumn and Bluebell were going to tell him she'd gone to bed early.

James was right on time, waiting outside in the cream 1990s Rover Mini he shared with his mother. Her bag was already in the car — she had sneaked it into his boot at his request the day before — so she hopped straight into the passenger seat, gave him a peck on the lips, and then they were on their way.

"Where are we going?" Maddie asked, excitedly.

"Ware," he said. Maddie had suspected the market town would be their destination. It was a short drive from their village, just ten minutes or so, and it was quaint and beautiful. "Our hotel is called the Velvet and it's gorgeous. It has a restaurant that has pretty good reviews so I reserved a table there for eight o'clock, but we absolutely don't have to eat there if you would rather go somewhere else."

"Sounds good to me," Maddie said. James pulled onto a country lane, then he reached for her hand. She cradled his palm with her own, stroking his wrist with her thumb.

"I think my mum might be on to us," he said. Maddie snapped to attention. "Don't panic, it's all good. She didn't say it, but I could just tell by the way she was looking at me. She didn't seem to believe me when I implied I was meeting a stranger for a first date, in fact, she asked me what you were up to this evening. It was . . . pointed."

"Oh, God!" Maddie groaned. Jennifer and her own mother had been spending more time together recently, visiting each other at home, and popping out for coffee and brunch. If Jennifer suspected, it was only a matter of time before she spoke to Emma about it. Perhaps they'd compare notes on this evening.

"Maddie," James said, squeezing her hand. "I want you to think very carefully about why this bothers you so much. The idea of people knowing about us, I mean."

Maddie sighed and shook her head. She already knew why it bothered her so much, but she didn't want to have the conversation until James had told her what his plans were. She didn't want her fears for the future to sway his decision.

"Are you embarrassed of me?" he asked. Maddie stared at him, aghast.

"Are you kidding?" she asked. "Why the fuck would I be embarrassed of you?"

"I don't know," he mumbled. "If it's not that, I can't figure it out."

Maddie supposed that made sense. She felt terrible. She wanted to tell the whole world this man was hers, that she was his, but she wanted to be sure they really did belong to each other. She didn't know what to say, so she held his hand up to her mouth and kissed it.

"I'm not embarrassed of you," she said.

"Then what's going on?" he asked.

Maddie sighed and stared out of the window. She too did not understand why she was feeling like this. She just knew that before she told everyone the details of her personal life and how happy she was, she absolutely had to be sure that this was for keeps, and she wasn't yet. So much was up in the air, there was so much about their future that was unclear. The people who loved her would ask her questions and she had no idea how to answer them. They would have concerns and she would have no idea how to calm their fears. James loved her family and telling him this might change his mind about what he wanted to do, and Maddie cared too deeply about him to let that happen. She sighed. It was a mess. Right on cue, James spoke.

"You know I'm crazy about you, don't you?" James said. "I could follow you around for the rest of my life just trying to make you laugh and I'd be the happiest man on the planet."

Maddie turned to look at him. He was staring intently at the road, blinking rapidly. She got the distinct impression he was holding back tears.

"You've changed my life, Maddie," he said. "I never, ever thought I would feel at home again in the village. I had such a happy childhood until we lost Harry. Some of my greatest memories were made in that home, on these streets, and then it was all gone, in an instant. When I came back here I couldn't wait to leave again, but now . . . there is nowhere in the entire world I would rather be than here with you."

He was holding onto her palm so tightly that their hands were sweaty, despite the snappy January air and an ancient car heating system that worked intermittently.

"Mum and I stayed in together the other night. We sat and watched TV together and laughed. That might sound stupid if you do it all the time, but for us, it was so important. I went to the shop to buy ingredients and we cooked together. When she went to bed, she said goodnight. If you'd told me six months ago my mum and I would share a joke, that we'd laugh together, that she'd kiss my cheek before she went to bed, I'd never have believed it. I still can't believe it now."

Maddie gave in to her own tears. James, whose eyes were mercifully focused on the road, did not notice.

"I know we were going to wait to have this conversation over dinner, but I can't hold it in anymore. I just want to be with you. Properly be with you. Here, at home. I want you and me and our tiny village and 'the big house'. I want your gorgeous family and my mum, Pigglesworth and Stevie Licks. I just . . ." He slowed as they entered Ware, and took the opportunity to look at her. Maddie self-consciously wiped her face with her sheer sleeve. It did little to dry her cheeks. James groaned. "Tell me those are happy tears," he pleaded. Maddie laughed and nodded, feeling pathetic. He rewarded her with the floppy side-smile she knew she'd never get enough of.

"I was out there looking for something that was here the whole time," he said, suddenly serious once more. He indicated to pull over, and Maddie saw their home for the evening, the Velvet, a short walk away, at the top of the high street. James artfully parked the car, but did not turn off the engine. Instead he unbuckled his seatbelt and turned to face her. He stared straight into her eyes. "I'm falling in love with you," he whispered, reaching out to touch her cheek. He frantically brushed away her tears with his fingers, then cupped her face in his hands. Maddie laughed again, swiping frantically at her own face.

"I'm sorry," she said.

James leaned in to kiss the tip of her nose. "Don't apologise," he murmured. "But I have to ask, why are you so worried about people finding out? Are you sure you're not embarrassed of us? Of me? We're from such different backgrounds . . ."

"God, no!" Maddie said. James looked sceptical. "I promise, James, there isn't a single part of me that's embarrassed of you."

"Then what's wrong?"

Maddie shrugged. "I don't know why I'm like this. I'm just . . . scared."

James looked thoughtful. "These are big feelings." He shrugged. Maddie smiled and nodded. He was right, they were. The biggest happy feelings she had ever felt, in fact. Her tears were warranted. "You are mine, aren't you, Maddie?" he whispered, self-doubt creeping across his features.

Maddie desperately wanted to say yes, but she couldn't. Before they tumbled into this mess of emotions, she needed to be absolutely sure he'd let go of the part of himself that longed for something completely different, something she could not — would not — give him. Her home was here, with her family. She had long since given up wanting anything except to be beside them. Sure, they would travel away from her — away from the house and Bowie's resting place — for periods of time, but Maddie had no desire to do that. She knew who she was and she knew what she wanted. She just wasn't one-hundred-per-cent sure James did.

"Are you mine?" she asked, searching for words he'd said to her once. "I thought you belonged to . . . adventure, unpredictability and the open road?"

243

His eyes crinkled in their corners and he smiled seeming, suddenly, to understand. "Is that what you're worried about? That I'm going to run away, or one day I'll wish I had? Mads, I haven't given a single thought to travelling since . . . I can't remember the last time I thought about it. I know this is all happening so quickly, but my heart is here, with you. I really hope you'll believe me. It'll break me if you don't. I wish I could bottle up the way I feel and show it to you somehow. You'd never have to ask me if I was yours ever again if you could physically see it in front of you. I promise."

There was something so desperate in the way he was talking to her, as though he might explode if she didn't believe him. It was exactly the tone she needed, exactly what she had been hoping for. She really, truly believed he had changed his mind, and of his own accord. She grabbed his hands, still pressed against her face, and nodded. "Then I'm yours," she said, smiling a little stupidly. James grinned goofily, and Maddie knew, in that moment, they were the two happiest idiots on the planet.

* * *

She had thought she'd want to get out and roam the streets of Ware with James, but when she saw their room at the Velvet, she understood why he'd booked the restaurant downstairs. The hotel was small, with only six bedrooms. Theirs was on the third floor of the tall, narrow townhouse. It was painted a deep, royal blue, and had a four-poster bed and a freestanding tin bath set before two giant windows. They looked out over the high street.

"We can give people a show later, if you like," James quipped. Maddie laughed, running her hands across the oak furniture and admiring the art on the walls. There were long candles set in brass candleholders dotted around the room, and a teeny, tiny log burner in one corner. The bed covers looked thick, heavy and expensive.

"James, this is too much," Maddie said, overwhelmed.

"Do you like it?" he asked. Maddie nodded, touched by the thought he must have put into choosing somewhere he knew she would like. "Then it's not too much," he said, dropping their bags and joining her at the window. Maddie caught sight of a flash of red and tracked a robin with her eyes. It landed on the sill and stared through the window, hopping happily from side to side. She smiled and turned to James, who was also watching the robin, no doubt whimsically concluding this was a visit from his own brother in the same way she was adamant it was a message from hers.

She squeezed his arm to get his attention and gazed up at him. "It must have cost a fortune," she said.

"Stop, please." He reached for her hand. "I wanted to treat you."

Maddie felt a little guilty, but she also couldn't help but beam. Internally resolving to take him away somewhere at her expense as soon as she could, she stood on her tiptoes and pressed her lips to his, snaking her arms around his waist and pulling his body close to her own. James wrapped his arms around her shoulders and they stood like that for a good few minutes, connected everywhere, kissing greedily. As they did, Maddie marvelled at how happy she felt and how quickly things had turned around. Just a few short months ago, she had been lonely, anxious and lacking hope. She felt like a brand-new person, like anything was possible, and the future was no longer a means to distract herself from the pain of the past, but something to look forward to.

Eventually, James pulled away. "I hate to break this up because I am actually gagging for you, but I'm also starving," he said.

"Quickie?" Maddie suggested. His eyebrows shot up in surprise, and she felt a flicker of excitement course through his body, his desire pressed against her torso. He pushed her back towards the bed, grinning. They toppled upon it, giggling happily, their bodies entangled. James set about undressing her immediately, ripping off her jeans and pulling down his own trousers, his urgency evident in the pace of his breath and the speed of his actions. She, too, was breathless with desire. She manoeuvred him away from foreplay and insisted he enter her immediately, moaning with relief when he complied. Despite their agreement, their sex was not quick, it was slow, tender and passionate. Maddie hadn't thought this side of their relationship could get any better, but their conversation in the car had freed something within her, and the romantic setting — the mood lighting, the privacy, the luxurious bed — added to the intensity of the experience. The sex lasted well over an hour, but Maddie didn't want it to end. She couldn't get enough of him. The moment his body left hers, she wanted him back again.

"I promise we can do it all night," James said. "But I need feeding or I won't have the energy."

Maddie laughed at that and it made him smile. They re-dressed quickly. As they did, Maddie worked hard to squash a feeling of foreboding, a concern bubbling up from somewhere deep within her, determinedly trying to douse her fiery happiness. She had barely known this man for four weeks, but she was falling in love with him, and he with her. She was heading for a level of happiness she had never dared dream she'd know. She only wished it was with a man who hadn't wanted something else with such mad passion so recently. It didn't make her feel safe. Maddie had no fear of James cheating on her or disrespecting her in any way — if he did either of those things she would hurl him out of her life in a heartbeat — but she *was* worried she would hold him back and he would grow to resent her. She was concerned she had accidentally presented him with an ultimatum that, if he stuck to his original plan to live abroad most of the time their relationship would end, and so — while languishing blissfully deep in the throes of obsession that so often comes with a budding romance — he felt like he had no choice but to stay here and foster it. Perhaps he even wanted to. Her concern was that he would regret doing so when the novelty wore off.

"Ready?" He interrupted her deep thinking. Maddie nodded, smiling at his reflection in the mirror. He stared at her for a few seconds, as though it was the first time he'd ever laid eyes on her, before marching determinedly towards her and wrapping his arms around her from behind. He pulled her close. "God, you're so gorgeous," he said, his breath against her neck. She felt him harden, his erection pressed against her bum.

"Stop." Maddie groaned. "Or we'll never get out."

He kissed her then held out his hand for her to take. They made their way to the restaurant downstairs.

* * *

They both chose pasta dishes. Maddie opted for a tomato-based bake, James selected a vegetarian creamy mushroom and courgette carbonara. Maddie chose the wine, a bottle of red, and they settled in by the fire, the only two punters in the Velvet's quaint, kitschy restaurant. Because he was hungry, James ordered bread with vinegar and olive oil, then he fidgeted impatiently, his face twisted in discomfort.

"I haven't eaten all day," he explained. "I was so nervous about our chat tonight, I couldn't stomach anything."

"Why?" Maddie asked. She knew why she'd been nervous — she'd had no idea how he was going to answer her questions about him travelling — but she was sure she'd been clear about how she felt about him, so she didn't understand why he'd be worried.

"I don't know." He shrugged, thoughtfully. "Actually, I do. I've never asked anyone to be my girlfriend before. You've never made me worry about how you feel about me, so it's not that, but I've also never been in a situation where I could be rejected and I'd be bothered."

Maddie tutted. "That must be nice," she said.

"Sorry." He shrugged.

"Pretty privilege." Maddie sighed, shaking her head.

"Fuckboyery, more like," James said, wincing in clear mental discomfort. "I was so ordinary at school, so gawky and awkward. Invisible, really. I don't know what the hell happened when I went to university, but suddenly girls found me attractive. I grew into my looks, I guess. Started dressing better, smelling better. I didn't know how to deal with it and I didn't bother to learn for a long time. I just did what I wanted and never thought about the consequences. I'd spent so long feeling miserable in the wake of Harry's death and because of my issues with Mum, I just didn't care about anything but myself. The way I look helped bring people to me, sure, but that wasn't what made me push them away. I've done some things I'm not proud of. Ghosting and the like. I had no business messing around with anyone, given my insides were all over the place. When I think about it now, it makes me feel terrible."

"Hard to disagree," Maddie said. "It's easy to remain emotionally avoidant and push people away when you're fit and you know the next one isn't too far away."

James thought about that. "You're right, I reckon," he conceded.

Maddie thought they would scoff down their dinner and run back upstairs, but they took their time. They indulged in dessert — sticky toffee pudding for Maddie and a crème brulée for James — then he ordered an Irish coffee and she opted for a cappuccino made with oat milk. When they were done, the waiter asked if they'd like another bottle of wine, and they decided on a whim, since the restaurant was empty, to curl up by the fire with it and chat. Concerned by how much he had spent on the trip, Maddie insisted on paying for dinner. When they'd settled the tab, James settled himself on the comfiest-looking sofa, opening his arms so that she could nestle in the nook between the top of his chest and his shoulder.

"So," he said, sighing happily. "When — and how — are we telling everyone?"

Maddie groaned. As happy as she was that things were finally sorted out between them — that they were doing this, without a doubt — she was not looking forward to her brothers and her parents finding out about her secret relationship. Her parents would be ecstatic, her brothers, too, actually, but there was almost certainly a significant amount of teasing to come. For a while, they would make her and James the centre of attention, the butt of all jokes, and, albeit for a nice reason, Maddie was dreading it.

"Tomorrow?" she suggested. James looked surprised, but he nodded, happily. Maddie grinned. She hoped her urgency might banish any fears he had that she was embarrassed by him. Although she was very much enjoying where they were at, there was a part of her that longed for the future, for a time when she didn't yearn for the weight of James upon her every moment of every day. A time when they were just James and Maddie. Maddie and James. A time when there were no surprises associated with their togetherness, because it was old, certain, and accepted. She hoped one day someone might consider her experienced, might ask her for advice the way she sought support from Autumn. She was so close she could feel it, she just needed to take the plunge.

* * *

They were up half the night, so they slept in late, leaving the hotel exactly on check-out time. They put the bags in the car and then strolled, hand in hand, around Ware. They stopped for a coffee and some breakfast, munching on vegan pastries as they browsed Ware's tiny gift shops and bookstores.

"In the next bookshop we go to, I'll give you five minutes to choose five books and I'll buy them for you," James said. Maddie laughed.

"Why only five minutes?" she asked. "And, while we're at it, why only five books?"

"Because it's fun," he said. "It'll force you to make quick decisions. Perhaps you'll end up reading something you never expected."

"You're just sick of browsing, aren't you?" she teased.

"No," he said, in a tone that made clear he was lying.

"Are there no books you fancy?" she asked.

"I don't really read," he said. She eyed him, pointedly. "All right, I never read. I don't think I've read a book since school."

"You really don't know what you're missing," she told him. "To be fair, Marley never used to read, either, until Autumn got him into it. Now he constantly has his nose in a book."

"Maybe you'll do the same for me. Slowly morph me away from 'guitar man' and turn me into 'book man'."

Maddie tittered at that, though she was thoughtful. "You can be both. I'm still not sure I like the reduction of any of us down to our hobbies," she said.

"Me neither." James shrugged. "When I first came up with that concept, I was just trying to find a way to let you know I play guitar."

Maddie laughed. "And that you weren't a podcaster?" she added.

"Exactly that." He grinned. "With this curly barnet and the Chelsea boots and the travel, I do give off podcaster vibes. I didn't want you to get the wrong impression."

"It worked," she said, stopping outside a small, dimly lit second-hand bookshop. "Five minutes and five books, you said?"

James held up his hand to corroborate the numbers, eyeing his fingers playfully. "Not a second longer and not a single extra book," he said, warningly. "Your time starts when you enter the store.

"Right," Maddie agreed to the terms. "Are you ready, then?"

James nodded, checking his watch.

"Ready?" he said, watching the second arm approach twelve. "Go!"

* * *

They moseyed on home in the early afternoon. Maddie desperately wanted an extra night in Ware with James, but she knew their joint absence over two nights would raise suspicion beyond all reasonable doubt, and, for some reason, she felt like she should tell her parents herself what was happening between them. As they pulled up into the driveway, she saw Autumn's car parked outside and found herself hoping Marley wasn't there, not because she didn't want him to know, but because she'd rather stagger this revelation out.

Her parents were sitting in the kitchen with Autumn and Bluebell, each nursing a coffee. They stopped talking when James and Maddie entered, and Maddie got the distinct impression they had just been talking about the two of them.

"Hey, guys, how was the garden centre?" Autumn asked. Maddie recognised immediately that this was the excuse she had given as to why Maddie wasn't with her and Bluebell, and why she and James were returning to the house together. She didn't have the heart to lie. Luckily, James did.

"It was crap," he said. "We didn't get anything at all."

Maddie's parents stared pointedly at her, and she couldn't help it. She smiled. Her reaction made her mother's mouth twitch, and Maddie lost her composure completely. She rolled her lips in on themselves to try and stop herself from laughing, but it was no use. Autumn and Bluebell, diligently committed to the facade, did a great job of pretending they were confused, but her parents were ignoring them, folding their arms and shaking their heads in what Maddie knew was jest. She felt James' eyes upon her and, though she couldn't see him, knew, somehow, he was grinning, too.

"Which centre did you go to, James?" Emma asked.

"One in Ware," he said.

251

"Gulliver's?" Emma asked. Maddie knew this was a trap. James nodded. "That's the one."

Emma sat forward, pouring herself another coffee from the cafetière. "There is no garden centre called Gulliver's in Ware." She picked up her mug.

Maddie could no longer hold in her laugh. She guffawed dramatically, covering her mouth with her hand, embarrassed. James winced at being caught out, but was clearly amused. Maddie turned to look at him, and they stared at each other for a moment, breaking their gaze only when Maddie shrugged. She turned back to her parents. It was now or never.

"James and I are seeing each other," she said.

Emma clapped her hands and did a little squeak. "I knew it." She nudged Ben with her elbow. "Didn't I say something was going on between them?"

Ben nodded. He was staring at Maddie. His mouth was set in a smile, but there was something else behind his eyes. Concern.

"I'm so happy," Emma said. "Oh, you should have told us before! You know how much we love you, James."

Maddie rescued him. "We just wanted to keep it between us for a while."

"I bet these two knew." Emma gestured with her eyes to Autumn and Bluebell. Both women grinned.

"Fair play to you two," James said. "Keeping it secret all this time."

"Goes without saying," Bluebell said. "What happens in your relationship stays between you two and the two of us."

Everyone laughed heartily, and then, since she wasn't sure what she should do, Maddie took a seat at the table and poured herself a cup of coffee. James followed suit, and the table settled into comfortable silence. Maddie knew the questions would come, but that her parents didn't want to overwhelm her. They knew she hated being the centre of attention and wouldn't react well to a barrage of questions. Still, they would be coming. She could see it in her mother's eyes and, most worryingly, in her father's stance. Ben was still staring at her, his eyes still bursting with worry.

Whatever it was he had to say, it was serious.

* * *

Later that afternoon, after James had gone home, Maddie made sure she was alone somewhere her father could find her. She did a little bit of work arranging furniture and planning content for her social media platforms, and by five o'clock she was sitting in the orangery with a book and a cup of tea, waiting for her father to come in and check the strawberry plants. Maddie rarely ventured into the orangery. It was a new room and therefore one of the only rooms that had already been done — if she disregarded a couple of stone flower beds Pigglesworth had damaged that she still needed to fix — so there was hardly any need for her to frequent it. Ben was surprised to find her there.

"Hello, my darling," he said, feigning nonchalance.

"Pops." She nodded, folding the page on her book and putting it down. She watched her dad checking the vines, and felt as though her heart might burst. It was Maddie's sincere belief that Ben was the greatest man who had ever existed. He was quiet, kind and gentle, a logical and clever man, who'd do anything for anyone if it would make their lives better. Maddie was too young to remember when Ben had met Emma, but from what she'd heard — mainly from Bowie and Marley — his positioning as their stepfather had been slow and measured. He'd treated them sensitively and cautiously, starting as a friend of their mother's, then progressing to a friend of theirs, winning their trust and respect by taking things slowly, treating them respectfully, communicating openly, and never wavering from the commitment he'd made to always be there for them. Over time, they had grown to love him, started calling him Dad of their own accord, and stopped telling people he was their stepfather. Throughout

Bowie's illness, Ben had behaved perfectly, expertly walking the line between being there for Bowie and doing what was best for him, while also supporting his devastated mother and siblings through their turmoil and grief. Everyone felt incredibly lucky to have him, and Maddie did, too. She watched him pretending to care about the plants when she knew they were the furthest thing from his mind today.

She prompted him. "What's happening, Dad?"

He sighed and dropped his facade, turning to her, a strained grin on his face. "You always did know me well, my love." He sat beside her on the wicker sofa. Maddie didn't say anything. She didn't need to. "I suppose it's just that I've never seen you look like that." He clasped his hands. "So happy. Giddy, actually. It . . . scared me."

"Why?" Maddie asked, knowing the answer already.

"I don't want him to break your heart." He shrugged, wincing guiltily.

"What makes you think he'll do that?" She was aware she sounded nervous, but couldn't help herself. She, too, was terrified she'd end up heartbroken. She trusted her father's opinion, so she wanted to know if he thought that was a likely outcome and, if he did, what he was basing it on.

"Nothing at all," he said, smiling warmly. "Just a father's fear, I suppose. I hope you won't feel patronised. I used to have the same concerns every time there was a chance Bowie might get hurt. He was soft and gentle, like you. Marley, Pip and Bluebell . . . they're wild and strong. You're just like Bowie. You walk heart-first into everything you do. Your gentle side is so exposed, it makes me worry sometimes."

Maddie nodded, reaching for his hand. "James is a good man, Dad."

"Oh, I know," Ben said, confidently. They slipped into a comfortable silence, lost in their own thoughts. Maddie wasn't sure what her father was thinking, but she was wondering how long it would take to move past this part of the relationship process. She was eager for enough time to have passed for these fears her family had — that she'd get hurt — to be quelled. She wanted them to be as confident and happy about her and James as she was. Eventually, Ben shattered the silence. "Has he changed his mind about travelling, or have you agreed he'll go away and you'll stay together?" Ben asked.

"Perhaps I'm going with him?" Maddie teased. Her father chuckled, knowingly shaking his head. "He's staying," she said.

Ben nodded, clearly satisfied. "I'm sorry if my reaction in the kitchen alarmed you." He stood up, readying himself to leave. "You're a smart woman, Maddie. Every decision you make is measured and careful. I know you know what's right for yourself, and I'm pleased to say I agree with you. James is a charming young man, and it's clear as day he's crazy about you. As long as you're happy, my darling girl, I'm happy, too."

Maddie gazed up at him, grateful. "I'm so happy I could die, Dad," she said, a little breathless. It was not like Maddie to share how she felt so candidly, but she knew her father needed to hear it. He understood that making her happy was no easy task. It never had been, but it was even harder in the wake of Bowie's passing. She'd floundered in the depths of despair, then dragged herself into numbness, where she'd planned to stay. James had pulled her out of the purgatory she'd been languishing in. Maddie knew her father would understand how difficult that had been, and how special it made James.

She was right. Ben smiled, his eyes softening with the sincerity of her words. "And it's about damn time you were." Maddie grinned back. She saw his fears dissipate, his shoulders relax, the tension fall from his features. She nodded reassuringly and he turned, jaunting happily from the room.

CHAPTER SEVENTEEN

The next four weeks passed in a blur of drama that started and ended with Marley. Maddie's brother predictably over-reacted to the news she and James were dating. He swung wildly between teasing them and warning James not to hurt his little sister. Marley repeatedly checked that Maddie was happy, that James was taking care of her, and that Maddie's new boyfriend understood the complexities of her mind, how sensitive she was, and how unlike her it was to let someone new into her life. Maddie reassured him over and over again. She was happy. James was taking care of her. He knew exactly who she was, how delicately they were held together and how easy it would be to ruin it all. He cared about her, she was sure he would not risk ruining anything. He would not embarrass her. Her heart would remain intact. Marley could relax.

James took the whole thing in his stride, repeatedly reas-suring Marley that he adored Maddie. He had been unsure about the course of his life before, but had made up his mind now — this was what he wanted.

"If you want to know my intentions, mate, it's to stay here and fall so deeply in love with your sister I have no choice but to marry her," he said, one afternoon over coffee. Maddie blushed. Autumn, Emma and Bluebell cooed.

Marley glanced at Ben, clearly still uncertain. Ben grinned and shrugged his shoulders. "I know you know what that feels like." He gestured towards Autumn with his head.

"I know. I'm sorry I'm so tense about the whole thing," Marley addressed his whole family then turned to James. "It's none of my business, I get it, but it's just that you were so sure you wanted to go travelling before . . ."

"What better reason is there for a man to change the course of his life than for the love of a woman?" Autumn interrupted.

"That's pretty, who said that?" Marley asked, presuming she was quoting a book or a movie.

Autumn looked confused. "I did," she said. Everyone giggled.

"Sorry," Marley mumbled. "Sometimes I forget you're a writer."

Autumn continued. "Just look at you, Marley. Nobody could have predicted you would settle down — ever — let alone that you'd give up the stage for me."

"That's true." Marley pondered a moment and then shrugged, trying to hide a smirk. "I guess I presumed there were no other men as cool as I am."

"Well, clearly you were wrong," James said, his chest swelling.

"Chill out, both of you," Bluebell scolded. "Women give up their careers and their dreams for men and their children all the time. You're doing what would be considered the very bare minimum if Autumn and Maddie were to do it and I, for one, think you would be stupid *not* to be doing it, given you are both punching so far out of your leagues it's quite frightening. If you want to be congratulated for making a common-sense decision, you're in the wrong kitchen."

Marley and James visibly deflated. The women in the room laughed. From across the kitchen, James caught Maddie's eye and winked. She grinned. There was no doubt in her mind at all, this man knew her. She was in good hands.

* * *

257

Later that day, Marley found Maddie upstairs painting furniture and picked up a paintbrush to help. She knew he had come to talk to her, and she vowed she would let him, only because she knew he felt like he needed to. They painted in silence until he summoned the courage.

"I love you so much," he started, smiling warmly. Maddie nudged him affectionately with her elbow, wrinkling her nose in gratitude. Marley sighed, continuing. "Since what we went through with Bowie, that night we helped him say goodbye . . ."

He stopped, his voice cracking with the strain of his words. Maddie dropped her paintbrush and put her arms around him, forcing him into a hug.

"I know the impact that had on you," he murmured, squeezing her tight. "I know why you did it and I'll never regret it — it was the right thing to do. But I also know you martyred your own mental health for Bowie. You're the type of person who'd do absolutely anything for the people you love. It's so beautiful, there's such strength in that, but there's also weakness. I guess I'm just trying to make sure you're putting your heart in the right hands."

Maddie held him tighter for a moment, then pulled away. "What do you think?" she asked him, already knowing the answer.

"James is great." Marley threw her a floppy smile. "But nobody will ever be good enough for my hero of a sister."

Maddie winced. She hated it when he called her a hero. She knew his heart was in the right place, but she did not feel heroic for helping Bowie to end his life. She'd merely done what she needed to do for someone she loved — to free him from pain, fulfil his wishes and maintain his dignity. She would do it again, or variations of it, and if she would do *that* then Marley was right, there was absolutely nothing she wouldn't do for someone she loved, even if it hurt her heart, or meant she never got to see them again, or harmed her own mental health. She wasn't this way because she wanted to be a hero, it was just that when she loved someone, she loved them incredibly deeply.

"Does James know?" Marley asked, pulling her from her thoughts. Maddie vigorously shook her head. They had sworn they would never tell anyone, that the way Bowie had died would remain between the three of them: Maddie, Marley and Autumn. Maddie intended to keep that promise, no matter how hard she fell in love. She couldn't risk her parents finding out, or Bluebell, or Pip. They would never forgive her, she was sure of it. "Good," Marley said, sighing out obvious relief.

They sat side by side in the bedroom for a moment, engulfed in comfortable silence. Maddie was thinking mostly of James, of how lucky she felt to have found another good man to add to the good men she already knew, how safe she felt, how ordinary.

Marley continued. "You know, when James' brother died, Bowie offered to teach him guitar."

Maddie did know this. James and Marley had both told her several times, but she smiled and nodded and let him continue anyway, just because she liked hearing the story. It made her feel like things had come full circle.

"We felt really sorry for the kid. He was back at school within a couple of days, covered in stitches on his face and hands. Everyone was staring and asking him questions. Bowie invited him to sit with us in the sixth-form common room and told anyone who came near him to fuck off."

"Bowie did that?"

"Well, actually, the fuck off part might have been me," Marley admitted. "That's when Bowie started teaching him guitar at breaktime and in his lunch break. I'm so glad he kept learning after we left. It's so lovely, isn't it, having a little bit of Bowie's kindness left behind in someone else? But anyway, my point is that Bowie loved him then and he would have loved him now, if he were here."

Maddie agreed with that. "They'd get on really well."

"And he'd leave you alone about it," Marley added.

"He would," Maddie said, rather pointedly.

"He was a wiser man than me." Marley sighed.

Maddie nodded. "He was." Marley glared at her, feigning offence. Maddie hit his arm playfully. They chuckled, content with the truth. Bowie had been the wisest of them all, perhaps with the exception of Ben, who had taught their brother by example. Everyone who met Ben commented on his impeccable character, and those who had known Bowie had similar things to say. They were, undoubtedly, the best men most people had ever met.

"'What would Bowie do?'," Marley said. "I ask myself that every time I need guidance. I think it's served me well so far. It's changed my perspective. Helped me be a better boyfriend and father, and hopefully a better brother, too. It's extraordinary, when you think about it. Autumn's happy, Benjamin's happy, and it's all because of Bowie. He lives on in me through that, I think."

"It's not *all* because of Bowie. I'm sure you had *something* to do with it," Maddie teased, enjoying this brand-new take on things anyway. "But, out of interest, what's Bowie telling you to do now?"

Marley thought about that, his face suddenly extremely serious. "To leave you alone and make a brew." He stood up. "Do you want one?"

* * *

"Come for a drink with your mummies," Emma suggested one afternoon. January had rolled into February, and Maddie and James were hard at work on their hands and knees fixing the flower beds in the orangery. They had been working pretty much non-stop this past month and had done almost everything they needed to do. They had, together, sanded the porch and painted it, fixed the furniture and given it a new lick of paint, mapped out the garden so that they knew where the flower beds and benches would go, added new soft

furnishings — second-hand and vintage where possible —
to every room, posted job ads for yoga instructors and massage therapists, preened the lawn, built the pond, stocked the
pantry with non-perishables, created a menu of easy, healthy
recipes and determined what shopping they would need to
produce them. They still had two months to go until opening.
Maddie had her first and second batch of guests ready and
waiting to attend, plus a waiting list for future dates. And
they were ahead of schedule. That didn't mean Maddie wasn't
nervous, though. So, while she really wanted to go for a coffee
with Emma, James and Jennifer, she felt tied to the house.

"I don't know . . ." She looked to James for support. She
could tell he wanted to go — he'd been suggesting a meet-up
of this kind for a while — but she also knew he was aware how
stressed she was and would let her make the decision. She was
right, he merely shrugged.

"You can have one afternoon off," Emma insisted. She
held out Maddie's jacket, which she had obviously brought
with her from the kitchen.

"That's very presumptuous of you, Mum."

"It's a mum's prerogative to presume our children will
spend time with us when we demand it, especially when we're
feeling neglected," Emma said.

Maddie rolled her eyes. "Emotional manipulation. Nice."

Emma threw them a strained smile. "James wants to
come, don't you, James?"

"No," James said, but Maddie felt him nodding vigorously beside her. She tried not to find that funny, but she
couldn't help it. She smiled, biffing him on the arm with the
back of her hand.

"Come on!" he whined. "We can go for an hour or two."

"Please!" Emma pleaded. "I never get to see you anymore."

Maddie eyed her mother with mild amusement. Emma
was right — they'd hardly spent any time together recently.
When Maddie wasn't working she was nurturing her fledg-
ling romance with James. She did miss her mum. Still, she

faltered again, her eyes sliding between James and Emma, who both had their hands pressed together in a pleading gesture. "Oh, all right." She sighed, trying to hide her grin when James jumped up in the air and whooped. He held his hand out to help her up. "Two hours only," she warned.

"You're the boss," James said, as they headed for the door.

* * *

Ten minutes later, Maddie, James and Emma were strolling down the lane towards their sleepy village. To her surprise, Maddie began enjoying herself immediately. Her never-ending to-do list was forgotten — instead, the weight of James' hand in hers, the quiet stillness of the wintry lane and the promising hints of spring in the air flooded her senses and lifted her spirits. Her eyes chased a flash of red and she smiled. A robin was following them, hopping from branch to branch, chirping excitedly as he went. Maddie smiled, hoping that James might catch sight of it. They often bantered about the robin in her garden, about whether it was Bowie's spirit or Harry's. In the end she nudged him, gesturing with her head. He caught her eye, mouthed 'Harry', and grinned when she shook her head.

Maddie forced herself to tune in to her mother, who was chewing over her concerns about Benjamin entering show business. Maddie felt her nerves flood back. Benjamin had auditioned twice for a part in a play being directed by an old friend of Bowie's, Larry Ross. He was so excited he couldn't stop talking about it. Neither could Marley, who was now effectively a full-time, stay-at-home dad and chaperone.

"I think Marley thought he'd be bored," Emma was saying. "But he says he's as busy at home as he was at work."

Maddie had heard the same thing from Autumn. Now that she was the sole financial provider for the family, Marley had taken on the responsibility for all the household chores, giving Autumn more time to work. She also found she had more free time, which meant she had more time to spend on her own and with the people she loved. Their new life meant Autumn and Marley were more present at the big house than they had ever been. Though Maddie was busy, she loved having people she cared about close by and often stopped to appreciate the buzz of the house, since she knew it wouldn't last long. Emma, Ben and Bluebell had started excitedly planning their travelling adventures. They would head somewhere in Europe first, somewhere sunny and busy, then perhaps fly further afield. Ben and Emma had set aside the big suitcases in preparation and started making sure Maddie had everything she would need to keep the house going — they'd added her to the accounts for all bills and given her a list of vendors she could call if things went wrong. Maddie knew her parents felt better that Autumn and Marley were close by and would keep popping in. They also knew she had James, and despite the fact it was still early days, they often commented on how happy she seemed, usually while gushing about what a nice man James was.

Maddie refocused on her mum, who had hardly paused for breath since they'd left the house. "I'm having such a lovely time building a friendship with your mum, James. It's so much harder to make friends when you're older, isn't it?"

Maddie nodded, and felt James squeeze her hand supportively. This was something the two of them had spoken about, especially in light of James' growing friendship with Marley, who'd had lots of fickle friends he spent arbitrary time with every now and then, but nobody he was exceptionally close to, until he'd met James. He'd had a built-in best friend in Bowie, so he'd never felt the need to build platonic relationships with anyone else when his brother had been alive, and he hadn't had the heart to do so since Bowie had died. James hadn't given Marley much of a choice, though. Their shared interests and similar sense of humour had glued them together, and the two built a firm, fast friendship. They were so close, Marley had asked James to be a groomsman when he married Autumn. Maddie would be lying if she said she wasn't jealous. She wished someone might come along with whom she could connect with in that way. She loved her family and considered Autumn and Bluebell her friends as well as her relatives, but she was very aware she had nobody besides them. When she was out and about, her eyes would wander to groups of women giggling girlishly together, and she would wish she had a group of women she could do the same with. She had no idea where she'd meet a friend now, as she was certain most women already had their forever friends by the time they reached her age. Still, she knew she should do something about it. She had an incredible support network — a great family and a loving boyfriend — but there was something special about female friends, and while she could confide absolutely anything in Bluebell and Autumn, the fact they were all connected to the same family meant it wasn't quite the same.

Emma interrupted her deep thinking. "You should put yourself out there a bit more," she said. "I know you're shy, my love, but you're such a lovely girl. If you were in the right place at the right time a little more often, you'd meet some fabulous friends."

"Hard agree," James said, squeezing her hand again.

Maddie thought about reminding them she was about to launch a business. She was going to be busier than she'd ever been in her life, so she'd have less time than ever to make new friends. Her dad had also recently advised her to stop trying to get to the end of her to-do list, as it would never end now she was a business owner. She didn't have the energy to say all this, so she nodded and smiled. James squeezed her hand for a third time, and she knew he was reading her mind.

"Don't forget, you have me now," he said. "I'll be here to help with things, and you can have some of your life back."

Maddie grinned, nudging him gratefully. They hadn't yet talked about how this would work, but she had hoped he'd want to work alongside her to make this business a success. She was thrilled to hear him say that was his plan, too. The future looked fun and exciting. That made Maddie feel warm and fuzzy inside.

* * *

Jennifer was seated at a table in the café waiting for them when they arrived. She was thrilled to see Maddie and James, who she hadn't known were coming. She stood to give them each a hug, holding her son for slightly longer than she did the others. Their growing bond delighted Maddie because she knew how important it was to James. He talked regularly about the chats they were having and the barriers they were breaking down between them. He insisted their relationship had never been better, that his mother was willing to listen to any criticism he had of her past parenting with an open mind, and that he was confronting his own flaws when she raised them with him. Maddie had not realised at the time, but the weight of his crumbling relationship with Jennifer had weighed heavily on James. She could tell because he was different now — his laugh was lighter, his eyes brighter and he hardly ever frowned. Seeing them hug in this way, as though there had been no turmoil between them, made Maddie indescribably happy.

"Sit down," James said, pulling out two chairs for Maddie and Emma. "I'll go and order. Soya cappuccinos?"

"Yes please," they answered together.

"Good boy," Jennifer said, grinning with pride. She watched Maddie take her gloves off and blow into her hands. "I cannot wait for this rotten weather to break," she said, shaking her head in sympathy.

"Oh, tell me about it," Emma agreed. "Maddie likes to walk in the evenings, so she really struggles in the winter because she can't trudge the streets at nine o'clock at night."

Maddie theatrically stuck out her bottom lip, nodding sadly. It was true, she was never her best self in winter, and that was partly because her favourite form of exercise was undoubtedly walking. She loved the snow when it came, the way it glistened in the sunlight and crunched under her boots, and she liked crisp winter mornings. But she hated the dark because she never felt safe, so her evening walking ceased as the darkness expanded between autumn and winter — a thick, black, heavy blanket across an otherwise enchanted landscape.

"You should get yourself a dog," Jennifer said. "Most of them are daft as rags these days, but they offer a little protection, at least. A dog would make someone think twice, I reckon."

"That's a good idea," Maddie said. "We have Stevie, of course. I could walk her in the dark, I suppose, though I'm not sure she'd be much good if someone attacked me."

Emma laughed. "She might kiss them to death," she said, clearly doubtful.

Maddie smiled, content. For the first time in a long time, she felt as though things were moving mostly in the right direction, towards a happiness she finally felt she deserved. James' promise, mere minutes ago, to stand beside her and help make the business work had doused her remaining nerves. She knew what she was doing and where she was heading. She felt capable and strong.

Unbeknown to her, Maddie was sitting in a 'time before' moment. She had no way of knowing that everything was about to change. When she thought about it later, she'd swing wildly between wishing she'd never been so deluded and being glad that she had been, at least for a little while, more content within a relationship than she'd ever thought possible.

When Jennifer replied, she spoke her words pointedly. "Yes, but you won't have her for very much longer. When James goes away, he'll take her with him."

Maddie's heart somehow sank and quickened at the same time. She felt like it was beating backwards, as though it were trying desperately to go back in time. She felt her mother bristle beside her and knew Emma was seeking her gaze, but Maddie didn't dare look at her. She didn't want to make it obvious she was devastated by Jennifer's assumption James was still planning on leaving, either because he hadn't bothered to tell her he wasn't, or because there really was some separate, secret plan to go. While neither scenario was good, the first was obviously preferable, though that didn't make her feel at ease, either. As far as Maddie knew, things between James and Jennifer were great. There should be no reason he hadn't shared his plans for the future with her. She felt hollow, like someone had gouged out her insides, so when James returned and put a soya cappuccino and a red-berry croissant before her, she found them both so unappetising she had to stop herself from pointedly pushing them away.

"I got you a blueberry muffin, Mum," he said, returning to the counter to collect the rest of their order. Jennifer, who had not asked for food, nodded her appreciation to his back, her worried gaze settling on Maddie, who was quite sure she looked like she was going to be sick. She knew herself well enough to know what this would do to her. Any indication James was hiding anything from anyone would push her back into the safety of her solitude. He was back in seconds, settling himself in the seat opposite Maddie and beside his mother, so consumed by a giant raspberry-and-white-chocolate muffin he didn't notice the switch in the atmosphere at the table. He immediately set about devouring his sweet treat, pausing only to take little sips of his latte. Maddie couldn't bring herself to look at him, so she stared at a crumb on her plate, wishing she could return to 'the time before', swearing she would cling to it tenderly, fully appreciating its value and beauty. Her head was empty of all rational thought. She was catastrophising in a way she hadn't for over six years, back when life was bursting with uncertainty and every experience had been tiring and sad.

Eventually, Jennifer broke the silence. "I was just suggesting Maddie gets a dog to fill the gap when you and Stevie leave."

James froze, his mouth half full of food. His eyes darted immediately to Maddie, as she had known they would. She dared to meet his gaze, knowing he would read the fear etched in her expression. He chewed frantically, desperate to answer.

"I'm not going away," he said. There was only one right answer and that had been it, though it didn't make Maddie feel any better. This was an old conversation. She'd thought they'd moved past it, that everyone knew he was staying here and they were going to be together. Maddie's disappointment didn't shift. It lay heavy on her chest.

Jennifer stared at James, confused. "What do you mean, you're not going away?" she asked. "What about Italy? We were talking about it just the other day. You had that interview. You said they loved you!"

Maddie wanted to get up and walk out. She wanted to run through the streets and scream. She wanted to move to the woods and never see anyone again, or get in a boat and sail away. If she couldn't go back in time, she wanted to go forward six months from now, to a time when she would hopefully no longer feel the jumbled mess of emotions wreaking havoc with her blood pressure, leaving her feeling light-headed and weak.

"I told you not to mention this to anyone," James said.

Jennifer reeled. "I thought you'd have told them by now."

"I also told you it wasn't a sure thing," he said, his eyes still on Maddie. "That I probably wasn't going to do it."

"You said it was an incredible opportunity," Jennifer said.

James nodded pointedly. "I also said I don't want to leave Maddie."

"And *I* told *you* that if Maddie really loved you then you'd make it work," Jennifer said. "I said you'd be silly not to do it and we ended the conversation there. This is your dream, James. To travel and work. To live abroad, where every day is different. It's always been your dream."

James widened his eyes at his mother, pursing his lips in a pointed manner. Jennifer faltered, turning her attention back to Maddie.

"I'm sorry, I didn't mean to cause any drama. Maddie, darling, I thought you knew."

Maddie realised they were both telling the truth, but that didn't make her feel any better. She hadn't yet told James she loved him, but she did love him, and Jennifer's words were bouncing around in her brain.

'If Maddie really loved you then you'd make it work.'

"Oh, gosh, I'm so sorry," Jennifer said, her eyes bursting with concern. Maddie took stock of her facial features and realised she was dangerously close to crying. She blinked rapidly, shaking her head and trying to force a smile on her face, but she couldn't manage it. Beneath the table, she felt her mother grab her hand.

"Perhaps we should go," Emma said, squeezing. James nodded, moving to stand. "Just us," Emma said, her tone sharp. Her message was clear — *I want to talk to my daughter alone.*

James' eyes went wide. He stared straight at Emma, his gaze pleading. "This is a misunderstanding," he insisted, his voice cracking.

"I'm sure it is," Emma said, not unkindly.

James' eyes flickered to Maddie. "Oh, God, don't . . ." he whispered, breathless. He reached across the table, his palm outstretched, beseeching her to touch him. Maddie was reminded of the theatricality that first attracted her to him, but she kept her hands firmly under the table, where her mother's grip gave comfort. James wiggled his fingers, growing visibly frantic when she didn't respond. "Please don't," he said. "Yes, I had the interview, but only because I was curious. I wanted to see what would happen. This is a mistake, that's all."

Maddie nodded, swallowing hard. Beside her, Emma was texting someone. "Shall we go, darling?" she suggested, popping her phone back in her bag. Maddie nodded, letting go of her mother's hand. James shook his head, desperate, his own palm still open, his fingers splayed across the table like a sacrificial offering.

"I'll chase you if you leave," he said. "I'll get on my knees and beg, Maddie. I'll make a right dick of myself, I swear."

"Please, don't do that," Emma said, standing. "You know Maddie hates being the centre of attention. You can sort this out later, just the two of you. Right now, Maddie needs to go home."

Maddie took her mother's cue and stood, fumbling with her winter jacket and almost knocking over her abandoned cappuccino. James watched her. His expression dropped, his despair evident. His arm was still outstretched and he looked down to stare at the table. His mouth was slightly open, his hair stuck out the way it only did when he had run his fingers through it in frustration. He looked as far from his true self as he could possibly be — meek and small. That frightened Maddie in a way she hadn't been expecting. She'd never thought herself capable of destroying a man, but she could see now that she could ruin this one if she chose to. That might make some women feel good, feel safe, but it didn't make her feel that way. Instead, she felt the weight of the latest item added to her 'to-do' list — *Protect James' heart*.

"We'll talk later," she reassured him. He snapped to attention and gazed up at her hopefully.

"You're everything, Maddie," he said, choking on her name. Beside him, Jennifer put her head in her hands. Maddie nodded and faltered, as desperate to put some space between them as she was to hold him in her arms. She'd never felt so confused. Luckily, she had Emma to guide her. Her mother grabbed her hand and tugged her gently towards the door. Hand in hand, they left.

As she walked out of the door, she heard James draw in a breath, a tangible depiction of the torture he'd endure until he could make this right, and the worry he'd feel that he couldn't. It made her want to turn around, but instead she fell into step beside her mother, fat tears rolling down her cheeks. Through the haze of her despair, she could see Marley's car waiting on the corner. Her brother sat in the driving seat, watching them approach. Maddie wanted privacy, but she wasn't mad her mother had texted him — she didn't have the energy to walk home. She let Emma help her into the passenger seat. She avoided Marley's gaze. Mercifully, he didn't say anything. Instead he reached across to squeeze her hand, told her he loved her, then set off home.

CHAPTER EIGHTEEN

"Where's Autumn?" Maddie asked, more to make conversation than because she was genuinely curious. She was sitting at the kitchen table nursing an Irish coffee Marley had insisted she have. He'd just learned how to make them and wanted to show off his skills. Plus, he insisted she needed a stiff drink and a shot of caffeine, so this solved both problems. Maddie couldn't be bothered to explain she was yawning not because she was tired, but because she was on the verge of a panic attack and yawning was always the first symptom.

"She's taken Benjamin into London to meet Phil and Clara," Marley said.

"Bowie's old friends?" Emma asked, seeming surprised.

Marley nodded. "They've kept in touch over the years. We've seen them a few times. I didn't go this time because I am, quite frankly, exhausted."

Emma chuckled. "Stay-at-home parenting is not for the weak," she said, as though she had done it herself. Up until Bowie's illness had gotten so bad, when Emma could barely concentrate on anything else, she had been a drama teacher. She could have stayed at home if she wanted, but she had chosen to work because she loved her job.

"Tell me about it," Marley muttered. "It was easier when he was a baby, at least he stayed in one place. Do you know how many times he asked me 'why?' yesterday? Seventy-two." Maddie laughed in spite of herself. Her brother sighed and shook his head, visibly pleased he'd made her smile. She met his gaze and he smiled sadly, tilting his head to one side, clearly waiting for her to say something. When she didn't, he prompted her. "Whose arse do I need to kick?" He scratched at the kitchen table with his claw. "Please don't say James." He winced.

Maddie swallowed hard and nodded, unable to speak.

"What has he done?" His tone had changed. It was now low and threatening. The atmosphere was suddenly frosty, the frivolity gone. Maddie found herself feeling grateful. Truly, Marley would do anything for her. She could correct his spirit in a minute. She didn't need him to fight her battles for her, certainly not to get physical with anyone, but for a moment she basked in how protected her brother made her feel.

"It turns out he hasn't been completely honest with Maddie," Emma said.

"How, exactly?" Marley asked. Emma looked to Maddie to explain, but she felt too exhausted to say anything at all. She deferred with a nod back to Emma.

"It sounded to me like he's had some sort of interview and been offered some sort of opportunity in Italy and he'd expressed at least some desire to accept the offer to Jennifer. Does that sound about right, honey?"

Maddie nodded, forcing herself to elaborate. "We've already talked about this in so much detail. He was adamant he wanted to stay here. I've given him the option to go so many times, promised him we'd make it work if he did. I just feel . . ."

"Stupid," Marley muttered.

"Exactly," Maddie concurred.

"Not you, him!" There was something in the way Marley said it that made her take proper notice. He had inside information, Maddie was sure of it. She gave him her full attention.

"And me," he said, wincing a little guiltily. "He mentioned this to me a week or so ago. We had a bit of an argument about it, actually."

"Oh, Marley!" Emma said, her tone scolding.

"I know." He grimaced. "It's some agency he's been trying to work with for a while. Accommodation provided, a good salary, a visa, Italy in the summer, winter seasonal work in a chalet in Sweden if he wants it, a never-ending contract if he does a good job, destinations that change year-on-year, everything he's been working towards for years."

Marley stopped, his eyebrows knitted together in thought. Maddie felt she might hurl her mug at him if he didn't start speaking again soon.

"And?" Emma nudged him, frustrated.

"He said he'd had the interview just to see what would happen and they'd offered him the job. I was really mad he'd done that. I felt like he was going back on everything he'd promised you. I told him he shouldn't take the job."

"Did you get the impression he was going to go before you told him not to?" Maddie asked. This was the only part that was important to her. James and Marley were friends, so she didn't much care that James had confided in her brother, but she did care that her sibling's influence might have swayed his decision.

"I honestly don't know," he said. "He hadn't even fully gotten the words out before I was telling him it wasn't fair to leave you. I'm sorry, Maddie."

Emma rolled her eyes and shook her head. "You bloody idiot," she said. Marley nodded his agreement.

"You said you argued . . ." Maddie prompted, trying to maintain her composure. She was worried that if she showed him how upset and angry she was really feeling, Marley wouldn't tell her the whole truth, and she really needed to know what she was working with.

"Oh, yeah. He said that because he'd told me about it he was going to tell you about it, too, but I told him not to.

273

I thought it would make you nervous. He was adamant he should, but I told him it would make you jittery. In the end, he agreed I was right."

Maddie and Emma stared at Marley, their mouths agape. Maddie couldn't believe what she was hearing. It was not at all like her brother to get involved in her personal affairs. Not that she'd had many personal affairs for him to insert himself into, but, more generally, when it came to the private lives of his siblings, Marley was typically non-committal. Before this conversation, Maddie would have bet her own life Marley would have held up his hands and refused to comment had James brought something like this up with him. She couldn't believe it.

"Marley!" Emma admonished him once again.

"I know." He groaned, putting his head in his hands. "I'm so sorry. I thought I was doing the right thing. You've been so happy, Maddie. I've never seen you like this. I wished he hadn't told me and I wanted the whole thing to go away. This seemed like the best way to get rid of it."

"You bloody idiot," Emma repeated, wringing her hands in distress. "You've made this fifty-thousand times worse."

"I can see that," he said, eyeing Maddie sheepishly. "I was just trying to help."

"It was none of your business," Maddie said. She sounded calm, but she was seething. She knew he'd had her best interests at heart, but he had taken this entire situation to the point of no return. Now, Maddie could never be sure James had decided to stay because he wanted to. She would always wonder if her brother had swayed his decision. She felt sick.

"I'm so sorry," Marley said. "Truly, Maddie, I am. But I couldn't help myself. You've been so sad since Bowie died, I never thought I'd see you this happy. I've felt so useless these past few years, like I couldn't make you feel any better, and I guess this made me feel like I was doing something to help you. To protect you. I know it was wrong. I'm not trying to make excuses — I'm just trying to explain."

"None of what you said after the 'but' matters," Maddie said. Marley nodded. His eyes bored sorrowfully into hers.

"I'm sorry," he said again. Maddie sighed and nodded, cradling the dregs of her drink, which now tasted much more like whiskey than coffee. She took a moment to absorb what she was feeling. Betrayed. Infantilised. Misunderstood. Embarrassed. She had never in her life wanted space from her family the way she did right now. She contemplated packing a bag and walking away, never to be seen or heard from again. "Do you want me to leave?" Marley asked, his voice pitifully contrite.

"No." Maddie sighed. She was angry, but she couldn't bear the thought of casting Marley out, of sending him home. He'd done something stupid, but his intentions had been pure. He loved her, he'd been trying to protect her, but he'd overstepped the line. Maddie didn't need to lecture Marley on this. She knew he'd reflect and see it for himself. Failing that, Autumn would make sure he knew.

Right on cue, Marley groaned. "Autumn's going to kill me."

* * *

Later that evening, Maddie kept her promise and texted James, inviting him to the house to talk. She'd spent the last few hours sitting on her own in the orangery, mulling over how she was going to handle this. She knew James was going to insist it was all a big misunderstanding, that his earlier declaration still rang true: he had chosen to stay because it was what he wanted to do. He would tell her this new opportunity changed nothing, perhaps that Jennifer and Marley had blown their discussions out of proportion. He'd want to forget about it and move on, but Maddie knew she couldn't. She couldn't bear the idea she had kept him here. Trapped him. She loved him too much to do that.

From her spot in the orangery, she saw James trundle up the drive with Stevie Licks in tow. His head was low, his movements slow. He looked sad and scared, and she had to stop herself from jumping up and running to him. She forced herself to wait until he'd had enough time to get inside, then headed for the kitchen. She timed it just right. James was halfway across the room when she entered. He stopped, stock-still, clasping his hands together as though he was a naughty school child waiting for admonishment. She gestured towards the hallway and he nodded, waiting for her to lead the way, and followed close behind her, his footsteps heavy with fore-boding. Maddie was heading for the orangery, but as they passed Bowie's old bedroom, he grabbed her wrist, tugging for her to stop.

"Let's go in here?" he suggested.

Maddie was surprised. "I didn't think it was ready yet?"

"It's almost done. I really want you to see it. Please?"

Maddie relented, stepping cautiously towards the door. She already suspected she was going to be blown away. This was a cheap attempt by James to change the direction of the conversation by reminding her how thoughtful he was and how much effort he was willing to put into projects to make her happy. She should say no, but her curiosity got the better of her. James grinned and opened the door slowly and dramatically, standing back so she could enter first. She gasped. She was not disappointed.

He'd built a large bookcase from floor to ceiling, complete with compartments of various sizes for decorative impact. The casing curved around the room, so the bookcase continued between the top of the door frame and the ceiling, completely covering two walls. It was accessible by a sliding ladder, which Maddie could tell ran all the way around the room. She marched over to test it, sliding it backwards and forwards. She couldn't help herself, she beamed.

"How did you know I've always wanted one of these?" she asked.

He shrugged. "Women who love books always do," he said.

Maddie laughed softly, then turned to take in the rest of the room. In its centre sat a heavy-looking desk, fashioned from large slabs of tree trunk. It had been varnished a rich, mahogany brown. It was littered with trinkets, including a vintage banker's lamp, just like one she had commented on during their stroll around Ware.

"That's the actual lamp you liked. I went back and got it for you," James answered her questioning gaze. Maddie had thought as much. She nodded, turning her attention to several photo frames carefully arranged in one corner of the desk. She didn't dare look at their contents properly — Bowie was in several photographs and Maddie already knew they would make her cry. She admired a set of three wooden trinkets instead, each about the size of her fist. The first was a pig, the second a robin, and the third was a set of wooden bunk beds.

"I have some more to make," he told her. "I want to make a welly boot, to remind us of that day in the snow, and a little set of boxes with a carrot in them, to remind us of the time we played Carrot in a Box."

"Broccoli in a Box," she corrected him, trying and failing to suppress a smile. He chuckled, shrugging his shoulders.

"I can make a broccoli instead," he said. "I thought I could make them as we go through life, and you could add them to your new bookcase."

Maddie didn't know what to say. There was so much to take in. The rest of the room was tastefully painted a pretty light green, and decorated with patterned side tables, lamps with textured shades, floral vases and textured rugs. There was a squishy cream armchair that looked like it had been lovingly restored, dried flowers, a mantel clock with a ticking pendulum, and several plants of various sizes around it. It was beautiful. She took in a deep breath, searching for that familiar smell — the lingering scent of Bowie's cologne she was absolutely sure was in her head — and smiled when she found it. She was relieved. He was still here.

"Everything in here is second-hand," James said. "Rescued and repaired, just for you."

Maddie didn't know what to say. She turned on the spot in an attempt to take it all in. On her second lap, she noticed a hand-drawn, framed picture on one wall. She stepped towards it, and saw James tense.

"Benjamin drew that," he said. "I asked him for a picture of the house and this is what he came up with. I hope it doesn't upset you."

Maddie smiled as her eyes roamed over the drawing. She admired the house, and her family sitting on the porch. Pigglesworth Snortimer and Stevie Licks were there, as was James. There was another man in the garden, a blond man, drawn lighter than the others. His presence confused Maddie for a moment, then she realised it was Bowie. She gasped, and started to cry.

"Oh, no, please don't." James stepped towards her, reaching her in record time. He faltered before he touched her, clearly unsure if it was appropriate. She marched into his arms and held him tightly. "I didn't mean to upset you," he said, kissing the top of her head.

"You didn't," Maddie said, trying to compose herself. "I'm just overwhelmed."

James rocked her slowly from side to side, clinging to her like she might disappear. Maddie pressed her ear to his chest and allowed the thudding of his heart to soothe her. She felt herself calming down, the way she always did when he was close by. She cursed him inwardly, angry that she had to do what she had to do, and it was all his fault.

"You told me once this is where you come when you want to be close to Bowie," he said. "That you feel at peace here because you feel like he's nearby. I hope I've made this a comfortable place for you to enjoy feeling close to your brother."

"You have," Maddie said, stepping away from him. "Thank you so much. It's beautiful. I love it."

They stood face to face, staring at each other. The atmosphere cooled immediately. Things felt suddenly awkward, and Maddie knew it was because James could tell she was not reacting how she would if things were OK between them, which meant they still weren't. The room, though beautiful, had not been enough. He looked tense again, his shoulders pitched high, his face contorted with stress.

He prompted her. "Tell me." He looked like he might be about to cry.

"I want you to go travelling." Maddie felt guilty saying it. She knew she was betraying her heart, well aware he was about to argue the case for the exact opposite, but she was going to force him to do it anyway. She'd been thinking about it all afternoon and she could see she had no other choice. Letting him stay here when she'd come to believe there was a good chance he didn't want to was not an option. She was worried he would grow to resent her, that this love they shared would be poisoned by the experiences he hadn't had because she wouldn't go with him. He needed to go.

James shook his head. "No, you don't." He cleared his throat and Maddie knew he was trying to add some strength to his voice, though he looked meeker than she had ever seen him. "You don't want me to go, you just think I should," he corrected her. Maddie shrugged, too tired to argue. Both had the same outcome. There was no point in fighting about the terminology.

"If that makes it easier to swallow, then yes, I think you should go."

He blinked pointedly at her, leaning back slightly, as though trying to get a good look at her face. Maddie stood her ground. She straightened her features and held his gaze. She wanted him to know she was serious, that talking her into changing her mind was impossible. His gaze broke first.

"Don't do that," he said, running his hand through his hair.

"Do what?" she asked, genuinely confused.

"You're doing that thing you do."

"What thing?"

"Trying to protect me from the way you really feel by lying about it," he said. "I know you don't want me to go,

279

Maddie. But you're going to pretend you do because you think it's the best thing for me. Look, I know how hurt you were in the café. You felt like I'd kept something from you, like I'd told Mum something I hadn't told you . . ."

"Marley knew, too," Maddie pointed out. James sighed and put his head in his hands. He mumbled something, but Maddie didn't catch it. She continued. "So, yes, I felt pretty stupid. I have no qualms about saying that. And, no, I don't want you to go. I'm not going to pretend I do. But I still think you should."

"OK, so you're not doing the *exact* thing you usually do," he said, stepping away from her and starting to pace. "But just because you're not hiding your feelings doesn't mean you're not doing some variation of it. You're going to send me away for 'my own good', despite the fact it's not what you want, just in case I'm lying about wanting to stay and it hurts me down the line. You're going to hurt yourself to try to protect me. You're going to lock up your own feelings and try to put mine first, the way you always do for everyone, the way you have for years, and you're going to make yourself miserable because you'd rather do that than risk hurting someone you love."

Maddie was shocked. She knew James was an intuitive person, but she had not expected him to know her quite this well — as well as her own brother did. Just a few short weeks ago, in 'the time before', Marley had expressed his concerns about whether or not she was putting her heart in the right hands precisely because of this tendency of hers, and she had insisted she was sure she was. Now, here they were, her and James, discussing what he had done to cause her to revert back to harming herself on behalf of others, because seeing the people she loved in distress was the greatest pain she could ever imagine, and she'd rather die than endure it.

"I don't know what else to do," she said, exasperated. She was telling the truth. This was all she'd known since Bowie. She had helped her brother to die because he had wanted to. She had hidden her depression about it from her family because they had needed her to. Whenever there was an opportunity for Maddie to bear the burden of something to save the people that she loved, she would do it because she didn't know how to do anything else.

"I don't understand what's happening here," James said, stepping towards her and grabbing her hands. "I thought you wanted marriage and kids and all that good stuff."

"I do," Maddie said.

His eyes flickered back and forth. She knew he was searching wildly for an answer and then, as she'd known he would, he jumped to the wrong conclusion. He released her hands. "Just not with me?"

"Yes, with you!"

"Then what's the problem?"

"It's not what *you* want," Maddie said.

"Yes it *is*!" James said. Maddie stared at him. She didn't know what to say to that. They had talked about it, but still, she hadn't expected such a blatant declaration of his intentions, and it had rendered her speechless. She watched his features soften. He gazed down at her, worry written all over his face. "You don't believe me, do you?"

Maddie faltered, then shook her head. She didn't know what she believed anymore. James turned away to throw his hands in the air in exasperation. "I had the interview just to see what would happen. It was stupid, but I've been striving for that kind of job security for so long, I just wanted to prove I could do it if I wanted to. Then I got it. I contemplated it for a split second, and then I decided on you. It's not as complicated as you think it is. There's no hidden meanings or subconscious regrets, I swear!"

"You told me before that the only time you ever felt yourself was when you were travelling," Maddie reminded him.

"That was true until you."

"So, what, you've just changed your mind?" she asked.

"Yes!" he said, clearly exasperated. He stepped towards her again, his eyes pleading. "You changed *your* mind, Maddie.

I'm pretty sure a husband and a family were the last things you thought you wanted when we first met. Are you going to try to tell me now that my appearance in your life didn't force you to consider it more deeply?"

She didn't know what to say to that, because it was true. Until James, there had been no cause to consider what she wanted, because getting married and having children had seemed so far removed from potential future prospects there had been no point. Meeting James had changed her mind — she had fallen head over heels in love, and when she'd carefully considered it, taken the time to ask her heart what it really wanted, it had been a resounding *yes*.

"Why is this different?" he goaded her. "Why are you allowed to change your mind, but I'm not allowed to change mine?"

Maddie shrugged despondently. "I don't know."

"Great," James muttered, turning away again. He continued to pace back and forth. Suddenly, he stopped, his features laden with dread. "Is this over?" he asked her.

Maddie shook her head, blinking rapidly. That wasn't what she wanted, not at all. "I hope not," she said.

He stared at her. Maddie saw his eyes fill with tears and knew he was about to cry. She didn't know what to do next. Her head felt jumbled. She was immeasurably tired and was being forced to endure the very thing she hated — watching someone she loved in distress. "So, you want me to go and live in another country," he said. "But you want us to stay together?"

Maddie nodded, only because that seemed closest to the conclusion she was coming to. She hadn't had time to properly draw up a plan, but this solution seemed like it might be the best of both worlds. She wouldn't feel like she was holding him back, but he would still be hers.

"Even though I've told you I don't want to go," he said.

Maddie nodded again. "You *do* want to go," she said. "You just don't want to go without me. If I told you I'd come with you, that I'd give all of this up and go with you, you would go, wouldn't you?"

"Of course I would, but you don't want to, so I'll stay here with you," he said.

"But I wouldn't give up the recovery retreat for you," she said. "If you said you were going travelling and it was over if I didn't come with you, I would let you go."

"So," he said, petulantly.

"So," Maddie echoed. "That's what is making me uncomfortable. You're giving up your dream for me."

"So?" he said again, irritated this time. "Maddie, it doesn't matter what you would or wouldn't do in a hypothetical role reversal. This, right here, what is happening now, is the true situation. This is real life. The only thing that should matter is that the man standing in front of you wants to be with you wherever you go. I promise you, I would happily spend the rest of my life doing exactly what you want to do, worshipping every bit of ground you choose to walk on, and I'd be giddy through all of it."

"Exactly! You're so wonderful. Perhaps you should be with someone who wants what you want instead of being with someone like me."

"Someone like you?" He stepped towards her. "Maddie, you're the greatest human I have ever met. You're sweet and goofy and kind and funny and caring and devoted. What you're trying to do is both the sickest and the sweetest thing I have ever known anyone do for another human — though it kills me to say it, because I wish you would stop. You're beautiful, and I love . . ."

She put her hand over his mouth. "Don't," she begged. She couldn't bear to let him say the words. Not here, like this, in a tone laden with sadness and out of desperation instead of giddiness and glee. He said them anyway, but his voice was muffled and hardly intelligible, so she closed her eyes and pretended she hadn't heard them. After a moment or so, she let her hands fall listlessly by her sides and forced herself to look at him. His lips were pursed tightly shut, and all the hope had gone from his face. She knew he was finally understanding there was nothing he could say to change her mind. She wondered if he, like her, was marvelling at the fragility of happiness. It certainly looked like whatever he was thinking about was as tragically flawed as the concept of love — which Maddie had come to realise was blissful only when it didn't shatter the heart. When it did, it was pure torture.

They stared at each other for a little while. She thought he might try to touch her, or say it again, but he didn't. Instead, he waited until he was sure she wasn't going to say those all-important words back to him. Then he turned and walked away, leaving her alone in the purest declaration of love he could ever have given her: the beautiful new version of Bowie's old bedroom.

CHAPTER NINETEEN

The next fortnight was wretched. Maddie was sick of herself. Her head pounded constantly from crying so often, and she could tell from the way her jaw ached that she'd started grinding her teeth in her sleep again. She was constantly restless and exhausted. She longed for the days when she had considered being obsessed with James and unable to have him torturous. Compared to the torment she was feeling now, those feelings had been a walk in the park. This thing they were doing now, this was real torture. The closer they got to James' departure date — which was, according to Emma, the day after Autumn's and Marley's wedding — the more disconnected they became. They barely spoke, could hardly look at each other, and yet Maddie found herself falling deeper and deeper in love. The mere prospect of his absence was enough to grow her feelings for him. She felt constantly terrible. She yearned for him every second of the day, for the warmth and strength of his embrace, for the heat of his breath against her neck.

"Are you sure you're doing the right thing?" Bluebell asked one morning, handing Maddie a coffee. Maddie felt her eyes fill with tears. She swallowed hard and nodded, rubbing her hands across her face, looking for some way to adequately describe the pain she was in to her sister, a woman who had never really been in love. Nothing came to mind.

"I haven't seen you this sad since Bowie," Bluebell said. Maddie nodded. That was an accurate assessment. The unhappiness was different, of course, but it was just as putrid. It consumed her every waking moment in the same way. "Maddie, are you *sure* you are doing the right thing?" Bluebell asked again.

Maddie nodded. "Honestly, I really do think it will be better for James if he sticks to his original plan and goes travelling."

Bluebell eyed her sceptically. "What about what's best for you?"

Maddie shrugged. "That doesn't matter."

"Madison Whittle!" Bluebell gasped. Maddie winced. In her entire life, she could count on one hand the number of times someone had called her by her full name. The words hit her like a slap in the face, largely because they brought her biological mother crashing into her brain, along with the qualities she knew Julianne had possessed. Stubbornness, dismissiveness, an avoidant attachment style. Maddie wasn't comfortable being reminded of her, and the realisation she might have inherited some of her mother's worst traits made her feel a little bit sick. For her entire life, Maddie had been consistently compared to her father, but if there was one thing her father would never do, it was abandon a person he loved, or push them away, or dismiss their sadness — all things she had been doing to James for this last week. She decided then and there she needed to get herself back into therapy. For her own sake, as well as everyone else's.

"You, of all people, absolutely deserve to be happy," Bluebell said.

Maddie dared to look at her sister, despite the fact she was pretty sure her gaze would cause her tears to spill over. She was right. "I love him," Maddie admitted. "And I want him to be the happiest he can be, whatever that means for me."

Bluebell's face softened. She reached for Maddie's hand, squeezing it tightly. "Sissy, you are so unbelievably selfless, and I wish I was more like you, honestly, I do. But you have a life to live, too."

Maddie nodded thoughtfully, though she wasn't really thinking. She already knew there was nothing Bluebell could say that would make her change her mind. She loved James too much to tie him to a life he never wanted for himself. As hard as it was, she had to let him go, even if that meant they couldn't make things work between them — which was the conclusion she was coming to as time wore on. They could barely stand to be in the same room together, so it was looking increasingly unlikely he'd bother flying home from Italy to visit her. Maddie's heart, which felt like it had been sitting low in her chest since that day it had been shattered in the café, sank lower still. She felt so sorry for herself.

"I can't tell you what to do, but I do wish you'd listen — I know I'm right," Bluebell said, topping up Maddie's mug. "I've never been in love, as you know, but I've met a lot of men in my time, and hardly any men are like James. If you let that bisexual, guitar-playing vegetarian with a cute dog and a talent for handiwork, who also happens to be madly in love with you, leave and go to Italy, you will regret it for the rest of your life."

Maddie didn't say anything, she just stared straight ahead. Bluebell stared right back, as though challenging her sister to disagree with her. Maddie couldn't, she wouldn't. She already knew sending James away would probably end their relationship, and that she would miss him for ever. But if he met another woman in the future, made a family and found happiness, which she was sure he would, she'd have done the right thing for him and that would help her through. She felt a little more like her biological mother than she'd ever hoped to feel, but fuck it. Everything she had now besides her father, including the woman in front of her, she owed to Julianne making a decision as difficult as the one she was making now. Her biological mother had concluded she was not the best thing for Ben and Maddie, and she had probably been right. Maddie couldn't imagine having a better life than the one she'd had. The decision must have been difficult — at least Maddie hoped it had been, as it was far too painful to consider the alternative — but Julianne had made it regardless because she had known her partner and baby daughter would be happier in different circumstances. That was what Maddie was trying to do for James. This situation had given her a new perspective on a very painful part of her past.

Eventually, Bluebell sighed. "You know me, Mads, I'm not one to simp over any man, but you have a really good one there. I'll drop it after this, I swear, but I am begging you, from the bottom of my heart, please don't throw it all away."

* * *

Maddie spent the morning locked in her bedroom thinking about what Bluebell had said. Because Bluebell was usually so unserious, any frank conversations she chose to have with her siblings were usually important and therefore should be heeded. This one was no exception. Bluebell was staunchly feminist and extremely unforgiving when it came to men acting shitty, so if Bluebell thought she was making a mistake by letting James go, there was a good chance she was.

Still, she was struggling to get out of her own way. Every time she convinced herself that perhaps she should set aside her concerns and be selfish for once, she'd envision a day in the future when James would come to her and accuse her of holding him back, of tying him to a life of normalcy instead of one bursting with adventure.

Around lunchtime, she forced herself to stop crying, doused her face with water, and left her room to head for the kitchen, before anyone found her once more in a state. She was frustrating her family, she knew that they all wanted her to relent. She'd done so much to hide her issues from them over the past six years — bearing the burden of her sadness alone to prevent causing them any stress or harm. They didn't realise this situation had been the final straw, tipping her over the edge into full-blown sadness again — to them it looked like she was being unnecessarily dramatic and difficult. Those were not words anyone typically associated with Maddie.

She was not expecting to find anyone upstairs, but she ran into James in the hallway. His jeans, typically big on him anyway, were baggier than ever. His sweatshirt hung loose. He'd been avoiding eating at the house and Maddie had assumed it was because he didn't want to be around her, but it looked like he'd lost his appetite completely. He was tired and consumed, and it was written all over every part of him.

"Hey," he said, stepping as far to one side as he possibly could. He was carrying a book and headed for his bedroom. He did not stop.

"James!" Maddie heard herself say. She wasn't sure where it came from. She'd had absolutely no intention of saying his name, but there it was, echoing around the hallway and stopping him in his tracks. He sighed and turned to face her, planting his eyes on hers. Maddie made her way towards him, bidding herself not to touch him. She didn't want to give him false hope. They stared at each other and she saw his expression change briefly from sadness to hope, then to resignation, then land right back on sadness. All in a few seconds.

She didn't know where to start, so she gestured to the book. "You've taken up reading?" He turned it around so that she could see the cover: *Rome — The Unforgettable City.*

"Your dad gave it to me," he explained. She didn't know what to say, so she nodded. He let the awkwardness linger for a moment, then continued, "I've never been to Italy, but I've heard it's quite refined. I need to brush up on my general etiquette."

"You're English, James — you'll be fine. Nobody expects any better from us," Maddie joked. He chuckled half-heartedly.

They tumbled back into uncomfortable silence. Through the floor, they could hear the giddy laughter of her family in the kitchen. Maddie wanted to join them more than anything, but had to have this conversation with James. For the sake of everyone, not just the two of them, Maddie needed to clear the air.

"I never meant to hurt you," she started, her voice barely more than a whisper.

"I know that," he said. "I mean, you didn't, not really. I hurt myself by being a bloody idiot. What's happening now is the consequences of my own actions. Indulging the idea of taking the job in the first place, even if it was only fleetingly, talking to your brother, taking his advice when he told me not to tell you about it. That was all my fault. I should have known better."

Maddie didn't want to object to his explanation because it was true, but she wanted to acknowledge that her own complicated personality had not helped the situation.

"Another woman would probably accept your explanation and move on," she said, wincing guiltily.

James stared straight into her face. "And I would not be in love with that woman," he said. "I adore every single bit of you, Maddie, even the part that's making you do this."

Maddie nodded sadly, tearing her gaze from his. She had not expected him to be so understanding. She'd presumed his stony gaze and silence this past week had been because he was angry at her, but it sounded more like he was mad at himself.

"I don't want to spend the next few weeks like this," she said.

James shook his head, closing his eyes and covering his face with his free hand. "Me neither," he said, sighing. "Being so close to you and not being able to touch you is driving me mad."

"You can touch me whenever you want," Maddie said, reaching out to grab him. She tugged gently on his wrist, forcing him to uncover his face and the tears he was trying to hide from her. She had thought in the beginning that James was not an emotional man, but knew now that he was. He had been close to tears several times in just a few short months, but this was the first time she'd seen him actually cry. It devastated her. "Come here." She pulled him towards her. He complied, burying his head in her shoulder and resting there. Maddie ran her hand through his hair, enjoying the feel of his breath against her skin. She kissed his cheek and sighed.

"Can I stay in your room tonight?" she asked. She felt his breath catch in his throat, his body tense. "We're still together, aren't we? I thought we were. We're wasting so much time, James. I want to spend as much time with you as possible before you go," she explained.

He stood up straight to look at her. "You can stay with me whenever you want," he said, parroting her earlier words. Maddie raised a small smile, cupping his face with her hand.

"I love you, James," she said, staring straight into his eyes.

He gazed back, his eyes wet with resignation. "I love you, too." He pulled her closer. "More than absolutely everything else. More than I ever thought possible. More and more, with each day that passes. I love you, Maddie. I only wish I could prove to you how much."

* * *

In the weeks leading up to the opening of the retreat, Maddie posted a job vacancy for a handyperson, someone to take over James' role when he left. The salary and benefits were good, and they'd get his room, of course. She needed someone who had some skills and — most important — the right values. Someone who was kind, courteous and cared about people. She was inundated with inappropriate applicants, some of whom slipped through the net, which led to her interviewing them by accident. One man turned up wearing a tuxedo and proudly told her he'd never held a hammer in his life. There was a woman in her eighties who insisted she could handle the manual labour that came with the role, and an eighteen-year-old whose first question was 'Do I still get paid if I'm off sick?'.

To ease Maddie's growing anxiety, Marley promised he'd help out until a replacement for James could be found. He was still pretty useless when it came to proper DIY, but good with any heavy lifting and moving, plus he'd be great company. His promise made Maddie feel slightly better, and she was grateful he'd offered to help despite not agreeing with her sending James away.

Nobody did.

When it came to James, things were better between them. They celebrated Valentine's Day like any normal couple would. They were flirty and playful. They went on dates and took sunset strolls hand in hand in the garden. By early March, he'd stopped begging her to let him stay and she'd stopped sidestepping conversations about his travelling. She regularly asked him about his plans and he'd answer without adding the caveat that he still didn't want to leave and would stay if she asked him to. Now that he was on good terms with his mother again, James would alternate his evenings, spending one night with Maddie and the next night at home. During the evenings they spent together, they made love all through the night, whispering declarations of love so frequently that the words almost lost all meaning. They felt natural and ordinary, so true and accepted they were no longer a declaration at all. Over time, Maddie felt better about the way her voice sounded when she simply said those three words, without the need for clarification of her position by sticking the word 'but' into the middle of a longer sentence. She loved him, it was that simple — she'd told him a thousand times before and she'd tell him a thousand times again. He knew where he stood and so did she. There was no need to add anything else.

In the daytime, they worked. Though James understandably didn't want to get involved in replacing himself, he did help Maddie find yoga instructors, meditation experts and massage therapists. There were dozens of them in the local area, all looking for regular work. Over time, Maddie hoped to add more animals to the grounds — chickens, ducks, goats, perhaps a dog. The retreat would be a sanctuary for those looking to focus on getting better, to relax and spend time with people who knew what they had been through. Maddie would do most of the cooking and cleaning herself, though she accepted she might need to hire someone at some point. It would be hard work, but the level of dedication required would feel worth it to the new hire if she hired the right person. They would understand that commitment came with the territory, that they should be stressed because they were working with vulnerable people and trying to make their lives better. She reiterated that part, hopeful she'd find people who genuinely cared about the health and well-being of their guests.

Aside from that, Maddie had re-enrolled in therapy. In the wake of everything that had happened with James, she had realised her happiness had become intrinsically tied to him, and that was not a good enough life for Maddie. She wanted to be strong, secure and happy of her own accord. She wanted to finally beat her demons. She wanted to heal properly, so that any decisions she made were in spite of the hardships she had faced in her life, not because of them. She no longer wanted to be led by the damage that had been done to her by circumstances out of her control — her mother leaving her and Bowie dying. She wanted to get better, and accepted that would take more time and effort than she had invested thus far. She was apprehensive at first, but knew she'd made the right decision after her very first session. This was the only way.

As the weeks wore on, Maddie's feelings of anxiety started to dissipate and she rediscovered her passion for her project. That was in part because her family had stepped up spectacularly to help. Together, they had improved every imperfect nook and cranny. The house and its gardens had never looked so good.

Even Pip was lending a hand, travelling home most weekends to assist where he could. In mid-March, the day before Marley's and Autumn's wedding, he dedicated his afternoon to helping Maddie paint her bedroom, which looked tired compared to the rest of the house. Maddie loved her room and always had. It had been hers for a really long time. She had grown up there, morphed from a little girl into a grown

woman. She'd cried within its confines, pondered and won-
dered. Most recently, she had fallen in love there. Truly, it felt
like a sanctuary to her, a safe space. Now that her books and
Bowie's had been relocated to their new home on the bookcase
James had built especially for them in Bowie's old bedroom,
Maddie couldn't wait to reclaim her space.

Instead of getting the stepladder so that he could reach
the very top of her bedroom wall, Pip had hoisted Benjamin
onto his shoulders and given him a paintbrush. Her nephew
was making a terrible mess of things, but he was also having a
wonderful time, so Maddie didn't mind so much. There was
no real need for this room to be perfect — nobody would see
it except for her. The sentimentality of her nephew's contri-
bution meant more to her than a flawless finish. Maddie lay
on her bed, watching them.

"Have you had any thoughts on a name for the retreat?"
Pip asked, stepping sideways so that Benjamin could reach a
new part of the wall.

Maddie didn't answer right away. She was too busy
basking in the joy she felt at having Pip home so often. He
was doing so not just to help her out, but also in order to
spend time with Bluebell and their parents before they left for
Venice. Their impending departure made Maddie feel nervous. Soon, there would be Whittles spread all over the place,
and the house would be virtually empty. She swallowed hard,
resolving to worry about how much she would miss them
later. This was supposed to be a happy time. "Yes, we have a
name. Didn't I tell you?" she asked. Pip shook his head.

Benjamin stopped painting, peering down at his uncle.
"A name for what, Uncle Pip?" he asked.

"For this house," Pip said. "When Aunty Maddie opens
her special hotel, it'll need a proper name."

Benjamin looked concerned. Maddie laughed.

"You can still call it 'the big house' if you want to,
Benjamin," Maddie reassured him. His eyes lit up and he graced
her with the dopey grin she loved, the one he had inherited

somehow from the uncle he'd never met. How appropriate, given what she had decided to name the retreat.

"We're calling it 'Bowie's Place'," she said. Pip's face broke into a smile, his eyes filling with tears. Maddie grinned. Every Whittle she'd told had been overwhelmed at the sentimentality of the gesture. "It just felt right, somehow. I'm doing all of this in his memory and using the money he left me, after all. I can't believe I didn't tell you! James and I came up with it a few weeks ago."

Actually, she had suggested it and James had agreed it was a good idea. Despite his impending departure, this had somehow become their project. She trusted his business sense and appreciated his instincts.

"But I like calling it the big house," Benjamin whined, shattering the moment. Pip and Maddie laughed.

"This will always be the big house," Pip said, lifting Benjamin off his shoulders and stepping back to admire the terrible job he had done with the painting. "Nice work, buddy. Go and find your daddy, would you? I need to talk to Aunty Maddie."

Benjamin nodded and ran from the room, paintbrush still in hand. Maddie closed her eyes, praying her nephew did not drop it anywhere or rub it up against anything. She did not have the energy for any more fixing. When she opened her eyes, Pip was watching her, clearly concerned.

"What?" she asked, already knowing the answer.

"You know what," he said. Maddie sighed, shaking her head. "Is there any point in me trying?" he asked. "Have you really made up your mind, Maddie?"

Maddie nodded, resolute. She didn't feel anxious about this conversation. Pip was doing his brotherly duty. He'd most likely been encouraged to come and talk to her by their mother. He would take Maddie's answer as the absolute truth, and wouldn't hassle her too hard about it.

"Then I'm not going to do you the disservice of distrusting you, or bother wasting my time," he said, heading for the door.

"Thank you," Maddie called after him.

Pip stopped suddenly, turning back to look at her. "Don't thank me, Mads," he said, gently. "I don't think I'm doing you a favour by letting you put yourself last again. There's safety in predictability, I understand that. You can control the pain that doesn't get to take you by surprise the way it did when Bowie died — but you lose so much other stuff. Stuff I think it's worthwhile having."

Maddie winced. Bowie's death had not taken her by surprise in the slightest. She had been there, had orchestrated it, and yet the pain she had felt had been debilitating. She could not imagine how hard it would have been had she gone to bed with everyone else and woken up to find him gone. So, yes, perhaps she really was trying to avoid the type of heartbreak that takes people by surprise, because she had never felt it, and she honestly didn't know how she would ever survive it.

Pip faltered, shuffling uncomfortably. He drew in a deep breath, and continued. "I think you're making a massive mistake, Mads. I feel uncomfortable saying that, but I have to. You know I've always accepted that you know best what you want for yourself. I've never argued with you, not once. But I need to tell you that I think you're doing the wrong thing. And I want to remind you it's not too late. James is desperate for you to ask him to stay."

Somehow, Maddie knew he was not done, so she waited, watching him, wondering how he'd grown up so suddenly right before her eyes without her noticing it.

"You could insist you're only changing your mind to prevent Marley from wrecking the house with his terrible DIY skills," he said, eventually. "I was downstairs earlier and James was trying to teach him how to hang a picture . . . Maddie, this is not hyperbole — we will have no house left if you let this go on for too long."

Maddie laughed, wiping away the tears falling from her eyes. She was upset not because of what Pip had said, but because of the way he'd said it. He sounded like Bowie, both in the tone of his voice and the sentiment in his words, and she knew for certain in that moment that if Bowie were there he would be saying the same thing in the same way — gently, with a hint of humour to soothe her ego. That realisation hurt her. She had trusted Bowie implicitly. The way she trusted Pip.

Her little brother sighed, smiling kindly. "Promise me you'll really think about this?" he said, eyeing her with obvious fondness.

Maddie smiled back, and nodded. "I will. I promise."

To her surprise, for the first time since this nightmare had started, she found she actually meant it.

CHAPTER TWENTY

The morning of the wedding dawned clear and bright. Maddie awoke just before the sun rose. She fully expected to be alone in the kitchen, but found Autumn sitting at the table nursing a coffee. She must have driven over early, Maddie concluded. Perhaps she had been unable to sleep? She didn't have the energy to ask.

"Morning!" Autumn sang, in a manner that was exceptionally cheery, even for a bride.

"Good morning, Mrs Whittle," Maddie teased. Autumn rolled her eyes, dutifully pouring Maddie a coffee.

"You know full well I'm not changing my name," she said.

"Marley said you were thinking about double-barrelling them," Maddie said, sitting down and sipping gratefully from her mug.

Autumn nodded. "We were thinking about that, mainly because Benjamin is Whittle-Black and we wouldn't mind all being the same. But, truthfully, I couldn't care less — I just want to marry him."

Maddie feigned surprise. "If the old Autumn could see you now," she said.

Autumn laughed. "I reckon she'd be flabbergasted, but only because she never thought she'd love a man this much."

Maddie beamed, and the two women fell into comfortable silence. Maddie stared deep into her coffee cup, lost in thought. She wasn't thinking about anything deep — the timeline for today, how cute Benjamin would look in his suit, how excited she was to wear her bridesmaid's dress — a floor-length, black-satin, halter-neck gown she'd bought on a whim a few years ago from a vintage shop but never had a reason to wear. She finished her coffee and reached again for the cafetière, noticing only then that Autumn looked teary.

"Hey!" Maddie stood and went around the table, putting her arms around her friend. "Are you OK? What's wrong?"

"Nothing," Autumn said, laughing a little. "Oh, nothing, Maddie, I'm being so silly. It doesn't even make any sense."

Maddie let go of Autumn and sat beside her, pouring her another coffee. She knew Autumn was trying to drop this conversation only because she felt silly about whatever was on her mind, not because she didn't want to talk about it. Maddie pushed the mug towards her and watched her take a sip. She felt suddenly flooded with love for her friend, who looked so happy and yet so sad all at once. She nudged Autumn with her elbow. Autumn smiled.

"I get so tired of wittering on about the same thing," she said. "But on days like today, Bowie's absence is even more startling than usual. Not just for me, for Marley, too. He's generally OK these days, but whenever there's a celebration, Bowie is on his mind all day. That feels strange today, given the irony of the situation. Today wouldn't be happening if it wasn't for his absence, and yet almost every single person in attendance will be wishing he was here, including Marley and me. It's so confusing. There's no blueprint, and I find that so frustrating."

"I understand," Maddie said, because she did. The tumultuousness of the past few weeks had made her miss her brother more than ever. She longed for his wise words, his steady support, his hugs. His face swam into her mind unbidden — that dopey, sympathetic smile he'd reserved for the many conversations they'd had about being introverted and shy, and how it had held them both back. Her heart ached, but only because she felt so lucky to have had him. She too wished he was here, not least because her situation would be so much easier to navigate if he was here to help her sort through the way she felt. She cleared her throat, forcing herself to continue. "He was a massive presence in our lives. We loved him so very much. It's only natural we all default to thinking about him when important things happen. He doesn't deserve any less."

Autumn nodded a little frantically. "Oh, God, I know. I'll never forget him, or how wise he was, how kind, how sweet and funny. It just makes me sad, I guess."

"That all makes sense," Maddie reassured her. "And it's not silly, Autumn. Like you said, there's no blueprint for any of this. You and Marley found yourselves in such an extraordinary situation, of course you have no idea how to feel. As time goes on, I'm finding the best way for me to deal with my feelings about losing Bowie — is just to sit with them. If I'm sad, then I let myself be sad. If I miss him, then I let myself miss him. Sometimes I say the words aloud, as though he can hear them. I still tell him I love him every single day."

Autumn smiled sadly. "Me too." She wiped her tears away and sat up straighter, drawing in a deep breath and sighing hard. "I just really wish he was here."

She rushed the words out, as though she absolutely needed to say them, but wanted to do it as quickly as she possibly could. Maddie smiled reassuringly, squeezing her hand. There was nothing she could say to that.

A flutter of wings by the window caught Maddie's attention, drawing her from her thoughts. A robin had landed on the windowsill. It was staring out across the garden, as though it was waiting for something. The weather was turning, the sunrise was rippling through its feathers, and it was puffed up, seemingly proud. Maddie smiled and shook her head, trying desperately to rid her mind of celestial conclusions, but she couldn't help herself, it was too comforting.

Autumn followed her gaze. She caught sight of the robin and smiled. "Ah, that robin. It appears everywhere. Here, in our garden at home. Marley insists it's the same one. I keep trying to tell him it's not, but he says it's Bowie, that he follows us everywhere."

"Do you think that's daft?" Maddie asked, hoping Autumn would say yes. She felt silly for connecting frequent visits from robins to Bowie's lingering presence and she'd appreciate being shamed out of it, though she had to admit it did give her comfort.

Autumn thought about that. "Bowie would think it was ridiculous," she said, grinning. Maddie laughed. Autumn was right, her brother had been incensed by any such silliness for most of his life, convinced that death was the end of everything. He had insisted several times before he'd died that he would not come back to visit them, so they should not look for any sign he was trying to communicate with them from the afterlife. But Maddie knew that if he could, he would. He had loved them too much. He wouldn't be able to help himself. The robin turned and peered through the window. Autumn tittered, amused. "I don't know what I think," she admitted, watching the little bird dance back and forth. "But I know it gives me comfort to think he might be here."

Maddie smiled at that. She wholeheartedly agreed that it was a nice thing to think, even if it did sound absurd when you said it out loud. She squeezed Autumn's hand again, her eyes still on the robin, and whispered, "We love you, Bowie."

Right on cue, the bird tapped the window with its beak, fluffed up its feathers, skipped to the edge of the window-sill and flew away, singing heartily to the morning sunshine. Autumn and Maddie stared at each other, their eyes wide with wonder, then laughed.

* * *

Because Autumn and Marley wanted a fuss-free, relaxed wedding morning, their official civil ceremony — technically their proper wedding —was booked for the following Monday morning at Hertford Registry Office, with only Ben, Emma, Katherine and Benjamin in attendance as witnesses. Their wedding in the garden, which was happening at four o'clock, was technically a non-legal blessing, though Marley and Autumn had made it clear they viewed saying their vows in front of the people they loved most in their world and in their favourite place on the planet as the most important part, whether it was licenced or not. Autumn's mother, sister and baby niece had set off early that morning and were due to arrive at lunchtime. Autumn insisted she wanted to do nothing that morning except sit in her pyjamas and drink champagne with Maddie and Bluebell, a plan Maddie could get behind. They put on a pop playlist and, despite the fact they were in no rush, started lazily applying make-up and styling their hair. Autumn and Bluebell spent most of the morning chatting idly about their hopes for the future. Autumn wanted more of the steady predictability of her life at the moment. She was really enjoying having Marley at home. It had given them more time together, revived their friendship and invigorated their relationship. Bluebell, by contrast, longed for adventure. She yearned to dance with strangers, for isolated beaches and sunsets so beautiful they took her breath away.

"What about you, Mads?" Bluebell prompted her.

Maddie thought hard about that. "Obviously I want the business to be successful," she said. "But I'm not measuring that in monetary terms. I just really want to help as many people as possible."

Bluebell nodded, her eyes flitting to Autumn. "How are you feeling about James going away?" she asked.

"Bluebell," Autumn warned, passing her an eyeshadow and gesturing to her eyelids. "We all know how she feels about it. Today is not the day."

Maddie was grateful for her 'almost' sister-in-law, the only member of the family besides her father who had not tried to persuade her to ask James to stay. Maddie knew that was not because Autumn didn't care, but because she trusted Maddie to make her own decisions. She'd made it clear she was there if Maddie wanted to talk, then left it at that.

"Fine," Bluebell muttered, opening the eyeshadow pallet. "Do you want glitter?"

Autumn tutted. "When have I ever wanted glitter?" she said, clearly amused.

"It's your wedding day!" Bluebell pointed out.

"Exactly," Autumn said. "I want to look more like myself than I ever have before. Marley is marrying me, not someone who looks like me."

Bluebell smirked. "I'd be careful about saying that if I were you — you've let yourself go a bit recently."

"It is not too late for me to ban you from my wedding," Autumn warned.

Bluebell reeled theatrically. "Please don't even joke about that — I couldn't handle the FOMO."

Maddie and Autumn laughed.

* * *

The morning progressed just like that — relaxed, peaceful, joyful. Katherine, Lilly and Daisy arrived slightly behind schedule, closer to one o'clock than midday. Autumn spent the first half hour calming down her mother, who she insisted did not need two hours to get ready — and could sit down and have some lunch. Emma had prepared an entire kitchen table of Autumn's favourite foods — vegan scones, cucumber sandwiches, falafel and hummus, fried potatoes, spicy stuffed peppers, vegetable couscous, pasta salad, carrot cake, chocolate cake, and lemon drizzle cake. There was enough to last the entire family at least three days. Maddie was amazed.

"When did you do all this?" Maddie asked, incredulous.

"I did some of it yesterday and some of it this morning. Dad helped, too."

"Where is Dad?" Bluebell asked.

"He's with Marley, Pip, James and Benjamin," Emma said. "At Autumn's and Marley's house. Apparently, they're terribly organised and have been ready for hours. He said they're sitting in their suits playing video games."

"Do they have food?" Autumn asked.

"No idea," Emma said.

"Tell them to come up here," Autumn suggested. The women at the table stopped eating and stared at her. "Fuck tradition, it means nothing to me. If they want to come up here, tell them they can."

Maddie met her mother's gaze, shaking her head knowingly. If the offer was extended to the men, they would be here in a heartbeat, eating their food and causing a ruckus, overly excited by the weight of the day. Maddie couldn't imagine anything better. She missed them, truth be told, and she suspected Autumn missed them, too. This was a special day. When things were special, Autumn wanted to be with Marley. With everybody, actually. For a woman who had spent the first thirty-two years of her life feeling completely alone, she was surprisingly family-orientated now.

"I'll text Dad," Maddie said, picking up her phone.

"Tell Jennifer she should come, too?" Autumn suggested. Maddie nodded dutifully, typing out her text. Autumn grinned, satisfied, happily stuffing a falafel into her mouth. "You better eat as much as you can," she warned her mum through a mouthful of food. "They'll set off immediately, and when they get here, they'll clear this whole table in about fifteen seconds."

* * *

At two o'clock, while the rest of their family set out chairs and decorated the altar with flower garlands, Maddie and Bluebell helped Autumn step into her dress — a crêpe, champagne-coloured midi dress she'd found in a vintage shop. It had a delicate sweetheart neckline and puff-ball sleeves. It was romantic and feminine, whimsical and elegant, beautiful and timeless — all words Maddie would use to describe Autumn. They helped put the finishing touches to her hair and make-up — a pretty pink lipstick and a crystal headband to hold back the Hollywood waves they'd diligently curled into Autumn's straight, brown hair with a straightening iron — before stepping back to admire their work. Maddie was speechless. Autumn looked breathtaking.

"You have never looked more like yourself," Bluebell said, her smile wide.

Autumn grinned, turning on the spot. "I feel very pretty," she said.

"You're gorgeous, Autumn," Maddie found her voice.

"Thank you," she said, sliding her feet into strappy gold sandals. "Bluebell, can you help me tie my shoes? Maddie, would you go and get Marley, please? I want him to see me before everyone else."

Maddie nodded, setting off in search of her brother, wiping happy tears from her eyes as she went. She knew why Autumn had suddenly decided they should have a 'first look', a private moment for the two of them to share. Marley was struggling with his grief today. Maddie had seen it in his eyes when he turned up at the house. Autumn wanted some uninterrupted time alone with him to check he was OK. Perhaps she too needed to cry. It made Maddie emotional. Their love for each other was so wholesome, so pure, she felt lucky she got to witness it, and was immeasurably happy that her brother and her friend were the ones who got to experience it. She composed herself between the living room and the kitchen, because she didn't want to panic Benjamin. As it turned out, her nephew wasn't there. Maddie presumed he was off with Emma somewhere.

Having finally finished setting up the garden, Marley, Ben, Pip and James were sitting at the kitchen table. They stopped talking when she entered, their expressions sheepish.

Their sudden silence threw Maddie off. She stalled in the doorway, her eyes roaming over the four of them.

"Hey, Mads!" Marley said, wincing guiltily. She knew he was afraid she had heard what he'd said. Clearly, whatever they'd said was not for her ears. She narrowed her eyes at him, irritated.

"Autumn wants to see you," she said, gesturing to the living room with her head. "She's ready to go. She wants you to see her first."

Marley was clearly surprised, but stood straight up, quick and eager, hurrying ungracefully towards the door. As he sprang excitedly past her, Maddie grabbed his hand. He stopped, stock-still, his eyes wide with worry. "Brace yourself. She's literally the most gorgeous creature I've ever seen in my life."

Marley smiled and nodded. He faltered for a moment, then leaned forward, kissing her gently on the cheek. "Love you, sis," he said, squeezing her arm affectionately. The gesture was clearly an apology of sorts, an acknowledgement that the men shouldn't have been talking about her. Frustratingly, Maddie felt her anger dissipating. She had never been good at staying mad at people she loved for very long.

"I'm going to check on Emma and the others," Ben said, standing. "Pip, would you help me?"

"Why would you need me to help you check on Mum?" Pip asked, confused. James avoided Maddie's gaze. He was staring at the table, nursing a tumbler of whiskey, his shoulders hunched, his features pale. Whatever he was about to say, her family was pressuring him into it. Maddie muttered several swear words under her breath. She really didn't need this today.

"I think I've forgotten the way," Ben said, pointedly taking Pip's beer from him.

"To your own bedroom?" Pip frowned. "You should really get that checked out, Dad."

Ben biffed Pip on the arm with the back of his hand. "Upstairs," he said. "Now."

Pip stood, turning to Maddie and rolling his eyes. "I tried." He kissed her on the cheek. Maddie smiled at him gratefully. She waited awkwardly in the doorway until they had gone, then headed for the table, sitting down in the seat beside James, who was still refusing to look at her.

"What's up?" she asked, in an even tone of voice.

James lifted his head and planted his eyes on her. As uninterested as he had seemed a minute ago was as fixated as he appeared now, his eyes boring into hers, his face fraught with tension. "*What's up?*" he repeated, glaring at her. "Are you seriously making small talk with me, Maddie?"

Maddie sighed, shaking her head. "We've been over this. I don't know what you want from me, James. I can't rehash this all over again. I really want to enjoy today."

"I never asked you to," James said. "It's your brother and your dad, Maddie, they're the ones trying to force us to talk."

Maddie felt bad, because that was most likely true. Until just a moment ago, he'd looked like he wanted to be absolutely anywhere else, so it was plausible that he felt forced into this. She thought about getting up and leaving the room, but that didn't seem fair. They had so little time left to spend together, she didn't want to avoid him, or fight, or sit in stony silence, so she reached out and grabbed his hand, squeezing it tightly. He accepted the gesture, raising their clasped hands to his mouth and kissing her fingers lightly. "I'm sorry," he said. "I want to enjoy the day, too."

They sat in silence for a few minutes, their hands still clasped together, their bodies tilted towards each other. Maddie didn't know what James was thinking about, but she was growing increasingly excited to watch Marley and Autumn marry each other, and for an evening of good food, drinks and dancing. There were caterers arriving later to prepare the wedding breakfast and they'd be joined by just a few close, personal friends. Maddie could hardly wait.

"I should go and get ready," she said eventually, dropping his hand. "Will you save me a dance later?"

"Abso-fucking-lutely I will," he said, sipping from his tumbler.

"You know, I've never slow-danced before," she said, thoughtfully.

James considered this for a moment. "Me neither!" he admitted, grinning. "We can do it for the first time together."

Maddie nudged him affectionately, standing and smoothing down her pyjamas. Time was pressing on. She needed to finish her make-up, style her hair and slip into her bridesmaid's dress. She paused to admire James for a second, so handsome in his brown suit and paisley waistcoat, his hair tamed especially for the occasion. He smiled up at her, his eyes crinkling in their corners, his lips strained, but trying.

"What did they want you to say to me?" she heard herself ask. "Marley and my dad, I mean?"

"Oh. They wanted me to ask you one more time to let me stay," James said, shrugging gently. "I tried to tell them I didn't need to. You know I will always be waiting for you to change your mind, that I would come back in an instant if you asked me to — but they thought you might need to hear it again."

Maddie smiled sadly. She'd thought as much. "I'm sorry," she said.

He shook his head. "Don't apologise. It was valid input from two of the greatest men I've ever met. Two men who love the women in their lives in a way I've never seen before. I appreciated their input, Maddie, I really did. It's just that I already knew it wouldn't work."

* * *

Two hours later, Autumn and Marley were officially married. Maddie sat beside her family and watched the couple say their vows, holding the hand of a riveted Benjamin. He was so excited to be dressed up that he had promised to be a very good boy and stay silent during the ceremony. He succeeded except for when he had to hand Autumn and Marley their wedding rings, which he did while chattering away to them all about his 'very important job'.

As the newly married couple made their way back up the aisle, hand in hand, the guests threw confetti cut from dried flower petals, their eyes sparkling with proud tears. Autumn and Marley were halfway along when they gave up walking and stopped to bask in the affection of their families — hugging, kissing, squeezing hands. Maddie watched Marley turn and gaze upon Autumn, shaking his head, his eyes wide, as though he couldn't believe his luck. She saw them mouth 'I love you' to each other, they kissed, then Marley's eyes flitted to the bottom of the garden, where Bowie was buried. Autumn's and Maddie's did the same. Maddie was quite suddenly overcome with emotion. As her gaze travelled back to the happy couple, she caught Autumn's eye without meaning to. Autumn glanced between her and James, and a wordless communication passed between them, sister-in-law to sister-in-law. *If I can survive Bowie dying, you can live through James going travelling.* Maddie nodded her understanding, reaching for James' hand and squeezing. He stopped throwing confetti and pulled her to him, lifting her up a little bit and kissing her passionately. For the first time in several weeks, Maddie felt her heart flutter happily. Autumn was right, she could survive this. And she would.

* * *

They cut the cake right away because Benjamin wanted a slice. It was a two-tiered Victoria sponge cake baked by Emma, complete with edible flowers. Jennifer said it was the best cake she had ever eaten and implored Emma to give her the recipe before she flew to Venice next week. Emma promised she would. Then Katherine asked if she could have it, too, so Emma said she would write up the recipe for anyone who wanted it. They stood around on the porch and chatted in this manner until the sun began to set. Emma pitched open the orangery doors for those who wanted to sit inside. Ben lit the firepit, Marley retrieved blankets and Autumn asked the catering company if they'd mind making everyone a hot chocolate. The vibe was cosy and comfortable.

At seven o'clock, they sat down in the dining room to eat dinner, which was delicious and plentiful. The waiters brought out plate after plate of some of the most flavoursome food Maddie had ever eaten — tomato soup with truffle oil, mushrooms in white wine sauce on sourdough bread, chickpea-and-cucumber salad, stuffed peppers, cauliflower fritters with mango chutney and spicy fried rice, then chocolate brownies, raspberry mousse and sticky toffee pudding for dessert.

"I have never been so satisfied," James said, polishing off a second chocolate brownie. "I could sit here and eat for the rest of my life and I'd be happy, I reckon."

"Hard agree," Pip said, rubbing his stomach and groaning. "What an experience. Are you all ready for the speech of the century? Because I am not."

The table tittered happily, nodding in mutual agreement. They were ready for a speech or two. Why not? Marley went first, expressing his thanks for their attendance, his delight at marrying Autumn — "the most beautiful, driven, smart and funny woman I have ever known" — and taking a moment to give thanks to Bowie, who was never far from his thoughts and always in his heart. Ben went second. He called Autumn his third daughter and suggested she should call him 'Dad' from now on. Autumn tearfully agreed, hugging Ben tightly to her before he retook his seat. Bluebell gave a speech in which she encouraged Autumn to concede that destiny had brought her to the Whittles by laying out the 'evidence', which was mainly a series of spooky coincidences. Maddie thought Autumn would roll her eyes and put it all down to luck and good fortune like she always did, but her friend surprised her by yielding with a teary nod, causing Emma to cheer heartily. Last to go was Pip, who gave a long speech he'd littered with rude jokes and swear words. Luckily, it contained just the right amount of sentimentality, which meant he made it all the way through without Emma admonishing him for it, though she did throw him a pointed glance at the end. He winked at her and gestured to the rest of the table, who were all applauding long and loud, except for Benjamin. He was oblivious, sitting with his headphones on watching a cartoon on Marley's phone.

They took a break to have coffee and then the evening guests started to arrive. Maddie's shyness took over as she bid every new person a polite hello from the corner of the orangery, where she was sitting beside James, who was doing an excellent job of keeping her engaged in conversation, so she didn't feel awkward about not socialising with people she didn't know outside of a working environment. They talked about how wonderful the day had been, the deliciousness of the food, how incredible Autumn and Marley looked, and how heart-warming it was to see them together. As they people-watched, they saw Marley catch Autumn's eye from across the room, witnessed them each hone their gaze on the other, saw Marley wink, a happy smile fixed upon his face, and then Autumn grin like a fool in response.

"Fucking hell, they're like something out of a romance novel," James muttered.

Maddie laughed, because it was true.

* * *

Over the next few hours, as the group got merrier and the music got louder, people automatically migrated to what appeared to have been designated as the dance floor — the very centre of the orangery, beneath the same twinkling fairy lights that adorned their tree every Christmas. Pip and Marley had suspended them from the orangery ceiling. Maddie and James initially avoided dancing, but when the first slow song hit, James held his hand out for Maddie to take. He nodded reassuringly when she faltered, suddenly convinced that absolutely everyone would watch them if they did this, that she would be the centre of attention.

"Nobody exists except us," he said, staring straight into her eyes. Maddie nodded reluctantly and let him pull her to a relatively empty part of the room. Her mum and dad were already there, swaying in time to the music. Before they could look at her, Maddie wrapped her arms around James' neck and buried her head in the nook between his neck and shoulder, eager to shut the world out. She drew in a deep breath, inhaling the scent of him, knowing it would calm her nerves. James held her tightly to him, murmuring the words to the song just loud enough that only she could hear him. She quickly forgot there were other people in the room, that real life existed. Despite the weight of what they were doing, their first ever slow dance, and the last one they'd likely do for a long while, Maddie lost herself completely in the moment, so, when the music ended and she felt someone tugging gently at her elbow, it took her a moment to come back to reality.

"May I?" someone asked. Maddie felt James release his grip on her waist. Suddenly, he stepped back. The room was not in focus, Maddie was still somewhere else, dancing on a cloud among the stars, but she saw James nod. Maddie wanted to tell the interrupter to go away, to leave them alone, but when her brain joined her body back in the room, she realised that it was her very own little brother. Pip stepped towards her, took her suspended hands in his own, and started swaying, encouraging Maddie to do the same.

They danced on the spot for a moment, twirling slowly around and around. Maddie was no longer hiding her face, she was distracted from her embarrassment at being on display by torturous thoughts about James. This time tomorrow, he would no longer be there to help her block the world out. There would be no nook to protect her, nobody to whisper sweet nothings against her skin. James would be away for at least three months before he could visit her for a weekend. It could be potentially longer, if the agency said they needed him to stay. This moment, right now, was a new 'time before'. They had but a few precious hours left to spend together. She knew this was a wedding and she was supposed to socialise, but she just wanted to be with James. She was irritated that Pip was interrupting them.

Her brother seemed to read her mind. "I'll give you back to him in a minute, but I need to talk to you first."

Maddie sighed and shook her head, fairly sure she knew what this was about. She had sensed last night that Pip wasn't content with the conclusion of their chat in her bedroom. She was so tired of having this conversation. She wished they would all leave her alone. Right now, their repetitive arguments felt like a real waste of time.

"Please don't, Pip," Maddie said, her eyes filling with frustrated tears.

"You know I normally wouldn't, Maddie — but in Bowie's absence, I have to." Maddie was thrown by the mention of their older brother. She blinked her tears away, using her eyes to question him.

"What has Bowie got to do with this?" she asked, breathless. Tired and irritated, she found herself angry at Pip for bringing him up.

"I know what you did for him, the night he died," Pip said.

Maddie's eyes went wide. Her heart quickened, the world slowed down, the room felt small. She was no longer sure whether she was swaying because she was dancing or because she was going to faint.

Pip held her a little tighter, holding her up on her feet. His mouth was set in a hard straight line, but his eyes were soft, his expression gentle. "You did the right thing," he reassured her. "I have never, ever doubted that for a single second."

"I don't understand . . ."

"I was going to do what you did," Pip said, sighing deeply. "That night, when he was begging us to help him, I

313

wanted to. I couldn't stand listening to him in pain anymore, watching him slowly suffer and die, so I went to bed with everyone else and then I sneaked downstairs and tried to find his tablets, but they had already gone. I crept to his bedroom, and I heard you, Autumn and Marley in there with him, so I went back to bed, and I waited."

"Why didn't you come in?" Maddie asked. Silent tears of shame and sadness slid down her cheeks. She knew they would alarm anyone who saw them, so she hid her face from view, turning her brother so that she was facing the wall.

"I didn't really want to see it," Pip said, wincing guiltily. "I knew it would fuck me up. I was doing it to help him, but he had you guys. He wasn't going to suffer anymore, and that was all that mattered."

Maddie whispered Pip's name. She was dangerously close to sobbing. Her brother had been so incredibly young back then, just eighteen years old. She couldn't believe he had borne this burden alone all this time.

"Why didn't you tell me you knew?" she asked. She could tell by his smile that Pip already had an answer for that.

"Ever since we lost him, whenever I've been in a situation where I didn't know what to do, I ask myself what Bowie would do. Marley does the same thing, and I know why. It helps me. It's been my way of keeping him alive, I guess. In the depths of my grief, when I really wanted to tell you that I knew, I'd ask myself what he would do, and I felt like he would stay silent and support you from afar. Like he would keep what he knew to himself, unless he really needed to come clean."

Maddie agreed. She could not recall a single time Bowie had inserted himself in a situation that did not require his input. The biggest interference he'd ever orchestrated was bringing Marley and Autumn together, and he'd only done that for their own good. Stubborn and damagingly independent, Autumn and Marley needed each other, but they would never have found their way to each other on their own.

"I'm doing the same thing now," Pip said, drawing her attention back to him. "Calling on Bowie to stop you from making the biggest mistake of your life, Mads."

Maddie gazed up at him, realising all at once that she had not been imagining it in her bedroom the day before. Pip was making a concerted effort to be more like Bowie, and it looked good on him. He was more extroverted than Bowie, more brash and insistent, but the steady attentiveness and calm delivery of advice her older brother had deployed was being expertly emulated by the youngest Whittle sibling. Maddie found herself trusting him, and interested in hearing what he had to say.

"I know why you're doing what you're doing," Pip continued. "It's the same reason you let Bowie go that night. You're trying to do what is best for someone you love. But this isn't Bowie all over again. Bowie wanted to go. James does not."

Maddie closed her eyes in a poor attempt to stop her tears. She wished she could explain how ardently she longed to vacate her own head. She desperately wanted to let go of her fear that she would make someone she loved unhappy, but she didn't know how to. Right on cue, Pip started talking again.

"Look at him," he said, squeezing her hands in an effort to encourage her to open her eyes. He was watching James, who now sat at a table in the corner on his own, his shoulders slumped low, his eyes sparkling with emotion. Maddie followed his gaze. Her heart sank at the sight of him. "Does he look happy to you?" Pip asked.

Maddie shook her head.

"That's why you're doing this, right?" he asked her.

Maddie nodded, her heartbeat quickening. "He doesn't want an ordinary life," she said. "He wants adventure . . ."

She stopped because Pip was shaking his head and she knew, somehow, that her little brother — who she had loved mainly because he was vivacious and silly and unserious up until this point — was about to spell this out to her in a way that would make her feel like she'd made a big deal of something that was nothing. He was going to save her from herself. And she would love him all the more because of it.

Pip gestured to the middle of the room, where Marley and Autumn danced, their eyes locked on each other, their foreheads pressed together, their faces glowing with adoration. Maddie's face broke into an involuntary smile. She had never seen two people look more giddy at the sight of each other. It made her heart swell. "Look at them," Pip said. "On the face of it, Marley has given up so much for Autumn. Remember Mum's reaction when he told us he was leaving what we considered his dream job, after he'd struggled for years for a way back in? Remember his insistence that we should leave him alone, that he was making a decision based on what was best for his family? Well, he's never been happier, and I can absolutely guarantee that's because Autumn and Benjamin and the life they have built together is the real dream. Their happiness as a unit is the ultimate goal. The three of them together, as a family, that's the real adventure."

Maddie had never thought of it that way. It was true, her brother's heart had always been on the stage, but she had never seen him happier than he was right now.

"You can have that," Pip whispered, gesturing once more to James.

"What if he resents me in the future?" Maddie spoke her fears aloud.

"Autumn could say the same thing about Marley," Pip said.

"Marley wouldn't do that, though."

"Neither would James," Pip said. Maddie gazed up at him, searching for any hint of uncertainty, but there was nothing. He seemed completely resolute. "We all agree on this," Pip said, gazing pointedly around the room. "Even Autumn, though I know she hasn't said it to you. We're your family, we love you, we trust you to make your own decisions, but we also want you to be happy. We *all* think James means what he says. That he's the right man for you. Even Dad, despite how worried he is. And if he were here, Maddie, Bowie would, too."

Maddie felt her eyes fill with tears. Pip smiled gently down at her, his lip quivering tellingly.

"Please, for your own sake, go and put him out of his misery," Pip whispered, his eyes flitting to a forlorn-looking James. Maddie followed his gaze, her heart soaring at the sight of the man she loved. Pip squeezed her hands and looked down at her. He had the same dopey smile spread across his face that Bowie had so often gifted her with when they had chatted. "If this is about making him happy, then you have to change your mind — I can absolutely guarantee that man will never be happy ever again unless he has your permission to be by your side," Pip said, with a satisfied nod.

Maddie was crying, but she smiled in spite of herself. Somehow, Pip had done it. Maddie no longer felt that sending James away was the right thing to do for either of them. In fact, it felt utterly absurd. She resisted the urge to drop her brother and run to James to tell him she had changed her mind, pulling him into a hug, instead.

"Thank you, Pip," she whispered, holding him close.

He squeezed her tight and kissed her head. "Don't thank me," he said. "Thank Bowie."

EPILOGUE

Two weeks later, as March prepared to roll into April and Spring was in full swing, Maddie and James made their breakfast in the kitchen and took it outside to enjoy on the porch. It was just three days before the recovery retreat was due to open. The lawn was lush and moist with dew, the sky tinged pink with the remnants of a truly spectacular sunrise. Maddie watched James and Stevie Licks skip happily across the lawn on their way to free Pigglesworth from his pigpen. As they raced back towards her, she acknowledged that she had never been happier in her entire life.

Though he had been gone for less than a minute, James kissed her on the cheek on his return. "I love you," he said, grinning happily.

"I love you, too," Maddie sighed, tapping the seat beside her. James shifted the blanket she had draped across her lap and sat down, tucking them both in beneath it. He poured them coffee while she topped their oatmeal with raisins, maple syrup and banana. When they were ready, they clinked their mugs together in celebration of a new day, a morning tradition that had somehow started. Maddie hoped it would continue. Satisfied, they settled in to watch Stevie and Pigglesworth exploring the garden while they ate.

Maddie had expected the house to feel big and empty when everyone left — Bluebell and her parents had flown to Italy, Marley and Autumn had taken Benjamin to the Lake District for a honeymoon of sorts, and Pip had gone back to London to continue his role as part-time communications manager and full-time activist — but the house was still bursting with love. Freed once again from the shackles of an impending departure, Maddie and James were experiencing a new phase of their relationship, one in which they got to indulge their excitement for the future. Their preparations for the retreat were almost complete. Eager to broaden her social circle, Maddie had joined a village book club with Jennifer and had re-taken up yoga. Her life felt full of love and adventure. She didn't have time to worry, she was too busy doing things she enjoyed. 'The time before' was gone. She and James had fought their battles and they had won — this was 'the time after'. After confusion, after mistakes, after heartbreak, grief and loneliness.

"Look at us," James remarked, halfway through breakfast. Maddie didn't know what to say, so she smiled and snuggled closer to him, in silent awe of the fact that a life neither of them had ever dared dream for themselves would soon be theirs. Maddie had never expected that she would find someone she felt like herself with and trusted so much with her heart. James had never fathomed he could find love, contentment and happiness in the village where he had grown up. For both of them, it felt like a real adventure. "It doesn't get any better than this," James murmured, balancing his bowl on his knees, his free hand reaching for hers beneath the blanket. They ate the rest of their breakfast in comfortable silence, completely content with the state of all things.

They had just finished eating when they were joined by a familiar friend — the robin.

"My brother is here."

They said it together, before laughing at their own absurdity. They fell quickly back into a satisfied silence, turning back to the robin to watch him pottering around the garden. He spent a few minutes dancing around and sussing them out, before heading for the stack of raisins, which Maddie already knew he could safely eat. These days, he ate with them almost every morning. Playfully squabbling over whether his appearance was a sign from Bowie or a visit from Harry was part of Maddie's and James' daily routine. It was one of their private jokes, one of the first steps they had taken towards becoming a proper couple. Maddie grinned. They had personal banter — things only they found funny because 'you had to be there'. James put his arm around her shoulder, squeezing her tight.

They watched the robin pinch a raisin, then fly onto the lawn to eat it. He tossed it around with his beak, breaking it up into manageable chunks, before making quick work of it and returning to the table for more. Before pinching another one, he sang them a small song. His growing confidence made Maddie smile.

"Listen to him sing! You are Bowie, aren't you?" Maddie said. The robin watched her, bobbing his head. Maddie nudged James pointedly. She opened her mouth to tell him that settled it, but a flutter of feathers and a flash of red in the tree to her left caught her attention. She turned to investigate. James followed her gaze.

Sitting on a branch, basking in the sunlight, was a second robin redbreast.

Maddie and James turned to each other, and smiled.

THE END

320

THE CHOC LIT STORY

Established in 2009, Choc Lit is an independent, award-winning publisher dedicated to creating a delicious selection of quality women's fiction.

We have won 18 awards, including Publisher of the Year and the Romantic Novel of the Year, and have been shortlisted for countless others. In 2023, we were shortlisted for Publisher of the Year by the Romantic Novelists' Association.

All our novels are selected by genuine readers. We are proud to publish talented first-time authors, as well as established writers whose books we love introducing to a new generation of readers.

In 2023, we became a Joffe Books company. Best known for publishing a wide range of commercial fiction, Joffe Books has its roots in women's fiction. Today it is one of the largest independent publishers in the UK.

We love to hear from you, so please email us about absolutely anything bookish at choc-lit@joffebooks.com.

If you want to receive free books every Friday and hear about all our new releases, join our mailing list here: www.joffebooks.com/freebooks.